FIVE
Enchanted Roses

ROOGLEWOOD PRESS

Raleigh, NC

© 2015 by Rooglewood Press

Published by Rooglewood Press
www.RooglewoodPress.com

Printed in the United States of America

All rights reserved. No part of this publication may be reproduced, stored in a retrieval system, or transmitted in any form or by any means—for example, electronic, photocopy, recording—without the prior written permission of the publisher. The only exception is brief quotations in printed reviews.

ISBN-13: 978-1-942379-03-4

This volume contains works of fiction. Names, characters, incidents, and dialogues are products of each author's imagination and are not to be construed as real. Any resemblance to actual events or persons, living or dead, is entirely coincidental.

Book design by A.E. de Silva
Cover illustration by Julia Popova

Table of Contents

FOREWORD

WHEN MY team and I first began discussing ideas for the second annual Rooglewood Press writing contest, we unanimously agreed that "Beauty and the Beast" would be the perfect topic. After all, I thought, does a better-loved fairy tale even exist? Always one of my personal favorites, this story stands out as one of particular loveliness, ripe for the retelling. So we went forward and announced the contest, with me blithely referring to our chosen theme as "the most beloved fairy tale of all time."

I was wrong.

Indeed, I was shocked to discover how truly polarizing the story of "Beauty and the Beast" can be. While many would claim it as their favorite, many more derided it as a glorified tale of Stockholm syndrome, while others composed harsh critiques of the Disney version (as though the movie were an accurate representation of the original, which is far from the truth).

This derision in no way hindered the success of the contest, however. Many of the same writers who disliked the fairy tale sent in excellent retellings, using the contest as an opportunity to "correct" those aspects of the tale they disliked. But as I read the submissions and pondered anew the age-old story, I began to consider what quality makes this fairy tale appeal to me as one of the most beautiful and most profound. In the end, the best explanation I found for my own love of this story was a short line written by G.K. Chesterton in his famous essay, "The Ethics of Elfland."

> "There is the great lesson of 'Beauty and the Beast';
> that a thing must be loved *before* it is loveable."

Ah! There it is at last. This is not a tale of Stolkholm syndrome, though modern readers have been quick to jump to this interpretation. The original intent of the story—the core truth that makes "Beauty and the Beast" bloom so brightly in the garden of Grimm's and Perrault's collected tales—is simply this: It is a tale of redemption. It is a tale of the unloved being loved and, miraculously, becoming lovable.

"Beauty and the Beast" is a story of grace offered to the undeserving, of Beauty giving herself to the ugly and despised Beast not because he compelled her, nor even because he asked. For in the end, Beauty herself realizes the Beast's need and returns to his side just in time, even as he lies dying, offering him her heart and her hand. So is the Beast redeemed.

Is the tale a perfect one? By no means. Allegory dressed as a romance will always face certain difficulties. But the profound themes captured in this narrative remind the reader that there is hope for all. Yes, even I, at my most beastly, may be offered love and grace at the last. So will this story continue to be cherished—and sometimes despised—by readers for generations to come.

"Beauty and the Beast" will also continue to be retold, as new authors explore its various facets and interpretations. As the *Five Enchanted Roses* contest progressed, writers found much room for individual creativity, exploring the classic themes and inventing new ways to express them. The volume you now hold is the result of many months' worth of reading, sorting, discussing, and culling, both by me and by the fine readers who served as judges. Together we selected these five stories, each a unique reflection of the individual author who wrote it.

To open the collection, I give to you "Esprit de la Rose," a story which, when I first began to read it, made me scratch my head in curiosity. Beauty and the Beast . . . and *pirates?* What a crazy notion! And yet, as I read Kaycee Browning's swashbuckling tale, I could not help but smile and turn pages quickly to find out where she would take this mad idea of hers. As I read on, I watched her neatly fit all the important themes of the original fairy tale into their places, while simultaneously keeping the whole story so fresh, vibrant, and completely unusual, I could not predict how it would turn out. A madcap adventure with plenty of spooky thrills along the way, this first story opens the collection by dashing all reader-expectations to the ground and building them up again into something new.

But when you turn the page and progress to the next story, you'll find another mood entirely. Savannah Jezowski paints a gothic adventure with broad strokes of contrasting lights and darks. "Wither" is sometimes a truly frightening tale, and sometimes truly comical. Striding through a forest of ghouls, zombies, and blood-sucking monsters is our intrepid heroine, Lilybet, whose feminine name belies her practical, sturdy nature. As I read her story for the first time, she won my heart completely—more easily, perhaps, than she wins the heart of the Beast. Savannah's story is a close match to the original, but set in a world so unlike any I have ever seen before that I could have believed the plot to be entirely of her own invention.

It was Jenelle Schmidt, however, who truly turned the fairy tale on its head in her clever retelling, "Stone Curse." At every opportunity, this talented author reversed the familiar storyline. Unlike the Beauty of the fairy tale, Jenelle's heroine *begins* her adventure at the Beast's castle, setting out from its cursed grounds on a quest to rescue her father. Our Beast is not terribly beastly either, and is in fact a kind, sympathetic character, who does not deserve the fate that has befallen him. He may not even be the true beast after all, for it is not he who needs the redemptive grace that is at the heart of the original. But I cannot say more for fear of giving away a wonderful plot full of the unexpected. This is an adventure peopled with endearing characters, and its ending can bring a tear to the eye.

An enthusiastic message sent by the judge who read it before me raised my expectations high before I even began to read "Rosara and the Jungle King" for the first time. Those expectations were not disappointed. Dorian Tsukioka's beautifully written story deviates furthest from the source material, at times reading more like an original South American myth than like "Beauty and the Beast." At its core, however, the themes remain true—the brave beauty, the humbled beast, the sacrificial act of love under the looming shadow of death. The atmosphere of the Amazonian jungle is redolent with magic and mystery in a retelling that will surely linger in readers' imaginations long after they have set the book aside.

Standing in stark contrast to "Rosara" is the final offering in this collection. Throughout the contest, I wished to find a story that communicated the same mood, tone, and feel as the original fairy tale. A story that, while still a retelling, followed the pattern of "Beauty and the Beast" near to perfection. I found that story in "The Wulver's Rose." Though this last story cleaves closest to its source, Hayden Wand manages her share of surprises. She gives her Beast a motivation even more compelling than that of his traditional predecessor, so that readers are desperate to see him succeed in his bid to win his Beauty's heart. The eighteenth-century Scotland setting is lightly touched upon, given just enough authentic detail, but never so much as to distract from the truth—that this story is a fairy tale. A true fairy tale with a heart of gold.

These five authors have each poured a bit of themselves into these variations on the ancient theme, thus becoming part of an ongoing literary legacy. "Beauty and the Beast," whether your favorite or least favorite of the popular fairy tales, must certainly leave its mark. It is my wish that these new interpretations found in *Five Enchanted Roses* will impress upon you the truth of the original story: hope for the hopeless, grace for the graceless.

For Beauty must ultimately redeem her Beast.

Anne Elisabeth Stengl

KAYCEE BROWNING

ESPRIT
DE LA
ROSE

To Grandad: For living a life filled with adventure, laughter, and love.

And to Mimi: For shining Christ's grace and hope wherever you go.
I love you!

CHAPTER ONE

SHE CLUTCHED the rail with white-knuckled fingers, straining every sense yet hearing only the snap of sails and rush of water. Though it was midday, the *Sister Wench*'s wake looked like spilled ink spreading beneath a veneer of broken glass. Fingers of shadow seemed to stretch toward the gray horizon, shifting beneath the water, growing angrier . . . and stronger.

Cecilia quickly turned her back to the rail and leaned against it, breathing hard as her stomach roiled. Every crewmember within view gaped at the ocean, stock-still in the midst of forgotten duties, leaning against rigging high above or kneeling on the deck with rags clutched in their motionless hands. The clouds were angry too. They seemed to be shoving and pushing each other, vying for the darkest seat in the sky in order to watch the ship below.

Cecilia was no sailor, but even she knew that something uncanny was going on. Across the quarterdeck, Captain Lester gazed out across the blackened sea, one hand limply gripping the tiller. He did not move. She opened her mouth to shout but reconsidered. Instead, holding her cap to her head, she picked her way through shrouds and rigging to approach him. "Father."

He glanced at her from the corner of a red-rimmed eye. Cecilia leaned to the side to glimpse his other hand. A nearly empty wine bottle threatened to slip from his lax hold. She shifted to stand in front of this stranger who was her father, forcing him to see her. "Why is the water black?"

"It can't have . . ." Captain Lester murmured. He looked her full in the eyes for a moment, and his chin firmed. His hand clenched the tiller. "Mr. Walker!" he shouted. "To the quarterdeck, if you please!"

Mr. Walker, the quartermaster, stumbled onto the quarterdeck, pointing wildly at the black ocean. "Captain! Captain, why . . . ? I thought—"

"I know. Take the tiller, Mr. Walker," Captain Lester replied. "Cecilia, come." He strode to the companionway and descended its steep steps. Cecilia scurried after him, following her father into the captain's quarters, wincing as he let the door slam against her. She shut it quietly.

Captain Lester stormed across the room and sat down at his desk, staring at a thick, lumpy mound of cloth on its surface. He looked as though he might be sick.

Cecilia approached the desk to get a closer look. At first she saw only cloth. Then lightning flashed outside the paned window, and something simultaneously flashed between the folds. Part of the cloth fell aside, revealing the edge of a beautiful mirror. Its glass reflected perfectly, almost too perfectly, revealing crisp and harsh images. Pear-shaped diamonds adorned its frame, glittering even in the murky light allowed by the storm clouds.

Such a mirror must be worth a fortune.

"What is this, Father?" Cecilia asked. Why had her father not sold it when they restocked in Tortuga only a week ago? They had met no ships since leaving Tortuga's port, so he must have possessed it while they were there.

"It's why the sea's turning black," Captain Lester said. "I stole this from the Fee, and now they're coming for me. They might be coming for my whole crew. For *you.*" A light seemed to dim in his red-rimmed eyes. He turned his back to the mirror and stared out the window, watching the dark ocean begin to throb and pulse with the shifting of the shadows. "I unwrapped it only to make sure . . ." His voice trailed off into hopeless curses.

Lightning flashed again, and a myriad of colors momentarily beamed from the mirror's diamond edge, dotting the cabin walls. When the colors vanished, the darkness seemed even deeper.

"The Fee," Cecilia repeated. She did not know the word, but somehow the way her father spoke it filled her heart with terrible foreboding. "What are the Fee? What are you talking about?"

Captain Lester gulped. "They're monsters. Vicious, ruthless . . . they punish those they deem wrongdoers but reward those who help them." He glared at the mirror. "I swore I'd never get into religion, and then I go and work for them. Same thing, really. And it's hellish."

The more he explained, the more confused Cecilia felt. "I don't understand, Father! You worked for them? Why? How? Exactly what is that thing?" She pointed at the mirror.

"It summons them. I stole it, and now they've been called . . ." Captain Lester ran his hand over his thinning hair, knocking his battered tricorn hat askew. Cecilia opened her mouth to ask another question, but the captain's low murmur stopped her. "That's what we do, Cilla. The crew and I. I'm no privateer for England; I'm a privateer for the Fee. Ah!" With this exclamation, he turned a stricken glance her way but could not meet her eyes for more than a breath. "I should've left the mirror on land when I had the chance! But you see, Cilla, the Fee have gold and riches, and lots of it, too . . . I had to keep it, don't you see?"

Cecilia could only shake her head. "No, Father. I don't see." His ramblings made little sense, and she was too confused to decipher them.

A strangled yell broke through the silence on deck as another lightning flash illuminated the stern window. The crew's shouts and screams echoed with the thunder. Without another glance at Cecilia, the captain rushed from his cabin.

She stepped to the window and peered upward. The ocean was completely dark, empty, like a throbbing void barely visible against the expanse of gray skies. A thorn of lightning split the sky, and once more the tiny rainbows repelled the darkness then vanished.

Cecilia felt her eyes flooding, blurring her vision of the ocean and sky until all swirled together into a dark, writhing fog. Her father had his faults—so many that he would hang if certain people caught him! But Cecilia believed that, deep down, Captain Martin Lester must be a good man. He cared for this creaky old ship and for his men. From what little she had seen and heard, he was (mostly) fair when he dealt out wages to the crew. He was even willing to ferry his impertinent daughter across the ocean to England.

Or so he said. At present, weeks after leaving Bermuda, they still sailed the Caribbean Sea. She gave her head a quick shake. No, he would not lie to her. She would not believe he was a bad person.

Blinking away tears, she again glanced at the mirror. Would the Fee—whoever and whatever they were—would they *kill* her father?

Almost without thought, she wrapped the mirror firmly in the cloth, clutched it to her chest, swung the door open, and bolted up the companionway steps, stepping on her skirts and nearly falling more than once. "Father!" Her voice could not be heard above the shouting crew. "Father, please!"

He stood beside the tiller, a spare man of medium height, feet braced, chin high. "Please, you don't have to die!" she said, and held the wrapped mirror out to him.

Mr. Walker yelped and leaped backward, eying the lump of cloth as though it were a death sentence. Captain Lester stared blankly at the proffered mirror.

Cecilia rushed on, her words spilling out so quickly she might almost choke upon them. "Return the mirror to the Fee. Apologize. If they disapprove of wrongdoers, surely they will forgive you if you take the right course of action!"

Captain Lester shifted his feet, his brave stance crumbling. "Cilla, the Fee aren't—"

His eyes widened, staring beyond Cecilia.

She turned. The water surrounding the ship burst upward, rushing toward the sky like an upside-down waterfall. It arced above the topmost sails to form an inverted bowl over the ship, caging the vessel in an impenetrable prison. With the sky now obscured, the ship plunged into a blue darkness, its sails hanging limp in a dead calm. Multi-colored lights began appearing inside the wall of water, human-sized, perhaps slightly larger, and level with the ship's deck. Red, green, violet, and more—all beautiful, and all painful to look upon. Cecilia forced her eyes to keep looking. Squinting and blinking, she peered at a silver-hued glow, wondering and dreading what she might soon see. As her eyes adjusted, she beheld the head and torso of a woman, the tail of a sea creature.

They were mermaids. They were the Fee.

How beautiful they appeared, with their flashing eyes and lustrous hair! But the beauty felt strained, as though it might burst into ugliness at the slightest breath. No one spoke for nearly a minute. Cecilia struggled to breathe and risked a glance at her father.

He drew a quivering breath then stepped toward the starboard rail, doffed his hat, and bowed awkwardly before the silver-haired Fee who somehow looked bigger than the others. "I'm Captain Martin Lester of the *Sister Wench.* Who might I have the honor of addressing?"

The creature regarded him with cold eyes. "We do not reveal our names to pirates."

Cecilia winced and stared at the back of the captain's head. He hated that title. *Don't be a fool, Father,* she silently pleaded with him. *It's just a word . . .*

Captain Lester thrust the cloth-wrapped mirror toward the Fee as if it were a sword. "The proper term is 'privateer,' ma'am, and you'd do good to remember that!"

Cecilia pressed her hand to her face. Oh, why did he have to be such a buffoon?

A sneer twisted the Fee's silver lips. "Indeed? Do privateers rob their employers and expect to go unpunished?"

Captain Lester lowered his arm. "No . . ."

"Well then," the Fee said, her voice weirdly prim and dreadful at the same time. "I believe punishment is in order. It's only fair. We have always seen fit to reward your spying, and now we see fit to punish your trespass."

Captain Lester donned and straightened his hat. "I accept whatever punishment you deal me."

"Your courage is admirable," the Fee said. "Return the stolen item and await justice."

Shuddering, Captain Lester uncovered the mirror and let the cloth fall to the deck. The diamonds shone in the stormy light, scattering prismatic color across the faces of the seething Fee. Thunder bellowed, and Cecilia thought she heard horrible insults in its echoes, though the cage of water muffled the full sound.

The Fee reached out her arms, the current of the water-wall forming foamy shackles around her wrists, and wrested the mirror from Captain Lester's hands. Lightning lit the ocean cage, and thunder crashed, and this time Cecilia knew she heard words.

Punishment. Punishment. Punishment.

One by one the Fee vanished, diving silently from the walls of water into the ocean outside the darkness of the dome, until only the silver Fee remained. She pointed the mirror glass at Captain Lester. Lightning flashed, and the mirror reflected a small beam of light.

A whirlpool appeared in the wall of water directly in front of Captain Lester. Nearby crew members shouted and scrambled as far from him as possible, grasping anything their hands could find to protect themselves from the turbulence the whirlpool would certainly cause. The whirlpool widened and deepened. The ship began to pitch back and forth, side to side.

"Go in. You have no choice," the Fee said. With a flick of her tail she swam out from behind the whirlpool, still pointing the mirror at the captain. She remained unaffected by the water's turmoil, her face impassive.

But then she smiled. And it was a smirk of complete, cruel satisfaction.

Cecilia's fists clenched. Slowly she edged away from the tiller. The Fee had not yet noticed her. The mirror shone starkly in the Fee's light, casting unnaturally vivid colors across the quarterdeck: the blues too deep, the greens too bright, the reds too harsh. The Fee loosened her grip on the mirror, tilting it, and swept it to the side, its glass still facing Captain Lester. The whirlpool tilted, surging toward him, following the motion of the mirror.

The mirror controlled the whirlpool. It must, surely it must! Cecilia took another step toward the Fee. If she could take the mirror . . . If she could somehow snatch it from the Fee's hand and shatter its glass, perhaps she could make the whirlpool disappear.

Another step. The Fee tilted the mirror again. The edge of the frame emerged through the water-wall, droplets falling from the glittering diamonds to the deck. The whirlpool surged forward.

Cecilia made a dash across the deck and grabbed the mirror with both hands. The Fee shrieked, slinging her arm backwards with unaccountable strength. Cecilia, her grip still firm upon the frame, felt her feet leave the deck, her side strike the rail.

Then she toppled and lost her hold on the mirror. For a moment she floated, suspended in the water-wall, and saw the ship's blurry deck, her father's ashen face . . . Then, jerked horribly to the side, she felt the world spin into a blur. Her lungs burned; water and motion and darkness were everywhere.

The whirlpool swallowed her whole.

CHAPTER TWO

EVERYTHING WAS muffled. Her head throbbed and her nose felt thick, clogged, unable to draw breath. She gasped and heaved, forcing her throat to suck in gulps of air despite the scratched and torn feeling in her mouth. Lying on her stomach, her face turned to one side, she relearned how to breathe.

Once air flowed through her lungs, she stared at her own hand. Only then did she try to remember why she was shuddering and why she was scared. Then she noticed the floor beneath her hand.

It wasn't the weathered deck of her father's ship, nor was it the sandy stretches of a beach. It also wasn't gold. Father John Francis said that heaven was gold, and if she had died, she assumed that's where she would go. So she couldn't have died . . .

The wood was red. Not the deep brown of the pau brasil trees she had seen near Tortuga. No, this was *red*. Screaming red. Cut-throat red.

Cecilia took another deep breath. She pushed herself off the ground and onto her feet.

The world rocked. Cecilia stumbled and slammed into a set of heavy bars. She held herself against the bars for a long moment, listening to the familiar creak and toss of buoyancy. She was on a ship. A red ship. She blinked and focused on the bars. Bars . . . like prison bars . . .

Cecilia's mind surged out of its fog. She stood in a small gaol lit only by the strangled light of a dying candle in an algae-covered lantern hung from the low ceiling. Bars made up the entirety of one wall. Rotting hay littered the floor, its dull yellow a stark contrast to the eye-aching red. Water dribbled through a crack in the curved back wall.

She stumbled to the cell door. It was locked. She rattled the bars with all of her strength, but they did not give way.

"Hullo?" she called, blinking into the darkness outside of the cell. Her only light source was the lantern. Everything was the same red wood. Why was it red? Was it blood-stained? Cecilia shuddered and hastened to assure herself that the blood would be brown at this point, but the thought did little to comfort her. "Please, let me out! Hullo!"

Nobody answered. Cecilia shoved her hands through her soaked hair, pushing the tangled locks out of her face. Her head felt light, disoriented, unable to process her surroundings, much less her terror. Her skirts and petticoats were heavy, sopping wet, yet she did not feel cold.

Exhaling a shuddering breath, she sank to the floor. The reek of moldy hay hit her nose, bringing tears to her eyes. She blinked them back. She couldn't lose control. Not now. Everything would be sorted out soon. There had been some sort of misunderstanding. She had dreamed a horrid dream, fallen into this nightmare . . .

Eventually her tears subsided, and the moldy smell served to clear her head of fog. Cecilia took a few calming breaths. She crawled to the curved wall, which appeared to be the inside of the ship's hull, and pressed her eye to the crack, peering out of her cell into the world.

Ocean. Although she could see nothing but darkness, she suddenly knew that she was in the bilge of this ship, far below the water line. She scrambled away from the crack, expecting torrents of water to burst through and flood the room. Nothing happened. Even the dribble had stopped.

What is this place?

She crept back to the crack and peeked out again. No matter how she strained her eyes, she saw only the same darkness that had surrounded the *Sister Wench*. It was black and hopeless. How could she tell if there were Fee in the water?

Cecilia pushed herself away from the crack and stood up, more carefully this time. Kicking aside the straw, she sought for something, some clue or tool that could help her escape the gaol. She found nothing but composting hay. She gagged at the stench and pushed the slightly fresher hay over it. Still coughing, she sat down and stared at her shoes, watching the water droplets leaking from her gown fade into the floor.

She didn't know how long she sat in a daze, but she snapped out of it as soon as she heard laughter.

"Get down here, Billy! You ain't getting out of it neither. Cap'n's orders and all," a gruff voice said, followed by a deep guffaw. He sounded British, though poorly educated.

A smoother voice replied with a more polished accent, "It's *William*, thank you very much. And I absolutely despise checking the bilge. It's filthy down there. Besides, it is logical to assume there is no one in the ship's gaol. We would have heard the shouting."

Cecilia opened her mouth to shout, but natural caution held her back. She didn't know who these men were, and she was completely helpless and unarmed. She waited.

"Oh, there ain't no one there, but you still get to go and check. I sent in a report to the cap'n, and he said ye had to! He also poked fun at your being a blue-blood and all." The gruff one chuckled again.

William swore both at the gruff speaker (whom he categorized as 'churlish low-life' among other more colorful titles) and at the captain ('the idiotic Frenchman'). An eerie blue light appeared in what seemed to be a passage between bulkheads, and she saw that the bilge was empty but for her cell.

However, at the moment more urgent matters preoccupied her mind. No matter what she might do, this William person was going to find her. What was it her father had said her first day aboard the *Sister Wench*? *"Just keep your head high and act confident-like. The others will leave you alone if you pretend you know what you're doing."*

Clearing her throat, Cecilia called to the light, "Hullo? Is anyone there?"

She heard a startled gasp then pounding feet. The blue light emerged from the passage and reached Cecilia's prison, causing the walls to appear lavender. Any greeting Cecilia had intended to speak upon seeing William vanished. She clapped her hand over her mouth to hold back a scream.

William wasn't human. His body *was* the blue light, the nasty color of dried foam clinging to sand. His clumpy hair seemed to ooze. A black blob throbbed and pulsed in the place where his heart should be, dark and squirming like a dying squid.

William stopped in his tracks, and his face mirrored Cecilia's own expression. "You—you are solid!" he gasped.

Cecilia pressed her hand tighter to her mouth. His teeth reminded her of the slimy stones lining the lake behind her old home, stones she avoided because of the leeches clinging to them. Only with great effort of will could she force herself to speak behind her trembling hand, whimpering, "What *are* you?"

William stared at her for several moments longer. His soggy eyes blinked. Then he bolted out of sight. The cramped cell almost seemed brighter without the glow shining off of the wet, ghostly man.

Cecilia let out a breath she hadn't realized she was holding. A horrifying thought crossed her mind: What if she had gone not to heaven but to . . . some awful hell? Cecilia grasped at the rosary hidden beneath her dress, rubbing her trembling fingers over the familiar shape through the cloth. Could this be purgatory?

The light appeared in the passage again, this time far stronger. She dropped her hands and clenched them at her side. Shouts and footsteps echoed through the ship. The blue light intensified, forcing Cecilia to blink, her eyes stinging again as if they had just been doused in salt water.

William appeared first, but after him swarmed a crowd of the monsters. Cecilia cried out and scrambled backwards, pressing against the wall. Each creature was unique in its hideousness. Though they looked like watery men, she believed their skin would have the texture of a crab's shell. Their hair seemed nothing more than seaweed draped over their heads and held down by their hats, and their teeth might have been stolen from a dead shark. But worst of all were the throbbing black hearts visible through the blueness of their skin and clothes. Everything about them felt rotten.

The creatures grabbed at the bars and shook them, gnashing their teeth at Cecilia. Some shoved William forward, jostling him toward the door.

"Get it open! She's in my omen!"

"And in mine! I want her first!"

"Come here, girl! I'm finally going to be free!"

"Everyone needs to remain calm," William said, his voice shaking and difficult to hear over the noise. Someone slammed him into the bars and ordered him to open the door. "We should all try to be rational about this. We need to talk to her!" William protested.

Demands and insults flew at him, ending in a muscular ghost pulling William off the ground and shaking him. "Let her out, lobsterback, or I'll squeeze your heart 'til it bleeds as red as this cursed ship!"

"Put him down, Jack," a familiar voice shouted. Cecilia scanned the crowd until she spotted a monster slightly less horrifying than Jack making his way toward the two. He jerked William out of the large ghost's grasp. "Billy's right. We need to talk all this out, and somebody oughter tell Cap'n."

"Franklin. Brilliant timing." William sniffed and dusted off his clothes, sending splatters of water to the ground where they sizzled before disappearing.

"Get out of this, Frank," Jack growled, taking a step toward him. Frank simply glanced up and grinned at him, flashing crooked teeth the color of black pearls. Jack shook his fist. "And don't you even think about telling the captain. He's got no rights in this. If he even shows his ugly face here, I'm going to—"

"What, *je t'en prie*, will you do, my dear Jacques?" a voice with a decidedly French accent intoned.

Cecilia strained her eyes trying to catch sight of the owner of this new voice. She couldn't see anything beyond the line of specters immediately outside her cell. Everyone fell silent. Jack glared at Cecilia, shoved William into the wall, and stormed away.

The voice lost the heavy French accent, speaking now with barely a hint of it. "William, please unlock our guest and lead her to my cabin. Frank, I should be most grateful if you will find and annoy Jack. I'm irritated with him. And I believe the rest of you have duties to perform. This ship won't sail itself, after all. Well, it *will*, but that's no reason to stand about and gawk like schoolchildren at a menagerie. It's just a solid female human, after all. It's not as if we've seen nothing of the sort in—oh, years! Step lively now."

The ghosts scrambled away, casting forlorn glances back at her before disappearing into the passageway. Frank grinned and winked before dashing off after the retreated Jack. Cecilia stepped away from the wall, trying to find the speaker. She saw no more than a tricorn hat and the swish of a long black coat.

William offered a small smile, rendered no less hideous for its friendliness. "I apologize for the fright you've undergone, my lady. And I also apologize for being the one responsible for your . . . er . . . abnormal welcoming party. You must understand, I was quite shocked upon seeing you here."

Cecilia attempted to smile in return, but it was difficult to smile in the vicinity of that throbbing black heart. William pulled a key from his pocket and unlocked the door, swinging it open with a *creeeeak.*

Suddenly unwilling to leave the only shelter within sight, Cecilia drew a heavy breath. With no alternatives available to her, she stepped out of the cell into this dreadful, red nightmare of a ship.

CHAPTER THREE

WILLIAM BECKONED for Cecilia to follow him and led her out of the gaol, along the short passage, and into the underbelly of the ship, his rippling glow lighting the way. Nothing seemed to be stored in the bilge: no sails, rope, ammunition, water barrels, or food. Did these monsters live on air or . . . or were they even alive?

Despite these thoughts her fear subsided, or most of it anyway. She studied the back of William, feeling both curiosity and revulsion. When she looked past the dripping hair, the black heart, and the slimy blueness of his skin, he appeared oddly normal. He was thin and tall, his face gaunt and sickly but commanding. He was probably around twenty, barely older than she was.

"I'm terribly sorry, but you really must climb up," William said, wringing his hands as though he could not believe his own audacity in asking a woman to climb a ladder. Cecilia blinked back at him, confused, then realized she had been staring, and that he had probably already mentioned the ladder with no response from her. He no doubt thought her slow-witted.

She attempted a smile. "Oh, certainly. I can climb."

William nodded and nimbly scrambled up ahead of her. Cecilia followed close behind. They emerged onto another red deck, this one divided by bulkheads yet appearing mostly empty. William led her aft to a companionway which they ascended to a main deck lined on both sides with cannons larger than any her father had owned. Looking up and around, she counted three scarlet masts rising into a canopy of dense fog. This ship was much larger than the *Sister Wench*. "Is this a man o' war?" she asked.

"She was," William said, his tone melancholy. "A fighting frigate, all 110 feet and 26 guns of her. This way now." He led her toward one of two ornate red doors set on either side of the companionway stairs up to the quarterdeck. As Cecilia obediently followed, she got a clear look at him by daylight, and her steps faltered in renewed horror.

His hair now looked like slithering eels, his coat appeared to be made of a moth-ridden sail, and he smelled like putrid seaweed. She forced herself to approach him, trying to see what she had seen before.

"Right in here, my lady," William said, and opened the door, revealing a darkness far more violent than William's blue glow.

Cecilia shivered and peered inside. Her eyes stung, but she kept them open and forced herself to focus on the room.

A gray sun shining through a glass-paned window revealed the silhouette of a figure wearing a long black coat, and yet beyond the window, all was dense fog and dark ocean. The room itself, what could be seen of it, was shockingly elegant. A Persian rug covered the floor, the table and chairs were ornamented, and gilded chests were shoved against the walls, practically screaming to be opened and the riches inside perused. Dim candles glimmered in the heavy stillness of the cabin.

The man spun around. Cecilia gasped at the sudden movement.

"*Ma chère*, we do not have all day. This would be true whether or not you stood gawking stupidly in my doorway, as there *is* no day here. But I assume you are more intelligent than you currently appear, and thus I shall also assume that you understand my gist."

Despite the amused condescension coating his tone, something oddly alluring in his voice roused Cecilia out of her discomfort and piqued her curiosity. Perhaps it was the strange combination of matter-of-fact sarcasm and a French accent.

"William, *merci*. Leave." His tone was curt and final. William bowed, backed from the room, and closed the door.

Cecilia sucked in a breath, her curiosity extinguishing like candlelight in a storm, and spun about to stare at the closed door as though it were an impenetrable barrier.

"I suppose this is all rather frightening," the captain said. When Cecilia, bracing herself, looked back around at him, he gestured for her to sit in a stiffly upholstered chair. Even as he made the gesture, he knelt before one of the chests and retrieved from its interior two tin mugs. After staring at them for a moment, he huffed, tossed them back into the chest, and then rummaged further, emerging at last with two goblets.

Numbly, Cecilia took the proffered seat. She eyed the captain, trying to steel herself before her first glimpse of his ghoulish looks, which were sure to be worse than William's. William was horrid enough, but at least he produced a blue aura. This man, by contrast, dimmed any candlelight and sunlight that might have touched him.

The spectral captain spun from the chest and placed the goblets and a bottle on the table. Cecilia gazed up at him, trying to discern his features.

She couldn't. The darkness of his heart seemed to have spread, shrouding his face and body in inky blackness. She could see the faint impression of a straight nose, a twisted smirk, and long fingers. Otherwise, his shirt, his trousers, his overcoat—all were dark like his skin.

Somehow, his entirely shadowed body was even more awful than the soggy figures of his crew. It brought to mind images of the suffering and demons and hell that Father John Francis had warned about from his pulpit.

"Do you have a name, Mademoiselle?" the captain asked as he uncorked the bottle and poured. Cecilia recognized the dull smell of wine, like metallic blood. It reminded her of the Fee and the whirlpool.

Her stomach quivered, but she accepted the goblet he handed her and held it tightly with both hands. Rallying herself as best she could, she answered the captain's question. "My name is Lester. Miss Cecilia Lester."

The shades of black on his face seemed to shift as if he raised an eyebrow. "An English surname? And your English is flawless. Yet you look Spanish to me."

"Mother is . . . was," Cecilia stammered. "But I grew up in St. George's Parish."

"Ah. Bermuda, a British colony. And you are of mixed nationality, yes? *Tres exotique.*"

Cecilia's fingers tightened around the goblet's stem. She suddenly found she didn't care about anything but getting answers. She set the goblet aside and leaped to her feet, glaring up into the black space vaguely shaped like a head. Words wouldn't form, so she simply stood her ground.

The captain chuckled and tilted his head to view her better. "*Exotique.* That was a rather poor choice of wording, given the circumstances. Though I meant it as a compliment. *Ma chère*, you have the great misfortune to find yourself aboard the punishment vessel of our mutual friends, the Fee— home of despairing and accursed men-turned-monsters. Welcome aboard the *Rose*. I hope you do not intend to stay long."

Cecilia stared at the captain and felt him returning her gaze, though she could not see his face. At last, feeling strangely satisfied, as though an important question had finally been answered, she sat. "So all of you were . . . are people?" she asked.

The captain nodded. "*Mais oui*. Our appearance is part of our punishments. As if being stuck on this appallingly colored ship is not punishment enough."

"The Fee were going to punish my father," Cecilia mused aloud. Worry for her father, his ship, and even his crew rushed into her mind, casting out her momentary calm. Did the Fee spare him? What if they assumed he had been behind her attempt to take the mirror? She gripped the arms of her chair. Had she only made his situation worse?

"Your father? How did you come to be here, then?" the captain asked, settling gracefully into the chair behind his desk, his goblet in one hand.

Perhaps motivated by fear, perhaps by her relief at not being killed, or perhaps simply to distract herself from the dark form of the captain, Cecilia poured out her tale as hastily and effectively as she could. She explained how her mother had died of influenza, how she'd been left destitute. She told about how her father had come to St. George's Parish at last, finding her in the care of kindly Father John Francis, the only man in all the village willing to take in a privateer's daughter. Captain Lester had promised to carry her back to England by the end of the year . . . to London, where he claimed he had a respectable sister who might just be willing to take in the daughter of her less-than-respectable brother.

She told of her weeks aboard the *Sister Wench*, enduring rough and rowdy men, bad weather, and the inconveniences of shipboard life. At last they had taken on supplies at Tortuga, an island overrun by pirates and rampant with degradation, depravity, and despair. Cecilia had observed the port from the safe distance of the *Sister Wench's* deck, having no desire to venture ashore. She had been truly happy to put Tortuga astern and embrace the rollicking waves of the ocean again.

Finally, her tale nearing its conclusion, she spoke of her discovery of Captain Lester's thievery, of the beautiful mirror that belonged to the Fee, of the wall and the whirlpool—and of her reckless decision to steal back the mirror in an attempt to save her father.

The captain listened silently, nodding his shadowy head throughout the story. When Cecilia fell silent, her temples throbbing at the telling of her own tale, the captain spoke again, his voice surprisingly soft:

"You were very brave, Mademoiselle Lester. Not many would have done what you did. Attacking one of the Fee! *Tres vaillante.*"

Cecilia did not feel valiant. She hardly knew what she felt. Lost, perhaps. She took up the goblet and, suddenly parched, took a tentative sip. The wine tasted acrid in her mouth, and she wished she'd not tried it. "Please," she said, setting the drink aside, "did I accomplish anything at all? Did they kill my father?"

"*Non.* The Fee do not kill," the captain said, his accent growing heavier. "They only punish, and their punishment consists of turning men into monsters and casting them aboard this ship. Newcomers always appear exactly where you appeared—in the cell down in the bilge. Had your father suffered the Fee's punishment, he would have been with you."

"I see," Cecilia replied. She eyed him for a moment, then said, "You seem to know quite a lot. Do you know anything about the mirror? How did the Fee find my father?" She squinted at him suspiciously. "And how do you know about them?"

"Light," the captain replied immediately. "That is how they found your father, or so I would surmise. If light touches the mirror's glass while in the world of mortals, the Fee can appear in that location. So long as it is in an ocean, *bien sûr*. If the mirror were brought on land, they could sense the mirror but they could not go to it."

Cecilia sat in silence for a long moment, pondering. Why, *why*, hadn't her father left the mirror in Tortuga? If he truly wished to be rid of his servitude to the Fee, he should have left the mirror on land, buried it in the ground, or even sold it. He would have been safe!

Her father's verbal rambling before the Fee attacked came back to her: *But Cilla, the Fee have gold and riches, and lots of it too . . . I had to keep it, don't you see?*

Cecilia clenched her hands, her ragged fingernails biting into the skin of her palms. "Why am I not like the rest of you?" she asked, her voice scarcely above a whisper. "Why am I not . . ." A monster? A ghost? A horror of water and slime? Cecilia struggled for an inoffensive word, though she knew that the captain would only chuckle at her. "Blue. Why am I not blue?" she finished finally.

True to form, the captain did laugh, sounding as though he had been young at the time of his cursing, no older than thirty or somewhere thereabouts. When he finished laughing, he said, *"Je ne sais pas,* Mademoiselle Lester. I do not know. What does your omen say? There is no need to fear; I promise to tell no one, and I will endeavor to help you fulfill it."

"My omen?" Cecilia asked.

"Oui. I understand why you did not share in your initial story. It is often disturbing. But, *ma chère,* nothing good will come of keeping it secret. I can help you." He sounded earnest, and his French accent grew heavier. Cecilia suspected it only did that when he became too emotional. Her mother's Spanish accent had been the same.

Cecilia reached for the wine goblet once more. Anything to distract her from thinking about her mother. She peered into the goblet's bowl. It smelled like her father, and the previous sip still tasted foul on her tongue. She put it back. "I don't know what you mean," she said, aware that the captain was staring deeply at her, though she could not see his eyes. "The men were shouting something about omens down in the hull. What were they saying?"

The captain suddenly cleared his throat. "Where are my manners? I must introduce myself! My name is Pepin-René Marc Daviau. It's quite long, and I rarely bother to recall all of it, so please call me Pepin. Then again, call me Captain, as I am your superior, but you may *think* of me as Pepin, if you like."

"Daviau?" Cecilia asked. A conversation with her father not two weeks prior rushed back to her. "The privateer?"

He huffed. "There is no need to insult me. *S'il vous plaît*, use the term 'pirate.' It is far less offensive."

Cecilia sat back in her chair, staring at the shadowed figure with new awe and fear. This was the man who rode into Tortuga and pillaged it, stealing everything—from the gold of other pirates to wooden beams from fallen homes—just to toss it all into the ocean. This man defeated an entire fleet of British warships by tricking them into a kraken's nest. This man held the entire pirate world, even her father, in a constant state of reverence and terror. They whispered his name only after several bottles of rum, and even then they glanced over their shoulders and hissed for silence.

She wasn't surprised that he had run afoul of the Fee; she *was* surprised that they had actually managed to punish him. Though, after looking at the cabin—which more closely resembled a king's court than a captain's quarters—and remembering the way the men quivered and obeyed, it seemed the punishment had affected him little.

"I suppose your father told you stories of me?" Pepin asked. Cecilia could almost hear the smug grin she was sure he wore beneath the darkness.

"He told me you sank to the bottom of the ocean along with the *Bête de Diable* during a battle off the coast of Florida," Cecilia said.

A torrent of what was no doubt French invective flew from Pepin's mouth. Cecilia drew a sharp breath, frightened and suddenly glad that she did not understand French. He stood and began pacing furiously across the cabin, never pausing his tirade to draw breath.

Finally he calmed himself and turned toward Cecilia. "*Excusez-moi*, Mademoiselle Cecile. It is not every day one receives word that one's *imbécile* fath . . . first mate decided to go after the Fountain of Youth, following a map that was *clearly* a trap set by the British, which then results in the destruction of one's friends. *Sacrebleu, quand je sortirai d'ici . . .*"

He ranted on in French while Cecilia, suspecting it would be perilous to interrupt, waited for him to finish.

He stopped at last and bowed to her. "Mademoiselle, I again bid you welcome aboard the *Rose*. We sail an endless ocean, and landing is impossible. Food and drink mystically appear in the galley. It tastes horrid, but none of the ghosts have died from it, so have as much as you please. There is a room for you below. At least, I assume there is. Cabins always seem to appear when some new poor soul arrives, though by rights the ship shouldn't be large enough for another. It will be dry and stuffy, with an aroma that calls to mind images of the ocean. Particularly the fish part of the ocean. Most particularly the dead-fish part of the ocean. There's only one port we can anchor in, and we could not enter it before you came because we needed a solid person. But now that you are here . . . well, we shall see. Perhaps we can return you to your father."

As he spoke he motioned for her to rise and, without touching her, somehow managed to propel her toward the door. "The ship is yours to roam, though I suggest avoiding most of the men, especially Jack. They would be unpleasantly happy to meet you. William and Frank are good sorts though. Also, stay away from all of the rooms other than your own, all of the lower decks, and whatever you do, stay away from the little room in the bow. That is where I keep the insane ones. Don't touch anything that looks odd. Don't touch anything that looks normal. Other than following these few trifling rules, feel free to do whatever you want. Good day. Or night. Whichever you wish to call it."

He bowed again and ushered her out, shutting the door firmly behind her. So Cecilia found herself standing alone in the endless fog and contemplating the mystery that was Pepin-René Marc Daviau.

CHAPTER FOUR

THE NEXT morning . . . or evening—it was truly impossible to say which—Cecilia awoke with burning eyes and a throbbing head. Several agonized moments passed before she could bear to allow herself to remember where she was. When the memory came, she wished she might fall asleep again. The nightmares she'd experienced in sleep would be a welcome relief!

But instead she lay in her hammock, gazing at the red boards above her until they blurred. Last night both William and Frank (good sorts according to Captain Pepin, if his word could be trusted) had escorted her down the companionway and through what seemed like miles of winding passages between bulkheads before arriving at the door of her cabin, which, they said, had appeared suddenly upon her arrival. Reason told Cecilia that it shouldn't exist at all.

Exist it did, however, beyond all reason, and her two ghostly escorts had urged her to remain inside. She wondered now, upon waking, if they had forgotten all about her. At the same time she wondered whether her door was bolted on the inside or outside.

She blinked. Her vision cleared, but the stinging remained. Cecilia rubbed her eyes and sat up, careful not to overturn the hammock. Staring blearily around the room, she took in its wooden walls and floor, a clothes chest against the far wall, a flickering lantern on a hook (had it burned all night?), and a bolted door—all perfectly ordinary other than the blood-red of the wood. A small space and spare in its furnishings, but ultimately she felt Captain Pepin had exaggerated the cabin's unpleasantness. She doubted she would have slept at all had she smelled dead fish all night. The room actually smelled strangely pleasant, like flowers in the spring.

As she thought back over her conversation with the captain, her mind focused on a single word: *omens.* Why had Captain Pepin avoided the subject? Somehow, now that she considered the topic, she knew it was important. Why else would he shy away from it? He had been forthcoming about everything else . . . or had he? She wasn't certain.

She had been tired and frightened last night. She was tired and frightened now, but determined, too. She rose to pace across the room, running her fingers through her hair to undo her frazzled braid. When she turned back she noticed a tortoiseshell comb lying atop the clothes chest. Within a few minutes she had combed and braided her hair and secured it with her limp hair ribbon. She checked her wan reflection in a polished brass mirror above a vermilion dressing table, then poured warm, scented water from a china pitcher into a basin, washed her face and hands, and dried them on a soft white cloth.

It was then she noticed the gleam of daylight falling on her reflected face. Had that window been there a moment ago? She pressed her face to its wavy glass to peer outside, then, noticing a latch, opened it wide and leaned out, breathing deep as salt spray dampened her cheeks. Dense fog curled and smoked above the black ocean, twisting like a shark savoring blood.

Somehow her cabin was located high in the bow of the ship on the port side. Above and to her right extended the bowsprit, with its spider web of lines and a small sail filled with wind. She looked down and sucked in a breath. Though the water was dark and shadowed, it, unlike the captain, still held its definition and shape. She watched the bow cut into a wave then rise amid foaming currents and spray. The fog obstructed her view ahead, but even so she knew that the *Rose* was moving faster than any ship she had ever heard of. No breeze could propel a ship, certainly not one the size of the *Rose*, this quickly. Perhaps in a strong following wind a normal man o' war could sail at half this speed, but how could there be wind in such a dense, inert fog?

She needed answers.

Cecilia latched the window then turned to face the door. She'd not wanted to know if she was locked in, but the time of discovery had come. She tried the latch and found that it gave. Did her stomach lurch in relief or in dread? For now, surely, she must step out into the terrible unknown and leave behind the relative safety of this red-glaring room.

Pausing with her hand on the handle, she took a few calming breaths before holding her head high and swinging open the door.

"Oi! Eh, Billy! She's up!" a gruff voice shouted.

Cecilia yelped, jumped backwards into her room, and slammed the door. She heard guffaws of laughter and a thick English accent swearing profusely. Frank and William.

She sighed. Why were they here? Had the captain ordered them to spy on her? The thought was annoying, but at least it hadn't been Jack or one of the others waiting outside her door. With a start, Cecilia realized how likely a possibility that was.

Frowning sternly, she swung the door wide again and found herself staring into the grinning face of Frank and the scowling face of William. "What are you doing here?" she demanded, crossing her arms over her chest.

"Thought you might be hungry, my lady," William replied, holding out a plate of food. "I'm sorry at its appearance, but it truly was the best that could be found down in the galley today." He glared at Frank. "Except for that cake this fool decided to eat."

Frank shrugged indifferently. "Stale, it was! You wouldn't want to give the missy a stale cake, would you?"

"No, but I do not like handing her a plate of mush either, you peasantly bumpkin!" William snapped.

"Now listen here, you little—"

Cecilia quit listening to the argument. She glanced down at the plate of food then raised an eyebrow at William. Mush? What did he mean? Half of the plate was piled with fresh-baked bread, and the other side held porridge with cinnamon dashed on top. Hesitantly, Cecilia stuck her finger into the porridge—maybe it *tasted* like mush—but no, it was as delicious as it looked, lightly sweetened with honey.

She took the plate from William and quickly ate the bread. The two pirates did not notice her until she plucked from William's hand the spoon he had been pointing at Frank's throat. She ate several more bites, pleased that at least she would not go hungry on this ship. Then she noticed their silence and glanced up, momentarily embarrassed about eating her food so quickly before recalling that they were pirates and probably didn't give an empty rum bottle about manners. "What's wrong?" she asked.

Frank grimaced. "I can't believe you tried the gray stuff. It's awful."

Cecilia glanced down at the plate, her spoon poised over the half-eaten serving. "The porridge? No, it's delicious."

William stared at her, considering. "You ate the moldy bread."

Cecilia blinked. "It wasn't moldy."

"I think the sun's getting to her," Frank said morosely.

William sneered. "What sun?" He glanced back at Cecilia. "You *are* feeling well, aren't you?"

Cecilia set the plate on the floor and planted her fists on her hips, glaring at both of them until they took a few steps back. When she was little, she had seen her mother do the same to her father, and he always staggered away too. "Oh, I'm feeling well considering I just awoke on a cursed pirate ship. Why shouldn't I eat the food? It looked and tasted delightful."

William and Frank exchanged glances then shifted until they faced each other, shutting Cecilia out of the ensuing conversation.

"I don't think she's lying."

"Why would she lie, you bumbling beehive? Of course she's not lying!"

"Is it because she's solid? Or because she's insane?"

"You're one to talk about insanity! She is clearly not the mentally unstable one aboard this vessel."

"Maybe she's just stupid."

Cecilia cleared her throat, pursing her lips. They continued to argue, ignoring her.

"Do you think we should tell the captain?" William mused.

Frank shook his head, flinging droplets from his stringy, wet hair. "No need to bother him."

"But we can't just let this anomaly go unspoken . . ."

And so they bickered, gaining in speed and volume as though they never intended to stop. Her stomach properly satisfied, Cecilia's thoughts returned to her confusion and questions. She needed to find the captain.

"If you two are finished debating my mental capacities, I have a request to make," she announced. Both men snapped quiet. "Thank you. I'd like to speak to Captain Pepin. Would you please lead me to him? *Now*, if it's not too much trouble."

William fidgeted. "Apologies, my lady. The captain is currently unavailable."

"Aye, you can't go see him, miss. He's busy," Frank seconded.

Peering around them, Cecilia glimpsed, at the end of a short passage, a companionway up to the main deck. "The captain ordered you to stay with me, correct?"

They nodded quickly, pleased at the apparent change of subject.

Cecilia stepped past them and made her way to the stairs, ignoring their protests. "If the captain ordered you to protect me, you probably ought to come along as I explore."

As Cecilia set her foot on the first step, William burst out, "My lady, what did the captain tell you last night?"

She glanced back at him. "What do you mean?"

His ghoulish face seemed to darken, and he cast a quick look from side to side, as though afraid of eavesdroppers. Lowering his voice to a whisper, he said, "About the *omens*."

Cecilia's eyes widened. She returned to face the two soggy men. "He didn't tell me anything. He shied away from the subject, actually."

William and Frank exchanged a look.

"What are the omens?" Cecilia persisted. "Can you tell me?"

They turned toward her. They nodded. "Yes," both said. William added, "You'll have to help us though."

"And keep it shushed up, will you?" Frank inserted, his voice a whisper. He glanced over his shoulder. "Don't want the captain to know about this."

This was certainly intriguing. "What do I need to do?" Cecilia asked.

"Follow us," they both said. Without another word, they turned and rushed into the darkness, their watery forms making little noise, like the sea just before the first breaths of a storm.

Cecilia glanced at the stairs for a considering moment then hastened after William and Frank. She needed to know what the omens were and why the captain had tried to hide them from her.

Pepin-René Marc Daviau prided himself on being the laziest person aboard the ship. There was something powerful and invigorating about being a captain who did nothing. True, the men didn't seem to appreciate it, but they couldn't really do anything about it, now could they?

Pepin glanced down at his shadowy arm. He flexed his fingers. A thrill swept up his arm and into his head, causing the world to blur momentarily. Well, they couldn't do anything about it yet, anyway. He held the power. He was the captain.

For now.

Irritated at the thought, Pepin swung his legs off his desk and strode toward the door, trying to tell himself that he didn't *actually* care about going out in what passed for sunlight in the weird, floating world of the *Rose*. He told himself that his dark, expressionless form didn't *actually* bother him. Pepin grimaced ruefully and exited the cabin.

He met several quick glares and disdainful huffs from the ghosts scrubbing the decks nearby. One made a fist and cracked his knuckles.

Pepin rolled his eyes, though no one could see it. He knew the men hated him. He knew they would kill him the moment they had the chance. However, was a little subtlety about these particular sentiments too much to ask? It wasn't *his* fault the Fee created the *Rose* to move at speeds proportionate to the misery of her inhabitants. Blaming him was most unfair. William and Frank were the only two who showed him any respect. Even then, were they simply biding their time, waiting to betray him?

Pepin shrugged the thought away as he climbed to the quarterdeck. There, striking a pose with feet braced and arms crossed, he eyed with affected disinterest the men below him on the main deck. Some were on their hands and knees, scrubbing furiously at the red boards. He had given them the choice of scrubbing until the boards shone white or practicing curtsies for five hours. *Sacrebleu,* one of them was trying to curtsy! Pepin burst into laughter at the sight.

He heard muttered curses and swearing from the men behind him. They were angry. Fine. This would only make the ship move faster.

Beside him the tiller moved of its own accord, as if a huge, invisible finger nudged it from side to side; and the ship cut through the water with speed far greater than any normal vessel could attain, as if the Fee themselves were slashing through the ocean and creating an easy path. Pepin shuddered, thinking back to his last conversation with them. The Fee must truly want Mademoiselle Lester to enter that shack . . .

Mademoiselle Lester. Cecile. What was she doing right now? Pepin had sent William and Frank to watch over her, but she had struck him as an extremely thoughtful type. William and Frank . . . if they shared a single thought between them, it would be a miracle. What if they failed to carry out his plan?

What if she *read* the omens? What if she realized . . . ?

In a flash, Pepin was clattering down the companionway, his dignity cast to the four winds. He cursed his stupidity; why had he let William and Frank guard her? He should have watched over her himself. He should have postponed his lazy meandering to another day.

A day when he would no longer be a monster.

CHAPTER FIVE

AFTER DESCENDING a series of ladders, Frank and William led Cecilia at last to the stinking bilge of the ship, the same level in which she had first awakened in a cell on the *Rose*. Cecilia vaguely recalled climbing only one ladder during her ascent the day before, but she shoved this puzzle into the recesses of her brain for later contemplation. Captain Pepin's warning that she shouldn't venture into any of the lower decks rang in her memory. Nevertheless, she bravely followed the two ghosts until they stood at last before a certain door.

"'Ere we are!" Frank announced, indicating the door with a sweep of one arm.

He reached for the handle, but William grabbed him and jerked his hand away, then glanced back at Cecilia apologetically. "This room can be somewhat disconcerting. Rest assured, you are on the ship, and nothing is going to happen to you."

Cecilia stared at William before shifting her gaze to the red door. "What do you mean? Is it dangerous?"

"No," William said. "Just . . . eerie."

This was little enough comfort. But Cecilia was offered no chance to dwell on her anxiety before Frank thrust the door open, causing William to stumble to the ground, swearing.

Cecilia took one glimpse through the doorway and forgot everything else. She dashed into the room, spinning, her braid bouncing around her shoulders and threatening to come undone.

London glistened around her. She knew it was London, though she couldn't say how she knew. She'd never been to a great city before, but Father John Francis had told her stories of the city of his birth. Stories which had led her to dream of a beautiful place like no other. And this *felt* like London as she had dreamed it would be. The cobblestone street glistened with a recent rain, reflecting the clouds in the creamy sky. Beautifully old and even older buildings lined the streets and towered each above the next, vying for her admiration. It was exactly how she had imagined it.

Cecilia blinked at this thought. No, not exactly. There were no people. Only buildings and streets and skies.

She stared at the cobblestone street then rubbed it with the toe of her shoe. It was flat. The stones held no variation in height, though they *looked* like they did. Cecilia walked over to a building, and her hand touched a solid wall that should have been empty air.

Cecilia closed her eyes and stepped back. When she dared look again, she could see that all was not as it seemed. Here, a brief image of herself flickered in the gray sky . . . there, a glint in the stone, illuminating the building that should have been behind her.

It wasn't London. It was a room, but a room that was a mirror. A strange mirror . . .

The Fee.

She shuddered and turned to question Frank and William, pausing when she noticed that they had not yet entered the room. Frank inched across the threshold, out of the dim redness of the rest of the ship and into her London, his gaze darting to every corner, a frown etched between his brows. William's eyes were shut tight. He opened them briefly before slamming them shut again, twitching his head as if trying to negate an argument.

"What's wrong?" Cecilia asked.

William's eyes popped open. Frank snorted. "What's wrong? That's a good one. Don't see how you're holding up so well when you've never . . ." Frank paused. He groaned. "Aw, don't tell me. First the food, now this room? What do *you* see?"

"London," Cecilia said, glancing back at the street—no, the mirror. "It's beautiful," she added to herself, her whisper strangely loud in the silence.

"I would hardly describe London that way," William said. He opened his eyes. They widened, and he shuddered but kept them open. "But I wouldn't mind seeing London now."

"What do you see?" Cecilia asked. "Is it bad?"

Frank's frown deepened. "It's bad," he murmured. He offered no further explanation.

"Well then!" William said, abruptly changing the subject. "This makes everything easier! My lady, do you see the chest in the far corner of the room? It will be hard to spot at first."

Cecilia glanced at the corner. She saw only a swinging silversmith sign and the street. Wait . . . the street *did* look a bit odd. The depth wasn't right.

Cecilia, moving a little uncertainly, made her way to that strange, warped corner. As she drew nearer, she discerned the shape of a chest.

Kneeling, she groped for its latch. She opened the chest.

The lining of the chest was the same red as the rest of the ship. Cecilia scowled at the color, hating to find it here in her vision of London. But she forgot the garish hue when she noticed the book—a shabby, leather-bound book at the bottom of the otherwise-empty chest. Cecilia plucked it up.

"Aye, that's it!" Frank said. "Bring it here, miss! We'll tell you about the omens with it!"

Cecilia started for the door then halted, holding the book against her heart. The two ghostly sailors seemed far too eager. Had they brought her here to fetch this book for them because they were too afraid to enter the room themselves? Were they lying to her?

Remaining where she stood, Cecilia carefully rested the book across her arm and opened the binding. "I think I'll take a look first."

William started forward then yelped and leaped back as soon as his boot crossed into the room. Frank's brow furrowed. "Miss Lester, please come out. We'll explain it all to you."

Ignoring their protests, Cecilia lowered her gaze to the worn pages before her.

They were crammed with hurried writing in blotchy red ink. Barely legible words covered every inch of every page, down the center, along the sides, upside down. Some were crossed or blotted out, others written with smearing ink, and others with hardly any ink at all, pale and small. She struggled to wrest any order or meaning from the bizarre scrawls, and after a few moments noticed that every line of writing contained a name followed by two phrases. Cecilia began reading the lines she could decipher, the ones written with a bold and decisive hand.

Lawrence T. Witten: Impatience for his wife—Silence the Solid Woman
John "Jack" Peterson: No Compassion for Life—Murder the Solid Woman

Michael Forest: Torture—Maim the Solid Woman

Adam P. Brown: Manipulating selfishly—Betray the Solid Woman

Rojo Cortez: Cowardice under pressure—Abandon the Solid Woman

Cecilia gasped and lifted her gaze from the book. She stared at William and Frank. They blinked mournfully back at her. "Why the Solid Woman?" she asked. "Why do these all involve something horrible happening to the Solid Woman? To . . . me?"

They made no reply.

She glowered at them and pressed herself against the far wall. Staring at the pages again, she struggled to recognize some sort of organization or pattern in the names, seeking the captain's omen or William's or Frank's. But she recognized none of the names.

However, she did notice that the majority of the names were crossed through. She wondered at this, and then realized that it must be because they had died. There weren't as many sailors aboard the ship as there were names in the book. How men made of water and ink managed to die, she could not imagine.

She continued to scan the names, flipping through pages hastily, trying to ignore the rising panic in her stomach at all of the atrocities the omens outlined.

Torture the Solid Woman. Drown the Solid Woman. Assault the Solid Woman.

With a shuddering breath, Cecilia started to slam the book shut. But something stopped her. There on the page was a name that was neither crossed out nor blood-red. It was fading, almost invisible, written in black ink that appeared comfortingly ordinary. She might have missed it had she not been so weary of red.

Charles "Curly" Tanner: Liar—Almost Solid

"Who's Charles Tanner?" Cecilia asked, closing the book with shaking hands. She snapped her head up to glare at William and Frank, but then shrieked and stumbled backwards, tripped over the hidden chest in the corner, and collapsed against the wall.

The captain stood behind William and Frank.

Pepin forced his breathing to steady, trying to make himself appear less forbidding and thus alleviate the sudden darkness his appearance had caused in the room. Cecilia looked ready to faint but for the defiant gleam in her eye. Her curiosity regarding the omens was only natural, and her swooning would serve no purpose.

The two imbeciles before him, on the other hand . . .

"Franklin. William." Pepin was pleased at how soft his voice sounded. The two pirates shuddered and tilted their heads to glance at him out of the corners of their eyes. Pepin crossed his arms and leaned casually against the wall. He examined the mirror room as though only just noticing it. "Why would you bring Mademoiselle Lester to such a dreadfully dull part of the *Rose?* This is hardly a considerate gesture of hospitality."

"Uh . . . well . . . you see, sir, we . . ." Frank stammered. William trod on his foot, causing the oaf to shut his mouth.

Pepin raised an eyebrow. "*Mais non*, I do not see. William, would you care to explain?"

William, to give him credit, put on a brave face. Though it could be only so brave while wet, dripping, and framed by slimy black hair. "She wanted to know about the omens," he said.

"You could have explained them without coming here."

William's watery skin rippled. "Didn't think of that, sir," he replied, his voice wavering, betraying the fear he was no doubt attempting to quell.

Pepin waved a lazy hand. "Fair enough. You're both fools. Run along now. Mademoiselle Lester will be along shortly."

William and Frank stood for a moment before gathering whatever senses they possessed and scurrying away from him. Cecilia clutched the book to her chest. Pepin frowned at this. Her expression struck him as odd. Her lips quivered, and a lock of thick hair slid over one eye. Cecilia was scared, and for some reason this seemed wrong.

No, he knew why it felt wrong. The dark hair, the trapped look, the helplessness . . . She looked like his mother on that day so long ago . . . .

"We're simply going to talk," Pepin said, focusing on the situation. She didn't relax. Indeed, she looked as though she might be ill, so dark were the hollows around her eyes. "Are you well, Mademoiselle?" he inquired politely.

Cecilia nodded. She tightened her hold on the book as though fearing he might snatch it from her. At last she broke the strained silence, saying, "Why didn't you tell me all of the horrible things about the omens? What are you planning to do to me?" Her voice shook.

Pepin adjusted his stance. He must appear less threatening. He could not have her throwing herself overboard. "I did not tell you because I did not want you to be frightened. Cowards prey on weakness. The pirates aboard this ship would have sensed that you were easy loot and would have attacked. By acting as though the omens did not bother you—for what else would they have assumed we were discussing last night?—you made them wary. What with your being solid, they might have assumed you had unknown powers that could fend them off."

Cecilia shifted her weight, looking down at the floor of the room. She scuffed her shoe along the ground, tracing a pattern only she could see. Pepin observed her, tilting his head to one side, wondering what she made of this strange mirror room. The men saw terrors, their nightmares made reality. When Pepin had first arrived on the *Rose* and was given her captaincy, the Fee had suggested locking men into the room to make the ship sail faster. Pepin had agreed. The ship had skimmed the water like a skipped stone, gliding and glorious, the fastest Pepin had ever traveled in his life. He had loved every second of it.

Until he unlocked the door to be greeted by a seething Jack and a pile of gaunt blue bodies. The poor sailors had nearly died of their own terrors all because Pepin wanted a little speed! Even now he saw the Book of Omens clutched in Jack's hand, sizzling black blood dripping from its leather cover to the floor and vanishing into the nothingness that was Pepin's nightmare.

Pepin forced his thoughts away from that rather disheartening memory to focus on more amusing matters, such as Cecilia's current confusion. She continued to stare at the ground for several more seconds, various emotions flitting across her features—sadness, anger, disbelief. She jerked her head up and looked directly into him, almost through him. He shoved away the urge to shudder and met her gaze.

"Unknown powers," she said, her voice level. "I'm a worthless, penniless, and friendless woman, barely out of childhood. What powers might I possibly have?"

Pepin smirked at her analysis. He would hardly have described her that way. *Exquise! Magnifique! Charmante!* would have been his chosen adjectives. "Oh, you have no powers in reality," he said with a shrug. "But sailors are a superstitious lot." He indicated the book clutched in her hands. "What did you read inside?"

"You know very well what I read!" Cecilia exclaimed, her voice losing the control she had gained during her brief silence, growing higher in pitch. "You know that all of those men want to hurt me! No doubt *you* want to hurt me!" With an effort she mastered herself, her jaw firm and tight with tension. "You're just waiting to do it."

Pepin chuckled dryly. "I swear to you, Mademoiselle Lester, I have no intention of hurting you."

"Then tell me your omen," Cecilia said.

Pepin fidgeted. *"C'est une situation délicate.* Embarrassing."

Cecilia's eyes narrowed. Hair fell over her face again. "Tell me."

Pepin sighed. He dropped his head and waited a few moments before standing straighter and meeting her eyes with what he hoped was a cool, clear, open-hearted gaze. "My omen . . ." His voice trailed away. He took a step forward into the black chasm of the room. The pit surrounding him seemed to fade under the intensity of Cecilia's gaze. "My omen says that to be free of this curse, I must fall in love with the Solid Woman and she must love me in return. Only then will I be free."

CHAPTER
SIX

ECILIA STARED at the captain, at the shadows where his eyes must be. For once he appeared completely serious, even somber. She became suddenly aware of how greasy and wind-blown her hair must look, how filthy her dress was. A hot flush rose in her cheeks, and she would have given anything to hide it. Just because he claimed that he needed her to love him didn't mean she must necessarily reciprocate his feelings. Must she?

No. No, she couldn't love him. How could she love someone she couldn't see? How could she love a notorious pirate, such an evil person?

How could she even contemplate such a notion?

Pepin seemed to arrive at the same conclusion. He let out a dramatic sigh. "Alas! I know it is a hopeless task! Well, at least half of it. I believe I shall soon fulfill, if I have not already fulfilled, my own part of the equation."

Cecilia shivered at his last words. Their tone was biting, derisive, as if he couldn't believe himself. A surge of pity rushed to Cecilia's head, forcing her to blink away the pressure in her eyes. Because he was right: She knew both too much and too little to ever love him. It was a hopeless task.

A hopeless task . . . The phrase struck Cecilia suddenly, and she frowned. *A hopeless task*. She considered the horrible omens she had just read and suddenly felt as though she held in her hands a particularly troublesome sailor's knot. As though somehow she were meant to untie it.

Meanwhile, Captain Pepin stood before her, having just made his improbable declaration. She must offer him some form of answer. "I am . . . I am so sorry," she began.

Pepin huffed and pressed a hand to his heart, cutting her off. "*Mais oui*, pour salt water on the wound, will you? No, no, make no apology! 'Tis a mere flesh wound, not a blow to my heart or soul or anything important!"

Cecilia felt oddly guilty. "I did not mean to hurt you," she said, furious at herself for how hotly she blushed. "I was insensitive, but I . . ." She held up the leather book. *A hopeless task*, she thought once more, and could not keep herself from asking, "Do you think the Fee intended all the omens to be hopeless?"

The shadow of Pepin's face turned weirdly quizzical.

Cecilia continued: "I'm not supposed to be here. The Fee did not expect me to fall into the whirlpool. Could it be that they never intended for you to find a Solid Woman, and thus never intended for you to be saved? Because if so, that is cruelty beyond any I have witnessed!"

"Indeed it is," Pepin replied dryly. "And what is more, I believe you are correct. I have considered it many times myself. The *Rose* sails an ocean that is not of earth, not of heaven, not of hell . . . not of anything except punishment with no offer of hope. Everything in this eerie netherworld has been taken and arranged by the Fee at some point. The men, the disgusting food, the *Rose,* small islands, treasure, other ships—"

"Other ships?" Cecilia interrupted. "There are others?"

"Mais oui, other ships with other cursed men searching for escape. We run across each other occasionally. And we fight. Such fun. As I was saying, the Fee—"

"Fight each other?" Cecilia exclaimed. "Why would you fight each other? Are you not all trapped together in this world?"

Pepin raised his arms defensively. "How else are we to find out if they have a Solid Woman?"

"You could try talking!" She sounded like a screeching fishwife in her own ears, but the captain did gall her so. Besides, the thought of being caught in a battle between eager, bloodthirsty ghosts provided incentive beyond mere courage. "By fighting each other, you do exactly what the Fee want you to do. Why give them the pleasure?"

Pepin shrugged. "You can trust no one, Mademoiselle Cecile. Not in this world, nor in the other. Who deserves trust?"

"It's Miss *Lester,* Captain Daviau," Cecilia said, biting the words out aggressively. Just when she had begun to think some decency remained in him, he began talking like the very pirate all the tales made him out to be! Well, he could disregard her opinions, but he would not disregard her dignity.

"But of course, Mademoiselle." Pepin flourished his tricorn and bowed extravagantly. "Propriety may be dropped among friends, but not between those who are courting."

Though she knew he must be teasing, Cecilia hastily exclaimed, "That is absolutely not what I—"

Yet again he laughed at her ire, waving a shadowy hand to hush her protests. She wished then that she had not provided him the satisfaction of watching her rise to his bait. Oh, what an aggravating condemned ghost-soul was he!

Pepin's voice lost some of its mocking amusement, turning momentarily serious. "Last night," he said, "I mentioned the one port at which we can dock, *oui*? We sail there now. There is an enchanted cabin on the island that will let no one pass inside without someone solid. Now that we have you, we can enter. I do not know what will happen then, what waits for us inside that cabin. But I feel it is a better option than your being tortured or murdered or skinned and fed to alligators."

Cecilia's eyes widened. "Is that one of the omens?"

Pepin chuckled. "Were you not listening? Did I not just say you would have to fall in love with me?"

Cecilia stared at him for a moment, but then realized it was yet another joke. She felt her mouth pull in an attempt to smile. It felt absurd, but then it also didn't. "You're hardly an alligator," she said.

"*C'est vrai.* I am but a shadowed monster with a pulsing black core. Nothing like so bad as an alligator."

Cecilia might have sworn she saw Pepin wink, and she ducked her head.

"Though if the port turns out to be nothing," he continued, "if you might garner the merest crumb of sympathy for me, I would be most obliged."

Cecilia raised her chin and allowed Pepin to glimpse the smile she had sought to hide. She hadn't intended to, but something about the tone of his voice softened all the harsh feelings she had, up to now, nurtured toward him. She could discern no reciprocal smile on his face, but something told her he was pleased.

She pursed her lips then, as a new thought rose unbidden in her mind. The Fee were liars, promising hope and giving pain. They must have told Pepin about this port and about the need for a Solid person. What if nothing happened? The ghostly men would want to beat her and assault her and kill her and . . . What would she do? Surely Pepin would protect her, especially if she somehow managed to fall in love with him. But was it possible to *make* oneself fall in love?

She supposed not. After all, if one could, it would stand to reason that one could make oneself *not* love someone as well. And then Cecilia's mother would never have fallen in love with the pirate that was Cecilia's father. Not if she could have helped it.

For the sake of her sanity, Cecilia forced these thoughts away. The port *would* work. She would *not* fall in love with a pirate. And she *would* make it safely to London and the home of her father's respectable sister.

"When will we arrive at this port of which you speak?" she asked.

"I am not entirely certain," Pepin admitted. "The distance changes every time, but this might have something to do with the fact that the *Rose* only ever sails about aimlessly. And attacks other cursed ships." The last was added with a barking laugh.

Cecilia, disliking the mockery in that laugh, narrowed her eyes at the shadowy specter that was Pepin. "You say the *Rose* sails aimlessly?" she said, a sting in every word. "My father tells me that a ship takes on the spirit of her captain."

Pepin's shadow rippled, and the room grew darker. Cecilia's eyes felt a sudden sting, as if an invisible ocean wave had just slapped her. She blinked and tried to focus on the words Pepin was murmuring under his breath: "*Esprit de la Rose.* Indeed."

The next moment, however, he seemed to shake away the gloom, and the room lightened. "I should go and see if we are nearing the port," he declared. "And I need to deal with Frank and William. But first, I feel you must make a new acquaintance."

He sauntered out of the room, leaving her alone with her dream of

London and the book. The pain receded from her eyes, and she could think again. In a panic she dropped the book into the chest and slammed the lid. Then she dashed to the door of the room and, standing on the threshold, called out into the redness, "Wait! Where are you going? You cannot leave me here!"

He came back into view so suddenly that Cecilia suspected he had purposely waited for her to scream at him. He bowed low. "My sincerest apologies, Mademoiselle Lester. As I should have said to begin with,"—he made an elegant sweep with one arm—"do follow me."

CHAPTER SEVEN

APTAIN PEPIN led Cecilia up from the hold to a deck that may or may not have been the one on which her cabin was located. From there he walked along a passage that seemed to follow the length of the ship toward the bow, though she couldn't be certain in the near-darkness. Apparently the ghosts felt no need to hang lanterns since their own blue bodies gave off such a glow.

"Wait!" she protested, lifting her skirts so that she might more easily overtake the captain. "Are we heading toward the bow? You told me not to venture that way." Although, she realized, recalling the view from her cabin window that morning, she might already have done so.

"You'll be perfectly safe, Mademoiselle," Pepin called back over his shoulder. *"Allez!"*

Still holding her skirts in both hands, Cecilia hustled after him, her stinging eyes struggling to see in the gloom. "You said it's where you keep the *insane* ones!" she persisted.

The captain paused before a door, which seemed to lead to another room that could not fit on this ship, just like Cecilia's own strange cabin. If she didn't know that the *Rose* was enchanted—or cursed, rather—she would have thought it a door leading out to empty air and a cold drop into the sea.

Pepin's face remained as inscrutable as ever, but she could have sworn he grinned at her. "Speak calmly to it. No sudden movements or loud noises and you will be fine. *Je vous promets.* I promise you." With that, Pepin reached out and caught Cecilia by the elbow. He swung open the door and, before she could so much as utter a protest, pushed her inside.

Cecilia yelped, spun around, and rattled the latch, but she heard only Pepin's bark of laughter and the click of a bolt sliding shut. She was trapped!

"'Ullo, there."

Terror clutched her by the throat. Cecilia whirled about, pressed her back to the door, and saw . . . not quite what she'd expected.

A young boy—perhaps ten years old but no more—sat in the corner on a white stool. All around him the room was dark, and she could make out nothing of its contours or features. But a gentle aura surrounded the boy, revealing his thick curly hair, which was sky blue and bushed around his face. His expression seemed to have worn a mischievous grin for so long that it now had trouble supporting his confused frown.

She blinked at him. He did not look insane.

"You're solid!" he exclaimed. A curl fell in front of his eyes as he bounded from his stool. Unlike everyone else aboard the ship, he didn't look remotely terrifying. He was blue, yes, but he wasn't slimy or malformed.

"Yes . . ." Cecilia replied hesitantly. "And you look different."

"I know. Why are you solid? How did you get solid?" His aura followed him as he crossed the little distance between them. He glared at her suddenly, his expression wary. "You didn't follow your omen, did you?"

"I never had an omen. I came here solid because I inadvertently took the punishment meant for my father," Cecilia explained, speaking as softly as she could with her heart pounding in her chest. What was this? This boy did not even *sound* insane! "Why do you look different?"

Comprehension crossed the boy's features, and he grinned suddenly, revealing a chipped front tooth. "You're the one in the omens, ain't ya?" His smile disappeared. "I'm really sorry about that, miss."

Cecilia shivered. His sudden solemnity was unsettling. "Who are you?" she asked.

"My name's Curly," the boy said. He stuck out his hand. "Curly Tanner. What's your name?"

"Miss Cecilia Lester," she replied, shaking his hand and offering a small smile. "How old are you, Curly?" She let go of his hand, but not before noting how normal his skin felt.

He scratched his head, jostling his curls. "Not really sure. I've been here for a while . . ." His voice trailed away, and he glanced back up at her with a cheeky grin. "If I had decided to follow my omen, I would have chopped your hair off!"

"What?"

He nodded vigorously. "Oh yes, miss! Your hair's really long and nice and dark, so I would have chosen to chop it off, braid and all! I'd either do that, or I would have ripped up your dress, or maybe I would have tripped you into a pile of dead fish or something."

"I . . . don't understand." If she hadn't already been backed against the door, Cecilia would have taken a wary step away from the blue boy. Maybe he *was* insane.

Curly went on as if he hadn't heard her. "You're lucky I decided to do the opposite of what my omen said and not play cruel jokes on people. You would have been in *big* trouble if I weren't such a 'rebel cur dog.' That's what William likes to call me." The last sentence ended with an explanatory nod.

Realization knocked into Cecilia like a blistering wind. "So . . . so you're breaking the curse by simply doing the *opposite* of your omen?"

Curly started whistling and crammed his hands into his pockets, but his curls gave a nod in the affirmative.

"But I . . ." Cecilia frowned. He *did* look far more ordinary than everyone else aboard the *Rose*. She couldn't dismiss this as the ravings of a mad boy. "Does the captain know? Why isn't everyone breaking the curse?"

"It's not as simple as all that, miss," Curly said, his voice carefree though he eyed her circumspectly. "It wasn't just *not* doing my prophecy. It was *trying* to change. The way I see it, your outside isn't worth loving until your inside is. That's what my pa always told me, and I thought about that, and well . . ." He shrugged. "I'm getting better."

Cecilia waited, sensing he had more to say. Curly tossed his hair out of his eyes and looked her boldly in the face. "When I started to change, lots of people tried to do what I was doing. But it didn't work for them. They—Jack, mostly—got real mad at me and tried to hurt me. They thought it was another one of my jokes. The captain, though he was plenty angry that it hadn't worked for him too, made sure to protect me. He put me in this room, and he tells everyone I've gone insane. He, William, and Frank are the only ones who know I'm fine. They bring me food and stuff to do."

"But the captain implied that you were truly insane. He cautioned me against movements and noises and told me to speak calmly to you. Why would he do that?"

Curly grinned. "I'm not insane, miss. The captain wanted you to meet me. He does things like that. He says one thing but really means the other, and he'll trick you into all sorts of stuff you'd never have imagined yourself doing. It's just his way."

An unbidden image of her father convincing her when she was only twelve years old that rum would help her grow, then laughing when the true effects of the drink took hold, crossed her mind. She shoved this thought away only to follow it with the memory of her mother screaming her father out of the house because of the incident. She understood Mother better now.

"I wouldn't take it too hard, miss," Curly said. "This is good, don't you see? He had to get you to talk to me and still keep his story that I'm insane, in case anyone overheard him. Jack likes to spy on him, and it would be bad for both me and you if Jack knew I was right in the head!"

"I suppose it would be," Cecilia mumbled.

Curly reached out suddenly and took Cecilia by the hand. It was a simple gesture, full of honest comfort. After a moment of hesitation, Cecilia squeezed the boy's fingers in return.

"I know why Cap'n wanted you to see me," Curly said. "You're solid and I'm nearly solid. He needs you to help us find a cure."

"You seem to have found a cure already," Cecilia pointed out.

Curly made a face. "I thought I had. I know I'm changing. But it didn't work for any of the other men, and I don't know why. It doesn't make sense." He brightened. "But now that you're here, I'm sure we can work something out! I'm sure you can figure out how to save us all!"

"Maybe."

"Aw, come on, miss. You got to! You're the only hope we've got left! You've got to help us."

Cecilia studied the boy, taking in his blue-tinted skin and freckles and bouncy curls. He was so young and he was trying so hard. Perhaps Pepin had meant well by manipulating her into meeting the child. She smiled at the thought of the captain saving the life of a ten-year-old boy. Deep down, he *had* to be a good person . . . even if he did believe in attacking before speaking.

"I'll try," Cecilia whispered.

Curly beamed and gave her hand another squeeze. "That's all anyone can do, miss. Try."

CHAPTER EIGHT

"WE'VE ARRIVED."

"We've arrived, *Captain*."

Jack turned an ugly sneer Pepin's way. His quivering ink-heart pulsed with sudden loathing. "*Captain*," he snarled.

"*Très bien*, my dear Jacques." Pepin mockingly applauded. "Go and tell the rest of the men."

Jack stormed across the deck and down the companionway, leaving Pepin alone on the quarterdeck. He squinted through the ever-present fog and could vaguely make out the shape of a jagged rock. The quay jutted out like an embedded thorn from the calloused skin of the stone, craggy and misshapen. Pepin raised his gaze and followed the outline of the slope until his gaze reached a point where the shack rested. He couldn't see it, but he knew it was there.

He shuddered and turned away.

You've got to do it, he reminded himself. *Weather that storm when you come to it.*

Recovering himself and assuming an attitude of nonchalant disregard, Pepin watched his crew crawl like flies over deck and rigging, trying to find something petty to critique. But he couldn't muster the energy. Odd—usually fault-finding bolstered his spirits.

Pepin shrugged and made his way down to the main deck, wondering if Cecilia had spoken with Curly yet and whether she would be more furious or less. Judging by what he knew about her, probably less furious. She was not like other women he had known. There was something in her eye he'd never seen in anyone else. She was both thoughtful and brash, and much braver than he would have given her credit for based on her petite and pretty appearance.

Frank and William had told him that she had seen London inside the omen room. The room usually showed everyone's deepest fears, so it would stand to reason that Cecilia saw her greatest dream. But why London? Why was she so determined to leave whatever life she'd had in Bermuda for a new one in such a city? Her life must have been terrible. Either that or she was running from something.

If the latter were the case then Cecilia reminded him of exactly one other person—himself. But this would imply that he hated her. He certainly did not hate her.

Though she'll hate me before this is all over . . .

Cecilia sat down on the beach and rubbed her aching feet, glaring ruefully at her discarded shoes. Her feet were sore and blistered, no doubt from sleeping in her shoes and dashing about all day. She gingerly dipped her toes into the cool water, relieved when, after the first salt-sting, the gently lapping waves soothed her burning blisters.

She felt watching eyes from the wharf. None of the crew members bothered her here on the sand, though they stared at her with expressions ranging from mild annoyance to barely contained hatred as they sat and lounged upon the rotting planks. But they could not follow her onto the island, not even so far as the sandy beach. Apparently the sand disagreed with the watery build of the ghost-men.

With a shudder, Cecilia forced herself to look away from the ghost-lined quay and out to sea, reminding herself yet again that she was solid. She fidgeted in the damp sand, little caring about dirtying her dress or getting soaked. These were minor inconveniences compared to the freedom of movement she now enjoyed. What a relief it was to be free of the *Rose* and her confining spaces!

Thank you, merciful Father, she thought, and fingered her rosary, perhaps a little more fervently than was her habit. The rosary was a gift from her mother who, though raising her daughter in a Protestant English community, had given her as much proper Catholic upbringing as possible. Cecilia carefully counted the beads now, first making the Sign of the Cross, then whispering the Apostles' Creed. From there she moved on to an *Our Father*, murmuring the words in Spanish as her mother had taught her.

"I might have known you were the praying type," a now-familiar French accent drawled behind her.

Cecilia startled, dropping her crucifix, and turned to gaze up at the shadowy captain, who approached along the strand of beach. She blinked then offered him a short nod. "What are you doing on the sand? The other men cannot bear it."

The captain laughed and settled on a flat rock near to her, stretching one long leg before him while he leaned an elbow on the upraised knee of his other leg. "Mademoiselle, if you have not yet noticed, *I* am not like other men."

Cecilia pursed her lips and *hmmed* noncommittally. He certainly did not need her affirmation to inflate his ego.

"You pray to God, yes?" Pepin pressed. He indicated her mother's rosary with a wave of his hand. "Your face looked like thunder. That may have been the angriest *Our Father* I have ever observed in all my days!"

Cecilia fingered the worn necklace once more, looking away from the captain to gaze out at the foggy sea. "I do not mean to be angry. Or disrespectful. But sometimes . . ."

"Sometimes a mortal soul feels the need to shout at God and not to pray, *oui*?" Pepin chuckled. "Every soul experiences this at some point in life, Mademoiselle. Otherwise, I would doubt that particular soul's humanity. Which is saying a great deal, coming from me!"

This speech might have shocked Cecilia a few short days ago. But her life had progressed far beyond such little surprises now. "Do you shout at God?" she asked curiously, tilting her face up toward him.

"*Non, jamais*. Never," Pepin replied, a mock-terrified tremor in his voice.

Cecilia laughed. Both her mother and Father John Francis would have been horrified to observe her sitting so calmly beside a spectral ghost and laughing at his irreverent conversation. But the laughter lightened Cecilia's heavy heart. "How do you pray then, Captain Pepin?" she asked.

Pepin shrugged. His cheerful demeanor seemed to dampen, and salt stung Cecilia's eyes. "My mother raised me in the Catholic church, though she was not Catholic herself. She often went on about all of the ways she disagreed. *C'est très déroutant.* Confusing, yes? I left the church when my father . . . when I followed my father out to sea. I do not pray often now."

"Your mother raised you Catholic but she was not Catholic herself?"

Cecilia asked. "Why would she do that?"

Pepin shrugged. "I suppose she assumed that some religion was better than none at all. Especially when it came to me." Glancing at Cecilia's face, he laughed and added, "She was English. She ran away to France after becoming pregnant. It would not do to have her good and pious family discover that their youngest daughter conceived a child out of wedlock."

"Oh!" Cecilia exclaimed, her face flushing at the turn of the conversation. She smiled slightly, trying to hide her unease. "I suppose our stories are similar then. My mother was born in the Spanish colonies to a rich family, but when she married a poor English sailor, they disowned her. Father moved her from Florida to St. George's Parish and then he left. He never visited, though he knew of me, until I was nearly three years old."

She attempted to laugh, as if the fact were amusing, but it wasn't, so she hurried on. "Mother and I always attended service at the local Protestant church, but she clung to her Catholic upbringing. A few months ago she fell ill and . . . I wanted to write to my father as soon as she took to her bed, but how can one send messages to a man at sea?" Cecilia struggled to keep the bitterness out of her voice, but the shift in the shadows of Pepin's face, indicating a raised eyebrow, informed her that she had failed. She shrugged and shifted her gaze back to the horizon. "He returned to Bermuda three months after the funeral. I asked him to take me away. He did. And now I find that it is hard to follow a righteous path alone."

"And your father . . . he was taking you to London, yes?" Pepin asked. "Pardon my curiosity, but what precisely draws you to London? I personally find Paris much more inviting."

"My father has a sister in London. I'm going to stay with her and her husband. They don't approve of his privateering, so I'm sure I'll like them." She paused. "If I ever meet them, that is."

"Ah, yes! The *respectable* sister. You mentioned her during our first conversation. And why would you not meet them?"

The captain seemed startled and sincerely worried. It was gratifying, Cecilia admitted, to feel that he might hold some concern for her. She sighed heavily, however, and shook her head. "Captain Pepin, you know as well as I that the Fee are liars. What if this mysterious cabin does nothing? Or if it does . . ."

Unable to finish, she began wiping her grit-covered hands on her skirts, attempting to clean them. "Will you take me to London?" she asked, struggling to keep her voice steady. It was a simple question but terribly important! And Captain Pepin was such a selfish man . . . "If the curse is broken, will you escort me safely to my father's sister?"

Pepin nodded his head in a slight bow. "*Mais oui.* It would be my honor, Mademoiselle."

Cecilia felt her face grow warm at his sincerity, at the unaccustomed kindness in his voice, so strange coming from that featureless face. She glanced up at him but felt tears springing to her eyes, so she quickly looked down again. "Thank you." She stopped trying to wipe her hands clean and let them come to rest in her lap. For a short time the two shared a companionable silence.

Pepin snorted suddenly. "Privateer. *Si ridicule.*"

Her eyes stung, not with tears but as though they burned with salt. Cecilia blinked back the pain until she could look quizzically at Pepin, surprised by his sudden shift in mood. "Better than being a pirate."

Pepin chuckled darkly. "Oh, *ma chère,* surely you like pirates! Have we not been a most charming collection of hosts to you?"

Cecilia offered a weak smile, glancing up at the looming figures lining the wharf. They, seeing her look their way, shuffled and quivered, their black hearts trembling as though in a silent chorus of violence. "Charming," she whispered, and closed her eyes quickly.

"Be that as it may," Pepin continued, his voice snapping back to its usual drawl, "I am still curious. Why leave Bermuda at all? Surely you had friends."

Cecilia was silent for several breaths. How should she explain it to him? Or, a better question, *should* she explain it to him? She decided she should, though she couldn't think of a reason other than pure instinct. She would question her sanity later.

"No, I had no friends," she said after a moment. She buried her toes in the sand. "Other than Father John Francis, of course. He was very kind. But everyone else in my village thought that I was odd at best. At worst, that I was a pirate's illegitimate daughter. Needless to say, not many people sought out my company."

"Why would they think you odd?"

Cecilia moved her feet, making mounds of sand rise and fall. She ducked her head, letting a few loose strands of hair hide her face. "Naturally, the children lacked their parents' prejudice. Whenever I visited the main part of town with my mother, I would play with the children and invent stories for them. Stories of adventure and sea serpents and . . . mermaids." She sighed. "The little boys and girls appreciated it. The parents did not."

Pepin snorted. "Well, I think you are brilliant. And as I am the smartest person I have ever met, I assure you that you may trust my opinion on the matter."

Cecilia did not reply, but a slow smile spread across her face. She continued to push her feet through the sand, trying to focus on the grating feeling between her toes instead of the grateful feeling in her heart. Indeed, was it mere gratitude that she felt? For while she sat here in the captain's strange but admittedly charismatic company, her heart knew a lightness she had not experienced since before her dear mother's death. Could it possibly be that she'd found a . . . a *friend* in this vain, bizarre, spectral apparition of a man?

She opened her mouth to speak, but William's panicked voice suddenly cut through the air:

"Captain! Captain, mutiny! *Mutiny!*"

CHAPTER NINE

PEPIN LEAPED from the ground and ran toward the wharf. He could hear shouts and curses echoing off the boulders beyond the beach and the wharf. He swore to himself. Why did they have to mutiny *now?*

At the edge of the beach he took a deep breath and spun around. Cecilia, who had scrambled to her feet and hastened after him, cried out in surprise and skidded to a halt, nearly colliding with him. "You are probably going to want to stay here, Mademoiselle," he said. "Mutinies are dull affairs, and it would be the height of rudeness for me to allow a lady to undergo such boredom."

Cecilia stared up at him, momentarily confused. Then her jaw set, and he had to stop himself from grinning . . . not that she could see a grin on his featureless face. "You could be killed!" she protested. "Am I supposed to stand by and watch you be cut down by those monsters?"

"*Mais non,* you could see nothing from this vantage! You might hear it though." Pepin allowed his grin, but then turned serious when her lips only pursed tighter, her knuckles whitening as she clenched her fingers around her quickly grabbed shoes. "Stay on the beach, Mademoiselle," he said. "They can't hurt you on the sand, and I can put an end to the boring opera that is a mutiny much faster without your being made a target, *comprenez vous?*"

Cecilia wavered for a moment then nodded once. Pepin turned and climbed the stony rise leading from the beach to the rickety quay. The entire crew had gathered there, pointing cutlasses, daggers, pistols, and muskets at him. Pepin swaggered toward them, heaving a great, long-suffering sigh.

"A party, *mes garçons?* You know that's not allowed until your chores are done," he drawled, swatting aside a sword that was a breath from his throat.

The sword swung back toward his face. The shadows of Pepin's face twisted in a smirk. The owner of the sword growled, baring his slimy teeth. It was Jack. "We don't want any part of this, *Captain,*" he said, liquid dripping like blood from the sharp ends of his canines. "The Fee may have given you powers, but you're spent. You can't fight all of us at once. I reckon we could even take the girl from you."

The rest of the sailors swore their agreement, surging toward Pepin, though they retained a ring of distance between themselves and the captain. Pepin heard a muffled whimper, and his gaze slid to the side, spotting William and Frank with cutlasses pressed to their necks. Pepin acknowledged this with a chuckle. "Scared of William and Frank? I expected more from you, Jacques."

Jack took a step closer, his sword level with Pepin's chin. "You've been using us. Don't think we've forgotten how you trapped us in the mirror room! Don't think we've forgiven you. We all want to be free. What gives you the right to liberate yourself with the girl?"

Pepin flicked invisible specks of dust from his coat. "It may interest you to know that, should my plan work, we might just free all of you." He watched Jack carefully from the corner of his eye.

The men guffawed. Jack sneered. "I'm sure of it." He waved his free arm. The crowd parted, and the ghost who had been curtseying so prettily earlier that day came forward, carrying a large sack that writhed and wriggled as something inside struggled to escape.

Pepin felt his grin disappear and his control slip. The port darkened, and the men closest to him staggered back a step.

In a fluid motion Jack sliced the sack, and a strangled cry escaped. The sacking fell away, revealing Curly, gagged, his cheek and shoulder bleeding red from the cut. The boy thrashed and squirmed, but his hands were tied together and his legs still caught up in the sack. His gaze met Pepin's, and Pepin knew that the boy had been crying. Vaguely he heard Jack saying something, and he saw the sword move from his own throat to Curly's.

Everything went black. An energized, rippling force like a gale lit by flashes of lightning surged through Pepin. He felt it draining him, hurting him, but he did not stop. His vision filled with something like fire, and he forced all the energy building up inside him to channel into a single terrible blast.

Jack dropped his sword. He saw what was coming, and his eyes rounded in terror. He turned and started to run through the crowd but knew already that he was too late. The captain, though not as strong as he had once been, was not as weak as he had guessed.

Jack took no more than four steps. The world surged, and he heard strange noises—screams, wind, laughter, storms, a weird lullaby, and more screams.

Then . . . silence.

Light filtered back through her vision, and she realized she was not actually closing her eyes. Cecilia blinked. Her eyes felt scorched, heated red dots blinding her. She gasped and clapped her hands over her face, breathing heavily, forcing herself to face one problem at a time. First breathe, then see.

She lowered her hands and slowly lifted her eyelids. Her head burned, but it was bearable. Her vision cleared.

A blue wall arched above the wharf in a crescent. For a moment Cecilia thought she was back on her father's ship surrounded by the Fee's magical water. But no. This wall was different.

It was the crew, stacked like bales of sagging hay, sleeping soundly. Even Curly slept, though he looked much more peaceful than the crew, despite the gag and the rope. She could see the rhythmic waves of their breathing, but none of them made any effort to move.

Except for William and Frank. Those two were standing, mouths agape, staring at the pile of men all around them. As if united in thought, they pivoted suddenly, but they didn't face Cecilia.

Cecilia followed their gazes. She covered her mouth with both hands to stifle a scream.

Pepin lay on the soaked wharf, panting. Droplets of crimson throbbed in his chest, outlining the pulsing squid-like heart that had heretofore been indiscernible from his shadowed figure. Red lines tore across his body, pooling in places like bruises after a fight. His fingers were creased with them, as if blistered from a punch. They slid down his chest and legs, giving fatigue a color. But worst of all were the pools around his eyes. Black eyes rimmed in red shone from their sockets, giving him the aspect of a demonic skeleton.

Cecilia forced herself to look at him, slowly lowering her hands. Her mouth hung open. She tried to think of something to say, but the only words she could recall were *red, black,* and *beast.*

Pepin heaved himself to his feet. The red pulsed brighter before fading. "Get Curly," he snapped at Frank and William. "All of you hide on the island. I doubt the rest of the crew will be feeling up to a sociable natter and a spot of tea when they awaken." He chuckled dryly, though he didn't sound amused.

"But, sir," Frank protested, "we can't walk on the land. It makes me go all . . . all *runny.*"

"*Sacrebleu*, must I do everything for you imbeciles?" Though his words were as biting as ever, they lacked Pepin's usual vitality. He staggered a pace or two, drew himself up, and latched hold of William with one hand, Frank with the other. "Ready, *mes amis?*"

"Um," Frank gulped, and then both of them yelped as ripples of black shot through the captain's arms, passing from his hands into the two of them, flowing up to their shoulders and on into the rest of their bodies. Even as Cecilia watched, their watery outer forms solidified until they were almost, though not quite, as dark as the captain himself.

Gasping out a string of French expletives, Pepin stepped back, his heart heaving red once more from the effort. "Now!" he gasped. "Pick up the boy and go!"

Not waiting to be told twice, Frank and William, slightly unsteady on their newly solidified limbs, scrambled past the pile of men on the wharf. Frank hoisted Curly over his shoulder, and dashed around Pepin and onto the rocky ground, stumbling over boulders and rocks until they disappeared around the curve of the hill. They didn't look back.

Cecilia suddenly wished she could go with them.

"*Allez*, Mademoiselle," Pepin said. He stumbled off the wharf, heading in the direction opposite to that taken by his friends, moving at a jerking, uneasy pace at first, but slowly gaining speed and strength. Soon he was striding along with his shoulders back, assuming his familiar jaunty attitude, though Cecilia suspected it was no more than a feeble show. Lines of red pulsed from his heart out through his limbs, like veins made visible through the shadowy skin.

Cecilia cast an almost longing glance back at the *Rose*, but the glare of the red ship only reminded her of the strange transformation taking place in Pepin. She shuddered and ran after the captain, pausing only to shove her feet into her shoes. "Where are we going?"

He pointed to the highest peak of the craggy rocks that made up the island then dropped his arm to his side wearily. "The cabin is at the top. No one has been able to enter it, but as I said before, I think a Solid person might be able to. I don't know what's inside, but it is the only hope we have."

Cecilia paused. "You realize that if this doesn't work those men will *kill* us?" Somehow she wasn't frightened, but she knew she would be frightened as soon as a sword was pointed at her throat the way Jack had pointed his sword at Pepin. Her heart trembled at the too-recent memory.

"Well then, we had better hurry to ensure that they are still asleep when this fails. Then we can take the *Rose* and run," Pepin said over his shoulder.

Cecilia's brow wrinkled in a worried frown. This was complete insanity. If she had known that the entire crew was ruthless enough to threaten a little boy like Curly, she would have . . .well, she would have . . .

She would have come anyway. The captain was right. They had no other choice.

But what about Curly? a voice in the back of her head whispered. *He's different. He's changing. Why didn't it work for the other men? Were they too evil? No, William and Frank . . .*

It didn't matter. She had promised Curly she would try, and this was their only hope. Pulling her hair back from her face, she darted after Pepin. He stumbled now, and his breath came in deep pants and stifled grunts.

"Are you well?" Cecilia asked, tentatively reaching out her hand.

He wrenched away from her. "Fine."

Cecilia frowned at him but didn't press the issue. Offering comfort to a pirate who had professed to love—or nearly to love—her felt unnatural anyway. Besides, she had no wish to touch the swirling black-and-red-ness.

Questions burned through her head like a forest fire, and though she wanted to stop herself, she couldn't help but ask, "What did you do back at the wharf? How did you make all of the men fall asleep?"

Pepin did not turn around. The red in his back pulsed brighter. He continued to climb.

"They mentioned some sort of . . . power?" Cecilia pressed, ignoring the voice in her head warning her to leave well enough alone. "Is that what happened? Why do you have that power and they do not?"

"Had," Pepin said, his voice sounding strained but otherwise normal.

"Pardon?"

"*Had* that power, not *have* that power," Pepin corrected. He shook his head and *tsked* sadly, but Cecilia was not about to be so easily put off.

"You don't have the power anymore?" she demanded.

"*J'en ai marre!*" Pepin burst out, causing Cecilia to start and stumble on the boulder she was struggling to climb. She opened her mouth to demand an explanation, but he simply waved his hands dramatically in the air as he ranted. "Why does no one listen to me? I am brilliant! I am a genius! I have the answers to every single problem, and still nobody gives me the respect I deserve." He sighed, resigned. "I suppose it is my humility. It entices people to tread all over me. Like a doormat. Or a dead slug."

Cecilia shook her head in disbelief as she pulled herself onto the boulder. "You are avoiding my question."

Pepin tilted his head sideways as though deeply considering her statement. "I suppose I am. And look! There is my reason!"

Despite herself, Cecilia let her gaze follow his pointed finger.

It was the cabin, or rather, a shack. The walls slanted inward, and the whole thing balanced upon a precarious ledge, placed unevenly along the rocky terrain. The middle of the roof sagged heavily, as though just waiting for the slightest excuse to collapse and end its miserable existence. Forcing herself not to scramble away at the sight, Cecilia realized that they stood on a crusty cliff high above the ocean. If they fell, they would die.

She glanced sideways at Pepin. The eerie, frightening red remained pooled around his eyes, though it had faded everywhere else. She shuddered. *She* would die, certainly. She would go to heaven to join her dear mother. She could not guess what would happen to Pepin.

For some reason this thought caused her to forget the drop and the water and the cliff.

"Shall we?" she said, brushing past Pepin and striding toward the shack.

The door appeared to be the only section of the shambling structure that was unlikely to collapse upon touch. It stood firmly bolted with a bejeweled chain and lock unlike anything Cecilia had ever before seen.

"This is the key the Fee said would unlock the door. But only to a Solid person. It has not worked before," Pepin said, reaching into his satchel and pulling out a key, which glimmered in the pale sunlight, flashing starkly against his red-streaked hand. "Perhaps you could touch the lock as I try to make it work? I do not know what else to attempt."

Cecilia set her hand on the lock. It felt completely normal, cool and slightly damp, with flecks of almost-unnoticeable rust scratching her fingers. Slowly, reverently, Pepin placed the key into the lock. He paused for a moment then twisted.

The chain clattered to the stone. The door opened with an ominous creak.

The inside looked exactly as the outside implied: dank and falling in on itself. Cecilia made to enter, but paused when Pepin did not move. He bowed slightly and gestured toward the room. "Apologies, but I do not know if I can enter first. The Fee implied that horrifically horrible punishments would ensue should this law be disobeyed."

Cecilia shivered, but nodded and tentatively stepped through the doorway, the moldy floorboards shuddering beneath her feet. She stood in the center of the shack and heard Pepin enter the cabin behind her. Nothing happened. She stared deep into every corner, wondering if there could be an invisible chest hidden here like in the mirror room on the *Rose*. But she saw nothing on the floor or walls. "Captain, I don't think—"

The door slammed shut behind her.

Cecilia spun. Pepin leaned against the door, arms folded casually, but the intense pulsing of the blood-like streams through his body screamed danger.

"Captain Pepin?" Cecilia took a step toward him. "What is happening?"

He didn't answer for a moment, but when he did Cecilia wished he hadn't. The redness pooled around the bottom of his face, shaping into a mouth. A gaping, skull-like mouth made of dripping liquid. "To you or to me?" he asked finally, his voice coated with his customary amusement and arrogance.

"What . . ." Cecilia found her mouth suddenly so dry that she could scarcely form words. "Please tell me."

He leaned his head back against the door. The mouth disappeared, as did the overlarge circles around his eyes. "What is happening?" he whispered. "I am betraying you, Mademoiselle Lester." He reached into his satchel and pulled out the mirror. The mirror with the beautiful diamond frame, the very mirror her father had stolen, the mirror that had caused all her subsequent trials, flashing as though with its own inner light. Pepin pointed it at Cecilia.

Cecilia's eyes burned and burned and *burned,* as though they were melting out of her head, and she screamed at the pain.

A harsh wind roared behind her. Cecilia's head whirled; everything went blurry, colors that didn't belong in the shack streaming together, and her eyes throbbed. The walls shook, and the roof clattered, flashes of dim sunlight slicing through its loose boards. Something blue twisted in front of her, growing and growing, spiraling all around her. Water droplets hit her skin. Cecilia tried to run, but she couldn't move. She couldn't look away. The water stretched closer to her, always spinning. Her soaking dress pulled down on her shoulders.

"Pepin!" she screamed.

He didn't come.

The whirlpool touched her. The stillness shattered. She thrashed around, her arms flailing wildly around her head. Her vision started to blacken, and the last image she saw was the captain kneeling on the cabin floor, the shadow fading from his body and his features coming into focus, his skin becoming healthy flesh and his hair a flaming red.

CHAPTER TEN

SOUNDS DRIFTED through Cecilia's mind, morphing into colors, the colors into feelings, the feelings into memories. She couldn't quite reach complete coherency, but she kept thinking of her mother, and her head hurt terribly. The pounding grew worse in her temples, scattering the frail images and echoing the sounds. She squeezed her eyes shut, trying to hold onto the remnants of the dream, but it was too late. Her head hurt too much.

The sounds disappeared at last. Moaning, Cecilia opened her eyes. She found herself lying on her stomach, arms stretched over her head, with her face pressed against a cold marble floor. Blinking, she pushed herself upright and scrambled to her feet.

She was surrounded. The Fee circled around her, floating above her. No, not floating—*swimming.*

Cecilia's eyes widened and she held her breath, twisting around and struggling not to scream. She stood in the center of what appeared to be an underwater court, as if a king's castle had been built upon sea foam and sunk completely unharmed to the ocean floor. The Fee continued to swim around her, their eyes identically cold and their faces identically beautiful. Cecilia's throat began to burn. She looked up. A ceiling painted with infant merpeople hung above, dipping slightly in the center where an ornate chandelier floated, its weird candles glowing under the water.

She couldn't swim up. Cecilia let go of her breath, her lungs heaving for air. She expected to drag in a lungful of water. She expected to die. Instead she found that she could breathe. And this was almost as terrifying as the prospect of death.

What is happening to me? The desperate thought screamed through her mind even as she took a second shuddering breath. Slowly she lifted her hands toward her hair, which was floating in front of her face, her dark locks acting like a blindfold. Cecilia paused then grabbed all of her hair and twisted it violently, securing it in a knot. She seemed able to move freely in this place, and her feet remained solidly on the floor.

"Why am I here?" she asked the Fee. Her voice seemed to flow a bit more slowly underwater but otherwise sounded weirdly normal in her ear.

They stopped circling. The one directly in front of her undulated forward, a familiar smirk twisting her serene features. Cecilia recognized her. She was the silver Fee who had spoken to Cecilia's father . . . Was that only two days ago?

"You are here because Adam Brown fulfilled his omen and completed his bargain with us," the silver-haired Fee said.

"Who?" Cecilia asked.

The Fee continued: "His full name is Adam Pepin Brown, but he prefers his more ostentatious moniker."

Adam Pepin *Brown?* Cecilia's thoughts swirled. Pepin had used the mirror to alert the Fee to her presence, causing the whirlpool to appear and bring her here. He had said he was betraying her, his voice so hard and cold. He had changed back into a human. For fulfilling his omen.

Adam P. Brown: Manipulating selfishly—Betray the Solid Woman

The image of the scrawled writing in the omen book flashed before her mind's eye, leaving a numb indentation of pain. Cecilia shook her head wordlessly. No. No, this could not be! Pepin said that his omen required her to fall in love with him! He had said that he himself was already in love! He had said . . .

He had manipulated her. He had manipulated her to save himself.

"Now you understand," the Fee said, her voice a strange sibilant whisper. She sounded as distant and chilly as ever, but Cecilia heard laughter in her words.

"What am I doing here?" Cecilia persisted, her voice much stronger than her spirit felt.

The Fee smiled. "We're rewarding you." She swam closer until she floated only a few fin-wafts away from Cecilia. The Fee's silver tail swished below her, gently pushing her up and down as she hovered in front of Cecilia. She smiled. "You have been terribly abused by life, have you not?" As the Fee flung her hair behind her shoulders, her face seemed to glow with righteousness. "A man you trusted betrays you for his own selfish reasons, manipulating you into believing you were saving everyone. A little boy begs you to save him, knowing full well there is nothing you can do. Your father robs us, leaving you to suffer the consequences. Your mother sickens and dies, and nobody in your village would even help dig her grave. You grew up lonely and . . ."

"Father John Francis helped," Cecilia said, interrupting the Fee. The Fee's eyes flashed dangerously, but Cecilia forced her chin to lift and her eyes to meet the icy gaze.

The glow faded from the Fee, and her mirthless smile returned. "The priest was only fulfilling his duty. And did your father come to the funeral? Or was he away robbing more innocent souls of their possessions?" She swished her tail, slapping a current of water at Cecilia. "That is your flaw: You believe there is good in everyone. But this is not the truth of the world."

Cecilia opened her mouth to protest but could find no words.

The Fee nodded. "Everyone realizes it sooner or later. Your Captain Pepin has known it ever since his father threatened to murder his mother unless young Adam agreed to serve as a decoy for him in an attempt to fool *us*. It's a pity you only learned it upon being used in one of our omens. You could have lived a long and prosperous life had you not been daft."

Cecilia didn't know how to refute this. She didn't know if she could or if she even wanted to. The Fee had proven her statement. Everyone in Cecilia's life had turned out rather beastly. The proud villagers, the rowdy crew, her absent father, Pepin . . .

Not Father John Francis, a voice whispered in Cecilia's head. *Not Mama.*

The Fee interrupted her thoughts. "Everyone is so *ugly*, are they not? Always thinking of themselves, always struggling to gain more, always destroying any remnant of true beauty that flits across their narrow-minded paths. It is a tale as old as time itself, a tale of selfishness completely and utterly destroying the good."

The Fee flicked her tail upward and lowered her head until her face drew level with Cecilia's. "You, Cecilia Lester, are one of the few examples of goodness in existence. You trust because you choose to believe the best of people. You love because you look past the sting of ugliness to see the beauty beneath. Foolish though you are, you are still good. You deserve better than the world has given you. You deserve to punish the world for what it has done to you."

She gestured toward the ring of Fee surrounding them and observing the conversation through ice-cold eyes. When she turned back to Cecilia, the smile on her lips made Cecilia remember (with a shudder) the day she'd watched a cat pounce on an injured bird. "Just say the word, Cecilia, and you can become one of us. You can become immortal—a force that condemns the evils of the world! You can become justice. You *deserve* it. Just say yes, Cecilia. Say yes and join us, your sisters."

The Fee's eyes glittered with . . . in any other person, Cecilia would have called the emotion portrayed in their depths "joy." But just now her mind envisioned that cat tearing into a fledgling bird, playfully ripping feathers away as the blue wings stained scarlet.

She stepped away from the silver Fee and stared around at the others. When Cecilia first heard about the Fee, she had assumed they were demons or angels or some other supernatural being. When they surrounded her father's ship, condemning him for his crimes, she had thought they must be angels. When she had explored the *Rose* and discovered the omens, she had decided they were demons.

Looking at them now, she knew they had once been like she was: human. The one with the red tail had a nose perked up a bit more than the silver one's. The one with the green hair had smaller eyes than the Fee next to her. The lavender Fee had a larger mouth than the yellow one. Yet, they all wore the same expression. They all looked the same. Beautiful. Proud. Cruel.

If she consented to join them, would this happen to her? Would she become like them? Would she spend eternity destroying the world for destroying her?

Cecilia scowled, but nevertheless her spirit hesitated. Why was it such a repulsive idea? After all, that bird had been injured when the cat found it. The world was an ugly place. It had condemned her mother for falling in love with the wrong person, even though she had never broken any law made by God. She had been married, and it was her husband's selfish choices that killed her. Had he stayed with her and helped her raise Cecilia, perhaps the doctor would have come instead of ostracizing her like the rest of the village did. Perhaps her mother would have been healed!

The bird would have lived had it been healed.

The silver Fee smiled encouragingly, but Cecilia saw only the anger lurking behind her perfect face. This Fee, whose name Cecilia did not know, had scoured the oceans for such a long time, long enough to become a legend, all for the sake of punishing the world. And what punishments did she inflict? Trapping men in the form of monsters, urging them to fulfill dreadful omens that could never be accomplished. She cared nothing for morality or justice or beauty. She was completely and utterly selfish.

Perhaps Cecilia's mother would have lived had her father made better choices. Perhaps Pepin would not have become a pirate had his life been different. Perhaps the world was filled with selfish and ugly people.

Why, then, was this perfect mermaid the ugliest being Cecilia had ever seen?

"No," Cecilia said.

A sneer replaced the Fee's smile.

"No!" Cecilia said more firmly. "I'm not going to punish anyone. I do not wish to become a Fee. I do not wish to become like you." She paused for a moment, breathing deep draughts of the strange water in which she stood. Would refusal mean sudden drowning? A terrible fate, but still better than that which the Fee urged her to accept. "Besides," she continued, "I doubt you truly want me to be a Fee. You simply want to get me, the Solid Woman, out of the way. If I stay in your world, I might free some of the men. If you let me escape back to my world, I might tell others and try to return. And if you kill me, you break every vow you've ever made. So I wonder . . . what will you do with me now that I've refused? In truth, you have no option but to send me back to my world!"

The silver-haired Fee stared at her for the space of several silent heartbeats. Then she waved a hand.

A beam of light flashed through the water. Cecilia scrambled out of the way, suddenly aware of the pressure from the ocean and the slowness of her movements. The Fee waved her arm again and shot another flash toward her. Cecilia kicked and swam as fast as she could. She ran into something and her eyes opened wide. A red Fee grabbed her arms and thrust her backwards. Cecilia struggled, her eyes wide with terror, noticing the tight ring the other Fee had made around her and the silver Fee. She was trapped.

She twisted and faced the silver Fee. There was no smile of encouragement now, no spark of emotion in those eyes. Just an icy monster staring down at her like a guardian of hell, holding a writhing circle of flames in her hand.

"You should have accepted the deal," the Fee said, speaking in the coldly dismissive voice she had used when addressing Cecilia's father. "Now you are no better than the rest of the world. Being separate, like us, is the only way to fix the sin. You cannot sympathize with them. You cannot love them. They don't deserve it."

The Fee raised her arm, the fiery ring burning in the water, reflecting all around Cecilia until she could see nothing but flames. Cecilia wanted to close her eyes, but she forced her lids to remain open. She would die bravely. She would die knowing she had made the right decision. Her mother would be proud. They would be together soon.

When the flash came, Cecilia gasped and her eyes shut.

But she felt no pain. Nothing burned. She felt water around her and the stares of the other Fee.

She opened her eyes and staggered back. A man with bright red hair and a tricorn hat stood with his back to her, shielding her from the Fee. His outstretched arm held a cutlass to the silver Fee's throat.

Looking completely stunned, the Fee dropped the fiery ring, and its flames extinguished. Her silver eyes were wide with shock before slowly fading back to their usual aloofness. "Mr. Brown," the Fee said. "Are you unhappy with your humanity?"

"*Oui, Madame!*" Pepin replied in his familiar drawl. "I've found it doesn't suit me at all. I'd like a refund."

CHAPTER ELEVEN

THE FEE smiled, though it looked more like a snarl. "Your power was gone. You spent it saving that defiant child. You were dying. You would like to die, Mr. Brown?"

Pepin's voice lost its mockery. "If that is what I must do to save Mademoiselle Lester . . . yes."

"You cannot save her!" the silver Fee cried. She swished her tail, pushing herself higher than Pepin, away from his sword. "Fate is decided by the individual. Miss Lester has already chosen her path, and she has chosen the path of destruction." She growled savagely down at Cecilia.

Pepin lifted the cutlass to point once more at the Fee's neck. "Let her go. Take me instead."

All of the watching Fee went still. The silver Fee gazed upon Pepin, her expression empty but for the slight quirk in her brow. Cecilia became aware of the pressure of the water, the pounding of her heart, and the unaccountable truth that was life. She did not wish to die. She just wanted to go home . . . though she hardly knew where home was anymore.

The Fee's smirk slowly returned. "You never fail to perplex us. Very well, Mr. Brown. Your request has been noted."

She flicked her hand. The other Fee swarmed forward, grasping and tugging at Pepin. Pepin swung his cutlass, but it was sluggish and useless in the water. The Fee wrenched it out of his hand and flung it beyond the silver Fee, where, with a final glint of steel in the wavering light, it fell out of sight.

Cecilia kicked forward, trying to grab Pepin, but was jerked backwards. She clawed and struggled against the Fee holding her, scratching and kicking at any flesh or fin she could find. The Fee hissed in her ear. A shock pulsed through her body, forcing her to be still. She could move nothing except for her eyes. Her hair, which had come undone from its knot during the fight, floated over her face, blocking her view.

She heard the Fee shrieking and Pepin yelling. Then he too fell silent. That silence was like a heavy stone plummeting in Cecilia's heart. The Fee gripping Cecilia tugged the dark hair out of her eyes and used it to painfully jerk her head backwards, so that she had a clear view of the silver Fee floating above the mayhem below.

"You ask for Miss Lester's . . . salvation." The Fee hissed the word like a taunt. "I repeat that fate lies within the individual, not within any outside force. Therefore, I will allow Miss Lester a choice."

She waved her hand toward Pepin, and the mirror wafted from inside his coat to her hand, cutting through the water. The Fee pointed the mirror's glass toward Cecilia, and an orb of light appeared in the center of the circle formed by the Fee, causing their light to fade. It glowed softly golden, like the glimmer of the distant chandelier. Despite the pain in her neck, despite her dire predicament, Cecilia felt safe while staring at the orb, as if she were gazing into the eye of a friend.

"This will take you to safety," the silver Fee said. "You will be in your own world. You need never think of this one, or its inhabitants, again. You have earned this."

Cecilia felt the Fee release her hair. She half-floated, half-walked forward, the shock leaving her body, her gaze focused wholly on the friendly, beautiful orb. The light flickered playfully as she neared it. Just as Cecilia reached out her hand, she saw a flash of red in her peripheral vision and abruptly came to herself.

She spun and faced the silver Fee, though her gaze fixed instead on Pepin, who was locked in struggle with two other Fee, one of which had a hand clamped over his mouth, disabling speech. His long orange-red hair floated around his face, bright, alarming, and stark, even more eye-catching than the tail of the silver Fee who floated directly above him. But his shockingly blue eyes shone more than anything, brighter than his hair, brighter than the Fee, and brighter even than the orb.

He met Cecilia's gaze. And then he winked. As though with that single gesture he could tell her that everything was all right, that she should go, that this was all one great lark.

"You said I had a choice," Cecilia said. "This is but one option."

"Our previous offer stands," the silver Fee replied.

Cecilia snapped her gaze away from Pepin's and stared into the stony face of the Fee. "And what of Captain Pepin?"

"Mr. Brown has now twice crossed us. He will not be shown mercy."

"A sentiment you are incapable of extending!" Cecilia spat.

The assembled Fee stiffened, and she heard their muttered hisses. She pressed on, advancing slowly toward the silver Fee, kicking herself higher. Her skirts billowed around her but did not impede her movements.

"You claim to abhor sin, and yet you agree to kill him in exchange for me. Shouldn't you reward him for his bravery? For his self-sacrifice? And as to crossing you twice, he actually fulfilled his omen! He betrayed me." Cecilia swam above Pepin now, though she kept her gaze locked on the silver Fee, pointing at her.

"Your omens are wicked! Sin will not redeem sin. I know this better than anyone, as you so reminded me a few minutes ago. The cruelty of my neighbors did not induce me to abandon my mother, but to stand by her. Your omens will fix nothing, and I think you know that. You create them out of spite, never intending to help or instruct. Your motive is hatred, not love. I reject everything you stand for. You sicken me. I will not be like you. I will never become a Fee!"

The Fee's eyes flashed. "So you have said before. Why do you continue to mock us? We are gracing you with mercy because of your goodness. Go through the orb!"

"I will," Cecilia said.

With those words, she made a last lunge through the water and drew level with the Fee. This time she did not underestimate the silver Fee's strength. This time she knew very well the powerful grip the Fee would have upon the mirror. So, this time when she caught hold of that diamond-studded frame, she simultaneously brought both her feet up and kicked off against the Fee's stomach.

The creature gasped in surprise and pain, doubling over even as Cecilia, the mirror clutched to her heart, sped back down toward Pepin and the orb. The two Fee holding Pepin, startled by the turn of events, loosened their hold just enough that Pepin struggled free, elbowing one captor in the face and flipping the other upside-down.

Cecilia grabbed him by the arm, and they swam, kicking and flailing, toward the orb. Then its light surrounded them. They spun around and around, and the water pressed against them, and all of the Fee screamed and cursed as though the water were hellfire.

Cecilia's hair and gown suddenly weighed far more, and she fell onto the ground in a puddle of the water streaming from her clothes. The mirror clattered on wooden boards beside her.

Pepin was human. The hands clenched in front of him were human. The arms attached to them were flesh-colored and freckled. The lock of hair falling in front of his eyes was red. He was human.

Why did the fact of his humanity feel wrong? Ah yes. If he were back in the Fee's netherworld he would be dead, not human. Or maybe he would be a dead human. But being a dead human rather than a dead monster would hardly be an improvement. Dead was dead. But he wasn't dead, at least, not yet.

How was he alive? Unclenching his fists, Pepin pushed himself off the ground and stared at his surroundings. Cecilia sat on the floor, coughing and spluttering and sopping wet, the mirror on the floor beside her. They were back in that miserable shack atop the stony island. But what was different? It looked different.

Light. It wasn't gray anymore. Light filtered through the cracks in the sagging boards above his head, and light shone through the open doorway, which revealed a brilliant blue Caribbean unmarred by fog or blackness or Fee. Pepin's breathing felt lighter. They were out of the netherworld. They had returned to the real world. But how?

The Fee had said the orb would return Cecilia to her world, and when she dragged him along with her, they had returned there together. But something else was wrong here: the mirror.

He racked his memory, thinking through all of those horrid conversations with his father, scathing and useless save for the information the old man had provided about the Fee. If light touched the mirror, the Fee could sense it. If the mirror was on the sea, the Fee could go to it. But never, *never,* could the mirror travel out of the netherworld and appear on solid ground in the real world. His father had been very clear on this point. When traveling from the Fee's realm to the world, it *had* to appear on the sea.

Yet here it was. So much for *never.* And now he understood why he wasn't dead, why the Fee did not even now appear and drag both him and Cecilia back to their realm. While the Fee could travel anywhere in their own world, even on land, Pepin and Cecilia were no longer in the realm of the Fee. This cabin must exist both in the netherworld *and* the real world. Pepin and Cecilia and the mirror were back in the real world, on solid ground, and the Fee could not reach them here.

"My father once informed me that excessive coughing leads to disembowelment," Pepin said, turning suddenly to smile benignantly at Cecilia.

She narrowed her eyes at him and coughed again, convulsively. Her eyes flashed with anger through the wet strands of hair stuck to her face. She staggered to her feet, and Pepin's excitement began to give way to worry. He stepped backwards and held up his hands. "Mademoiselle, before you do anything rash . . ."

"You tricked me! You betrayed me!" She marched toward him, shoving her hair out of her face, her eyes as furious as when she had addressed the Fee. "You owe me an explanation at once, sir! At once, I tell you!"

Pepin took another step away. "*Oui. Absolument.* It will be a good explanation, I swear."

"It needs to be a *truthful* explanation," she persisted, folding her arms over her chest. For all her stance was one of intimidation, she looked like a frightened, wet child.

Sorrow tore away the remaining shreds of Pepin's glee. "I will be honest," he said. "I swear this to you." He paused for a moment. How to explain everything? How to explain the darkness and the anger and the desperation prompting every deceit, every lie, every evil deed? How to make her understand the oddness of his position as captain, the reasons behind his mystical powers?

The answer to all of these was simple enough: *Tell her.*

"Do you . . . do you remember our conversation about *esprit de la Rose?*" he asked Cecilia.

"No," she replied. Then, after a moment's thought, she added, "Or do you mean . . . how my father told me that a ship takes on the spirit of her captain?"

"*Oui.* Well, the concept of the spirit of the *Rose* is actually more than one of my many nonsensically poetic phrases. It is the reason I am the captain. It is the reason I had the power to overcome the mutinous crew. It is—" Pepin glanced away from her to stare at the shack's rotting wall. "It is the reason I gave you to the Fee."

Shifting his gaze to the damp floorboards, he explained: "When the Fee punished me, they made me the captain because I was never supposed to be punished. You see, my father forced me from my home to serve as a decoy in the event his service to the Fee failed and they should turn on him. But I am no man's decoy!" Pepin chuckled ruefully. "When opportunity arose, I stole the mirror and framed my father for the robbery. The Fee arrived, created the whirlpool, and prepared to punish my father, Daviau.

"However, just seconds before my liberation, he shoved me through the whirlpool in his stead. I appeared in the bilge of the *Rose*, a Royal Navy man o' war my father had recently sunk at the behest of the Fee. I first arrived as a Solid. I had no welcoming party as you did though. No one was there. I was the first placed aboard the *Rose*.

"An orb appeared in the gaol, and I went through. The Fee wrested the truth from me . . ." Pepin shuddered at the memory then hurried on. "They were conflicted over my fate. Some argued I should be sent back because I had been pushed in. Others argued that I should be punished since I was the one who stole the mirror. Eventually they compromised. They cursed me, but they gave me power—power to control the *Rose*'s direction with my mind and power to subdue the crew if necessary.

"Two days ago, the orb appeared in my cabin. I went through. The Fee were frantic, even more frantic than they had been about Curly. You were an accident they had not foreseen. I suppose children and Solid Women are hard to control, even for them. They offered me another deal: If I brought you to this shack and sent you through a whirlpool, they would give me the ship of my dreams and I could go free. I agreed. They gave me the mirror to alert them when we arrived."

He chanced a glance at Cecilia. She was no longer glaring. Her expression was solemn, her brow lightly puckered. Was that pity he saw in her eyes? Accusation? He could not read her, and he feared what effect his tale might have on her opinion of him . . . which must already be dismally low.

He continued to look at Cecilia, though he couldn't quite meet her eyes. "After I gave you to the Fee, I staggered out of the shack to see my new ship. Before, you understand, I thought the Fee meant the ship would truly be the ship of my dreams. But they meant it would be an image of my true spirit. I beheld it below the cliff, a black, ugly thing, a ship of my nightmares! The torn sails hung upon it like flesh on a carcass, and the holes and rot infecting the wood were visible even from a distance. I knew it would sail nowhere. I was human, yes, but I was still in the Fee's world. Still in the netherworld. I had assumed that 'freedom' meant a return to my own world. The Fee had not intended that at all."

Pepin forced himself to meet Cecilia's gaze. "It was not the darkness of the ship that sent me through the whirlpool to save you. It was the darkness of myself."

Cecilia said nothing. She strode toward him, and Pepin flinched, expecting the slap he knew he deserved. It did not come. She walked past him into the sunlight and gazed over the island, her back to the cliff. Then suddenly she turned and offered him the most beautiful smile. "Captain, you kept your word and saved your crew."

Pepin trailed after her and followed her gaze. Hope burst through his shame like the first sunbeam on the horizon after a stormy night. Even now on the quay the waking crew discovered their human bodies, stared at their hands, stared at each other, then whooped and leaped for joy. Beyond them the *Rose* floated, her sails a pure white and her boards an ordinary brown.

She was beautiful.

EPILOGUE

L ONDON WAS not the glorious, magical city Cecilia had always imagined. Certainly nothing like the vision she had glimpsed in the mirror room of the *Rose* . . . though that, she had known at the time, must have been idealized at best.

London, the real London, was a cold, wet, dirty, stinking city, as unlike her dreams as it could be. Very different, as well, from the beautiful balmy islands of the Caribbean. And her father's respectable sister, though coldly generous to her only niece, did not provide the home Cecilia had wanted. Most of the time Cecilia felt chilled, inside and out.

Sighing, she fingered her hair, considering whether or not she should start to pin it up as her poor aunt kept suggesting. Fashionable women of London wore their hair loose over the shoulders with the rest gathered into a high bun on the back of the head, an ornate headdress, and a short fringe of hair over their foreheads. But this style seemed so strange to Cecilia, and she preferred her simple braid and cap.

Lightning flashed. Cecilia moved to the window and pressed her forehead to the glass, watching the torrents of rain patter against the street. Though it was only mid-afternoon, the skies were dark and the storm was dense. She blew lightly and watched her breath fog on the cold glass. The blackness, the storm, and the fog reminded her of a ship, two bumbling pirates, a fog-shrouded island, and an enigmatic captain . . .

What was wrong with her?

Huffing a frustrated breath, she spun from the window and threw herself into a cushioned armchair, crossing her arms somewhat petulantly. There was no point in wishing or dreaming. She was here in London, just as she had always wanted. Her aunt and uncle were kind to her. Her father's sister was much more affluent than Cecilia had expected, and Cecilia, who had grown up poor, found herself suddenly surrounded by what she considered the height of luxury.

She dropped her arms, wilting into the chair. At least back in St. George's Parish she had felt purposeful. She'd had the villagers to resist, her mother to help, Father John Francis to talk to. She was useless here: too rich to work and too restless to enjoy society. If London society could bring itself to accept a privateer's half-Spanish daughter, which remained to be seen.

She sighed again and stood, intending to find her aunt and ask if there was *anything* she might assist her with, but thunder crashed and she turned to the window. She squinted, then scurried to the glass pane.

A man and a boy dashed through the streets. The boy wore a cap pulled over bouncy curls, and the man's tricorn hat failed to conceal his fiery red hair.

Cecilia bounded from the room, dodged past the housemaid in the hall, and threw open the door.

Captain Pepin stood on the threshold, his fist poised to knock on the door.

"Hullo, Miss Lester!" Curly exclaimed, grinning.

"Miss me, Mademoiselle?" Pepin asked with a grin.

Cecilia felt her face flush. She ushered them into the house and into the drawing room, ignoring the wide-eyed horror of the housemaid. After closing the drawing-room door, she turned to face them. Curly poked at an expensive vase, and Pepin casually tossed his soaked coat onto a high-backed chair.

Pepin whistled to himself as he strolled around the table, running a finger over the wood. "You are perfectly comfortable here, are you not?" Pepin asked. "Unwilling to leave? Completely in love with the latest gossip about this prim lady and that proper heiress, gowns that are all fabric and no heart, and bewigged fops who brave the dangerous seas of English tea parties? *Oui,* London is quite the adventure for all!"

Cecilia blinked at him and felt her smile start to diminish. His sarcasm was harsh, cutting, yet it didn't hurt. She agreed with each of his sentiments. "What are you doing here?" she asked.

Pepin jerked his gaze away from the table and approached her. His voice was serious when he spoke. "Have you ever heard of a pirate named David Jones?"

Cecilia shook her head.

"Neither had I," Pepin said. "Until a few weeks ago."

"Who is he?"

"Nobody. A nobody with a tiny vessel, a scrawny crew, and an uncanny ability to completely demolish any ship he comes across." Pepin's blue eyes bored into Cecilia. "I met him briefly in Tortuga. He—rather rudely I might add—informed me that the *Rose* did not belong to me but to the goddesses of the sea, and that I would be killed immediately and brutally because of my disregard for the wishes of the Fee. He added that he knows where you live and would soon come for you."

Cecilia sucked in a breath. Curly bounded over to them. "Don't be scared, miss! He's not all he wants to seem, I think. Cap'n beat him in a duel, he did!"

"Did you really?" Cecilia asked.

Pepin raised both eyebrows and opened his mouth to reply, but Curly's chatter cut him off. "He did! 'Course, he had help from William and Frank and the others, but he only got a little beat up! Jones had to run. He didn't even have a scratch though! Completely eerie, I say!"

Pepin glared at Curly, who grinned cheekily up at him. Cecilia, despite herself, giggled at their silent exchange.

Pepin raised a brow at her. "You find your imminent doom amusing, Mademoiselle?"

"I find your attempt to impress me amusing," she replied.

Pepin's smirk returned. "Attempt? Are you sure that is the correct word?"

Cecilia ignored his flirting. "You came to warn me?"

Pepin pressed a hand to his heart and assumed a shocked expression. "What do you take me for, *un coquin? Mais non!* We are here to take you aboard the *Rose* and find a safer place for you to reside while I deal with Jones."

Cecilia stiffened in surprise. "You're taking me away from here?"

Pepin nodded a bow. "Alas, I'm afraid there is no time for you to bid adieu to the queue of sniveling suitors you have no doubt amassed. We must leave immediately."

Leaving. She was leaving. She didn't know where she would go, but she was *leaving*. A rush of excitement, of joy, burst through her . . . followed quickly by surprise. She shouldn't be excited about these strange events. She shouldn't be excited about having a madman pirate searching for her. She shouldn't be excited to board a ship captained by a man who had betrayed her, or to sail with a crew, the majority of whom had once intended to harm her.

Yet she was excited. Was there any point in hiding it?

She beamed up at Pepin. "Let me pack some clothes and I'll be ready! May I leave a note to my aunt? Do you suppose this Jones is somehow connected to the Fee? Is the mirror still hidden? How are William and Frank? I rather miss them."

"Please be quick about it. *Oui,* but don't tell her too much. I am certain of it. Yes, I *do* have that much sense. They are as imbecilic as ever, thank you for inquiring," Pepin returned answers as rapidly as she had asked questions.

Cecilia turned to dash from the room but paused when Pepin spoke again. "Aren't you terrified? Aren't you angry at having to leave your dream life? I thought this would be difficult for you, so I brought Curly along. I figured if he grinned and showed his dimples, you would be persuaded, since my good looks are *clearly* not enough to persuade you." The last he added rather petulantly.

Cecilia stood still for a moment then glanced over her shoulder and said, "Terrified? Angry? Absolutely not." She bounded through the doors and dashed to her room, attempting to stifle the smile spreading across her face. She was embarking on another adventure, and life suddenly seemed beautiful again.

About the Author

KAYCEE BROWNING is a homeschooled teenager living in North Carolina. She wrote her first novel when she was thirteen and published a novel at age fifteen. When not writing, she is most likely amusing herself by reading, fangirling, hanging out with friends, or (occasionally) doing her schoolwork. She resides with her two amazing parents, her three awesome siblings, and her two bossy dachshunds.

To learn more about Kaycee, visit www.KayceeBrowning.com

WITHER

SAVANNAH JEZOWSKI

To my White Knight,
for loving me even when my crazy shows through

PROLOGUE

MOONLIGHT BATHED the Neverway in cold, unforgiving light.

At long last, Merchant Haverly recognized his surroundings. He smelled smoke and heard the river churning as it rotated the water wheel outside the village boundaries. He was nearly home.

In his haste he tripped on his own boot laces and crashed to the ground. He did not rise immediately but moved his trembling hands to cover his face. That monster had left him here, only a few dozen yards from the village boundaries, to deliver horrifying news. It had been a mistake, a dreadful mistake.

He had been on his way home from Pandorum, where he peddled his watches every year at the Festival of Lights. There was only one route over the mountains, and it led straight through the Neverway, a wilderness that began on Pandorum's side of the mountain and carved a narrow gap through the peaks before spilling into the lowlands on the other side. The bandits attacked his caravan late in the afternoon, driving the travelers from the road and into the wilderness.

For hours Haverly had stumbled in rocky woods, without any supplies, afraid he would never see his precious family again. He knew his village lay to the south, at the base of the mountains, but he had never been good with directions. In the gathering darkness, on his own, he did not climb down far enough.

Instead, he stumbled upon a towering wall of roses. He searched for a gate, but it appeared the briar wall grew untended, that whatever structure lay behind it had been long forgotten. He thought of his children then, his darling daughters, and of the gifts he had purchased, now lost to scoundrels. There had been books for his eldest, a doll with a painted porcelain face for his youngest, and a rose bush for his middle daughter.

He could not replace the doll or books, but it seemed the Ever intended to replace at least one of the pilfered gifts. He plucked a rose from the wall. Only one, to put in his pocket.

The wall had shuddered, and beyond the briar wall some terrible creature stirred . . .

Haverly shook himself to escape the memory, but it clung to him. He now knew that the nursery tales were not quite true. No stories could have prepared him for the real monster that lived in Briarstone Abbey.

He forced himself to rise from the ground and stood facing the village. He could see light from the electric lamps in the watchtowers spaced around the village wall.

He moved a hand across his face, chasing tears. It had all been a mistake. And his darling Sunflower would pay the price.

CHAPTER

1

Lilybet Haverly - The Merchant's Middle Daughter

I HAD never been fond of roses. But now I had cause to truly hate them. I sat near the hearth in the kitchen, watching as the embers turned black. Rosamond and Sookie were near me, squashed together on Mama's rocker. Rosamond cried as she played with Sookie's pale curls— even she, ever the optimist, could find nothing hopeful in our sister's plight. I could hear Papa in his room off the kitchen, weeping. The Spook, who found Papa outside the village and brought him home to us, had left long ago.

The rose that caused it all lay on the floor near the plank table, where I'd dropped it the moment Papa finished telling his tale. I had no inclination to retrieve it but left it crushed and wilting on the packed-earth floor. How could I not hate roses after this? How could I not hate *him*? Of course I knew what folks said about Briarstone Abbey, but I had believed the stories to be simply that—stories. Some people claimed the Abbey was inhabited by thieves and vagabonds, while others described ghosts and grotesque monsters.

It appeared the harshest rumors had been the most correct. There really was a beast in Briarstone Abbey.

I leaned forward, grabbed a poker, and began to viciously stir the embers until they sparked in protest. I shoved two small logs into the coals and watched as tiny flames flickered around them. Who would have thought a simple flower could cause so much trouble? I didn't blame Papa. If anything, Sookie was more at fault for putting him in mind of the roses. Everyone knows my opinion of roses, so when Papa asked what I would like as a gift when he returned from Pandorum, my little sister impishly recommended a rose bush.

I rose and paced to the window, where I eased aside the burlap curtain to peer outside. The moon shone brightly on the roof of the chicken coop. The Beast had allowed us one day. Then he would come to the outskirts of the village at midnight to collect his bounty. If we did not comply, Papa would be taken as forfeit.

I ground my teeth together. I could not let this happen. There had to be a way around it. My stomach roiled unpleasantly, and there was a pain in my chest too, the hollow pain of helplessness.

Behind me, the rocker stopped creaking. "We should try to sleep," Rosamond said, as if sleep were actually a possibility. I felt a thin arm slip around my waist and a head press against my own.

"Come to bed, Bet," Sookie pleaded, her voice muffled in my hair. She was two years younger and already tall as I was.

"You go up," I said. "I'll come soon."

"Come now," she pleaded. I turned, lifting my arm to wrap it around her. I kissed her cheek. She tried to look brave, but her eyes still welled with tears. We had already told her not to worry, that we would never send her away. Of course she said she was willing to go—that was her way—but I knew our father. He would sacrifice himself first.

I could not allow that to happen either. The girls needed him far more than they needed me. They could not endure the loss of another parent. The mere thought made me ache for them, even Rosamond, who often chafed me like the measles.

I would do anything for them, even abandon them.

"Go to bed," I whispered. "Both of you. I'll be with you soon." The lie stuck in my throat. We were unaccustomed to lying to one another, and my poor sisters did not think to question my promise. They trusted me.

As soon as they had gone up to the loft, I spurred myself into action. No one ever went into the Neverway without the Spook for a guide, not unless they wished to lose life and limb. I must be a fool for considering it, but I had no choice. Sookie was far too young to be forced into such a dreadful fate, not when she was already bound by a curse of her own. Even though her curse was not her fault, rather a case of mistaken identity (naked and bald babies do look rather alike), I would die before letting her rush headlong into another one.

It was time for me to do my part, to offer myself in Sookie's place and pray that I was an acceptable substitute. It was the only way to save both my father and my sister. I was strong, built for hard labor, not winning husbands. In our home I handled most of the physical, outdoor chores—gardening, chopping wood, maintaining our house and outbuildings—leaving the housework and cooking to my sisters.

This was something I could do. I was sure of it.

Still, the logic of my plan did nothing to dull the pain. The silence of the house cut like a knife to the chest.

I left the kitchen and tiptoed to the back of the house, where I pulled a small pack from a storage chest. Inside I put my supplies: a small torch, stone and flint, and a blanket. I returned to the kitchen and gathered enough food for several days. The only weapons I had easy access to were in the knife block on Mama's baking hutch. I had to move one of Papa's boxes to get to it. The box was filled with his tools, tiny gears and springs, and clock faces. He had a workshop, but he often grew lonely and preferred to work inside, to be near us.

I selected a butcher knife from the block and forced myself to turn away.

Pausing outside Papa's door, I tilted my head, listening. No sound met my ear, and I guessed he had finally fallen into an exhausted asleep. I longed to see him one last time, but I did not dare enter his room, not even for the rifle he hung above his dresser. I splayed my palm against his door and mouthed a silent, agonizing goodbye. Then I shouldered my pack and opened the back door.

I halted before I'd taken two steps out of the house.

"Lilybet!" Papa exclaimed. He came to an abrupt standstill only a few yards away, holding an oil lamp above his head. The orange light of the lantern cast harsh shadows across his square face, glinting on his narrow spectacles. It made him look vulnerable and ghastly at the same time. He wore his leather apron, sleeves rolled up over his elbows, as if he'd come from his workshop behind the house. When had he left the house?

"You startled me! What are you about?" he asked.

I had no answer. Behind him, a dark form separated from the shadow of the old oak along our snaking dirt path. I could not discern his face with Papa's lantern shining in my eyes. Around us, the night was crisp and silent like a forgotten graveyard in late November.

"What are you doing?" Papa demanded and lowered the lantern. He must have noticed my pack.

"I'm sorry, Papa," I managed. Without another word, I bolted into the darkness. I had already made up my mind. There was no going back.

There were no electric lampposts in the farming sector of the village, but the moon hung full and bright above me, and stars studded the sky. I could see well enough to find my way, even at a run. I knew I could outrun Papa, but I did not know about the fellow with him. Instead of following the gravel road that wound through the village, I cut across our neighbor's yard, choosing a more direct route. Behind me Papa shouted my name.

I knew exactly where I was going, to a section of the village wall near the southeast corner. This segment of wall was showing wear, developing chinks in the stone mortar that a person might get her fingers and toes into.

I had scaled the wall before, on a dare.

I skidded to a halt at the perimeter of the village, my heartbeat thundering in my ears. The wall loomed over me, about a dozen feet high. My fingers searched for the cracks. I found a handhold and heaved myself up. I could hear shouts behind me as I flung an arm over my head, searching for another chink in the wall. My feet followed one at a time as I tried to jam the squat toes of my boots into cracks much too small for them. My fingers hurt and I scraped my knees as I climbed, but I forced myself to keep moving upward. I grunted as I heaved myself over the wall and straddled it like a horse, and then paused to stare into the night, straining to hear. My skin prickled with awareness. We had walls for a reason.

The trees tossed their branches against the blue-black of the sky. I could hear the wind moaning through narrow canyon corridors, stirring dead leaves along the base of the wall. Safety lay behind me, and certain death out there. The Neverway was riddled with creepers, the living dead who perish without seeking the Ever Father's healing—the living dead who wander in endless torment.

They were not the real problem, however; I worried mostly about the flesh eaters.

Footsteps pounded against the ground, beneath me. "Hold off!" came a voice from below.

It was Victor, the village Spook. I groaned and closed my eyes. The gig was up. I wouldn't stand a chance of eluding him. Beyond the walls of the village, he had the advantage. I would be on foreign ground. Within moments he had climbed up beside me, a thin wooden staff tucked across his waist behind the straps of his suspenders. He sat beside me and pulled his staff free, balancing it on his lap.

"Hullo, Bet," he said. The greeting was casual, but his moonlit expression was not. He removed his cloth cap and scratched furiously at his scalp.

"Hullo, Victor," I replied warily. "I won't be dissuaded. You know what's at stake here." I swung my leg over the wall, intending to jump if I had to. I glanced at the shadows beneath me and reconsidered that notion. I could easily break an ankle.

"Don't you do it, girl!" Papa gasped from below. "You get down here. Snappish!"

"Your father is right," the Spook insisted, his voice taut. "You should reconsider. This is not the way."

Perhaps his opinion would have counted for more had he offered me an alternative. I twisted to look down at Papa, who had set the lantern down at his feet. Puffing hard, he braced one hand against his knee and the other against the wall. His head leaned back so that I could see the grimace on his face.

Victor sighed. "I don't believe you've thought this through. Have you a weapon even?"

"Butcher knife," I muttered.

"Ah." That little word carried a world of hidden feeling.

"Eh? What are you saying?" Papa cried. "You bring her down. You hear me?"

I watched Victor, but he was gazing out into the Neverway. "Perhaps I might come with you and have a chat with this . . . this *beast*," he said.

I breathed a sigh of relief. He did not intend to hinder me. He intended to chat with this beast. Perhaps trounce this beast with his staff. And I jolly well couldn't say that I blamed him. I wouldn't mind doing some trouncing of my own.

As far as Spooks went, Victor came very well recommended—all the way from Pandorum. I had often wondered why such a fellow would come to a small village in the middle of nowhere. Whatever his reasons, I could not deny that he was good at his work. He would be a strong ally when facing a monster.

"Thank you," I finally whispered even as I shook my head. "He said Sookie was to come alone. If you were to show up . . . well, he might . . ." My gaze flickered down toward Papa, who was valiantly trying to climb the wall. He lost his grip and thudded back to the ground with a yelp. I winced. "I will be all right," I said with more feeling than I felt.

"Says the girl with a butcher knife."

I flushed, the heat stinging my ears. "Besides," I continued, ignoring him, ignoring Papa's labored grunts below. "If I am very good, this *beast* may let me go after I have paid off Papa's debt." By the Never, it should not take long to pay for a stupid rose. I might even be home in time for Sookie's birthday. *Her sixteenth birthday.*

"He might," Victor agreed quietly. "But it is just as likely he might not."

I swallowed and clenched my fists. "Better me than Papa." I looked down again, on the village side. Papa had climbed barely two feet off the ground. I could see the top of his bald head, shiny in the moonlight. He often claimed that my antics had caused him to lose all his hair so young.

The thought pained me.

"You have to know," Victor began. His tone demanded my attention. "I realize you mean well, but running away is only going to injure your family. And if you die?" His expression remained resolutely blank. "Well, they will never forget it."

I felt a chill sweep through me; he spoke as if he knew. Something moaned nearby, and I stiffened. Papa gasped and thudded to the ground once more while Victor held a finger to his lips and stretched the arm holding the staff out in front of me. But he needn't have worried. I knew enough about creepers not to startle them. They were dangerous only if frightened or angry.

Two hunched figures stumbled into our line of sight. The creepers moaned incessantly, following the perimeter of the wall. We sat in silence until they shuffled off into the darkness, unaware of us. They left something foul behind on the air, like an aftertaste of the afterlife.

"Lilybet, don't do this!" Papa called, his voice lost and childlike, as if he already knew he had lost me.

I repositioned, preparing for my descent. I hooked my arms over the top of the wall and braced my feet against the side of it. "Victor, please," I beseeched him. "I must go."

He turned toward me and leaned down so that Papa would not hear. "I know," he whispered. "Keep to the north road. It will take you right to the top of the mountain. The moon is full tonight and will be your friend. Stay out of the trees." He reached for one of my wrists and squeezed. "And go *quietly*."

"Thank you," I whispered back as I pulled my arm free. "Look after Sookie, will you? Keep her away from the Spinner." I did not have to explain why. We all knew about the curse.

"I will try."

Knowing it was the best I would get from him, I began to lower myself down.

"Betty, don't do this!" Papa shouted. I heard a thud, as if he had pounded the wall with one hand. "I'll go instead! I'll go! By the Never, Bet! Victor, *do* something!" There were tears in his voice.

I ground my teeth and tried to ignore the writhing in my belly. I felt as if I were betraying him.

When I reached the ground, Victor called my name. I looked up in time to catch the staff he dropped for me. I tested the weight of it and nodded my approval. It was not too heavy.

I took a stabilizing breath. "I love you, Papa," I whispered, and pressed my fingers to the cold stone. I could hear him on the other side, weeping. Now would be an appropriate time for tears, but I never cried.

So I turned and set my feet to the north road. Behind me, Papa sobbed my name.

CHAPTER

2

Corwin - The Beast of Briarstone Abbey

I CROUCHED on the battlement of the southeast tower, listening to the night wind and to the voice of my conscience. Beneath me, Briarstone Abbey creaked and groaned, each sound as familiar to me as breathing, but the familiarity brought no comfort tonight. I had done a terrible thing. An unthinkable thing.

I had stolen a life.

In the past I would never have done something this drastic on my own. I would have sought counsel from my parents or aunts and uncles. But no one remained to speak against me. For years I had labored in silence— agonized in silence—nurtured by the memory of counsel. But, like my roses, memories last for only so long before they shrivel and fade.

My roses were withering away. Soon, I feared that I too would be nothing more than a long-forgotten memory.

I shifted, stricken with guilt as I remembered the horror on the merchant Haverly's face when I told him the tribute I required. He had been ready to pay for his blundering mistake, but he had not thought even me, a monster, capable of such monstrosity. Once I would not have thought myself capable of it either.

I lifted my head and sighed. With my fine-honed senses I could hear the wolfhound prowling outside the perimeter of the Abbey. I envied him. His job was so easy. Protect the Abbey. There was little to complicate his mandate besides an occasional gnawing need for food in his belly. Why could my task not be as simple?

Everything had become so tangled. I told myself that I had been just in seeking recompense for the merchant's theft. My roses were as precious to me as his daughters were to him. A life for a life. I wanted his youngest. I had watched Sunflower talking to her animals—to the chickens and pigs and stray cats. Her heart held enough room for all of them. I had never heard her speak ill of another.

I knew all about everyone in the village. Night after night, I went down to the perimeter and hid in the treetops and listened to people living their lives, laughing and loving and mourning and rebuilding. I would have gone mad long ago had I not been able to live my life through them.

Quarrel the wolfhound caught scent of something and dashed into the darkness. I leaned forward to keep track of him. I had the ability to throw out sound at a pitch too high for human ears, which allowed me to follow movement and catch sounds far beyond my natural reach.

My senses were as keen as ever, but my body grew weak. I could not survive much longer by watching the villagers. I needed something more, and I couldn't afford to be wrong. The consequences would be catastrophic, and not only for me. The world was on the precipice of change and knew nothing of it. I alone knew the truth, and the truth bound me like an iron cage.

I stood and prepared to follow Quarrel, in case he needed help. The days of waiting for help were at an end. The Ever had been afforded ample opportunity to speak to me, to offer aid as He had promised my forefathers long ago. He remained silent. I feared I was forgotten.

But there was no time for self-pity now. I could hear Quarrel's clawed paws scrabbling against the ground as he ran—and I started after him. I would have to close the distance before I learned what he had discovered.

I came upon the village Spook first. He was a frequent enough visitor in the Neverway, although he generally gave Briarstone a wide berth. Tonight, he was headed straight for us.

I swept the area around him, probing the darkness with my echoes. I found the girl several dozen yards to the west of him. At least I suspected it was a girl by the size and gait. She was on the north road, ten or fifteen minutes out, and carrying a torch. I frowned as I closed in on her, sweeping the area around her for danger. Living things give off a different echo than trees and boulders. Heartbeats, rapid breathing, footsteps.

I wondered that the Spook kept his distance from the girl, circling around her at times. Before she could catch sight of him, he would blend back into the trees. I watched for some time, but he appeared interested only in clearing her path. So I kept my distance and focused on the girl. I did not realize who she was until I moved in close enough to smell the merchant.

Had he sent Sunflower to me early then? I moved in closer, anxious at the thought of the tiny thing facing the darkness alone. I had planned to fetch her myself so that she would not be in danger.

But it was not Sunflower. It was the other daughter. The one who chopped wood and repaired fences and roof shingles. I could not remember her name—it was an unusual one. I paused a few dozen yards uphill from her, as she appeared on an open section of the trail. It was a wonder she could tell where she was going, even with the torch. She stormed up the mountainside as if intending to take it by siege. She was in for a rude awakening.

My thoughts churned. I was stunned that the merchant had flouted my wishes by sending me the wrong daughter. I did not want this girl. She was useless to me. I needed Sunflower. I needed her selflessness, her big heart, her quickness to love. I did not have time to train a girl who did not already possess a willingness to give of herself.

Perhaps it was justice for my sin that I end up with the wrong girl. I had deviated from my mandate, and though my reasons were honest, my sin was not lessened for the honesty.

I heard the Spook redirecting a couple of creepers downwind of me, diverting them away from the north road. I twisted my torso toward the sound of the girl clumping up the trail. I could smell her—the sweat on her skin, the village mud on her boots. I sniffed, forcing myself to work past her to other scents that might lurk in the darkness. Where was Quarrel? I had lost track of him, distracted by the girl.

Something putrid lifted on the breeze. I smelled blood and fear.

And Haverly's middle daughter was about to run afoul of it. With the Spook engaged and Quarrel missing, I had no choice but to intervene.

CHAPTER

3

Bet

I FOUND the creature just as I rounded a bend in the road where boulders ahead cut a stark line against the night sky. The area around me was mostly open and flat, with only scrubby-looking brambles or bushes. The moon shone brightly, illuminating the creature's bony back. It was hunched on the ground, snarling.

I stumbled backward, my torch and staff lifted in front of me. The creature had not yet sensed me. From behind, it was surprisingly humanlike, lithe, pale, and hairless. I knew what it was without having to be told—one of the flesh eaters. This was a ghoul, and it was probably eating now.

I did not breathe. I lifted one foot and gingerly eased it backward.

A stick snapped beneath the sole of my boot.

The ghoul spun to confront me, teeth bared and dripping blood. Its eyes glowed as if the sockets were filled with hot red coals rather than eyes. As those burning eyes fixed on me, I thought of the butcher knife in my sack and realized that to even use it I would have to get too close. No wonder Victor had scorned my choice of weapon.

The ghoul began to pace around me, darting forward only to fall back and continue circling. I circled with it, poised on the balls of my feet, sweaty skin sticking to my clothes. My breath came in short, ragged gasps. I considered dropping the torch to free up a hand but then reconsidered. The flame might prove a useful weapon.

It lunged, and I waved the burning torch toward it and yelled. We staggered apart, it howling in frustration, I in fear. The ghoul circled me again, slower this time, hissing through its teeth. Its eyes roamed over me from head to foot, like a butcher appraising a slab of meat. It darted forward as if to attack, and I swung the torch again, but the ghoul skirted around me, forcing me to stumble in a circle to keep it before me.

I realized then what it was doing. It was testing my strengths and weaknesses. This creature was *thinking*. It was learning me.

The next time the ghoul attacked, it came from above, lunging off a small boulder, and latched onto my staff with both hands. I dropped the torch as the ghoul's weight threw me backward, right off my feet. It sailed over my head, yanking the staff out of my hands.

I found my feet, dropped my pack, and bolted, knowing I had no other recourse. I could hear it behind me, gnashing its teeth, but I dared not look back. I lifted my arms to block low-lying branches and plunged into a dark stand of trees, using them as a means to put some distance between us.

At first I could see nothing, but the trees thinned abruptly, and moonlight broke through to offer me precious sight of the sloping mountainside. I kept ahead of the ghoul longer than I had expected to. My breath came in painful bursts, my heart smashing against my ribcage. It flanked me now, its glowing eyes bobbing in and out of my line of sight as it kept pace beside me.

It was playing with me.

Before I had time to consider my next move, the ghoul attacked. As it lunged for me, I fell backward and threw an arm over my face, screaming as teeth sank into the soft flesh of my forearm.

I crashed to the ground beneath it, but then the ghoul was ripped, screaming, away from me by some hairy creature much too large to be a common dog or wolf. I could hear them fighting in the darkness as I twisted and retched. Adrenaline coursed through my body, and something else, something that *hurt*. It was cold, ice cold, and burned its way into my arm.

I crawled for a while and then used a trunk to haul myself upright. The sounds of battle continued behind me, but I staggered away, not caring which direction I went.

I splashed into a creek of foul-smelling water and waded downstream until my lips trembled from the cold and my feet were nearly as numb as my injured arm. When I tried to crawl up the embankment, my legs gave out beneath me. Reaching out with my one good hand, I pulled myself up, using the roots of a massive cypress growing on the bank. But I only managed to crawl beneath the tree into a hollow created by the erosion of soil and time. I clutched my injured arm to my chest, blood leaking between my fingers, and drifted in and out of awareness, like the ebbing ripples of the creek along its banks.

Something stirred nearby, bringing me back to bleary consciousness. My breath frosted on the cold night air. I could hear it, whatever it was, shuffling closer.

I ground my teeth and prayed that the Ever Father would grant me a swift death. If I had to die, let it be quickly.

I looked up.

A shadow peeled away from deeper shadows and leaned over me. A shaft of moonlight settled on a face like death, as colorless as a corpse, as mutilated as a Creeper. Its eyes were milky white and fixed on me. My mouth fell open, but I did not scream.

"For a girl," the monster said, sounding annoyed, "you were surprisingly difficult to track. Using the river was clever."

I twisted and rammed myself deeper into the mass of soil and roots, digging frantically with my good hand. But the monster had other intentions. I felt him grab the back of my collar and tug. I flailed helplessly.

"Stop struggling," he growled. His fingers scratched my shoulder as I writhed, desperate to evade him. "You're killing yourself faster, girl!" He gave me another yank, hauling me out. I caught him with my fists a couple of times, but it was like hitting my knuckles against a brick wall.

"I will not hurt you," he said. I did not believe him and swung again. He grabbed me around the waist then and tossed me over his shoulder as if I were nothing. His shoulder dug into my stomach, driving the air from my lungs. I gasped and grabbed at the back of his shirt to find some way to reorient myself. I kicked, but my struggles were as nothing to him. Blood rushed into my swinging head, and a wave of blackness robbed me of all fight. I could hear his raspy breathing, could feel his body moving across the ground in a strange uneven fashion, almost as if he were lurching.

It was a dark, nauseating dream, and I was so cold.

"We're here," he panted. Twisting my neck, I peered about and tried to focus. I could see black walls rising from the darkness. Mist lay thick on the ground, curling as we eased through it. The beast heaved against a wrought-iron gate with his shoulder. My feet clanged against the metal. Muttering, he repositioned and used his other shoulder.

"This isn't the time!" he bellowed. "Let me in!"

The gate groaned and fell back, screaming on rusty hinges. I saw uneven cobblestones disappear into the fog as the monster walked a makeshift road guarded by stone gargoyles hulking on crude pedestals. Some animal darted around us and ran ahead. The air was oppressive and thick with the smell of wet dog and roses.

It would be roses, I thought as the darkness spirited me away.

CHAPTER

4

Corwin

I F SHE died, her blood would be on my head.

    I wiped my mouth on my sleeve. Her blood was warm, metallic, salty. The taste nearly sickened me, but the poison was worse. Like rot. Like drinking death.

I spat several more times, trying to rid myself of it.

The girl was blissfully unconscious. I had no desire to explain to her the seriousness of what had just happened. Had Quarrel not arrived when he did, she would be dead. She might die even yet if her constitution was poor.

I studied her, my eyes keen even in the darkness. Her complexion was dark and her limbs firm, accustomed to working. I lowered my nose and sniffed her neck. I could still smell the sun on her.

She would probably survive. She seemed hardy enough.

I had seen her confront the ghoul and must give credit where credit was due. She had come face to face with her own death with no begging or swooning. This one was a fighter.

I thought of the younger sister and tried to imagine how she would have reacted in this same situation. I considered hard, playing the scene from every angle. In no imaginable scenario could the little one have survived.

Gentleness and kindness had its place, but not in the Neverway.

Perhaps my first estimation had been hasty. After all, there was no leeway here for weakness, for frailty. Yes, I needed a woman who could empathize with my need, but I also required one who could survive the horror of the truth.

I pressed my mouth against her skin again, ripping into the soft flesh with my teeth.

I needed a woman who could survive the horror of me.

CHAPTER
5

Bet

I BOBBED to the surface of consciousness again. The ground was uneven beneath me. I could feel smooth stones, dirt, and something soft and damp. Moss, perhaps. I shifted and opened my eyes.

There were torches above me, but I must have been delirious, because they seemed to be floating on air, strung on nothing. I shifted my eyes and saw a wall of briars towering toward the sky, thick with the scent of roses. I heard frantic whispering, but I saw only one great shadow hulking over me, holding me down. I jerked.

"Be still," the monster grunted. I ignored him, struggling harder. "I said to be still!"

The burning ice had climbed to my shoulder. I no longer felt my arm. A pale head leaned over me. I saw a tangle of snarled white hair, a flash of milky eyes. Then he bent his head, and I felt the pressure of teeth. I realized the truth too late.

He was sucking my blood.

I thrashed against his hold but felt as if I were losing control of my own limbs. He never said a word, merely repositioned so that he crouched over me, using his heavy legs to keep me pinned down. He turned his head away from me and spat loudly. Then I felt his lips against my burning skin.

Bile clawed at the back of my throat as another wave of dizziness swept over me. If I must lose the contents of my stomach, I hoped I lost them all over him. But the ice in my arm began to recede and with it the nausea.

"I will take her to her chamber," the voice said. I strained my eyes but could not seem to focus on his face. "Keep her there until dawn."

I wanted to yell, to have a say in whatever terrible plans he had for me. But I could not seem to speak. I felt a heavy hand on my shoulder. "Be at peace," the beast said in a voice that did little to pacify me. "The paralysis will wear off. I've instructed the Lonely to give you something to help you sleep until it passes."

Merciful After, I did not want to sleep! I wanted to fight back, to defend myself. I saw no one approach, but a cup pressed against my lips and hands lifted my head. I could not fight the sickly sweet liquid filling my mouth any more than I could fight the numbing exhaustion that followed.

My dear father and sisters consumed my last thoughts.

I surfaced to heat and a musty, ticklish smell that pressed against me. I wrenched awake with a start. A vaulted ceiling arched over me and away into shadows. I blinked and gasped for steady breaths, lifting my head to better see my surroundings. I was alone in a massive chamber, lying on some sort of settee next to a roaring fire. I saw a large set of double doors and narrow arched windows covered by shutters. There were several tall wardrobes along one wall, and in the far corner a giant copper tub with feet fashioned like animal claws.

The smell bothered me again, and I shoved at the weight on my chest. It slid back scant inches, so I shoved more forcefully. The animal hide slid away from me and fell to the floor with a resounding thump. The smell dissipated, but my body protested each movement.

I groaned and took quick stock of myself. My arm throbbed, but when I reached to feel it, my skin was covered in a bandage. I could feel lace against my throat and lifted a hand to pull at it. I wore, not my overalls and work jacket, but a white nightgown. I felt clean as well, not covered in blood and grime. When had that happened?

Memories came flooding back on me, like a deluge.

I sat up too quickly and nearly fell off the settee, woozy and lightheaded. Cold hands caught and righted me. Startled, I turned to look, and my jaw slackened. I saw only rippling air where I expected to see a person.

I wrenched the other way and toppled off the settee onto the animal hide. Voices chittered around me too softly to be understood. They sounded like leaves shivering in the wind. As I sat up, I felt cold hands smoothing my hair and caressing my face, moving up and down my arms and even down to my bare feet. I yanked my feet away.

There was more chattering, like laughter. I felt a brief pressure against my cheek, as if it had been tweaked. Another shimmering entity appeared and offered me a pewter mug. I shook my head. I felt a surge of irritation that was not my own, and the thing shoved the mug toward my face.

I sniffed the contents. I could see a faint curl of steam rising from the top. Did they intend to drug me again? My stomach twisted at the thought and I shook my head. "Not yet. Please."

I expected an argument, but the shimmering being took the mug away and set it on a small table next to the settee.

The beings let me alone as I rose to my feet, clinging to the back of the settee. The room tipped but soon settled, and I dared to take several steps. I tried to remember the last moments before I'd succumbed to my wounds and the sleeping draught they'd given me. What had the Beast said? *I've instructed the Lonely.* Were these strange servants what he called the Lonely? I had never heard of such a thing.

It did explain the ghost stories, however.

The shutters on a nearby window suddenly slammed open and started banging, and a cold night breeze buffeted me. I saw shimmering as one of the beings—one of the supposed Lonely—hurried toward the window. The shutters seemed to have become jammed on something, and no matter how the Lonely pulled, would not close.

I saw darkness through the window.

Tears began to throb behind my eyes. I couldn't understand why I felt like crying now, when I had not buckled during the previous night's horrific events. I rarely cried, especially in front of strangers. But the pulsing of emotions did not subside. I found myself succumbing. After all, I'd had a night of it, and if I wanted to cry, why shouldn't I? Besides, I told myself, tears would make me blotchy and unattractive. Then perhaps my blood-sucking host would lose interest in me and send me home.

So I perched on the edge of the settee and wept.

Cold fingers brushed up and down my neck and shoulders, touching my cheeks, skimming away tears. I was not consoled. I hated crying and was convinced that my current weakness had something to do with these shimmery busybodies, some sort of lowdown magic. I grabbed the edge of the little metal table beside us and shoved it away. It clattered to the stone floor, splattering milk. The pewter mug rolled to a stop.

In the following silence I could feel them hovering. I swiped at my face with the back of my good hand as sobs subsided into choppy breaths.

One of the servants moved to clean up the mess I had made. I sighed, knowing I should not have knocked over the table. I stood up. "Oh, let me do that," I said in a choking, irritated voice. I hated how weak I sounded.

Once again I felt a surge of emotion that did not seem to come from me. It was stronger than before, now filled with something more than mere irritation. I sat back down, hard. Fingers patted my hair. After mopping up the mess with a cloth, the angry one disappeared with the mug and table. I turned my attention to the one still playing with my hair. "May I please have my clothes?" I managed.

The room felt suddenly empty.

I swallowed hard. Perhaps my clothes were no longer fit to wear. I had not considered that. "If I can't have mine, might I please have *any* clothes?"

This seemed to change things. The being, suddenly present once more, moved away from me to one of the wardrobes and returned with a gauzy gown in cream and gold.

I gaped in disbelief, heat creeping up to my ears. "Merciful After, haven't you anything—um, practical?"

She did not move, but I felt a sudden sense of distress. I could feel deep emotions from this one, emotions that ached like a raw wound. I did not wish to hurt her by being difficult, but how was I to fight off a bloodsucker while wearing a *gown*?

With no alternative offered, however, I heaved a sigh. "Very well." I may as well have said, "Do your worst."

I felt foolish, sitting there letting her dress me and play with my hair as if I were a helpless child. It wasn't until she was done that I had the uneasy feeling I was being dressed for *him*.

I tried to delay, but she whisked me toward a set of large double doors. The heeled shoes she had given me wobbled beneath my feet. I wavered at the doors, but she prodded me into the stone-walled corridor flanked with torches and boasting narrow slits for windows. I paused to look out one of the slits but could not see even the twinkle of a star. For some reason this bothered me. I felt as though I were in a foreign world where even the simplest laws of nature no longer applied.

It was one thing to imagine this place from the safety of my village. Actually being here was another thing entirely.

CHAPTER
6

Corwin

I WAS waiting when the Lonely brought her down to dinner.

The girl peeked around the door frame of the dining hall. She paused, glancing from the fire crackling along the north wall, to the long table made of wood planks, to the oil lamps illuminating the stone walls opposite the fireplace. Her posture reminded me of a wild deer, nose quivering, body poised for immediate flight.

She edged into the room. She did not seem to notice us waiting in the shadows.

The wolfhound bolted, ignoring my shout of protest. He scrabbled across the stone floor, skidded into her, and knocked her clean off her feet. She went down with a loud cry. I jolted forward, dismayed.

"Quarrel, get back!" The command came out as a snarl. The dog whimpered and ducked his head, tail between his legs, and dropped to the ground as the girl stood up. I paused and watched them. She clutched the sides of her skirts and breathed uneasily.

Quarrel whined and moved his nose imploringly toward her. Compared to her, in her pretty if now rumpled dress, he was hideous. Massive, wiry, and covered in patchy gray and black hair. Unsightly. Which is why I tolerated him. He was like me. With fur.

For a moment she strained her eyes to find me, but then she turned back to my dog, reaching out a tentative hand. He rushed to greet her, wagging his tail like a fool.

His head reached nearly as high as her shoulder. And he was making a complete ninny of himself.

"You are not as scary as you look, now are you?" she asked, sounding relieved. She rotated her hand to scratch behind his ear. The fool whimpered and kicked his ribs with one hind foot.

"So you'll talk to my dog but you won't speak to me," I growled, humiliated by his display. Quarrel whimpered and dropped to the ground, head turned back to look for me.

She lifted her eyes, following Quarrel's gaze, and scowled. "I'm sorry," she said, sounding irritated. "I didn't see you back there. In the shadows." She added that phrase with sarcastic emphasis. "You must be Papa's Beast."

I went cold all over. "The only beast in Briarstone Abbey is the *dog*," I said, barely managing to be civil.

Silence reigned between us but for Quarrel's whines and the murmurs of the servants.

"My name is Bet," she said at last, stiffly. "Lilybet Haverly."

"That's a ridiculous name," I retorted, on account of the beast comment.

Bet swayed but held her tongue. I snapped my fingers, and Quarrel lunged across the room, his claws clacking against the floor. He ran back into the shadows, to me.

"Who are you?" Bet asked, sounding strained.

"I am the master of this place. Everyone does as I command here."

"That's nice. But you must have a name," she persisted.

I lifted my gaze from the dog to study her. She was unsteady, shifting from foot to foot, but her jaw set in a determined way that suggested I would know no peace until I answered her. Now was the time to establish the hierarchy.

I sighed. "You may call me *Master*."

Something clattered. My head jerked in the direction of the kitchens. The mutter of voices rose, but when I swept a hand at the air, they fell silent. I felt them pulse in irritation, but they withered beneath my glare and faded into the shadows. I glowered a moment longer before turning back to the girl. "Dratted Lonely," I muttered.

"Lonely?" Bet echoed, arching one eyebrow. "I heard you say that name before. Why do you call them this?"

"They can neither speak nor be seen. That makes them Lonely." I took a steadying breath and privately acknowledged the unfairness of my impatience. In all honesty, I didn't know what they were either. I adjusted my cloak about my shoulders to make sure I was sufficiently covered, then took a step forward, leaning my weight on my cane. I stopped just shy of the circle of light cast by the candelabra. "Yours are called Twilight and Dawn."

"Mine? Oh, you mean the *Lonely*. Which one is the cranky one?"

I harrumphed. "That," I said, "would be Twilight." I felt a surge of temper course through the room. I cleared my throat and the assault retreated. I glimpsed one of the Lonely floating out of the room—obviously Twilight.

Ignoring her, I gripped my cane more firmly and eased the weight completely off my bad leg. "So tell me, Miss Haverly," I said, wishing I could make my voice gentler but knowing this was impossible, "did you come of your own free will?"

Something unpleasant crossed the girl's face, but she nodded. "I have no prospects, unlike Rosamond, who might marry a duke if she keeps her wits about her. And Sookie is too young for—for this."

I snorted, the sound echoing back to me. I steeled myself for what must come next. "You are not exactly . . . what I had in mind for a companion." I had imagined a demure and pleasant young maiden with a quick smile and trusting nature who liked to rescue stray animals.

For a moment the girl seemed speechless. "You want a *companion*?"

"Don't look so offended," I growled, pretending to misunderstand her hesitation. "You are not much better to look at than I am. And if I don't suit *you* then you can send your other sister—the one not pining for a duke." I waved a careless hand as if it mattered little to me.

Her expression shuttered, like a window abruptly closed. "That's impossible," she said coldly. "No, we are both stuck, I fear." She lifted her chin and stared right at me.

Now I was intrigued. I wanted to know what had elicited the change in her. Was it the insult to her looks?

"Perhaps we are well suited then," I pressed, keeping my tone disdainful and detached. "Tell me, why did you come here?"

Though a moment before she had met my gaze squarely, now she suddenly paled and looked away, her gaze searching out Quarrel's scruffy form as though for comfort. "I came to offer myself in my sister's place."

"Did you not consider the danger? I said I would come and get your sister, so that she need not face the Neverway alone. You must have known you would be risking your life to do this thing."

"I did." She still would not look at me.

It might surprise her if she knew, but I began to appreciate her decision. It seemed she had not come to me in a fit of temper, to deliberately plague me or disregard my demands. She came because she loved her sister.

This I found appealing.

"Since you have offered to take your sister's place," I began, trying not to falter over the words, "you must be informed of the facts. I am in need of assistance with a—with a delicate matter."

She glanced over then, her forehead furrowed.

I did not want to scare her away by telling her too much at once, but she needed to know the peril. She needed to know that much was at stake. I chose my words with care. "There is a danger here. At Briarstone. I need someone to share my life, to help me fight it."

"And you picked my little sister? *For that?*" she demanded, incredulous. "You are mad if you think I will believe this tale of yours. This is ridiculous!"

My thoughts on her capacity for intelligence aside, I could not believe her rudeness. "You have a bad temper, Miss Haverly, and I find your tone irksome," I managed, struggling to control my own rising irritation.

She sniffed. "If you wanted someone who wasn't irksome, you should have been more specific."

"I believe I was specific."

My words finally silenced her. She looked away from me, clearing her throat. I took the opportunity to study her. She was short but solid, with untidy hair and features that betrayed her rapidly changing moods. She also had quick wit and courage. Most people could not speak so bluntly to me. Even her father had cowered at my feet.

"Well," I said quietly. I shook my head side to side. "Well, I suppose you must find me irksome as well."

"Indeed," she agreed.

I reminded myself that, considering how I had taken advantage of her father in a moment of distress, her honesty—and bluntness—should not surprise me. It was not the reaction I had hoped for in our first conversation, but it was probably the reaction I deserved. "Which sister I picked does not matter now that you are here. If you are still willing."

"I'm sure I don't understand what you're asking."

I ground my teeth together. Merciful After, I had not believed such a trying woman existed! I tried to shove my emotions back where they would not interfere with what I needed to accomplish here. My tongue felt glued to the roof of my mouth. I peeled it loose by sheer willpower. "Miss Haverly, will you marry me?" The words stuck like stones in my throat.

Immediately the air felt oppressive. I watched horror take control of her features. I tried to shield myself from her revulsion, tried to imagine my heart as stone, unyielding, unbreakable. But the blood coursing in and out of that traitorous organ revealed the utter failure of my efforts.

It hurt. Of course it hurt.

"Do I have a choice?" she stammered.

I did not answer immediately. "Yes," I finally admitted.

"Then no," she retorted emphatically. "No, I will not."

I waited for a surge of anger but felt only despair. It was not all mine. The Lonely wept, and Briarstone's thoughts on the matter were quite clear. Every door in the Abbey began banging simultaneously.

There was much more I needed to say to this girl. But she was in no humor to hear the truth—not from me, and not tonight. I leaned heavily on my cane and limped toward the door with Quarrel hot on my heels. I turned my face from her so that I would not have to look at her when I hobbled past. "Pick up your plate, Miss Haverly. The Lonely will escort you back to your chambers," I muttered.

After what I had done to her, I should have expected no better.

CHAPTER

7

Bet

I COULD not believe that he expected me to marry him.

The Lonely tucked me into bed on the settee, but I lay awake, too aware of the hard bed, the smelly hide blankets, and the lack of sisters breathing nearby. I missed them more than I had thought possible.

At one point I rose to test the doors, but they were obviously locked.

In the morning, the Lonely fed me hard-boiled eggs and dried fruit. The sunlight refracted through the invisible servants as if through crystal, dotting the stone floor and walls in wobbling shards of color. They were like the prisms Papa had brought home for Rosamond one year, which now hung in our bedroom window.

After breakfast, Twilight made me take a bath in the tub and scrubbed me harder than I felt was necessary. Dawn dressed me in a beige dress that bunched beneath the bust and flared to my ankles. She then offered me a pair of brocade slippers. At least they were flats.

They led me through the Abbey, down long hallways and narrow staircases. I could see cobwebs in the windows, mildew on the stones, and stains on the carpeted runners that covered the floors. Eventually they led me to a doorway open to the outside. As soon as I passed through, the door slammed shut behind me, smacking me in the behind. I twisted with a yelp, but no one was there.

I had half expected to find Papa's Beast waiting for me, but as I surveyed my surroundings I realized that the Lonely and I were alone. I picked my way down a weedy path and turned back to survey the Abbey from the outside. We had apparently exited through a side entrance at the base of a tower. Briarstone Abbey seemed to have been constructed with minimal design beforehand, having windows in odd places and towers and parapets popping out at random. One side of the castle contained a massive stained-glass window, but many of its panes were shattered or missing. Battlements topped the many high towers, with ugly gargoyles glaring out over the Neverway.

I turned to take in the rest of my surroundings, from the path winding into an overgrown garden to the imposing wall of briars beyond it. I could see no end to the briars. They appeared to form a solid barrier around the Abbey.

I knew for certain then: I was completely trapped.

They made me return to the Abbey for a light luncheon of over-browned bread and cold ham, but the sun rose and set without a word from the "Master." The fact that he was waiting when Twilight and Dawn deposited me in the dinner hall only chafed me more. Why ignore me all day?

He was already seated at the far end of the table. When he motioned for me to be seated across from him, I complied noisily, scraping the heavy chair across the ground. At least there were a dozen chairs between us. I should be grateful for that.

I sniffed the air, glancing down. I saw it then, beside my silverware: a large black rose. Its petals were wilted and curling, the stem soiled with dark spots. I wondered what I was meant to do with it. It was probably intended as some sort of peace offering.

I left it be.

Awkward silence hung in the air between us. "How did you sleep?" he asked at long last.

"I didn't, thank you," I replied, just as stiffly.

Silence fell again. Two Lonely appeared from the kitchens with platters of food. I found myself only able to pick at the food they offered me. The meat was stringy and the vegetables boiled to mush. Apparently communicating was not the only thing the Lonely did poorly.

"I was wondering if you found my gardens."

I deliberated whether this was an accusation or his idea of polite conversation. "They weren't much to look at," I finally grumbled.

"Oh. I agree, they are . . . not as fine as they once were." He sounded annoyed. I could not see much of him. The oil lamps on the wall were turned down, and the two candelabra on the table stood at my end. "But it isn't for lack of effort. They're . . . sick."

I said nothing, shoving the dark stew around on my plate. Quarrel crept to my side, crawling across the floor as though he didn't want to be seen. I glanced up at my host from under my lashes and then slipped some gristly meat down to the dog. He swallowed it in one gulp.

"I require assistance in tending them," the Master continued, still on about his gardens, his spotty roses. "I cannot keep them on my own."

I sincerely hoped he was not about to renew our conversation from the night before. I had no intention of being his "companion." I glanced up at the cobwebs draping the beams above our head. The entire Abbey was falling down around his ears. I wondered if he meant for me to scrub the floors as well as water the creeper-loving roses. He didn't want a wife. He wanted a slave. I slipped another hunk of meat to the dog.

"Are you unwell?"

I glanced up. He had seen. "I'm fine," I said between my teeth. "I'm just not hungry." His presence seemed to have chased away my appetite.

His expression hardened. "I apologize if our humble fare displeases you." He lifted a chunk of the stringy meat and shoved it into his mouth with his fingers. We stared at one another, neither of us speaking as I watched him chew and swallow, and it suddenly struck me as odd.

"You *eat*?" I asked in surprise.

His pale, knobby hands lowered to the tabletop. "Of course I eat. I'm not dead yet."

Well, I'd already determined he wasn't a Creeper. "I thought you preferred blood."

His lips turned down. "Is that what they say now? That I'm a bloodsucker?" He snorted and shook his head from side to side. "Small-minded fools."

I bristled at the insult. I was *not* small-minded. "You're the one who introduced himself by drinking my blood!" I laid my arm across the oak tabletop and yanked up my lacey sleeve to reveal proof disputing my "small-mindedness."

"I wasn't *drinking* your blood!" he growled, slamming his hands down on the table. The dishes rattled; the candles sputtered. "I was sucking out the poison! If I hadn't, you'd be dead right now. Dead, Miss Haverly."

I felt suddenly cold. "Dead?" I echoed and replayed the events in my mind. I realized, unhappily, he was probably speaking the truth. "Oh."

He learned forward, and the lamps cast a hint of light across his prominent features, creating dark shadows where his pale eyes should be. "Oh, indeed," he mocked.

By the Never, how was I to know? I hadn't been exactly coherent at the time. I tugged my sleeve down and drew my arm back into my lap, frowning as I stared off to one side.

"Bloodsucker. What a notion!" he muttered. I glanced at him out of the corner of my eye and saw him cross his arms over his chest and glare in the opposite direction, sulking. I barely managed to strangle the impulse to laugh. It came out as an unladylike snort. I coughed, hoping to mask the blunder.

His gaze swiveled back to mine. "*What?*"

I didn't want to say, because I suspected I had done enough antagonizing for one night. He squinted at me, frowning. Then he shoved back his chair and moved toward me. I shrank back, my hands falling to grip the smooth arms of the chair. He did not stop until he stood right beside me, staring down at me.

He was so big. This was the first opportunity I had been given to truly study him. He was awfully pale, as if all pigment had been drained out of him. Even his eyes were milky white, with only a touch of pale blue in the irises. He had hairless, jutting brows and a fat, squat nose. His face was the wrong shape for a human, however, the jaw too square and jutting forward. And when he opened his mouth to speak, his teeth were those of a wild animal. He really was the ugliest living thing I'd ever seen.

"I wish to know what you are thinking. Why you laughed just now." It was a command, not a request, although he spoke softly enough.

I became uncomfortable in the silence. For once the servants were quiet, as if the entire Abbey were holding its breath. I swallowed hard, fidgeting. "We both seem to have bad tempers, is all."

"And you find this amusing?"

"I find it apropos. Contrary to your hopes that the better daughter might still be sent to you, I fear I'm the best suited." My voice had dropped to a whisper. If I hoped to be sent home, listing compatibilities was not the proper plan of attack. I tried to retrench, regroup my thoughts. If I intended to be home before Sookie's birthday, I didn't have time to make mistakes.

His expression no longer seemed angry, merely curious and perhaps a little wistful. "So." He said the one word as if that were all he intended to say. But then he cleared his throat and tried again. "So you will marry me then, Miss Haverly? I do need your help."

The air hissed between my teeth, loud enough he must surely have heard it. His gnarled hand settled on the table beside me, only inches from my folded hands. I stared at his long fingers, unable to meet his eyes.

"No," I said uneasily. "I have no intention of marrying a complete stranger. Most men introduce themselves before they start throwing around proposals of marriage."

This caused him to flinch. "It would make things *easier.*"

It would make things easier for him, certainly, but not for me. He had not put forth any sort of effort to spend time with me—and then, at a snap of his fingers, he expected me to capitulate to his wishes.

I had never been the capitulating sort. Besides, Rosamond had taught me enough about relationships to know that subtle problems before marriage meant certain trouble after. If I ever married—and I rather doubted I would—I planned to marry a man I could respect, who would respect me.

After what he had done, I could never respect the Master of Briarstone Abbey.

"There is more I need to tell you," he began, in a desperate way. "About the dangers here—about—"

"I don't want to talk about this anymore," I interrupted as I shoved my chair back and stumbled to my feet. "Please, may I be excused?"

He let me go without a word, but he looked wounded. As Twilight led me from the dining hall, I told myself it was impossible. He could not truly care for me after so short and unpleasant a time.

CHAPTER
8

Corwin

I WAS waiting for her each evening after that. She never once acknowledged the roses I left for her. She had been with me a week when I hunted for an entire armful of precious blossoms, stuffed them into a pewter pitcher, and plunked them down in front of her plate where she couldn't miss them.

When she arrived, Quarrel rushed to greet her and licked her face. She cupped his large face in her hands, grinning. "Hullo, there!" she exclaimed, clearly glad to see him.

I sat down, feeling stupidly jealous. Of the dog.

"I am told you've been poking your nose about," I said, not lifting my eyes from my meal. I attempted to use my fork, but the utensil felt ridiculous in my hands. "During the day you are free to wander about as you will, but the basements are *off limits*."

"The basements?" she echoed. "I am not sure I know where they are." She took her seat and immediately spooned half the contents of her plate onto the floor. I gaped at her, appalled. There would be no living with that dog after this. Granted, I did not exactly keep a proper household, but even I had my standards.

"On the contrary, I've been told you know *exactly* where they are," I retorted. I'd sensed her prowling around the corridor leading to the catacombs around midday. Our gazes locked and held. I could tell by the set of her chin that she was not about to be frightened into compliance.

"Will you at least tell me why?"

"You said you didn't want to talk about it. So, no."

"By the Never!" she sputtered, slamming her fork down on the table. "I meant I didn't want to talk about marriage. This is different. Where do you go all day long? Why can't I go down to—"

"You really are irksome," I interrupted, watching as Quarrel nudged her hand. She held out a biscuit, which he swiped shamelessly. "You'll spoil him."

"You have not answered my questions." She speared me with a glowering look. "It's time you 'fessed up. Why am I really here?"

"I have tried to tell you—repeatedly." I tried to skewer a gray hunk of turnip, but it skipped off my plate and across the table. I chucked the fork after it. I heard a second clatter and looked up to see Bet popping a bit of roast into her mouth with her fingers. She pointedly picked up another piece and shoved that in as well.

Well then.

I unclenched my jaw. "I have tried to speak with you, but you do not listen. You argue, and fuss, and growl like a bear."

"I have made every effort to listen, but I don't believe you have told me what you think you have," she said around a mouthful of meat. "You say you need help, but I spend my hours doing nothing at all."

I feared she wanted to know more than she was prepared to comprehend. I had delayed this long only because she managed to say something rude and unpleasant every time I angled the conversation in the appropriate direction.

I was not used to speaking to anyone who could answer me.

I grasped my cane and rose to limp toward her. She watched with narrowed eyes as I pulled out the chair next to hers and eased myself into it. Quarrel ran around her chair to sit between us, whining. I settled a hand on his head, enjoying its warmth against my calloused palm.

I finally looked up. Bet's attention focused on my hand cupped over Quarrel's head, her expression quizzical. Did it unsettle her to discover that even monsters have a need for comfort? My throat constricted, but I forced the lump down.

"Will you marry me, Miss Haverly?" I asked, just as I had every night since her arrival. "Because that is what I need."

Bet did not answer immediately. "I do not understand why I should," she finally said. "You will not even tell me your name." The candlelight danced across her face, reflecting in her eyes. They were blue like a dusky sky. I felt my pulse quicken beneath the intensity of her gaze. I thought she might be seeing me, truly *seeing* me, for the first time. Perhaps she was getting used to me, as I was growing accustomed to her. Was that not a good thing?

My insides felt tight, my breath short. Why then did I feel only more anxious?

I considered telling her all, but I was loath to undo what little I had accomplished. She would not believe the truth. I had seen enough of the villagers to know that they liked fantastical tales but did not truly believe them. I had seen enough of *her* to know this.

"My name is Corwin," I finally said, my voice nothing more than a whisper as fleeting as the candlelight. I felt a pulse of approval from the Lonely, almost as if they breathed a collective sigh of relief. She had heard truth enough for one night. I had waited this long, why would one more night hurt?

"Hullo, Corwin," she said. She took several fortifying breaths. "It's nice to meet you . . . I think."

"You think," I echoed. I allowed the ghost of a smile to touch my lips.

Still Bet stared at me. "I think," she repeated. "Yes, yes, I think." She must have immediately realized how stupid that sounded. With her short, unruly curls tucked behind her ears, I could see them turn pink. For some reason, I smiled.

That's what broke the spell. She saw my sharp incisors, my animal teeth, and sat back abruptly. I leaned away as well, feeling pained.

"Goodnight, Miss Haverly," I managed as I eased out of the chair and hobbled toward the doorway. Quarrel whined as if torn. I passed from the room without ordering him to follow. He stayed.

And I left alone.

CHAPTER 9

Bet

I COULD not sleep.

His name was Corwin. *Corwin.*

I paced the length of my prison, still wearing my green muslin gown. Twisted black and green ribbons laced down each side, and I tugged at their trailing ends, tying them into knots as I walked.

When Corwin finally said his name, he had looked almost ill. I could still feel his eyes on me, staring as if he never intended to look away. The dog, the Master, the servants . . . they all shared that haunted, untended look. They were all Lonely.

I shivered and rubbed my arms, my fingers brushing over the bruises and scabs. Scabs from his creeper-loving *teeth*! I should feel no pity for this monster.

But, strangely, impossibly . . . I almost did.

A loud noise tore through the Abbey. It sounded like a crack of thunder but felt like the felling of a tree. I froze mere feet from the arched doors. The floor trembled beneath me as the noise continued to rebound on stone after stone. I felt Twilight brush past me; I almost heard her movements. Sometimes when the Lonely moved I fancied I could hear them, but the sound was muted, like the echo of a footstep and not the step itself. She left the door ajar in her haste.

Dawn came up behind me, her cold fingers on my arm. She throbbed with fear as the rumbling beneath our feet continued.

From somewhere deep in the Abbey a voice cried out. At first I could not make out words, but I rushed to grab a torch from its wall sconce. Dawn clutched at me as I moved to peer into the darkness, my heart racing in my chest. Her grip tightened, but she lacked Twilight's strength.

My name echoed through the Abbey as the floor continued to shudder.

"Lilybet, help me!"

I knew that voice, and the sound of it filled me with blind terror. It was Sookie. My own dear Sookie!

I wrenched free of Dawn's fragile hold and dashed into the corridor. "Sookie!" I shouted as I ran. "Sookie, where are you?"

What was she doing here? Had she followed me? Or worse, was she a prisoner here as well? How could I have not known? How could I have missed her coming?

I neared an open door, but before I could reach it, the door slammed shut in my face. It would not open.

"Sookie!" I yelled as I ran further into Briarstone. I felt Dawn following behind me, her fear as tangible as the torch in my hand, as real as Sookie's voice screaming for my help. What was happening to my sister?

I heard stone grinding against stone as I rounded a corner in the hallway. I lifted my torch, scanning until I found an open passage in the wall. But the wall was closing as if it were a hidden door someone had just tripped.

"*Lilybet!*" Sookie's voice echoed through the opening.

Dawn caught my arm and pulled, but I lurched forward, twisting sideways to jam myself through the narrowing gap. Dawn tumbled after me. I found myself rushing down a windowless, winding staircase.

Something reared up in front of me. I could not stop in time but plunged straight through it. The air suddenly felt thick and smelled foul. I broke free, gasping, and whirled to investigate.

I did not know what I looked upon. It was like peering through a sheet of rushing water. Behind the rippling air I saw a dark shadow that *moved*, as if it pressed against the moving barrier.

The shadow began to leak into the stairwell. The air grew hot and smelled putrid like sulfur and charred flesh.

Choking, I swung the torch with both hands and backed down the stairs. Dawn plucked at my clothes, her terror battering against me, out of sync with my own galloping fear.

The shadow rose above me like a serpent coiling to strike. I opened my mouth to scream, but the sound was sucked right out of my mouth. My vision began to spot at the edges. Tears leaked from my eyes as one minute led into the next, building into an eternity I feared would never end.

What was happening?

CHAPTER
10

Corwin

BET HAD stumbled into grave danger.

Briarstone threw pictures into my mind with blinding speed. I glimpsed torchlight and a green dress. Rippling shadows. Stone steps, winding.

Bet was in the stairwell leading to the catacombs.

With a roar of panic I stumbled through the tunnels. I had sensed an impending assault but had not guessed how vital the danger had become. And how could I have known Bet would get herself caught up in the middle of it? But she would, of course! Stubborn, bullheaded girl! I cast aside my cane and ignored my pains as I ran. I was close, but was I close enough?

Let me be close enough! Don't let her die!

My thoughts thundered the prayer; the plea for help was instinctual. I should never have brought her here. Was this to be my punishment for taking matters into my own hands? Had I truly lost so much faith in my mission that I would risk the lives of the innocents I was sworn to protect?

In my haste, I stumbled against the wall when I reached the entrance to the stairs. I smelled burning and felt Dawn's terror hammering against my mind. I shouted for her to be silent as I began climbing.

Only a turn and a half and I found them. Bet hung in the air, surrounded by putrid shadows, a torch still clutched in her right hand. Behind her, the breach rippled where the underworlder had broken through.

The wraith was feeding.

I opened my mouth and blasted the creature with a wave of echoes. The sound was too high for humans to hear, but not for underworlders. The wraith recoiled and lost its grip on Bet, howling in pain as it turned on me.

Bet thudded to the steps, coughing, her arms outspread as she tried to catch herself. I lurched up beside her as the wraith recovered.

Strengthened by its feeding, the wraith had taken its solid form. It was thin, featureless. I saw the smoldering embers beneath the veil of darkness the wraith wrapped around itself in place of skin.

Briarstone came to my aid, wrenching stones right out of the ceiling and hurling them down on the underworlder. The wraith tried to avoid them but the barrage drove it back toward the breach. It began to lose control of itself, dropping its form and turning back to shadows as the laws of its own world demanded its return.

Like the pull of gravity, the Underworld tugged it back. The wraith could not resist us all.

Bet moved up beside me and looked as if she meant to thrust her torch at the wraith, but I shoved her back roughly. I would not risk her harming herself further. I flung another series of echoes and did not relent until the ripples swallowed the wraith whole.

Briarstone continued to pull stones from the ceiling, filling in the stairwell ahead of us. Imagining an invisible wall, I yanked at both sides of the rippling breach and knotted them together in the middle. From within the breach, the wraith flung itself against the weak point with renewed vigor, pummeling it again and again. Sparks exploded with each impact. But I'd had much experience and shifted my focus to block each renewed attack until the invisible wall solidified into stone and mortar.

Briarstone worked alongside me, groaning and shifting with each alteration, filling in the stairwell and changing the shape of herself to make sure the breach was completely sealed. Even then I could hear the wraith's muted screams.

I groaned and sagged against the wall. Dawn was instantly there. I could feel her weeping, her thoughts for me, not herself.

Bet stood across from me, her torch sputtering and hissing as it began to fail her. I stared at her, unable to believe she lived. I had rarely seen anyone survive a wraith attack. They were quick with their work. They didn't linger like the ghouls, who enjoyed the pleasure of the kill. No, wraiths ripped through people, sucked them dry, and discarded their husks.

I reached for her but stopped when she jerked away. "Can you walk?" I asked. "You must come with me."

Her torch hissed and failed her completely. We stood in utter blackness.

"You must come," I continued, as gently as I could manage. I needed to get her out of here. I needed to get us both out before I collapsed. Within moments my eyes adjusted to the dark, but I knew she would see nothing.

"Where is my sister?" Bet croaked. "I heard her screaming—" She broke off, as if either her voice or her will had failed her.

I closed my eyes, realizing then what had happened. I was such a fool. "She is not here," I whispered as I reached out once again. "I will explain, but you must come with me. Now. Please."

For a moment I thought she would refuse. But then she reached out a tentative hand, searching the darkness. I breathed a sigh of relief and grasped her hand in mine.

CHAPTER
11

Bet

CORWIN STAGGERED in the pitch darkness, dragging me alongside him. My throat burned as if I'd swallowed acid, and my head throbbed in pain. I kept one hand on the wall and clung to Corwin's hand with the other, but I still stumbled in blindness.

Ahead of us, barking echoed down the tunnel, growing steadily louder. Soon a torch appeared, and then another. The dual promise of Quarrel and light cheered me onward. When we drew closer, I saw that the torches were held by several Lonely standing right outside a doorway.

Quarrel barreled out of the darkness. Corwin released me and snapped his fingers before the dog was near enough to knock us over. The poor beast dropped to the ground, whimpering but obedient. I felt the Lonely tugging at my hands, trying to pull me through the doorway. I hesitated, but there were more torches within, so I stepped into the chamber.

The room stretched before me, long and narrow, with a higher ceiling than the tunnels. There were stone benches, tapestries on the walls, and torches flickering in wall sconces. I could see several alcoves branching off the main chamber, but they were dark.

Something thudded behind me. I whirled and saw Corwin on his knees, with several Lonely moving in around him. Quarrel pressed his head against his master's shoulder. "I am all right," Corwin said, hunched over and seeming to struggle for breath.

"What is happening?" I choked out. It hurt to speak, but I desperately needed answers. "Where is Sookie?" I felt cold hands take hold of me and let them guide me onto a nearby bench. I watched as several more Lonely moved into the chamber, filing in one after another. There were dozens of them.

Corwin lifted his head to look at me. If it were possible, he seemed even paler than normal, his eyes huge beneath his hulking brow. He was trembling.

Dawn offered me a cup; I took it but did not drink. "My sister," I pressed.

Corwin's throat convulsed as he swallowed. "She is not here. I swear it on my life. It was the wraith."

I wished I could be sure he spoke the truth. I did not see how I could trust him.

"It was a trap," he said, his voice cracking. "It was my fault. I should have . . . I should have told you sooner but I—I did not wish to frighten you away. I thought you would be safe in the tower. The wraiths hate light. They are strongest below ground, in the catacombs. I told you there was danger here, but I did not tell you how imminent the peril is. That was my error, and I beg your pardon."

I did not know what to say. I did not want to let his humility change my opinion of him, but it unsettled me deeply. "My sister is safe?"

He nodded.

I lifted the cup at last and took a tentative sip. It tasted bitter, but when I swallowed, it was as if I swallowed a breath of fresh air. I drank again, deeper, and closed my eyes as the tingling liquid slid down my raw throat. "That creature—that wraith? It is the danger you spoke of? There are more of . . . that thing?"

"Many, many more."

"Are we safe here?" I glanced about the room, at the Lonely huddled around us, shimmering in the torchlight. "Can it come back?"

He shifted when Quarrel bumped him under the chin, moving his hand to scratch the dog's ears. "They can return, but not here. These chambers are our sacred place. We call it Sanctuary. It has never been breached."

I glanced around, trying to take it in. The chamber was not much to look at for a sacred place, but I could see the signs. There were candles scattered around the room and old books on shelves. The tapestries on the walls seemed to have stories to tell. In a way, it was not unlike the chapel in our village: small, quiet, and somber.

I wanted to be furious, but I was also overwhelmed. There was too much going on here that I did not understand. Mostly I wanted to hold my sister in my arms and assure myself that she had not fallen prey to the horrors of this place.

Corwin cleared his throat. "If you ask any question of me," he said, "I will answer it. I owe you that and more."

"Yes, you do," I agreed. I drank from the cup again before setting it down on the bench. I breathed slowly and searched for the right words. "I should like to know who you are and what you are doing here at Briarstone," I said.

He sighed and let his hand slide from Quarrel's head down over his shoulders. "That, Miss Haverly, is a long story."

"I think it's time," I said. I would not let him put me off again.

His eyes darted over me, almost frantically. "Yes," he finally agreed, "I believe it is."

CHAPTER

12

Corwin

I DID not know where to begin.

Bet watched me, her short hair snarled around her pale face. I could not quite interpret her expression, but I appreciated that she gave me time to collect my thoughts.

I hated myself as fervently as I hated the underworlders. I saw now the folly of reticence. My cowardice had nearly cost Lilybet Haverly her life. I felt as monstrous as the villagers imagined me to be. Pushing Quarrel away, I tried to come to my feet, but my leg buckled and I jolted to the side, grunting in pain.

She was there instantly, ducking under my arm, close to my side. "Easy," she ordered in a gruff little voice. She waited. I took a tentative step, and she moved with me, bearing the weight of my arm across her shoulder. I didn't dare put much weight on her, but I lifted my foot and took a step, gritting my teeth against the pain, feeling the uncanny warmth of her stocky body against my side as we moved to the nearest bench. I sank down with a groan.

She ducked from under my arm and sat a few feet away. "So, are you going to tell me your story?" she asked as Quarrel moved to sit between us, looking from me to her. When she held out a hand, he rushed to lick her cheeks.

"I am a member of an ancient order," I began. I tried to shift into a more comfortable position. "Centuries ago, the Ever chose my ancestors to guard the Neverway. I am a Warden, as were my parents before me. We accepted the Calling, to keep the underworlders—the wraiths and ghouls—out of our world."

Her expression twisted in confusion. She did not quite believe me. "Where is *their* world exactly?"

"The Underworld," I whispered. "The Neverway is not what it seems. Think of it like oil and water trying to fit into the same container. They push against one another, correct?"

She nodded.

"Well, the Neverway is like the place between the oil and water. The fabric between realities. And the boundary is being *ripped* open. We call them breaches."

"The ghouls—and the wraiths. They're coming through the 'breaches'? From the Underworld."

"Yes."

"But why have we never seen this happen? Papa travels the Neverway frequently. He has never seen any breaches—or wraiths. Are they only here?"

Her logic surprised me. She was already leaping ahead of me, trying to put the pieces together. I had been wrong in the beginning when I thought her the wrong daughter.

She was the perfect daughter.

"At present," I managed, trying to keep my tone neutral, "the breaches are confined to the catacombs beneath Briarstone, although I suspect there are other weak places. I cannot account for the ghouls. They seem to be breaking out somewhere else; I have not yet discovered where. The Ever knew this area was a weak place. He built Briarstone to defend it and called the Wardens to help her. It was all planned long, long ago."

Bet continued to watch me, her eyes probing. I found I could not hold her gaze and looked down. I did not want her to know my thoughts, that I doubted the very foundations of my existence. My ancestors had fought bravely for centuries, and I would be the one to undo it all. I shifted to grip the bench on either side of me, knowing the stone should feel hard and cold beneath my touch.

But I couldn't feel it. I was as cold as the stone. Someday soon I would be as lifeless as this bench, as hard and cold and unmoving. My heart would be stone.

"I am afraid the Order of the Wardens is going to die with me," I whispered. "Then no one will be here to stand with Briarstone. I fear . . . I fear the Ever has forgotten me."

My fingers clenched, and I heard stone crumbling beneath my touch. My hands were white, covered in crumbled, chalk-like debris. I could see cracks in my skin. I was growing so tired.

I closed my eyes and searched Briarstone with my spirit. She towered proud and strong toward the sky, but I knew her too well to judge her strength by looks alone. In my precious gardens, black petals floated to the ground, wilting as they fell. Every petal was a sacrifice, a bit of her withering away. She was getting tired, too.

For this reason I had demanded a life from Merchant Haverly when he plucked a rose from the wall. A life for a life.

I exhaled. Inhaled.

"I think I understand, at least mostly," Bet said, breaking into my thoughts. I opened my eyes. She still studied me, a wrinkle between her brows. "But what *are* you exactly?" she asked. "You're not, well, human."

Here it was. She was finally ready to hear the last, most brutal truth.

I shifted forward, pushing myself upright. Bet jumped to her feet, startled. I lifted a placating palm toward her. "I think it will be easiest to show you," I said softly. I paused, and then turned my hand so that my palm faced up. "Will you come with me?"

Her expression changed from concern to distrust to lingering anger. At last she nodded. "I will come." She hesitated, as if she wished to say more. "I will come, but do I have to hold your hand?"

I sighed and curled my fingers into my palm. I could not blame her for refusing. I wanted her to like me—no, I wanted her to love me. She *was* the perfect daughter. But I had already asked too much of her, too soon.

Besides, in a few moments she would know the entire truth. She deserved to know everything. Once she knew everything, then she would have to decide.

I had no choice but to wait.

CHAPTER

13

Bet

WHERE ARE we going?" I asked when Corwin did not move toward the doorway but rather deeper into the chamber.

"Not far," he promised. He leaned one hand against the wall as he hobbled along on one leg. His body creaked and groaned.

Several Lonely went ahead of us into one of the alcoves, and Corwin followed them. The alcove seemed to be some sort of weapon room. Swords, knives, double-bladed axes, and even crossbows hung from iron hooks on the stone walls. He walked past all of these and entered a wide passage which sloped upward and into a dark chamber.

Quarrel and I followed close behind him. I could hear our footsteps echoing. Craning my neck, I looked up and was surprised to see faint light above me. We were in the room with the massive stained-glass window I had seen from the outside. I could tell that dawn was approaching by the gray light coming through the broken windowpanes. It must be several stories up, however, as we were so far underground.

The Lonely flowed around me with torches, moving into the chamber until they were spread all around. I followed their movements with my eyes, noticing the statues for the first time. The room was filled with them, filled with stone gargoyles like the ones I had glimpsed on the battlements.

"What is this place?" I whispered as Corwin led me deeper into the chamber.

"This is the heart of Sanctuary," he said as he pulled his cloak away from his shoulders and shook himself so that two massive wings peeled away from his body. They were leathery like the wings of a bat and tattered at the edges.

I felt my mouth drop open in surprise, but I had no words. He crouched and then leapt into the air, his wings flapping as they lifted him high, high into darkness.

I twisted in a circle, watching him until I noticed that the Lonely were climbing some sort of stone staircase to my left. Although it had no railings, I ran to join them, climbing round and round. The stairs led me to a wide circular platform directly below the stained-glass window.

Corwin waited for me beside another stone gargoyle. His hand rested on the gargoyle's shoulder. I moved around him so I could see. It was taller than I was by several inches and had two long stone braids trailing over its shoulders. Stone wings arched above the gargoyle's head. The features reminded me of Corwin somehow, but they were narrower, more feminine.

"We weren't always like this," Corwin whispered at last. "I was human once, like you, before I accepted my Calling."

I opened my mouth to question his statement, but then I felt as if my eyes were pulled to the other gargoyles scattered around the room. I had seen them all over the Abbey.

"Oh," I breathed, horrified. "They were *people?*"

"They were family." He sounded like a broken-hearted child, not like a monster, not like a Warden who fought demons from the Underworld. He was all of those things at once and yet none of them. "I am the last," he told me. "And someday soon I too will be stone."

I stared at him with fresh eyes. He was not what I had thought. He was not a monster but a man—a man who had refused to abandon his duty even when his loved ones fell by the wayside, turning to stone, broken beneath the weight of their burden.

I could not stand the idea that these people were turning into stone while fighting a battle none of us had known about.

Corwin moved his hand to rest on the female gargoyle's head. "This one was called Miriam," he whispered. He sounded as if he were crying. "She was my sister."

I gasped and covered my mouth with both hands. Sookie and Rosamond flashed before my eyes. I imagined them as stone and the thought made me ill. How could he bear it?

"Don't pity me," he continued, as if reading my thoughts. "I do what I must. I chose this. If I do not tend to the breaches, then everyone is in danger."

"My village?"

He turned to look at me at last, his eyes haunted. "Everyone, Bet. Everywhere."

I couldn't speak or swallow; I could hardly breathe. All this time he had been living in this place, trying to stop an apocalypse, and none of us had known. We had feared and resented him. We had told ghost stories about this place for our own amusement.

But for the sake of all humankind, Corwin had refused to give up. I considered how harshly I had treated him, how I had despised him and suspected him of unspeakable things.

I was the monster. He was perhaps the noblest soul I had ever known.

The room continued to brighten as morning crawled toward us. The first hint of sunlight began to slant through the window. Corwin moved away from the stone gargoyle that had once been his sister, hunkered down, and braced himself on the knuckles of one hand.

"The other night you asked where I come during the day. This is where I come," he said. "Miss Haverly, will you—"

But the first ray of morning touched the top of his head. As soon as it hit him, his body began to change. With faint crackles and hisses, his body transformed from pale flesh to hard stone. By the time the transformation was complete, he was like all the other gargoyles. Every part of him, even his clothing, had transformed into stone.

I stood alone, surrounded by the dead, surrounded by the Lonely. It occurred to me that he was not as alone as he thought. The Lonely glittered in the expanding pool of sunlight, casting shards of color around the room. Whatever they were, they adored him.

Quarrel came to my side and pressed against me. I did not believe the Ever would forget about Corwin if the danger was so great. He would have planned for this, as He had planned to protect the Neverway. I covered my face with my hands as I remembered Corwin's heart-wrenching proposals.

I could not be his only option. Surely, the Ever had something else in mind.

CHAPTER
14

Corwin

T HINGS WERE better than I had imagined they could be.

Bet's attitude changed. It took several weeks, but her sharp
remarks and explosions of temper began to dwindle. Soon she
began speaking to me with genuine interest. Now that she felt I did not
intend to threaten her with bodily harm, she became curious. Every evening
she pestered me with questions, grilling me until I had to send her to bed so
that I could do my rounds. When I woke at the end of each day to find her
bright-eyed and waiting for me, the aches began to fade. I felt my body
strengthening. I could walk without my cane for the first time in two years.

During the day, Bet had taken to working in the gardens, weeding the
paths and mowing down the overgrown flower beds with a scythe she had
found in one of the garden sheds. Even the roses began to bloom more
frequently. They were still black and sickly, but I no longer had to hunt for

them. They appeared everywhere. I allowed myself to imagine that things might truly get better, that I stood a chance of succeeding, even if it was a miniscule chance practically unworthy of mention.

But then the Spook arrived.

Bet had been with me for a month. It was nearly evening, but I was still in Sanctuary, and Bet labored behind the Abbey in the gardens. When trapped in stone, my senses were limited to what Briarstone could tell me. It was Quarrel who alerted Briarstone. She sensed his barking as the Spook reached the perimeter of the briar wall and banged on the rear gate.

I felt the roses shudder as Briarstone squared off against him. The briars spiraled up the gate, winding around the iron, tighter and tighter until the gate had become just another wall of thorns.

The Spook stood there and watched. He spoke. His words leaked back to me, slowly trickling through the castle, passing from one stone to the next until it reached my awareness.

I have a message for the girl.

I gauged the angle of the sun. One hour till sunset. That one hour seemed like an eternity.

What if the Spook began shouting and Bet heard him? She worked around at the other side of the Abbey, but she would surely hear him if he made enough noise. I wished she were indoors where it was safe—where I could control what she heard and saw.

I felt the Abbey rumbling as she tried to alert the Lonely that something was amiss. She did not always see eye to eye with me, but in this she did. We both knew that we didn't stand a chance without Bet. She could never, ever leave.

It's Sunflower. Tell her. Tell her it's Sookie.

I felt my heart sinking as the message trickled up to me. Bet could never know. She would leave me for her sister without a second thought.

CHAPTER
15

Bet

QUARREL'S INCESSANT barking battered upon my ears.

I rubbed the back of my neck with one hand as I tromped through the long grasses on my way to the shed. With the other hand, I propped the scythe I had been using against my shoulder so that the curved blade arched over behind me. As soon as I stashed my tools, I intended to see what was bothering the dog.

I had spent a good portion of the day trying to clear out the brush stifling the vegetable garden. Twilight had shown me where they grew their food, and it shocked me to see the state of the vegetable beds. It was a miracle Corwin had not starved to death long ago.

I hoped he would be pleased when he saw my progress. I could not give him what he really wanted, but that did not mean I could not help him in other ways.

Quarrel continued barking.

I broke into a light jog, enjoying the feel of boots instead of slippers or heels. After I destroyed my muslin gown the first day I worked in the gardens, the selection in my wardrobe improved. There were now tunics and leather vests, work gloves, and knee-high boots in the finest leather I had ever seen. Twilight and Dawn also provided me with trousers in various fabrics: corduroy, plaid woolens, and brocade, the latter clearly from fabrics once used for the gowns.

It amused me that they had butchered their gowns to make me some practical clothes. They'd done their best to please me, but it had clearly been a trial to give up their fancies.

Since the wraith attack I seemed to have passed some unspoken test. Somehow I had gone from petulant prisoner to something more. I was actually rather fond of the Lonely.

I heaved the scythe from my shoulder as I entered the stone shed beside the path winding to the kitchen door. I had no sooner hung the unwieldy tool on its hook when the door slammed shut behind me.

"Merciful After!" I spun around. A gust of wind must have blown it closed. I laughed at my startled reaction as I moved to push the door open again. It resisted my touch. I heaved against it with my shoulder, grunting.

Had I been locked in?

"Oh no," I breathed. I began to imagine the worst, wondering if another breach had ripped open with Corwin defenseless in Sanctuary.

"Unlock the door," I demanded and pounded on it with my fist. "I can help!"

I tried to remember how late it was. The sun had been dipping toward the mountain peaks when I decided to quit for the day. How long before Corwin woke up? By the Never, what was happening in the catacombs?

"Listen up, you," I shouted. "Let me out! I know you can hear me. I can help!" Once I would have felt ridiculous talking to a fortress as if it were a person, but not now. Now I knew there were things in the world I did not understand. If the Abbey would just let me out, perhaps I could make a difference.

I called her names. I begged for her help. I threatened and coaxed and fumed. Finally, the lock clicked and the door swung open.

Corwin stood in the gathering shadows outside the shed. I gaped at him, astonished to see him safe and sound. "What is happening?" I exclaimed. "Is it another breach? Are you injured?"

"Do lower your voice. Everything is quite safe," Corwin said. He stepped back to allow me to join him outside.

I floundered at his calm. I could still hear Quarrel barking, his howls short and frantic. "Well, I thought—I mean, the Abbey locked me in!"

"Occasionally Briarstone will do things to protect you," he continued, still annoyingly serene. He glanced over his shoulder and lowered his tone. "It's best simply to trust her."

"Trust her to what? Lock me up?" I planted my hands on my hips. "You cannot be serious. I am not the kind of woman you lock up to keep safe, Corwin."

His expression flickered for the first time. "No," he said, even more softly. "I know you are not, but there was no danger. Nothing for you to be upset about."

I should have been relieved, but instead I felt only irritation. Granted, Corwin no longer treated me quite like a prisoner. The Lonely no longer followed me around like nervous jailors. But I was still forbidden to leave the Abbey grounds. Considering Corwin's circumstances, I'd been generous in giving him allowances for ill behavior. But this was insufferable.

"What is wrong with Quarrel then? I can hear him howling plain as day," I accused, waving a hand in the general direction of the ruckus. "What are you not telling me? I have a right to know."

"No, you do not," he replied without a moment's hesitation, his voice once again a growl. "It is my responsibility to decide what is best for us." He turned and began to stalk away, his body lurching as he favored his bad knee. The tips of his leathery wings dragged in the grass behind him.

Us. I swallowed hard, suddenly uneasy. He said it so casually. *Us.* I knew exactly what he meant when he said it. And I didn't like it.

I hurried to catch up with him. "No matter your reasons or good intentions, I have a right to the truth! Why must you be so childish?"

He spun to face me. "You think *I* am childish?" he exclaimed, one finger pointed at me in accusation. "After everything I have told you, everything you have seen here, do you think so little of me?"

I did not speak immediately because my pride felt wounded. "Perhaps I should have chosen my words with more care," I conceded stiffly. "But how can you expect me to think better of you when you do not behave better?"

"I am not the one who behaves badly," he said. "I do what I must to protect us. You do what you do because you are stubborn. And foolish. And would choose to desert me the moment I gave you leave. In spite of all I have told you. In spite of how desperately I need you."

As he turned his face away from me, I felt my heart begin to thud. Here it came again, the dreaded proposal. Why must it always come back to this? Why could he not ask me to stay with him as a fellow soldier? Why must it be as a wife? I had grown to respect him. Indeed, I had. And I wanted to help him. But to marry him would require something I wasn't willing to give.

I waited for him to ask and prepared to refuse yet again. I felt as if something were straining inside me. I did not want to hurt him, but I simply could not marry him.

In the dying light of day, Corwin turned his face back toward me, his mouth twisted. The expression in his eyes plagued me. He looked as if he were about to cut off his own foot.

"I love you, Lilybet," he said.

I felt my face slacken in shock.

He winced and stepped closer. "Perhaps it is insane, perhaps it makes no sense, but I do. I am asking you to share my life." He hesitated but then reached an open palm to me. "I am offering you my heart. Is there no part of you that loves me back? No small part at all?"

I searched for words but could not find them. A simple *no* did not seem sufficient, not when this man—this beast—was pouring out his heart with such fervor. I looked inside myself, searching for that small part.

It was impossible. Wasn't it?

Even if I had grown to respect him, that did not mean I *loved* him. I pressed my lips together and said nothing. I did not want to cut him with harsh words, but I feared gentle words would give him hope.

It was Corwin who broke the silence at last, and he sounded defeated. "I see," he mumbled.

Something wrenched inside me. "I am sorry I cause you such pain, but I cannot give you what you want. Perhaps if you gave me more time, if you let me go home and see my family. I would return! I swear I would."

He stirred abruptly. "You cannot leave me!" Fear laced his voice. "I will die without you."

"Oh Corwin," I groaned. "No one actually dies from a broken heart."

He stared at me. "I will."

I had nothing to say to this. What was a girl supposed to say when a monster threatens to keel over if she withholds her affection from him? It was ludicrous. It was—

Someone shouted.

Corwin jerked in the direction of the sound. "Go inside," he ordered, spitting the words as though his mouth were once more full of my poisoned blood.

"Why? Who is that?"

"Go inside, Lilybet!" He seemed on the verge of panic, as if wraiths were about to jump out of the ground and consume me. The voice called again, this time louder. It did not sound like a wraith to me.

It sounded like the Spook.

Had Papa sent men to fetch me home? My heart lurched at the thought. No wonder Corwin was in such a panic. "There is someone here?" I demanded. "And you were not going to tell me?" I skirted around him and broke into a run.

"Bet, wait!" Corwin shouted. I heard him stumbling to follow. "Please wait!"

I ignored him and ran harder, pounding down the narrow path toward the gate. Around me the shadows continued to deepen. I rounded the corner of the Abbey and saw Quarrel ahead of me. He loped toward me as I made for the cobblestone walkway that led from the main entrance to the gate. I hastened past stone gargoyles and skidded to a halt as Quarrel moved to block my way. He growled at me.

"Come on, boy," I huffed and outstretched a hand. "Don't be like that."

"Bet, is that you?" someone called.

"Yes, it's me!" I shouted back. "Victor?"

"Yes," the voice said from the other side of the briars. "Your father sent me. I can't get past the gate."

"No, the Abbey won't let you in." I tried to move around Quarrel, but he snapped at me. I stumbled back. I did not believe he would actually bite me, but he was certainly upset.

"I need to speak with you. It's important," Victor said. "It's about your sister."

"My sister? Which one? What's happened?"

"Hang on. I will try to climb over."

I twisted to look behind me, but I did not see Corwin yet. Surely he would have caught up to me by now. "I don't know if you should," I warned. "Just tell me what's happened!"

"It's Sookie," the Spook said. "The curse has taken her."

It was as if a fist drove the air from me. "But how?" I managed. "Her birthday isn't for weeks yet—"

"The Spinner was mistaken about the particulars. It was that other girl's birthday. Not Sookie's."

I tried to comprehend this, but my thoughts tumbled over and over. Something moved in the dark gray sky, and I looked up in time to see Corwin, wings outspread, plummeting from above. He hit the ground so hard it shook, scattering pebbles in all directions. I turned toward him as he lifted himself up from a crouch, his wings unfurled behind him, tattered like an old flag whipped by violent winds.

Corwin stared at me, his shoulders hitching with uneven breaths. "Please," he gasped. "Please, don't leave me."

He looked bereft, his eyes fixed on me as if he were trying to memorize a face he feared he would never see again. The transparency of his emotions only frightened me more. I felt the panic building inside me. I could not do this anymore, torn in two different directions by my conflicting feelings for this beast.

He stumbled toward me, arm outstretched. I saw the rose for the first time.

"We were dying until you came," he said, the words shaking as they flowed from him. He held the rose toward me, not moving until I took it. "I've been trying to tell you how important you are. To us. To me. Please stay."

My fingers curled around the rose stem, the thorns digging into my calloused palm. "I need to go, Corwin," I said, my voice scarcely more than a whisper. "Victor says my sister is in trouble."

"I know," he said, "but if you leave, we will not survive."

He knew about Sookie. And he had planned to keep it from me. The realization struck me with such painful force, I almost dropped the rose. When I regained my ability to speak, I heard my own voice snarling through my teeth: "There isn't a trick you won't try, is there?"

I spun back toward the gate, having made my decision. I would leave now or die trying. "Out of my way, Quarrel."

He whined and nipped my sleeve, ripping it as he tried to hold me back.

"Bet, please!"

I ignored the agony in Corwin's voice, convinced it was all just a part of his game to keep me here. "Let me out!" I shouted.

Much to my surprise, the briar wall obeyed, peeling back, and the gate flew open as if hurled by invisible hands, slamming against the wall with a clatter of wrenching iron and cracking stone. Victor stumbled backward in the nick of time, his body poised for a fight. Behind him, two horses nickered and jerked against the restraints tying them to a tree.

I ran through the gate.

Corwin cried out behind me. I clutched the rose in my hand and fled.

CHAPTER
16

Corwin

I FELT my heart cracking down the middle, as if it were already an organ of stone and not flesh and blood. Briarstone began to tremble as I stumbled back into the Abbey. She sent me tumultuous images of the catacombs, of weak places bulging and straining as the pressure from the Underworld abruptly intensified. There were dozens of them all at once.

It was as if the underworlders knew that Bet had left me.

I stumbled through the main entrance. Dawn flew toward me. "Get out of here!" I bellowed to her. "Go!"

She hesitated, but when I shouted again, she disappeared down the hall leading to the kitchens. I followed after her toward the new stairwell to the catacombs. Every step was agony. Every step took me further away from the one person in the world who mattered to me.

But I didn't matter to her.

Briarstone moaned from the assault, snatching at my meager store of strength to fend off the attacks. They were happening everywhere simultaneously. I staggered and fell to my knees, trying to shore up the defenses until the attack dissipated.

But the assault only intensified. The pain ripped through my awareness as Briarstone began to shudder. She was breaking beneath the strain, already brittle beyond reason. Bet had been our only hope.

We were both going to die.

Sensing my distress, Briarstone moved beneath me, rearranging herself until a hole opened up beneath me. I plummeted into the darkness, into the catacombs. As I flung out my wings and let them fill with air to slow my descent, the screams of the wraiths filled my ears.

They began to spill into the catacombs, and with them came the stench of death.

I spread out my awareness, trying to aid Briarstone. Her thoughts were too frantic now for me to keep up with. I spread myself painfully thin, the pressure tearing me in too many directions. I tried to grit my teeth and continue.

I had lost Bet. I had broken my vows. I had failed my calling.

It was simply more than I could bear.

CHAPTER
17

Bet

I FELT his agony.

Victor and I had traveled barely half a mile from the Abbey. The shadows continued to lengthen around us, transitioning from grey to black. The wind hissed through the trees and pulled at my hair as I rode.

Corwin was in pain, so much pain. I could feel it like a knife in my chest. I felt his pain the same way I felt Dawn's sorrow and Twilight's anger.

Tears pressed against my eyes. I could not go back: I had to go to Sookie. My sister needed me.

But perhaps Corwin had not been exaggerating. He also needed me.

I pulled my horse to a stop and shouted for Victor as I swung my leg over and slid out of the saddle. I felt the ground shuddering beneath my feet. The Spook twisted to catch sight of me. His mare pranced in a circle until he urged her back up the path.

I looked back toward Briarstone, at the towers rising above the treetops. I heard a rumble like distant thunder. Was I foolish to feel this concern? Corwin could not possibly be dying of a broken heart!

I suddenly imagined him among the other gargoyles at Briarstone, unmoving, lifeless, and stone.

A different sort of pain filled me. This pain belonged to no one but me. I peeled back my fingers to reveal the flower I still clutched in my hand. The rose shriveled in my grasp, the petals peeling away like burning paper.

Withering.

Another wave of pain hit me. I closed my eyes and gritted my teeth against it. I felt it as if a tether somehow bound me to him and to Briarstone. Bullets of their pain ricocheted back to me, again and again.

"We shouldn't linger. Bet? Are you all right?" I heard Victor ask, but the echo of Corwin's pain would not go away.

What must it feel like to *him?*

CHAPTER
18

Corwin

I WOULD not die without a fight. I would make one last stand, the sort that could be remembered in legends.

Only I knew that my story would never be told. No one would remember my sacrifice. No one would remember beautiful, tenacious Briarstone and the day she crumbled to dust. No one would remember the day I turned to stone.

No one except Bet, perhaps. Would she remember us?

I landed in a crouch on the dirt floor of the catacombs. I felt the heat of the breaches as they ripped open, flooding the tunnels with the Underworld's sulfuric stench. Perhaps this had always been the Ever's plan. If He had chosen to leave this task to me, and me alone, I was duty-bound to strive on until the end. I had kicked against the brutal truth of my destiny for long enough.

It was time to embrace my destiny, to join my family at last.

As I plunged into the catacombs, I asked the Ever for one last portion of strength. I continued to give myself to Briarstone. I felt my skin splitting. The cracks were ripping me open. I saw the shadow and fire billowing up the passageway ahead as the wraiths ripped the Abbey open from the inside out.

I saw several of them spiraling toward me. I bared my teeth and stalked onward. I felt no fear. I had been born to do this. I would not stop until I had finished what was started by my ancestors long ago.

The wraiths hit me with blinding force, trying to drive me backward as I strove to drive forward. I bellowed and begged for the Ever's assistance as I hit the wraiths with my echoes. They shrieked, recoiled, and attacked again. One of them slipped past me, and I swung an arm. A portion of the tunnel wall broke free and crushed the wraith against the opposite wall.

The others recoiled, as if regrouping. I regrouped as well.

All these years I had waited, living on mere stories of glorious days when the Ever Father spoke to us. With me there had always been silence. But was this because He had abandoned me? Or because I had abandoned Him? Because I abandoned hope and embraced fear?

I thought of Bet and felt a wrenching shame that mingled with the agony. I'd had no right to bring her here. It was only just that I return the life I had stolen.

The wraiths attacked again. Even as they hurled themselves toward me, Briarstone threw an image at me, an image of another tunnel on the south side of the catacombs, overflowing with wraiths. I risked shifting my focus to help her rip apart the tunnel ceiling, caving in that section of the catacombs.

A wraith slammed into me and drove me back. Perhaps this was the moment when I would finally give my last. I was ready. I was willing.

I felt something then. A stirring in the air. Quiet and unseen.

I wasn't alone. Not really.

I knew suddenly what I must do, as if the words had been spoken to me out loud and not quietly impressed upon my thoughts. Perhaps I could still find a way to stop the wraiths. But it would require sacrifice.

I could still feel Bet. The connection was weakening. I knew that she would feel it too, knew that she would be blinded by pain she couldn't even understand.

I could not, *would not* bring her down with me. I could save her. Perhaps I could save them both—Bet and Briarstone. But I had to let go.

A life for a life.

"I'm sorry," I whispered, though I knew she would never hear the words. I closed my eyes and imagined the connection between us. I felt it, wrapped my awareness around it until it was all I knew.

Then I broke it clean in two.

CHAPTER
19

Bet

SOMETHING SNAPPED inside me. An awful calm settled in its wake, the calm of the blind and deaf. I no longer felt the pain. I no longer felt Corwin. I cradled his rose in my palms. I felt cold and bereft. As I stood there, the rose petals turned to ash and settled against my skin.

I gasped in horror.

"Bet, what is it?" Victor asked, jumping down from his horse beside me. I barely felt his hand on my shoulder. "What's happening?"

I lifted my eyes to the mountain. The sky darkened as if a terrible black storm swirled around Briarstone. But I knew it wasn't a normal storm. Somehow it was the result of a wraith army spiraling out of the Underworld, finally breaking free.

"He's dying," I cried as I let the rose stem and ashes fall from my hands and settle to the ground. Victor stared at me, uncomprehending. I caught my horse by the reins, grabbed a fistful of dark mane, and shoved my boot into the stirrup. "I have to return," I said as I swung my other leg over the mare.

Victor snatched the bridle. "You can't go up there. Whatever's happening, you can't stop it."

"You don't know that!" I tightened my legs, trying to force the horse to step around him. The wind began to pick up, beating against us, howling. But I feared it was not the wind howling. It was wraiths. I backed the mare away from him. "I need to go back."

"What about Sookie?" the Spook shouted over the wind.

If I abandoned Corwin now, they would all die. Sookie would be lost anyway. I couldn't help her until I helped Corwin. Because he couldn't save us on his own. And even if he somehow managed to stop the breach, if he didn't survive . . . if he died . . .

I couldn't stand even to finish the thought.

As if Victor read my answer in my expression, he stepped aside and released the bridle. "Then we will both go back," he said. "If that is what you must do."

It was as if an invisible weight lifted when I heard him say those words. I could not imagine a world in which Corwin did not exist. I could not imagine *my* world without him in it.

I yelled to the mare and leaned forward in the saddle.

CHAPTER
20

Corwin

I FOUGHT my way into Sanctuary, but the wraiths drove me back. They continued to swell in numbers, strengthening as they multiplied. I felt the chamber buckling around me as the wraiths forced their way inside.

Sanctuary had finally been breached.

Briarstone keened in agony, a sound that shook her very foundation, uprooting cellars, heaving towers, crumbling balconies. The underworlders drove me through the first chamber, through the weapons room, and into the chamber of my ancestors.

I was nearing the end. I would have to act soon.

My head swelled with Briarstone's torment. She knew what I was about to do, and she resisted me even as she crumbled around me. It was the only way. I could not hold on much longer.

What power remained in me I would give to Briarstone, feeding her every last drop of myself so that she could stem the tide of destruction before it set fire to the world. We would have to completely cave in the catacombs, but it might be enough to slow the advance.

I regretted only that I would never see Bet again.

I flapped my wings and rose into the air. Wraiths spiraled around me over and over again, as if trying to wrap me in a cocoon of fire and shadow. Outside the stained-glass window the sky crackled with thunder, the clouds streaked with violent lightening. I set my teeth and landed hard, smashing a crater into the platform floor. I dropped to my knees and held out my hands, my palms raised to the sky.

I could see Miriam's cold face in the wraith-filled darkness. Knowing I would soon join her gave me the comfort I needed.

I flung every part of my spirit into the stones around me, allowing myself to truly become one with them. I spread my consciousness throughout every corner, into every chamber, every tower. Briarstone wailed as I began to disappear, lost within her empty halls. I surrendered everything I was.

The moon rose over the Abbey. Along the briar wall, roses shuddered, scattering petals like dewdrops shaken from Quarrel's coat. The stone took me gradually, a tide creeping to the shore. I rode the swell of the coming darkness.

I embraced the stone.

CHAPTER
21

Bet

THE MARE skittered into an uneasy sidestep as we trotted through the mangled gate and onto the Abbey grounds. I swung myself out of the saddle. Victor cantered up behind me, shouting. I twisted. Not far behind him, pale figures peeled out of the trees.

"I see them!" I shouted. Not one but four ghouls emerged from the darkness, eyes glowing. How long had they been following us? I could hear them snarling, intent on the kill. I had never heard of their travelling in packs before. I wondered if they somehow sensed the trouble Briarstone and Corwin were in.

Victor dismounted and snatched a rifle from the saddle. He aimed and fired. One of the ghouls staggered backward, howling in pain, but it merely clutched a boney hand to its side and continued on. The Spook fired twice more before the thing collapsed to the ground. One of the others was nearly upon us. Having no time to fire, Victor grabbed his rifle by the barrel and swung it like a club.

I spun in a circle, searching for a weapon so that I could help. He would not be able to fight three of them. I snatched a rock from the ground and flung it as hard I could, aiming not for the ghoul Victor was fighting, but the one coming up behind it. My aim was true, but the ghoul barely jerked as the stone smacked into its chest. It swerved around Victor and barreled toward me with renewed determination.

Suddenly Quarrel burst from the darkness and caught the creature by the throat, ripping it clean off its feet. The ghoul clawed at the wolfhound, but Quarrel held it in a death grip. He did not let go until the thrashing monster fell still.

"Go!" Victor shouted to me. "We'll hold them off! Get out of here!"

I did not need to be told twice.

The front door hung wide open as I plunged into the main foyer. The day Corwin carried me up this path and through these doors seemed a lifetime ago.

I needed to find him. I knew where he would be. He would be with his family. He intended to die with them, in their Sanctuary.

But Briarstone rearranged herself so frequently that finding Sanctuary would be like finding one particular creeper in the whole of the Neverway. It would be impossible.

"Show me where he is!" I shouted as I edged into the darkness. I pressed a hand to the wall to follow as I moved. "Briarstone, please! I'm here to help!" I pounded my palm against the wall as I trotted past, hoping she would open a staircase for me like the one I had stumbled upon that night so long ago.

Ahead of me I heard a sound like metal rending and stone exploding. Down the corridor, a Lonely with a torch appeared and rushed to join me at the jagged hole Briarstone had ripped in her wall. It was Twilight.

"That's good!" I shouted as I snatched the torch from her hand. "More torches! Anything that will burn. They don't like light, so let's set the tunnels on fire!" I shoved past her, not waiting to see if she would obey. I trusted that she would.

I ran into the darkness, staring at my feet as Briarstone lifted stone steps beneath my boots, one at a time. Around me, the chamber felt as if it were ripping itself apart. Wraiths spiraled above me. They howled as Briarstone tore parts of the walls and ceiling free and smashed into them, trying to drive them away using any means possible.

I found Corwin on the round platform beneath the stained-glass window. He was on his knees, head bent, palms lifted to the sky as if he were pleading for the intercession of the Ever who had first given him this task. He was solid stone.

I ran toward him, dodging gargoyles and chunks of falling stone. I still did not believe that the Ever would give Corwin an impossible task. There was a way to survive this. There was a way to save Corwin. There had to be.

What did Corwin need? What had he always needed from me?

I remembered every proposal with aching clarity. Corwin had been trying to tell me since the day I arrived, the day he sucked the poisoned blood from my body: I was the one to help him.

Above, a wraith howled and began to descend on me. I ducked and rolled to one side as it spiraled past.

Will you marry me, Miss Haverly?

"He *is* Lonely," I whispered, the words snatched from my lips by the snarling wind buffeting the chamber. He needed love. He'd been asking me every day since the day we met. But why? What power or magic was there in love? It was a silly, senseless emotion. The sort of nonsense Rosamond indulged in.

Or was it?

Hadn't love for my family driven me to leave my home in the dead of night? Hadn't love made Corwin stay with Briarstone all these years?

Perhaps love wasn't so much about roses and romance as about choices and sacrifice.

The wraith recovered and angled toward me a second time. I swung my torch in an arc over my head as the wraith hovered above me, away from the burning fire.

I had been born a sister and daughter. Now I knew I was meant for something more.

Twilight appeared from the hole behind me, carrying two torches, and behind her more Lonely streamed into the chamber. I felt Dawn's presence among them. They flooded around me, waving torches in the air as other wraiths began to descend.

I lurched across the ground, scrambling to reach Corwin even as I waited for another wraith to descend on me. I gripped one of his stone hands and stared into his unseeing eyes. "Corwin!" I shouted. I squeezed his hand until my fingers ached.

The shadows began to tug at me, eager to destroy, eager to feed.

I whirled about, moving so that I stood between Corwin and the darkness. I swung my torch and cried for Briarstone to help me. I remembered Corwin, how he called the castle to him, bent her shape with his commands, refashioned her into the barricades he needed. I remembered the fondness in his voice when he spoke of her, the fierce loyalty she showed him in return.

I remembered the look in his eyes so short a time ago, when he confessed his love for me.

"I need you!" I shouted to Briarstone. The wind snatched my words away, but I tried again. "I can't save him without you!"

Only the howling wind answered me. Anger blossomed in my chest that she would ignore me at this moment of ultimate crisis.

"I love him too, you stupid hunk of stone!" I shouted. "I won't—"

My head exploded.

Briarstone burst into my thoughts, thundering against the inside of my skull. I saw halls and windows and stone flash before my eyes. She felt both ancient and young at the same time, as if caught between two poles of time. I thought of Sookie and Corwin, thought of how I felt torn between them, and I sympathized with Briarstone's plight. She snatched at this thought, at this familiarity, using it to bind herself to me. She spoke to me, but I couldn't understand her words, couldn't make sense of her thoughts. But then she thrust a picture into my mind.

Just as several wraiths whipped toward me I imagined an invisible dome surrounding us. I ducked and squeezed my eyes shut. I felt the terror of the Lonely, but I blocked them out and let Briarstone consume my thoughts. The force of this attack nearly drove the breath from my lungs. But I felt the fiends recoil. I opened my eyes.

I could see an invisible barrier shimmering above me, faint but tenacious. The wraiths continued to attack, hungry to feed, but I thought of my family. I thought of Corwin, of the unfamiliar but violent emotion burning in my chest. If Corwin believed there was power in love, then I did too. They wanted to eat?

"Feed on this," I snarled between my teeth.

I gave them love.

I fed the invisible barrier with every drop of love I had. I snatched at my memories of Sookie as a child picking flowers in the meadow, of Rosamond weeping into my shoulder because of some unrequited romantic interest. Of Papa bouncing me on his knee. Of Mama. Dear, sweet Mama.

Of Corwin, his eyes filled with longing and loss.

I gave it all.

But Briarstone whispered to me: *It's not enough.* I began to shake as the reserve of my memories ran low. *Give more.* The words implanted themselves in my mind as if she'd spoken them.

"I don't have anything else!" I screamed to her. Wraiths attacked with renewed fury, as if aware of my weakness.

Give more.

I felt myself buckling. My knees hit the stone floor with bruising force. I stared up at the shadows coiling above me, wondering if I had been wrong, if love was not the only thing Corwin needed.

I inhaled suddenly as a desperate thought took hold and flourished. There was one last thing I could do.

"I accept!" I cried. "I accept the Calling!"

Warmth washed over me, and I knew I had chosen well. I felt a sacred heat billowing around us, driving back the invisible dome, lacing it with layer upon layer of emotions I couldn't begin to describe. Heat and light filled the chamber. I closed my eyes as the Calling took me, felt it reaching down to the core of my being, refashioning me. I accepted the change.

The wraiths began to screech in agony. Light and love, to them, were as poison.

CHAPTER
22

Corwin

I INHALED.

Exhaled.

I found myself in a place of complete silence. I felt refreshed. Strengthened. If this was death, no wonder my family had left me so long ago. I opened my eyes and blinked.

I wasn't looking at a burning sunset or rippling fields of golden wheat or floating white clouds. I saw nothing that suggested the After.

I was looking at a girl. Only the sleeping girl was not the one I had left behind. I watched the breath ease in and out of her body, feeling perplexed and fascinated at once. Could this possibly be Bet?

Could it be anyone else?

Briarstone reached out to me, opening and closing doors in agitation, clearly waiting for me to wake up. I smiled and sent her soothing thoughts.

The doors closed, and peace fell in the Abbey. I sensed the Lonely nearby, but they too were quiet. I counted them, appalled to discover that many of them were injured, many were missing.

Bet blinked, as if sensing my stare, and opened her eyes. They were unusually pale.

I gasped as understanding dawned on me. "What have you done?" My voice creaked. I saw the other changes now, heightened cheekbones and eyebrows, broader shoulders, and wings the color of a walnut husk.

She sat up and blinked at me. The way the wings draped her shoulders made her look almost elegant. Strange, the idea of Bet Haverly being elegant. Usually she was clever and hard, like a swift kick to the seat of the pants. I liked her that way. But elegant was nice too.

"What have you done?" It startled me, the depth of sorrow surging through me. This was not what I had wanted for her, not at all. I had prepared my whole life to accept the Calling. She had been given only weeks.

"You needed me," she said, as if that explained it all. Her voice was deeper, but the inflections were the same. Her eyebrows lifted as if she expected an answer.

I swallowed the lump forming in my throat. "You came back because of me?"

She nodded, her eyes falling to her hands. She stared at them, flexing her fingers, then experimentally felt her injured arm, touching the scars that now looked like runes etched in stone. Her gaze shot back to mine.

"You are the bravest person I have ever known," I managed, the words sounding awkward. "You look . . . beautiful."

She offered half a smile and shrugged as if it didn't matter. I realized that to her it probably didn't. She was not that kind of girl. My gaze fell to the crazy brocade breeches she wore.

"You look better yourself," she said, quite matter-of-fact. "Not quite, er, *human,* but your skin isn't so pasty. And your eyes are clearer than I've ever seen them."

I shifted, embarrassed under her intense perusal. I found my feet, pleased to discover them solid beneath me. I stretched.

Bet joined me, her wings shifting as she did so. She lifted them above her head, gasping. "Now *those* I like!" she exclaimed in pure delight. She darted toward the perimeter of the platform as if she meant to test them at once. Beyond her, through shattered glass windowpanes, I glimpsed the faintest hint of orange caressing the mountain peaks.

I lurched forward and hauled her back by the collar. "It's nearly dawn!" I exclaimed, my heart in my throat.

She stared at me, her color changing several times before she shrugged me off. I could see the reality of what she had become sinking in. She was like me. We were bound by a different set of rules than the rest of the world followed. The cycles of the sun and moon would now control her movements.

When she spoke, however, it wasn't about that. "There's something important we need to discuss," she said. Her awkward delivery suggested that our discussion would be equally awkward.

I felt my heart quicken, throbbing against my ribs in its eagerness; a beating heart, not stone. I stared at her, mesmerized by her intense eyes and expressive features.

"I will not be locked in the garden shed," she said and raised a warning finger. "Never again."

My hopes fell. "I hardly think that was my fault," I grumbled, disheartened by the direction of our conversation. "It wasn't my *idea.* Exactly."

"You have a number of peculiar ideas, Corwin," she retorted dryly. "Such as sacrificing yourself to a demon horde. Briarstone plans to give you the scolding of the century, but I think she's tired just now."

Why did I get the feeling these two would soon be tight as thieves and tormenting me at every turn? But she was right. Briarstone was listing into complacency, as close to a state of sleep as she came. I let her go with my blessing. Even the Lonely were content for the time being. There would be time to lick our wounds later.

I heard the distant scrabble of claws over stone. Quarrel appeared and limped up the stairs toward us. I knelt as he approached, my hands reaching for the right leg he seemed to be favoring. He nosed me, his muzzle stained with blood.

"Oh no!" Bet exclaimed, dropping down beside me. She reached an arm around Quarrel in a hug. He whimpered, but his tail wagged with enough vigor to jerk his rear from side to side. I set his paw down, relieved. He had not been bitten.

"Good boy," I murmured, and fondled his ears.

"Corwin, I need to ask you something," Bet began. She pressed her face into Quarrel's side. A long paused ensued. "This whole falling-in-love thing is not my specialty," she mumbled. I had to strain to hear her and even then was uncertain I had heard her properly.

I held quite still.

She turned her face slightly. I could see her cheek and half of her mouth. One eye peeked up at me. "Will you marry me, Corwin?" she asked into Quarrel's side. As if he actually understood her words, the fool dog began to wiggle in excitement, bumping against her face so that she had to move away from him. "But, for tradition's sake," she continued in a more practical tone before I'd even had a chance to comprehend what I had just heard, "I do insist you speak with my father about . . . about *that*."

I felt as if she'd gut-punched me. Never in all my days would I have expected to hear these words from her mouth! Then the second half of her statement sank in, and I felt cold all over.

"By the Never, he will eat me alive!" I exclaimed, horrified.

"If he does, you would deserve it," she said. I knew I could never refute her logic. I deserved that and worse. But as I looked at her, I realized she was not punishing me. She was laying out new ground rules. She intended to stay; I could see it in her eyes, in the way she looked at me without judgment or fear.

My chest caught fire and I felt the weight of the ages easing off of me. I had not been forgotten, nor was I alone.

"Well? Have you nothing to say? About . . . anything?" she asked, sounding brusque even though her expression seemed strangely anxious.

"I love you," I said, and I laughed when fire rushed to her ears. She punched me playfully on the arm and beamed at me. After a moment, she reached out and took my hand. We both stared at our intertwined fingers as if neither of us quite knew what to think about it.

"Thank you," I whispered. If possible, her ears burned even brighter. Some things had not changed.

Just as the sun slipped through the windows, Bet looked up and smiled. It was a rare gift, the sweeter for its rarity.

I embraced the change, clinging more tightly to her as she experienced her first transformation. But I sensed no unease in her, no fear. Her awareness joined with mine, startled at first, then awed. I sensed her curiosity as her mind immediately darted out to Briarstone, already exploring. I stilled her with my thoughts, knowing the Abbey would not welcome meddling at this moment. Bet drew back to me, sighing but obedient.

I was no longer alone.

For the first time in ages, I felt human again. Bet returned to me something I had thought lost forever. The journey had been difficult, but had I suffered less, I would not know how to fully appreciate the gift I now possessed. She was the greatest gift I had ever received.

I knew the battle wasn't over. The seams of reality were sewn back together, but the scent of the Underworld still lingered beyond them. Wraiths lurked there. Waiting. Yet whatever evils would come, we had this moment. This here, this now. Perhaps it wasn't much, but it seemed like everything to me. I had not been forgotten after all, even though I had lost myself in the darkness.

I had plenty of time to muse on this revelation. Evening was a long way off.

EPILOGUE

THE SPOOK followed the blood trail the wolfhound had left behind, his steps slow as he moved through the old Abbey. He clutched a kerchief to the side of his head where he had been bludgeoned with a stone by the final ghoul. He had woken a short time ago, convinced that the wolfhound must be the only reason he still lived.

His eyes widened slightly as he climbed a wide set of stone steps and found himself surrounded by statues. In the center of them the wolfhound lay panting beside two huddled stone gargoyles. One of them looked suspiciously like Bet Haverly.

The scene was intimate. A great many things began to make sense.

The dog growled at him, but it was half-hearted. Victor stepped back to calm the animal's unease. He sensed no danger. Whatever had happened here was over, for the time being. Although he suspected Bet Haverly's work was just beginning. She would not be rushing home anytime soon.

"I suppose I'll find your sister, then," he said to the gargoyle that looked like the merchant's daughter, although he had no idea as to where he would begin. He let his gaze return to the wolfhound. "Thanks for the help, old boy." He saluted with two fingers.

As if he understood, the dog wagged his tail.

Victor left the Abbey. Although he searched, he found neither of his mounts. He could only hope they had made their way home and not into the belly of a ghoul. A warm rain streamed down his face, gently coating his skin.

He wished he had a better understanding of how he was to save Bet's sister. He was an expert on creepers and ghouls, not curses and Spinners and girls, but he had never balked at a challenge.

Victor set his feet to the road and ambled back down the mountain, into the Neverway. Above him, the rain broke and sunlight filled the sky. Somewhere in the Abbey gardens a rose bloomed, its scarlet petals blossoming like the first rays of morning.

ABOUT THE AUTHOR

SAVANNAH JEZOWSKI lives in a drafty farmhouse in Amish country with her Knight in Shining Armor, who is no less shiny after eight years of matrimony, and a loyal brigade of kitties, who may or may not sleep on the job.

Her work has been published in *Ray Gun Revival*, *Mindflights*, and in the student publication of *Fountains* at Pensacola Christian College. She likes books, faeries, writing hats, and having tea with her imaginary friends.

Visit www.SavannahJaysWorkshop.blogspot.com to learn more about Savannah and her work.

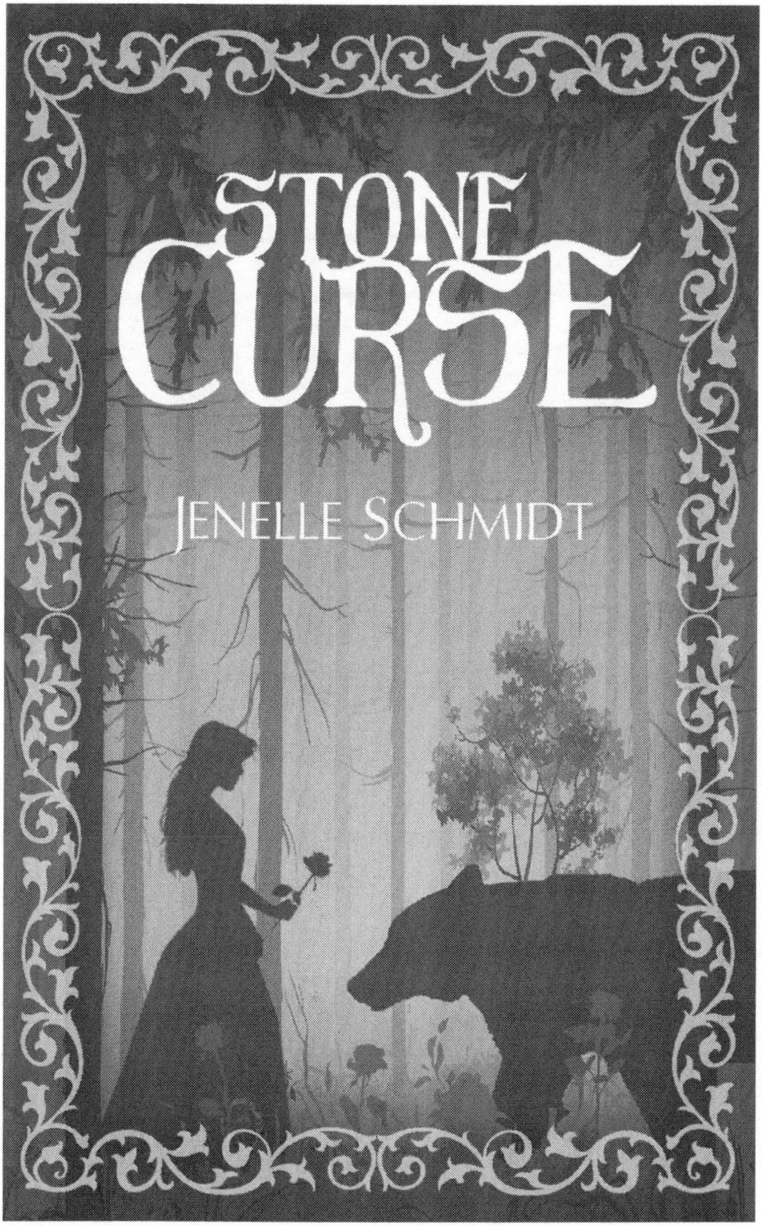
STONE CURSE
JENELLE SCHMIDT

For Leiana, Nathalie, and Brantland

CHAPTER ONE

T HE LONG stone hallways of Thorndale Castle stood empty and silent. On this overcast afternoon, only gray light fell through the high windows to bathe the castle in gloom. Once-brilliant tapestries, their colors now muted by dust, lined the walls and deadened the sound of Karyna's footsteps as she made her way to Princess Bellenya's vacant chambers. In one hand she carried a basket of dried roses, their heady perfume filling the air and disturbing the castle's eerie aura.

Karyna hummed as she walked, slightly swinging her basket so that it brushed against the skirts of her blue overdress in rhythm with the tune. The surrounding silence caused her no concern; she was used to it now. To be sure, when the curse first fell she had cried. And when most of the other servants left the castle, she had wept again in anger and despair. But her tears had dried up long ago; they served no purpose and solved no problems.

On the way to Bellenya's chambers she passed the great doors of the Throne Room and cast only a glance in their direction, being long accustomed to avoiding that room whenever possible. But three paces further down the passage she stopped short, her mind suddenly realizing what she had just seen.

Her skin prickling in sudden horror, she turned to look again, hoping she was mistaken. The basket dropped from her suddenly nerveless hand. Roses spilled out onto the floor. Petals scattered across the tile like drops of dried blood.

For the massive mahogany Throne Room doors, always so carefully closed and locked, were open.

Oh no! No, no, no, no! she thought desperately, though she was uncertain where the desperation came from. What did it matter that the doors were open? The curse could not spread. And yet Karyna's heart pounded wildly, and fear gripped her by the throat.

The darkness within the room oozed out into the hall like a physical being, carrying with it a musty scent of stale air and decaying flowers, nothing like the sweet aroma of her dried roses. This was the cloying stench of evil. Heart hammering with trepidation, Karyna peered inside. At the far end of the room a cautious glow of pale light lurked around the edges of the heavy purple curtains that covered the huge windows and forbade the sun entrance to this place.

Karyna rubbed her arms briskly and squinted into the shadows. Who would dare open these doors? She had no desire to venture inside. Just standing in the doorway brought painful memories crowding to the forefront of her mind. But she also had no wish to inadvertently lock someone into this room. This horrible room.

The moment of indecision passed, and Karyna crossed the threshold, her eyes quickly adjusting to the darkness. The expanse beyond the door was large, with high ceilings and tall white columns lining the perimeter. At the far end, two gilded thrones stood on a dais, ornate in their splendor, dusty from disuse. One throne held the statue of a crowned man wearing a startled expression, and before the other, a stone woman posed as if she had just sprung to her feet, her mouth open, her graceful hands raised in apparent distress. Even the folds of her sumptuous gown appeared as if frozen in motion. And scattered across the floor before the thrones stood more statues, hundreds more, all dressed in elegance and finery, all frozen in various postures of merrymaking.

Karyna averted her eyes. She had gazed upon them once before, and that had been enough.

She continued wending her way through the statues, trying to ignore the way her skin crawled and her every instinct screamed at her to run from the room and bar the doors. She could almost hear the swish of the elegant skirts, the echoes of laughter as couples joined each other on the dance floor, the chatter of a hundred voices making light conversation. And the terrible screams right before . . .

Karyna shook her head to dispel her morbid thoughts and instantly regretted it. Her unwary gaze fell upon one of the frozen faces. She averted her eyes, but the image lingered, refreshed as if she were seeing it for the first time. Every statue told the same story. No matter in what pose they were frozen, every face held an identical look of merriment turned to sudden terror.

Karyna made a soft sound deep in her throat and hastened her step. She hated this room.

"Hello?" she called out, her voice resounding in the deathlike stillness. "Your Highness? Is someone in here?"

She listened but heard no response. She crept through the maze of statues, careful not to allow even her skirts to touch them. It was a silly notion, thinking they might be disturbed, but Karyna couldn't help it. They were so lifelike, so perfect in every way despite their lack of color. It was hard to remember they were made of cold gray stone.

"Prince Barend? Hello?"

Karyna paused, drawing long breaths to calm her racing heart. Prince Barend was powerful and, at times, dangerous. It was best not to startle him. She peered through the gloom. Nothing stirred.

She paused, torn. Part of her wanted to leave immediately, but she had already ventured this far. Raising her chin, Karyna proceeded to the far end of the room. She bowed her head in a respectful gesture to the frozen king and queen in passing, then stopped before a statue positioned near the thrones.

It was not so splendid or grand as the others, just a baron unused to such finery. He had been a humble baronet before the queen chose Karyna to be Princess Bellenya's lady-in-waiting twelve years prior. Karyna had been only seven years old at the time. Her mother, a childhood friend of the queen, had just passed away, and Karyna did not know how she would have survived without Bellenya's friendship.

Her appointment had been a great honor for her and her family. Besides her father's new title, which effectively raised him from a commoner to a noble, Karyna was brought to live at the palace and be Bellenya's constant companion. She received an education alongside the princess and traveled with her. She also gained prospects of a more advantageous marriage—not that she had heeded that, being so young. She cared only that Bellenya was just a year older than she was, and that they shared many common interests. Once the initial shyness wore off, the two girls became closer than sisters and were inseparable ever after.

Karyna reached up and touched the statue's cold stone visage with gentle fingers. "Papa," she whispered. "I miss you." She gazed at him intently, as if the power of her stare could restore life and color to those cheeks, breath to those lungs, sparkle to those familiar eyes. Guilt clenched its fingers around her heart. "I'm sorry, Papa, so sorry. You wouldn't be here if it hadn't been for me."

He did not respond, but Karyna had not expected him to. Breathing one quick sigh, she wound her way out of the room, secured the doors, retrieved the fallen roses, and continued on down the hall toward the princess's chambers.

She entered Bellenya's apartments and halted, surprised by the sight that greeted her. A lovely young woman several years older than Karyna sat on the bed, her knees drawn up to her chin. She wore a rumpled satin gown, and her golden hair cascaded over her shoulders in gentle waves. Sniveling, she dabbed at her puffy, soulful eyes with a soggy handkerchief.

"Lady Ahren?" Karyna recovered from her surprise and felt suspicion flicker across her thoughts. "You're not supposed to be in here; you were told to stay out of this wing of the castle. Why aren't you in your own chambers?"

Lady Ahren looked up, her eyes filled with fear. "I was curious." She spoke defensively, but her tone lacked conviction. "I didn't mean any harm."

Karyna noted the heavy ring of keys clutched in Lady Ahren's hand, and her eyes flashed. "What have you done?"

"He . . . he got so angry."

"Who? Prince Barend?" Karyna crossed the room and gripped the girl by the shoulder. "Tell me what happened," she demanded.

"I just wanted to see them," Lady Ahren whimpered. "I've heard the stories. I wanted to see them. I didn't think it would hurt anything. But then the beast . . . he came up behind me as I opened the door and he . . ." The lady's eyes widened. "He got so angry! He went mad!"

A stone weight sank in Karyna's gut. With an effort she kept her voice calm. "Where did he go?"

"I don't know."

"Did he leave the palace grounds?" Surely he wouldn't. Oh, how she hoped he wouldn't! He knew all too well what would happen. But Lady Ahren's story filled Karyna with foreboding.

"I don't know!" the lady whispered. "He disappeared and I ran in here to hide. Nobody told me he was like that. I wouldn't have come if I'd known how horrid and ugly he is! No wonder Bellenya cursed him and ran away."

Outrage roared through Karyna's veins, growing hotter with every word from Lady Ahren's mouth. "How dare you!" she said, her voice thin and tense with anger. "Princess Bellenya could never do such a thing!"

"If she didn't do it, why isn't she in there?" Lady Ahren demanded, her chin rising as she glared defensively at Karyna.

"Because she was carried off by the same person who cursed the castle." Karyna clenched her teeth together to refrain from saying more. It would not do to insult Lord Worvenson's daughter out of hand.

She removed the key ring from Ahren's lifeless grasp and, taking her by the arm, marched her out of Bellenya's chambers and across the castle to the guest suite. Once there, Karyna told the girl in no uncertain terms to pack her things. "You were warned to stay away from the Throne Room." From the doorway she couldn't help adding, "Thorndale Castle is no place for fools."

With those words left ringing through the passage, Karyna turned on heel and marched down to the kitchens. Her frustration overtook her anger with every step she made. Lady Ahren was the latest in a long line of young women from the lesser nobility who had been sent to the palace in an attempt to break the curse. Nobody knew why the curse had been cast, or even if it was possible to break it, but that didn't stop the viscounts, barons, and even baronets and knights in every corner of Suvall from sending their daughters, sisters, cousins, and various other female relations. Karyna could not blame them: If true love were the answer like in the tales of old, the prize would be marriage to a prince and restoration of the kingdom.

So far their efforts had been in vain. Not one of the girls had lasted more than a month, and the curse remained unbroken.

Two years had passed since the curse fell, and the flood of prospective curse-breakers had slowed to a trickle. Few eligible young women remained to make the attempt: most members of the higher nobility stood frozen in stone in the Throne Room.

The situation beyond the castle walls was dire, Karyna knew. The minor nobles were not yet at all-out war, but the infighting and raids between counties had escalated in recent days. After two years without a leader, the country was slipping into chaos and its people lived in fear and uncertainty. Karyna believed it was only a matter of time before larger countries on Suvall's borders began eyeing it as a potential addition to their own kingdoms.

As she reached the final stair leading to the kitchen, delicious smells of baking bread wafted up to greet and comfort her. Setella, who was scrubbing the dinner vegetables clean in a bucket of cold water, looked up as Karyna descended the steps, and her tired eyes lit with a smile. But then, taking in the angry flush of Karyna's cheeks and the grim look in her eyes, the older woman pursed her lips in concern. "What's wrong?" she asked.

Karyna crossed her arms and leaned against the doorpost. "I found Lady Ahren in the princess's chambers."

"What was she doing there?" Setella asked, mystified.

"That's what I'd like to know." Uncrossing her arms, Karyna held out the key ring accusingly. "How could you be so careless?"

Setella wiped her withered hands on her apron and took the keys. With one forearm she brushed a few wisps of white hair away from her face, then sighed. "That one was looking to get kicked out."

"And I'm happy to oblige. But she may have been our last hope of breaking the curse."

"We don't even know if it can be broken." Her voice heavy with resignation, Setella tucked the keys into a pocket of the apron she wore over her drab gray dress.

Karyna crossed her arms again, as though fortifying herself against all the disappointments of the last two years. "I have to believe it can. And until it is, we must keep strangers from poking their noses where they don't belong."

"What do you expect me to do?" Setella asked. "I cannot be everywhere at once." She returned to the vegetables. Despite her age, Setella's hands did not shake as she attended to her work. "Look around," she said. "We used to have an entire kitchen staff; now there is just me. We once had gardeners, tree surgeons, and pruners; now there is only old Willem, and he refuses to go near the Queen's Garden. We had scores of maids; they have all left. Henry isn't much help, hiding out in the stables with the horses as he does, and refusing to set foot inside the castle. We're barely keeping our home together. We don't have time to be nursemaids to scheming viscounts' daughters."

The muscles in Karyna's arms tightened, and she fought to keep her voice calm. "I still think . . ."

Setella paused in her work and turned a motherly gaze on Karyna. "What would you have me do? I'm too old to try to be everywhere at once. I have no idea how Lady Ahren got her hands on my keys."

The old woman's words and tone deflated Karyna's anger, and she regretted her sharp words. "It wasn't your fault, Setella," she sighed. "I know that."

Setella offered her a weary smile. "We're all stretched to breaking, some days."

Abandoning her place in the doorway, Karyna stepped into the kitchen, snitched a slice of carrot, and leaned against the chopping block, munching pensively. It tasted bitter, however, and she swallowed it down with difficulty. "Despite her personality," she said flatly, "I had hoped Lady Ahren would be the one."

But Setella knew Karyna too well. "What else is bothering you?" she asked, eyeing the young lady before her.

Karyna bowed her head. "She said some horrible things about Prince Barend. And she blamed Bellenya for the curse. How can people believe such horrible things?"

"The curse did fall on the princess's eighteenth birthday," Setella reminded her.

"That doesn't mean she's responsible. She could never be capable of such evil."

"You don't need to defend her to me." Setella shook her knife at the girl before continuing her work. "I knew her even longer than you did. Like a granddaughter to me, she was! You're not the only one around here who loves the princess. Or the prince, either."

Karyna chewed on her thumbnail, caught herself, and instead brushed invisible dust from her skirts while her mind replayed the events of the morning. She jerked her head up in alarm and clapped a hand across her mouth.

"What is it?" Setella asked.

"Lady Ahren mentioned that Barend was there when she unlocked the Throne Room doors. She said he went mad and ran off." Karyna felt as though a knife cut her to the quick. How could she have forgotten?

"Ran off?" Setella stopped her chopping, and her eyes met Karyna's. "Do you think he left the palace grounds?"

"I don't know. The way she described his behavior, it's possible."

"You want to go after him?"

Karyna hesitated, but only for a breath. "Yes. But how will I find him?"

"Look for tracks, I suppose," Setella grimaced. "Lucky for you we had that late snow last night. If you don't see any tracks outside, he's probably in the castle somewhere, and all this fuss and worry is for nothing."

"If he is out there, what if I can't bring him back?"

"You managed just fine the night the curse fell," Setella said. Her voice lowered when she added, "And that other time." She made a shooing motion with her hands. "Take a rose with you. That seems to do the trick. And get going! We can't let him wander around out there on his own!"

Karyna allowed herself to be hustled out of the kitchen. She raced up the stairs to her little room and retrieved her warm cloak and sturdy walking boots. Then, still at a run, she hurried to Bellenya's chambers and retrieved one of her dried roses, tucking it inside a small satchel. Setting her shoulders and pulling the fur-lined hood of her cloak over her crown of braided hair, Karyna headed outside.

CHAPTER TWO

WORRY FOR the prince's safety crowded Karyna's thoughts even as she felt grateful for the surprise snowfall the night before. Instead of needing to ask Henry for help, she could easily follow Barend's tracks through the garden and, just as she had feared, across the invisible border.

A shudder coursed through her body as she passed out of the palace grounds and into the wild woods beyond. The curse did not affect everyone in the same way, and those who felt it most keenly were those who had been at the palace when the curse fell. To Karyna, stepping outside the palace grounds felt as if someone had placed an icicle on the back of her neck. To some it was like a wild buzzing of bees in their ears, and to others it was physically painful, like pressing through a tangle of thorny vines. For those entering the palace grounds, the sensation was milder. Those who noticed it at all agreed that it was similar to the feeling one experienced upon hearing the distant howl of a wolf: frightening enough to make one shiver and glance over one's shoulder, but not enough to cause terrified flight.

At first the tracks were spaced far apart, as though he had been running. But after she crossed into the woods, it seemed he had lost his sense of urgency. His tracks grew closer together and less direct. She followed the meandering trail for a while, finding it more difficult here under the trees, where less snow had fallen. Yet to a watchful eye, signs of his passage were evident everywhere: an overturned log, claw marks on several trees . . . and the bloody carcass of a deer. Karyna quickly looked away from the carnage, trying not to think about the prince eating raw meat like an animal.

Her boots swished through the slushy snow. There was a frosty nip to the wind, but Karyna could smell the fresh scent of spring on its back. Tender green shoots poked up through the snow, squirrels chattered, and the music of birdsong filled the trees above her. It was her favorite time of year, when the very air seemed infused with hope. However, Karyna could not enjoy the signs of spring; her objective was to find the prince and bring him home.

To her relief it did not take long to catch up with Barend. Tired from his initial burst of energy, he had apparently found a hollow in the underbrush and flopped down to rest. He must have heard or scented her approach, for when she spotted him he was already watching her. Deep in his chest a growl of warning rumbled.

Prince Barend was enormous—twice the height of a normal man if he stood on his hind legs, though he mostly stayed on all fours. His body was most like that of a wolf, though his four massive feet were more like a bear's, with sharp, dangerous claws. Shaggy black fur covered his body, and his snout was long and pointed. His eyes were those of a predator, yet they were also the only thing about him that remained even slightly human. Some called him a beast, though his appearance was more frightening than ugly. While inside the palace grounds, he had the mind of a man. Outside, however, he was wholly wild.

And yet Karyna believed she had seen recognition in his eyes the first time he left the palace grounds. She had run after him that day, confused and frightened but clinging to the fact that he had spoken her name before he fled and believing that, despite his appearance, he was still Barend. Neither one of them had known what would happen when he crossed the boundary line, and when in the forest he whirled to face her, she had known true terror. There had been nothing of Barend left in him. Karyna had frozen, babbling frantically, trying to remind him of who he was. Had she seen a flicker of awareness, of remembrance? When he lowered his terrible muzzle to her hair, she had known death was near.

But he had merely inhaled the scent of the roses woven into her dark braids and become docile and submissive, meekly following her back to the palace.

The second and only other time Barend had left the palace grounds was when his parents sent knights to attempt to bring him home. That had been even more terrifying to watch. Once across the boundary, Barend had gone wild and dangerous. Two of the knights were badly wounded before Karyna was able to get there, rose in hand, to calm him down.

Uttering soothing noises and taking care to make no sudden moves, Karyna now lowered the satchel from her shoulder. The beast emerged from the thicket and stalked toward her on huge, stealthy paws that made no sound even as they sank into the muddy ground. He snarled, pawing at the ground, then reared up on his hind legs and bellowed an angry roar. When Karyna did not react, he dropped heavily to the earth, still uttering menacing growls. His breath steamed in the cold air, and Karyna felt her heart begin to race as he stalked toward her.

Her fingers fumbled as she loosened the laces on the satchel. He was just a few paces away, now. His lip curled, revealing long, dagger-like teeth. Karyna's breath came quicker. She wrestled with the flap and heard stitches on the cover tear in her haste to get it open. She thrust her hand inside. The beast drew near, and by the gleam in his eye she knew he meant to kill her, even as he had killed that deer.

Karyna could not control the gasp of terror that escaped her lips as her fingers found the rose. Closing her eyes and clenching her teeth to keep from screaming, she pulled it out of the satchel and thrust it between herself and those terrible jaws.

A sweet aroma filled the air as though an entire rosebush had burst into bloom nearby. The beast quieted. His nose quivered, taking in the scent.

Why did it work? What hold did the roses have over him? How were they connected to the curse? Karyna had pondered these questions for two years, but she possessed no answers.

Barend put his nose out to the flower. The transformation was instantaneous, just as it had been before. The wildness left his eyes, and his entire being wilted. Karyna let out her breath in a sigh of relief. She pulled her cloak close around her with one hand and turned toward home. Barend followed her quietly, his gaze fixed upon the rose.

They were not far from the palace, for which Karyna was grateful. When they regained the confines of Thorndale's grounds, Prince Barend's eyes lit once more with intelligence and reason, and he swung his head from side to side.

"What am I doing here?" he thundered in confusion. "What happened?" He spotted Karyna near at hand and stared at her for a long moment. "You had to bring me back again, didn't you?" he asked. His voice was deep and rough, but it was a blessing the curse had left him any speech at all.

Karyna nodded mutely and held up the rose by way of explanation. She couldn't help asking, "Why did you leave the palace grounds?"

Prince Barend blinked in confusion. "I don't know," he muttered. "I remember seeing Lord Worvenson's daughter in the hallway, and . . . a darkness washed over me. I did not intend to leave the grounds. Forgive me. I know it must be frightening for you to have to come after me," he said, misinterpreting her melancholy expression. "There are others who could have been assigned this task."

Karyna shook her head. "Not really," she spoke without thinking, and then felt her face grow warm with embarrassment. "I mean, I'm the only one who . . . I'd be afraid someone else would—"

"Get hurt," he interrupted gruffly. "Forgive me again, dear Karyna. I do not mean to frighten you."

He turned and loped away before she could reply. She watched him go and felt vexation burn away her fatigue.

"That's not what I meant at all," she said to the empty air. "I only meant I'd be afraid someone else might hurt *you*."

Karyna had to search a bit to find Setella and inform her of the prince's safe return. The older woman was outside beating rugs when Karyna finally found her. Even after two years, Setella was reluctant to delegate the meaner chores to Karyna, though Karyna had reminded her often that rank meant nothing in an empty, cursed palace. Her skills as the princess's lady-in-waiting were wasted in a castle that housed no princess, and being a baron's daughter did not mean she should sit about idle while her home crumbled to pieces around her. Still, Setella and the other servants seemed bent on viewing her as the de facto mistress of the castle.

"You shouldn't be doing that," Karyna admonished.

"I couldn't sit still with worrying about you and the prince," Setella replied. "Are you hungry? I kept the stew warm over the coals on the hearth."

"I'm famished, though I doubt Barend will be taking supper." Karyna wrinkled her nose in distaste. "He already ate most of a deer."

Setella raised her eyebrows but did not appear as disgusted as Karyna felt. Instead of commenting on the prince's appetite or his lack of humanity she merely asked, "So the rose worked again?"

Karyna nodded and wrestled the rug off the line. Together they rolled it up and carried it into the palace. Back in the kitchen, Setella ladled stew into a bowl for Karyna, and cut a thick slice of bread, which she slathered with butter and blueberry preserves. Karyna dove into the food and for a while was too busy eating to converse. As she ate, the events of the day crashed down on her. She was weary in both body and spirit. Though her worry for the prince had lifted now that he was back inside the palace walls, in its place remained the constant ache she felt on his behalf.

She wondered too where Bellenya was, why she had not been found. And if she was safe.

"By the by, Henry escorted Lady Ahren off the premises." Setella smirked, handed Karyna a cup of water, and then disappeared into the pantry with the rest of the blueberry preserves.

"Good," Karyna whispered, and took another bite of stew. She would not miss Lord Worvenson's daughter.

"How did the prince seem when you brought him back? Is he well?" Setella called out as she returned.

"He's in his right mind again, but I'm worried about him." Karyna set down her spoon and rested her elbows on the table, something she would never have done before the curse fell. "I wish there was something I could do."

"I understand." Setella rounded the table and put an arm around Karyna's shoulders. "But we don't have enough information to act upon. And we can't very well go wandering around the countryside searching for shadows."

"I know." Exhausted, Karyna bent her head and smothered a yawn in her hand.

Setella removed Karyna's now-empty dishes. "Go get some rest," she advised. "Perhaps things will look brighter come morning."

Karyna nodded and returned to her own rooms, where she dressed for bed. Though exhausted, she couldn't fall asleep. Her thoughts kept swirling back to the curse, her father, Barend, Bellenya, and the mystery surrounding them all.

Eventually, too restless to relax, she got up and paced around her room. Her eyes alighted on the satchel hanging on its hook. She removed the rose from within it and sat on her bed, staring at the flower. She did not usually keep roses in her own room; they were for Bellenya's chambers, and even in Bellenya's absence she honored the princess by keeping the roses sacred, though she knew Bellenya would have called her silly for doing so.

At length, she placed the rose on the table near her bed. Its sweet fragrance filled the room, and Karyna drifted into a deep sleep.

She stood on the garden path under pale moonlight. Hurt and humiliation clawed through her heart; rage turned it to stone. She clenched her hands into fists and felt a sharp pain.

Numbly, she looked down and realized she had tightened her grasp on the stem of the rose she still held. The thorns bit into her skin, and blood dripped out of her fist.

She looked up, her teeth grinding together. Before her, dark and foreboding despite the moonlight, loomed the towers of her home . . . her chosen prison in which she lived alone. Alone with her anger, which whirled through her, an uncontrollable maelstrom of hatred and bitterness, she exploded into the night, a snarling, ravenous beast.

The next morning Karyna knelt in the garden, her long brown skirts pulled up into her belt to keep them out of the dirt. Her garments were not so fine as the gowns she had worn before the curse, but she liked to keep them tidy. Over her frock she wore an old apron with deep pockets for her garden tools. Her long black braid circled her head, hidden beneath a strip of cloth, though a few wisps of hair escaped and fell down around her face.

Snow lingered in shady spots, but the air was warm, as though spring had finally won its seasonal argument. Karyna was glad for the respite; she needed to be out of doors. She had not slept well, her rest plagued by nightmares. She had dreamed a strange dream last night—a dream of a once-loved place transformed into a haunt of sorrow and terror.

Her gloved hands dug into the soft, wet soil, and she shook the elusive remnants of the nightmare away by pulling early weeds. In two months the first roses would begin blooming, and she wanted to make sure the plants were healthy and the beds tidy.

As she worked, her mind spun. There was little she could do to end the curse, but she hated waiting around, hoping someone else would solve the problem. Barend deserved to go home to his family. And Bellenya must be found. Karyna worried about the princess above all else.

"Good morning, Karyna." Barend's deep, strangely elegant voice pulled

Karyna from her thoughts.

"Good morning," she replied, glad of the company. She rubbed her arm across an itch on her forehead.

"You have mud on your face."

Though his animal voice could be difficult to understand, he sounded amused. She craned her neck to look up at him again. "And you have leaves in your fur," she replied. "Did you sleep outside again last night?"

"It gets too hot inside." He shook his heavy coat as though to emphasize his point, jowls swinging and ears flapping.

Karyna stood and removed her gloves, tucking them into the pocket of her apron. "Here, let me help." As she started plucking leaves out of his black fur, Karyna hid a smile. She never would have dreamed she would be so familiar with a prince . . . albeit one trapped in beastly state. But after two years of isolation, a comfortable friendship had developed between her and Barend, transcending all class distinctions.

Barend twitched in embarrassment, but he did not move away. Karyna's fingers found a knotted mess of fur wrapped around a stubborn burr, and she began working it free. He stood quietly under her ministrations, neither quivering nor flinching even when she accidentally pulled too hard. He seemed so different here inside the palace grounds, strangely tame and yet powerful. She felt the warmth emanating from his body and wished everyone could see him as she did: gentle and lordly, a truly noble spirit.

Lady Ahren's cruel words from the day before rang in her ears, but she pushed them away.

"Do you remember anything more about what happened yesterday?" She tried to keep her voice casual, but her fingers suddenly felt clumsy. Barend did not like talking about anything related to the curse, and Karyna usually respected his feelings. But today she felt unable to keep quiet on the subject any longer.

Barend shifted his weight away from her. "It felt like that first night." He turned his huge head to one side, gazing off into some unseen middle-distance. "As though something physical and tangible swarmed out of the Throne Room and struck me. That is all I remember."

Karyna drew out the burr, then ran her fingers through the fur to remove the last knots and brushed away more leaves. This task complete, she knelt back down to attend to the flower beds. With her head bowed she gathered courage around her like a cloak. "Like that first night?" she repeated. "Can you remember what happened then?"

A growl rumbled in Barend's throat. "I cannot."

"Nothing? Do you remember what happened to Bellenya?" Karyna held her breath, hoping he would not stalk away and leave her questions unanswered. She hoped for a hint, a clue, something to give her an idea of why the curse had been cast, or by whom.

"Bellenya . . ." Barend lifted his head and gazed across the garden. "We left the ball to walk in the gardens. I remember talking, but I do not recall what we said. I remember returning to the Throne Room, standing in the doorway, looking toward Bellenya, and then . . ." His voice trailed off. He glanced at Karyna, who had stopped working, her eyes turned eagerly up to him. "No. I do not remember anything else. Something crashed into me, knocked me over, and the next thing I knew, I was as you see me now."

Karyna's shoulders slumped, and she looked down at her work to hide her disappointed expression. Barend pawed at the ground and let out a whuffling sigh. Karyna wanted to ask more questions, dig at the problem, try to find a solution. But she could tell Barend was done talking. She pressed her teeth together on the tip of her tongue and moved a bit farther down the row. The tension in the air faded.

"I hear you gave Lady Ahren quite a tongue-lashing yesterday," Barend remarked after a long silence.

"I did not!" Karyna protested. "I kept my words quite civil."

"You called her a fool."

"I implied only."

Barend rumbled with laughter. "You would make a splendid queen."

"Covered in mud and with leaves in my hair. Is that acceptable attire for queens in snowy Norvue?" Karyna cast him a quick, wry smile.

"In my homeland, queens can come from anywhere, even the gardens."

A strange, serious tone lurked in his voice. But when Karyna glanced up at him, he no longer looked at her but seemed to study one of her rosebushes instead.

Karyna ducked her head again and dug her fingers into the soil. A shock of cold struck her fingers, and she realized she had neglected to put her gloves back on. Though the soft wet ground was ideal for the work she was doing, it was also chilly due to the melted snow. A chuckle escaped her lips.

Barend stiffened and put back his ears. "I will leave you to your task," he said.

He stalked away before Karyna could reply. She watched him go, confused until she realized that he must have thought she was laughing at him. Had she inadvertently offended him? For the second time in as many days, she wished she could call him back and explain herself.

CHAPTER THREE

THE SUN rose over Wilshaw just as the old sentry arrived at his post by the north gate. Before he could get settled he noticed a figure emerging from the forest a ways down the road. He peered at it, squinting in an attempt to ascertain what was coming.

Out of the haze of distance rode a lone traveler. As he came closer, the sentry could tell he was a young man, probably from foreign parts. He rode a majestic sorrel horse and wore a fine cloak of dark green over a black shirt with loose sleeves and silver ties laced up its front. The sentry guessed that this was a nobleman of some prestige.

The young man reined his horse to a halt at the gate and hailed the sentry, his eyes earnest and kind with a sparkle of humor in their depths. "What town is this?" he asked, his voice lightly accented. The sentry told him, and the young man asked, "How much farther to Thorndale Castle?"

"Perhaps four days' journey, if you ride hard," the old man replied, mystified. "But you don't want to go there, lad. It's cursed."

The young man nodded seriously. "I know. But I hope to find a way to break the curse."

The sentry gave a bark of laughter devoid of amusement. "You think we haven't tried? We're on the brink of ruin and war. If we could break the curse, we would."

"Are things that bad?" The young man's eyes darkened in concern then filled with a determination that sparked unexpected hope in the sentry's heart. "What news can you share?"

"Rumor is Lord Fredrig finally managed to secure control of the regency," the sentry replied. "Whether he can make any changes for the better or hold onto the title remains to be seen."

The traveler looked thoughtful. "May I have leave to travel through your fine town?"

"I see no reason to stop you," the old man replied. "Mind you take care. The people here are wary of strangers and foreigners. I'd recommend you ride straight through and keep going. Perhaps you'll get a warmer welcome farther down the road in Hawksglen."

The traveler nodded his thanks and continued on his way. The old sentry watched him pass and then settled down on his stool with a sigh, knowing that exchange was likely to be his last interesting encounter of the day. He amused himself through the long morning hours by imagining all sorts of adventures to come for the enigmatic young man.

Her bitterness seethed around her, pulsing with a rhythm like ocean waves rolling up onto the shore and receding. She stormed around the large parlor and stared out the window that looked across the courtyard to the

forest beyond. A silent three-tiered fountain adorned with carvings of birds in flight caught her eye. A pang of sorrow lanced through her. Once this place had been filled with laughter. Now it lay dormant. White sheets covered the furniture. The halls lay silent, empty.

Why did no one come? Could it be that no one cared? Loneliness threatened to overwhelm her. She was like a prisoner in a cold dungeon, forgotten by everyone. Her loneliness was second only to her pain.

It had been two years, but her heart ached as though the wound were yet open and raw. It consumed her. Only when she poured her magic into the rose could she know any comfort or balm.

Climbing the steps, she returned to it: a single red rose floating in the air above a square glass vase (so thin and fragile that a glance could shatter it) adorned the center of her dressing table. The rose itself was a perfect specimen. A dark green stem, long and slender—leaves perfectly shaped— petals of the deepest blood-red, so soft they could be used to clothe a newborn babe. Even its thorns were objects of beauty.

She knelt before the table, her gaze fixed upon the rose.

Karyna woke, blinking sleep from her eyes. Her heart ached with remembered pain and bitterness as the nightmare faded.

Six weeks had slipped past since the incident with the Throne Room. The skies were blue, flowers bloomed in abundance, and the air was warm. But nightmares continued to afflict Karyna's sleep. She remembered nothing more than vague images upon waking, but these left her feeling tired and unsettled.

She stumbled out of bed and over to the washbasin, where she splashed water on her face and tried to dispel the final remnants of the dream. After clearing her head, she began her daily routine. It was late by the time she made it out to the gardens to tend the rosebushes. She had been keeping careful watch, attentive for any sign of pests or disease. The buds would be opening soon, an event Karyna looked forward to every year.

The afternoon sun shone warm on her back as she stepped outside. Blossoms adorned the fruit trees, and squirrels chased each other up and down their trunks. Karyna's eyes lit up as she spotted a group of butterflies fluttering around the lantana. The scents of the garden and the warm air filled her with joy.

The entire garden was Karyna's delight, but there was one rosebush she cared for with special attention. This glorious rosebush at the end of the path captured the attention of all who visited the Queen's Garden. Its blooms had been Bellenya's favorites, the same variety Karyna now painstakingly dried and placed in the princess's empty chambers. Cuttings of this rose had been brought to Thorndale Castle from Rivenloch Palace as a wedding gift to the king and queen from the king's mother.

As Karyna approached the bush she could see that many of the buds had burst open. But something was not right. She squinted at them, worried. The color of the flowers was strange. This bush always bore beautiful red blooms, but these flowers seemed too pale, almost gray.

A moment passed before she comprehended what she was seeing, and another moment after that before she believed it. Her earlier joy dissolved into foreboding. She turned and fled back to the palace.

"Setella! Barend! Help!" she shouted, racing through the halls until she found them both.

Mystified by the urgency in her voice and the panic in her eyes, they followed her outside. When they reached the rose garden, Barend and Setella stared in stunned disbelief. Every rose on the bush had turned to stone.

"It's spreading," Karyna whispered. Her worst fear, sprung to life before her. "The curse is spreading."

"What does it mean? Why would this happen now, after two years?" Setella asked.

"Perhaps the curse is getting stronger." Barend spoke in a low, angry growl.

"But why this rosebush? And why now?" Setella persisted.

Karyna twisted her apron in her hands, her mind spinning over the problem before her. A tendril of excitement and hope wound its way through her initial dismay. This was the first clue since the night the curse fell, and she did not want to miss its significance. A hunch began to play around the corners of her mind, growing in strength as memories of her recent nightmares flooded back to her. She gazed around the garden, her eyes scanning the foliage. Her heartbeat quickened as the hunch grew into certainty.

"Whoever cast the curse and kidnapped the princess is inside Rivenloch Palace," she said, her voice quiet but full of conviction.

Barend and Setella turned to look at her, their expressions uncomprehending. "Why would you think that?" Barend asked.

"The roses. These specific roses. There must be a connection. Why else would this bush be the only thing affected? It's all the way over here on the end of the garden farthest from the Throne Room, and none of the plants in between appear to be harmed. And," she hesitated, knowing her words would sound foolish, then plowed on anyway, "I've been having nightmares. They started the day I put one of my dried roses on the nightstand by my bed."

"What does that have to do with anything?" Barend asked.

"In the dreams I've caught glimpses of the person who cast the curse and kidnapped the princess."

At this Barend growled, sounding terribly animal. One could easily forget he had ever been a prince. "Who is it?" he demanded.

Karyna shook her head sadly. Her certainty grew as she spoke, but she knew her words sounded illogical, even insane. "I haven't seen her exactly, but I've . . . I've been her. I know it doesn't make sense, but dreams rarely do. I'm certain she's an enchantress, a powerful one. More importantly, I know that she is at Rivenloch Palace. I've glimpsed enough of her surroundings to recognize it."

She expected the others to reject her notion out of hand, but instead they looked contemplative.

"We always knew some strong magic was involved," Setella said slowly. "And Rivenloch is isolated and has been closed these seven years."

Barend's growling subsided, and his voice became once more that of a prince, though it rumbled in his beast's throat. "This could be why nobody has found the princess. Yet even if there was anyone left to send, it seems farfetched. How much stock should we really place in dreams?"

Karyna felt a desperation to act fill her entire being. Her mind raced ahead to the possibility of the curse's end. "I'll go!" she declared.

Immediately Barend growled again. "Absolutely not."

But Karyna could not be so easily thwarted. "Please! We could find Bellenya; we could end the curse!" She raised her eyes to the Throne Room windows, and impatience flooded her thoughts. "You could go home," she whispered, turning then and catching Barend's gaze. Even as she spoke, a pang of sadness tinged her excitement. And was that her sadness she saw reflected in the prince's eye?

"It's a two-week journey to Rivenloch," Barend protested. "Henry has said the roads are treacherous these days."

"I'll be fine. I can make the journey in ten days if I travel alone."

"I'm not letting you take a dangerous journey to an abandoned castle on the basis of a couple of dreams and a dead bush." Barend's voice deepened with his anxiety. "Besides, even if you get there safely, what are you going to do? You can't face down an enchantress alone. You're not a knight, and you have no magic to defend yourself. We're talking about someone powerful enough to reach out from two hundred miles away and touch this rosebush. I cannot allow it."

"You can't stop me," Karyna replied. She spoke quietly but with absolute certainty of her own mind. Nothing could stop her, not now. "You may be trapped here, and you may be a prince, but respectfully, Your Highness, I don't work for you."

"Karyna!" Setella said, her eyes wide with shock.

Barend's ears went back, and the dark pupils of his eyes widened. "If you're determined to do this, then I'll go with you."

Karyna barked a short laugh. "Don't be ridiculous!" She surprised herself with her own audacity. Barend was a prince, after all. But she could not seem to stop the words from pouring out of her mouth. "You know what happens when you leave the palace grounds. How could you hope to be helpful?"

Barend gave a growl of frustration. "You cannot go alone."

"You said it yourself: There's no one else. Setella, Willem, and Henry are all too old for such a journey." Her face softened then, her brow gently wrinkling. "Please, Barend. You must let me go."

Setella took Karyna's arm and patted her hand. "It is evening. Even if we do decide someone must travel to Rivenloch, this is not the time for starting a journey. Let us sleep on it and discuss it more tomorrow. Perhaps some of the nobles who sent their daughters would be willing to undertake the quest."

Karyna frowned. She had no desire to delay even a single minute. "Very well," she agreed, but she had no need to sleep on the decision. Her mind was already made up. She returned to the castle with Setella, her thoughts churning over the list of things she would need to pack and prepare for her journey.

She did not know that Barend watched her until she disappeared back inside.

In the misty predawn Barend climbed the exterior of the highest tower of the castle. Every muscle and nerve strained with exertion and focus as his powerful body flowed upward, a dark blur against the pale stone, his claws finding purchase in the gaps and chinking between blocks. Once a rear paw slipped on a gargoyle's head and gouged a chunk out of its ear. He heard the broken masonry bounce and skitter to the ground far below.

At last he reached the summit of the conical tower roof and crouched there, one forepaw wrapped around the sturdy flagpole at the top. His front paws were large and clawed but still retained a moderate amount of his human dexterity, for which he was grateful.

The air was dense and wet, as though the sky were trying to make up its mind about whether or not it should rain. Barend did not feel the mild chill in the air. His shaggy coat protected him, and Suvall never approached the sort of cold he had been used to in his homeland.

He gazed north, his heart yearning for home. A part of him was glad the curse prevented him from leaving the palace grounds. It meant he did not have to face his parents while wearing this horrible new form and face. When the reality of his situation had been made clear, Barend had sent them messages, hoping they might be able to find a cure. But magic was scarce in Norvue, and without the resources to combat such a curse, there had been little his parents could do.

At least here he could be isolated from the prying eyes, whispered rumors, and unkind words that were sure to follow him wherever he went. Outside Thorndale Castle, he would never be just Barend. He would be the cursed prince, the Beast, the pitiable creature. Yes, there were worse fates than being a prisoner.

A flicker of movement on the ground far below, near the stables, caught his eye and he peered through the mist, his senses on alert, his muscles tensed to spring into action if the need arose. His eyesight was keen, and he was able to see clearly what had caught his attention.

A mounted figure wearing a pale gray cloak and hood had just exited the stables and now galloped down the road toward the gates opening into the main road. Seeing the horse's mane and tail flash like silver in the early light, Barend bared his teeth in frustration. The horse was Pippa, which meant the rider must be Karyna.

"Stupid, stubborn girl," he muttered. Every fiber of his being wanted to race after her and make her turn back, but he knew he could not catch her before she crossed the invisible barrier.

Catlike, he bounded down to a flat part of a lower roof and crouched there in a crenellation of the wall to catch glimpses of the rider between obtrusive trees. What could he do? Karyna was pertinacious; she would not be deterred once she had made up her mind. He usually admired this trait, but he wished now that she was not quite so headstrong. Fear for her safety consumed him; he felt as though his heart were tearing in two. He cared for her deeply, though he had said nothing to her. He could neither bring himself to add such a burden to her shoulders nor bear to see pity in her eyes. It was better that she not know how he felt.

"What am I supposed to do?" he demanded of a grotesque beak-nosed gargoyle.

The gargoyle pointedly refused to look at him. Growling, Barend rose to prowl on the slate tiles. A question whispered in his soul, prodding him gently. It was a question he had avoided for two years, but now it hit him full strength. Did the Beast truly overpower him when he crossed the boundary, or, like a negligent jailor, did he allow its escape? Did he hide behind the Beast in order to stay sequestered in Thorndale Castle? He had ever considered himself a courageous man, yet was it the curse or his pride that kept him from leaving?

"It takes over," he argued, stalking back and forth. "I remember nothing once I'm outside the boundary."

Do you? the gargoyle seemed to ask.

"What if I hurt her? I can't protect her from myself."

Did you honestly not recognize her when she came after you?

He shook himself and uttered an animal roar. Karyna had reached the gates and turned south toward Rivenloch. Respect for her confidence and courage filled his heart. A part of him had known she would not wait to discuss the matter further. He had seen the look in her eye the evening before and understood it. Was this not why he had risen earlier than usual and climbed the front tower instead of the one at the back of the castle? Reckless though it may be, Karyna had made her decision. Now it was his turn to decide.

"I can't go with her. I'll only hinder her quest."

Karyna's figure vanished in the distance. Barend showed his teeth at the gargoyle, and a rumble of thunder rolled deep in his throat. His body flowed down the castle wall and over the ramparts with fluid strength.

He had made his choice: It was time to embrace the Beast.

CHAPTER FOUR

NIGHT FELL even as the lone traveler rode his horse into the courtyard of Thorndale Castle. A pale, waning moon hung in the sky as he swung down off his mount and ascended the steps to the great oak doors. He lifted the heavy iron knocker and rapped sharply, sending echoes resounding through the halls inside. He waited impatiently, knocking again several times before he heard footsteps coming.

An older woman opened the door and raised a candle to illuminate his face. He blinked at the sudden light.

"Who is there?" Her voice sounded apprehensive, but as her eyes scanned his appearance her fear visibly lessened.

The traveler touched his forehead with a little bow and spoke politely. "Good evening, mistress. I have come to speak with Prince Barend. Can you tell him that an old friend is here?"

The old servant's eyes grew worried. "I'm sorry . . . You are . . . from Norvue, my lord?"

He nodded, reining in impatience. "I am aware that the prince cannot leave the palace grounds. Please. I know he wouldn't refuse to see me after I've traveled all this way."

"Regardless, he's gone." The woman made a helpless motion with her hands and suddenly became talkative. "I am sorry, my lord, but there it is! My guess is he's gone to Rivenloch Palace, just south of Mirhaven. That's where Karyna was headed, in any case, and I'm assuming he went after her." The old woman shook her head with a grumble. "What either of them was thinking I'll never know. Karyna is—"

Losing patience, he interrupted her ramblings. "When did Barend leave?"

She stiffened. "Yesterday morning, my lord."

The traveler tried not to reveal his frustration and disappointment. This was the last thing he had expected to greet him at the end of his journey. But he was not one to let unexpected complications deter him. "My undying gratitude for this information, mistress." With a polite nod he turned and bounded down the steps. In one easy motion he mounted his horse and reined it toward the road.

"Wait! What will you do?" the servant shouted after him, nervous again.

The horse wheeled back to face her, champing impatiently, and its rider called, "If I hurry I might be able to catch them! Never fear: I intend to offer my help, such as it may be." The traveler gave another quick salute; then his horse spun toward the highway and broke into a canter.

In his heart the traveler knew he would not get far this night. His faithful horse, though loyal and tough, was weary from many days of travel. He smoothed its mane and gave its sweaty neck an encouraging pat. "Just a few more miles, Tarak, old boy." So they pressed on, alternating between walk and trot until the sun dipped low over the horizon.

In a matter of weeks the traveler would turn twenty-one, and he needed to find Barend before that day came.

The early-summer weather was lovely and nights were warm. However, Karyna's sense of adventure was nearly depleted. Sleeping on the ground had quickly lost all appeal, and endless days in the saddle were exhausting. She had spent two nights in villages, but usually inns were more than a day's journey apart. The legends of intrepid heroes never mentioned how uncomfortable and hard the ground was or how noisy nocturnal creatures could be.

But now as the afternoon of her eighth day of travel waned, she was within a few miles of Mirhaven, her journey nearly at an end. She straightened in the saddle and rolled her shoulders, trying to stretch her aching back and blinking exhaustion from her eyes. A tendril of worry at the thought of facing the enchantress wound its way through her thoughts, but she stubbornly pushed it away. There would be time to deal with that later.

"Almost to Mirhaven, Pippa," Karyna muttered. "Hopefully we'll be able to stay there tonight."

For lack of conversation, she had taken to talking to her horse. Karyna had once thought the halls of Thorndale Castle lonely, but now she knew true solitude. She found herself recalling and missing her interactions with Barend. Sometimes they had simply walked in the garden together as Karyna watered and weeded. At other times they discussed favorite music and plays, argued about philosophy, or laughed about their shared experiences as children. "Remember the time . . . ?" had been a frequent query, followed by fond and reminiscent smiles.

Norvue and Suvall had always been allies, and the royal families frequently exchanged friendly visits. Many times Karyna had accompanied Princess Bellenya for summer holidays at Norvue's palace, where the two girls played with the royal children. Karyna knew there had been hopes that the two kingdoms might be united through marriage, but such hopes died the night the curse fell.

Out here on the road she was more alone than ever before, having encountered no other travelers in the past two days. As a strange sense of foreboding fell over her, her sleepy reminiscences vanished into vigilance.

Shadows deepened, and the wooded path was empty. A twig snapped somewhere off to the left, and she flinched, making Pippa break into a nervous jog. "Steady, girl. Nothing to fear," Karyna said, but her voice sounded tense, and Pippa remained unconvinced.

Although her journey thus far had been without incident, Karyna had sensed for the past few days that she was being followed. Despite the lack of evidence, her fear deepened with each passing moment. She urged Pippa to a quicker trot, and the mare willingly lengthened her stride, ears flicking, muscles taut. The back of Karyna's neck prickled, and her stomach clenched in senseless dread . . . of what? Surely her imagination was running amok and Pippa was only sharing her fear. Desperately she strove to compose herself.

But then, close behind them an eerie howl rose, and another joined in weird harmony. Karyna cried out in fright, and Pippa, with a terrified squeal, charged off the path and into the woods. Branches whipped past, raking at Karyna. She leaned forward, clinging desperately to the mare's neck and barely keeping hold of the reins. The silver mane whipped across her face, making it hard to see.

"Whoa, whoa, girl!" Karyna gasped. "Steady, easy, whoa!"

She sawed on the reins, but to no avail. She gave up hope of controlling her horse and focused instead on merely hanging on. Terrible howls and yelping cries echoed through the trees, seeming to surround and close in around her. Then Pippa leaped over a fallen tree, and Karyna lost her balance and felt herself falling.

She hit the ground hard on her right shoulder, then tumbled to a sprawling stop and lay struggling to draw breath as the world spun above her and Pippa thundered on into the forest. A dim sense of urgency made her push herself upright and scoot backward to rest against a tree trunk. Once the pounding in her head slowed, she heard panting and eager whining; and as her vision cleared, she began to see gleaming fangs and dripping tongues.

The wolves had caught up to her, and now they circled, their eyes bright with hunger. Helpless, almost despairing, Karyna cast about for a stick she might use to fend them off. Her eyes alighted on a thick branch, and she reached out a trembling hand to grasp it and drag it into her lap, all the while knowing the futility of her actions.

"Well, what have we here?"

The voice was so unexpected that at first Karyna thought she had imagined it. She stared in disbelief as a tall thin man stepped out of the shadows, paused near one of the wolves, and rubbed its ear insouciantly.

Karyna blinked then looked again at the pack of creatures surrounding her. What she had mistaken for wolves were actually dogs, twelve of them—lean, vicious, and snarling, but not wolves. This should have relieved her, yet it merely served to alarm her further. Tightening her grip on the stick, her back still pressed against the tree, she pushed herself to her feet.

"I apologize if my dogs here caused you undue fright," the man said in a drawling accent. "They caught a scent and run off before I could stop them."

He came closer, and Karyna lifted her branch as a barrier. "They scared my horse," she replied stiffly.

"Your horse?" The man looked in the direction of Pippa's flight as he fiddled with the lace on the collar of his dark green waistcoat. He shook his long yellow hair out of his eyes. "It won't get far. That way leads to a dense thicket. If it don't stop, it's liable to get its tack all caught up in the thorns. Don't worry, we'll get your horse."

Karyna did not like the way he had phrased that last statement. "I would appreciate the help," she said cautiously. "But I wouldn't wish to be a burden to you, and your dogs might scare my horse even more."

"Don't worry about that; they'll stay back if I tell them to." He scratched his upper lip where a few days' worth of stubble grew. Karyna guessed his age at a few years older than she was. "You, uh, you out here alone?"

The question seemed innocent enough, but Karyna did not like the way he was looking at her. "Can you show me this thicket?" she asked, hoping to distract him from the question.

"Mm-hmm." A dangerous light glinted in the man's eyes. "Before we bother with any of that, I have to ask: What do you think you owe me for traveling through my wood? A pretty miss like yourself, you've probably got some ideas."

Karyna tipped the forked end of her dead branch toward the stranger, fear fluttering in the pit of her stomach. "Your wood?" She masked the fear in fury, her face a storm cloud of indignation. "It's no more your wood than it is mine."

A nasty smile twitched the corners of the man's lips. He took a step forward and Karyna, despite herself, shrank back. The dogs crept forward, their teeth bared in feral grins. Karyna's breath quickened and her heart throbbed in her ears. She adjusted her grip on the stick as panic flowed through her in a wave. Her thoughts careened wildly, yet no solution to her situation presented itself.

Then a monstrous roar echoed through the woods, and an enormous form leapt out of the trees, landing in front of Karyna. If not for the tree at her back, she would have collapsed in startled fear. But the creature crouched with its hindquarters toward her and faced the dogs. Karyna recognized that shaggy form and the rumbling growls.

"Barend!"

As if her cry shattered some invisible barrier, the pack of dogs attacked their unknown opponent. The battle was swift and fierce, the air filled with furious snarls, yelps, and cruelly snapping teeth. One of the dogs lunged toward the beast's hindquarters in an attempt to hamstring him, but Karyna jabbed at it with her stick until Barend knocked it away with a giant paw. Another slashed at his throat. Yet another sprang at the beast's forelegs, teeth snapping viciously, thirsty for blood. Tails wagging, yelping in the joy of the hunt, the pack assailed their quarry; but the tree at his back, and Karyna, prevented them from surrounding him. They retreated for a moment, panting and calculating.

The beast crouched, resting yet ready. Karyna felt blood pounding in her head, and her arms shook with fatigue and fear. Yet she held her stick with both hands. Dimly, as if through a fog, she heard the dogs' master shouting at them and encouraging them to fight on. Barend would hold them off; she could not let herself doubt him.

The attack returned in a rush of hot breath and sharp fangs. One of the dogs got around behind Barend and leapt on his back, driving its teeth into the thick, muscular shoulder. With an inhuman yell, Karyna swung her stick with all her might and knocked the dog to the ground. But in doing so she left the protection of her tree, a mistake she recognized when the creature recovered and turned on her, hackles raised and teeth bared. Her mouth went dry as she side-stepped toward another tree. The sounds of battle were suddenly muted to her ears, her whole being focused on this single predator threatening her.

The dog launched itself at Karyna. She raised her stick, but there was a wrench and cracking sound as the dry wood snapped, and the dog's weight and momentum knocked her flat on her back. For an instant she saw its flashing teeth and red maw—but its jaws snapped on empty air as Barend snatched it into the air. The hapless animal writhed and squirmed, then went limp and submissive with a pitiful whine.

Karyna scrambled shakily to her feet and glanced about, but the other dogs were either down or skulking off in defeat. Rumbling like distant thunder, Barend held the pack leader clamped in his massive jaws. Before him stood the yellow-haired man, his face a picture of fear and rage.

"Let him go!" The man's voice was high-pitched, verging on hysteria. "Hey! Let him go!"

The beast made a sharp, guttural sound deep in his throat, and the dog flinched and yelped. The man backed away, wild-eyed and visibly shaking.

"We'll leave the girl alone, I swear! You can have her! You're free to roam, hunt, whatever you please," the man gibbered. His eyes fixed on Karyna. "Witch of the Wood," he gasped, "spare me!"

Then he turned and fled. The beast dropped the dog. It dashed away, tail tucked between its legs, like a chastened puppy. The remaining dogs also fled after their master, leaving their fallen comrades behind.

"Barend," Karyna breathed. "Oh, you should not have come after me!"

Still rumbling, Barend swung his heavy head around, and those wild eyes gazed into hers. She began to shiver uncontrollably. Her teeth chattered together and she took deep breaths, trying to control her reaction. Having saved her, would the beast now kill her?

Seeing a flicker of recognition in his eyes, Karyna dared to hope. Cautiously, slowly, she reached out a hand and laid it on the beast's great, blood-smeared muzzle. He did not flinch away, so she laid her other hand on his ruff and twined her fingers in the thick, coarse fur. For a long moment they stayed that way, girl and beast.

"I can't take you home," she said at last, staring off into the forest. "Of course you knew that when you came after me. I'm glad you did," she admitted. "I don't know what would have happened if you hadn't." She turned her anxious gaze to his face. "Are you hurt? Will you let me help?"

Barend lay down and put his head on his paws as Karyna checked him for wounds. There was a shallow, easily tended gash on his shoulder. She wanted to clean and dress it, but she could do little until she found her horse and supplies.

"You'll be fine for now. Come on then; we'd best go find Pippa."

The sky above the trees darkened and the crickets' song became a full chorus. With Barend padding at her heels, Karyna wrapped herself tightly in her cloak. Its warmth about her shoulders felt reassuring despite the mildness of the evening.

She was even more glad of Barend's presence, for she would never have found Pippa by herself. Barend seemed to understand this, and he moved ahead of her, limping a bit as he led her to the horse.

Pippa had indeed managed to tangle her reins, and it took Karyna some time to get her loose. Eventually the frightened mare was freed and Karyna managed to calm her. She walked the horse about, patting her and murmuring soothingly.

"All right, Pippa, all right. You're safe now, girl, not to worry. You don't have to do anything more tonight. We'll set up camp here. I'll light a fire, and you can graze. I think I have a few carrots left in the saddlebags. With the thicket at our backs and Barend watching over us we'll be just fine."

The horse whickered and nudged at Karyna's arm with her nose. Karyna smiled, and set about tending Barend's wound. This accomplished, she built a fire and ate some of her rations. The meal was not satisfying but it was all she had. She comforted herself with thoughts of a hot meal in Mirhaven tomorrow.

Much later, just as she was falling asleep, the thief's words came back to her. What had he called her? Witch of the Wood? She would have to remember to ask about that when she reached Mirhaven.

She tried not to think about what might happen if there was nothing in Rivenloch at all. What if the nightmares proved nothing more than dreams? What if she found no enchantress, no Bellenya, no way to break the curse? Karyna shook the pessimistic thoughts away, refusing to believe that her efforts might end in a vapor of futility.

Darkness filled the woods around her as she spread out her bedroll. Once she closed her eyes, knowing that the prince was nearby, protecting her, Karyna felt as safe as she did in her own bed.

Sorrow clung to her like a heavy robe as she paced the empty, ruined halls, her chest heaving with silent sobs. Her eyes were dry, too dry, as though she had wept all her tears and none were left. She stumbled, but no one came to assist her.

Never before had she known such loneliness, such bleak desolation. Her hands hung at her sides, and her once-beautiful gown fell about her in tatters of purple satin. Her long black hair cascaded in unkempt waves about her shoulders. She no longer cared about her appearance, though she remembered it had once been important to her. What was the point? There was no one to see her wretched state.

Though it was summer outside, a winter of her own creation whistled through the corridors, a winter of bitterness. Her bare feet left bloody footprints on the frosty marble floors, but she no longer felt the pain or the cold. When she could bear it no longer, she would retreat to her tower, the one place where she could find any warmth, any comfort. There she would gaze upon her rose.

But for now she wandered the halls, unconscious of the mournful, unearthly wail tearing its way out of her throat and echoing down the halls. Her pain overwhelmed her, and she was deaf to her own grief.

It rained in the night, but Karyna awoke to a warmth that seemed impossible from the remnants of her cold campfire. She opened her eyes to find herself surrounded by long fur. The beast had kept her warm and dry. Vestiges of the sorrow she had felt in the nightmare hung heavy over her spirit, and she was amazed to discover that she remembered the dream clearly. In it, she had walked the halls of Rivenloch Palace. She felt triumphant despite the terrifying events of the previous evening: Her dreams were indeed leading her to her intended destination.

As Karyna stirred, Barend rose and backed away slowly. A strange emotion filled his dark eyes, one that Karyna was not sure she recognized. She felt her heart beat a bit more quickly and grew inexplicably embarrassed.

"Thank you," she said, "for keeping me warm last night."

The prince did not respond but turned and, after giving his coat a vigorous shake, disappeared into the forest. Karyna set about tacking up her horse, wondering as she did so why her hands were shaking.

CHAPTER FIVE

IRHAVEN WAS a quiet village bordered by thick forest. The town had grown up around Lord Pentworth's manor. Quaint shops lined its cobblestone streets, though many of them had boards across the windows. The few people outside in the early evening shot distrustful glances at Karyna and hurried past without giving the customary greeting. Karyna was not surprised. She had encountered the same suspicious reactions everywhere she stopped along her journey. The curse might have fallen on Thorndale Castle, but its effects crept throughout the entire country.

It was past midday when Karyna reached the inn, stabled Pippa, and went inside for a meal. She longed for a soft bed, but her purse was feeling light and she had the return trip to consider. The inn was a gray stone building with fresh thatch on the roof, and the interior was clean. Pleasant smells wafted from the back kitchen, and Karyna breathed deeply, her stomach rumbling a complaint. A girl about her own age with rosy cheeks and flaxen hair greeted her.

"Welcome," the girl said as Karyna entered the common room. "I'm Alys. Would miss like a room for the night?"

Karyna felt the tension lift from her shoulders. Alys's open, honest face was a relief after her encounter with the stranger in the woods. She shook her head. "I'd like a meal, but I won't be staying the night."

"Of course," the girl spoke cheerfully. "Anything to drink?"

"Do you have tea?" Karyna asked hopefully. Tea was not a common drink in Suvall, but Barend had introduced them to the Norvuan practice of steeping rosehips and other herbs in hot water, and Karyna had acquired a taste for it with honey.

The girl squinted, a puzzled look on her face. "What's that, miss?"

"Never mind." Karyna gave a regretful grin. "I'll take a mulled ale with my dinner."

"Very good, miss. Dinner won't be ready for about an hour. We don't have fancy fare, just pottage for the main course. But," she lowered her voice to a conspiratorial whisper, "the apple pie is very fine indeed."

Karyna's eyes crinkled at the corners. "It sounds wonderful," she said.

Alys hurried off, and Karyna seated herself on a bench at a table near the door. She leaned forward, propped her chin on her hands, and closed her eyes. It felt good to rest, even if only for a short while. She did not intend to stay long, just a quick meal and then she would be on her way.

She worried briefly about Barend. She had not seen him since that morning, though she knew he remained near throughout the day. All sign of him had vanished when she approached Mirhaven. She must simply trust that he had found a safe place to hide and wait for her. Though they could not communicate, he seemed to possess an uncanny sense of her needs and wishes.

So she tried to push that worry to the back of her mind. The quiet of the inn and Alys's friendliness comforted her soul, and she basked in the moment of peace, however brief.

A traveler entered the inn, shaking dust from his cloak. The common room was about half full, and he took casual notice of the clientele. A burly man sat near the door, evidently hired by the innkeeper to keep customers from getting out of hand. A trim young woman sat facing away from the door at a nearby table. A local, maybe. He dismissed her. Several other tables were also occupied by groups of locals, men who had stopped in after work, a few families. The inn's staff moved through the room with an easy rhythm. A boy, not quite yet a man, washed down a table; and a round-faced maid fairly danced between the tables, bringing people food and filling drinks.

It was by far the best inn the traveler had entered since crossing into Suvall. The atmosphere was more cheerful, less wary, though an undertone of suspicion still lingered in the people's eyes and their hushed voices.

In the moment required to assess his surroundings, the innkeeper appeared at his side, a tall, broad-shouldered man with receding white hair and an honest face. "Welcome, traveler," the man greeted him with an open but solemn expression. "Do you require food, drink, a bed for the night? What can my humble inn offer you this fine summer's eve?"

"Food and drink to start," the traveler replied. "And, if you have room, a place to spend the night. I've already lodged my horse in your stables." He showed the man his coin purse, and the remnants of wariness left the innkeeper's eyes.

"Excellent, excellent." He ushered his guest to a table and gestured to the girl, who had just returned to the counter. She grinned and hurried toward the kitchen with purposeful strides. "Alys will bring your dinner directly."

"Your daughter?"

"Aye." The innkeeper lingered, a curious look on his face. "You don't have the accent of a Suvallan. Where do you hail from, if you don't mind my asking?"

"I come from Norvue, friend. My name is Ritter."

"Norvue." The man looked thoughtful. "I've never visited there. The land of wind and snow, they call it."

Ritter chuckled. "Only in winter, though it's true our winters are long. Our summers are as full of flowers, sunshine, and balmy breezes as your own."

"Have you traveled here before, then? How do our countries compare?" The innkeeper leaned against the table with a friendly smile.

"I spent much of my time here as a child." Ritter looked thoughtful. "Norvue is far more rocky and timbered than Suvall. And of course," he paused, giving the innkeeper a meaningful glance, "magic is less common."

The innkeeper's eyes darkened. "Count your blessings then," he muttered and straightened as if to leave.

"The curse has affected you all the way out here?" Ritter asked.

The innkeeper moved his jaw as if chewing something tough then nodded shortly. "It's not the curse itself, mind. It's the squabbling, the raids, as every landholder in the country tries to grab a bit more for himself. Most of the time it's us commoners that feel the brunt of it."

"Oh? How so?" Ritter prompted.

The innkeeper scratched his chin, pondering. "The roads are dangerous, so merchants aren't traveling, which means trade is scarce. Luxuries are hard to come by. Mirhaven used to be a busy village and a neighborly place to live, but most folks couldn't make ends meet, and those of us left are barely scraping by."

"I'm sorry to hear that," Ritter said, feeling true sympathy for these good people thrust into such a plight.

The innkeeper forced a smile. "Well, we can still manage a modicum of hospitality. Here's Alys with your food and drink. If you need anything, just ask."

"My thanks," Ritter replied. "For now the food should be sufficient."

Alys set a trencher of pottage before Ritter, and he dug in hungrily. It wasn't the best food he'd ever eaten, but it wasn't terrible. The ale tasted more like water than anything else, but it quenched his thirst, and Alys kept his tankard full. When he was finished, Alys brought him a slice of warm apple pie. He took a wary bite and found it to be one of the most sumptuous things he had ever eaten. He glanced up and saw Alys lingering, watching him with a hopeful expression on her face.

"This is delicious," he said with heartfelt sincerity. "Your father said luxuries were scarce, so tell me: How is such a delicacy possible in times like these?"

Alys's cheeks dimpled in pleasure. "My own recipe, sir. My pa owns a stretch of orchards, so apples are the one treat we can manage these days. I'm glad you enjoyed it." She moved on to the next table and Ritter sat back and perused the room, sipping on the tasteless ale. A snippet of conversation caught his attention.

"I overheard a strange phrase as I entered your town. Who or what is the Witch of the Wood?" a female voice asked.

Ritter raised his eyes and scanned the room curiously. The young woman he had dismissed earlier now sat chatting with the innkeeper's son. Curious, Ritter strained to hear them better.

"... local legend ... two years ... celebration ..."

Ritter scowled. He could hear only fragments of the conversation. He got up and sauntered to a closer table. Neither the young woman nor the lad paid him any attention, and Ritter found that he could now hear their words clearly, though he still saw only the back of the girl's head.

"Two years ago? Are you sure, Nik?" The girl spoke quietly, yet Ritter immediately recognized education and culture in her voice. In fact, the voice seemed familiar . . .

"Yeah," Nik replied. "It was when all that strange business at Thorndale Castle happened. Anyway, it was a few weeks after that when strange things started happening around here too." The lad paused and made a wondering sound. "I hadn't thought about that before, how it all sort of started at the same time."

"What kind of strange things?" the young woman asked eagerly.

"People started seeing odd sights out in the forest and hearing weird noises—wailing and sobbing, that sort of thing. Mysterious lights out in the woods at night, and some even say they've seen a cloaked figure walking amongst the trees."

"They call her the Witch of the Wood?" the young woman interjected. Ritter risked a quick glance in her direction. She was leaning toward Nik, listening intently. Ritter frowned and wondered why anyone would be so excited about this kind of folk tale.

"They do." Nik shrugged. "All anybody knows for sure is something unnatural is out in the woods around Rivenloch Palace."

"Isn't the palace abandoned since the old queen died?"

Nik nodded. "It seems whatever's haunting the woods has taken up residence there." He shivered. "A friend of mine knew someone who dared his cousin to go spend the night there, but he said a great mass of thorns had grown up outside, and he couldn't get in. Don't know if he was telling the truth; I've never gone, myself. No sense looking for trouble."

"So you haven't seen anything of this enchantress yourself?"

"Not directly, but there's something out there. It's not just town gossip," the boy said with solemn earnestness. "You won't believe this, but the roses around here have all been turned to stone. Just the flowers, mind, not the bushes."

Ritter glanced over and—even though since stopping at Thorndale he'd hoped and expected to find her—felt a start of recognition as he caught a clear glimpse of her face.

He rose and was about to approach the young woman when the door to the inn slammed open with a loud crash. A well-dressed, golden-haired man entered and pointed an accusing finger at the young woman Ritter had been eavesdropping on.

"That girl," the man snarled into the startled silence, "is the Witch of the Wood!"

CHAPTER SIX

A HUSH settled over the room at the newcomer's announcement. All gazes fixed on Karyna. The innkeeper, having just returned to the common room, narrowed his eyes.

"Why don't you come in, Master Egan, and have a pint on the house?"

"I'm telling you, that girl is trouble. She needs to be locked up!" the man said, stabbing his finger at Karyna with every word.

Nik rose and edged away from Karyna. His expression had changed from friendly to suspicious. "She was just asking questions about the Witch," he added nervously.

"Now hold on a minute." The innkeeper raised a hand. "There's no reason to get excited. Let's all sit down and be reasonable."

"She attacked me on the road," Egan asserted. "She's got a beast doing her bidding."

"Come now, good master." The innkeeper raised his hands in a calming gesture. "The Witch of the Wood is just a story, everyone knows that. This young woman is a guest here; you can't accuse my guests of such things."

"She's a black enchantress," the man growled, his face contorted with rage. "Her beast nearly killed my Eska, my lead dog. Nearly snapped his back in half! He did kill several of my other dogs!"

A murmur rippled through the common room. Karyna cringed, her mind racing.

"Well, miss?" The innkeeper turned to Karyna. "Would you like to respond to this accusation?"

Karyna felt panic welling up, but she fought it down. "This man did approach me on the road," she admitted, but then she raised her chin with a haughty air. "He offered to help me after his dogs spooked my horse and she ran away. When he realized I was alone, he claimed I owed him compensation for allowing me to travel through his wood. He . . . insulted me." Her eyes flashed.

The innkeeper's expression grew troubled. "Then what happened?"

Karyna opened her mouth but closed it wordlessly. The silence in the room grew heavy and tense.

"I see." The innkeeper twisted his mouth to the side as though trying to avoid what he had to say next. "I'm no expert in these matters, and these are strong accusations on both sides. I'm afraid I'm going to have to ask you to stay here while we make the necessary arrangements. Nik, please show the lady to the private suite."

"What? Why?" Karyna burst out, leaping to her feet. "I was accosted on a free road by one of your people, and I am the one under suspicion?"

"These are troubled times, miss. I do apologize, but if you will not defend yourself, I have to wonder what you're hiding." The innkeeper addressed himself to his daughter. "Alys, please go fetch Lord Pentworth's steward. He will judge between these two."

"This is unbelievable!" Karyna bristled as Nik gingerly took her by the elbow and steered her up the stairs. "How can they believe his story?"

"Times are hard. We've all seen and heard unnatural things, things that scared away most everybody else," Nik muttered. "Master Egan is Lord Pentworth's son. Most of the people downstairs owe allegiance to his family in one way or another."

"I have important business." Karyna spoke stiffly, trying to sound like Princess Bellenya when she was being her most regal. "You must let me go."

Nik glanced at her out of the corner of his eye as he led her to the last room in the hallway. "Or you'll do what?" he asked. "Cast a spell on me, I'll bet."

Karyna let out an exasperated explosion of breath. "No, of course not! I don't have magic."

"You have a beast at your command," Nik's said, sounding both awed and frightened. He held a candle in one hand to light their way, and the light flickered as his hand trembled.

"Do you really believe that?"

The lad looked thoughtful. "Master Egan may not be my favorite person in the world," he said slowly, "but I've never known him to outright lie."

"Do you think I'm lying?" Karyna raised her eyebrows.

"No," Nik replied. "But I did notice you haven't denied it, either." He unlocked the door. "Don't worry, miss, I'm sure this will all get cleared up soon."

"With my word against Lord Pentworth's son's." Karyna sniffed, struggling to disguise her fear. "I'm sure I'll get true justice." She watched Nik flinch and regretted her sarcasm. This wasn't his fault, after all.

He pushed the door open and gestured for her to enter. Karyna gathered up as much dignity as possible and stepped across the threshold into her makeshift prison. To her relief, Nik offered her his candle before he closed the door behind her. As she heard the latch fall, Karyna felt a mixture of emotions threaten to overwhelm her. Her stomach fluttered at the thought of what the villagers might be planning to do with her. She had no way to convince them she was not a threat, for she would not betray Barend even to save herself.

Cold fury at the thought of Egan getting away with his villainy rose up in her throat, choking her and filling her eyes with angry tears. A part of her wanted to bang on the door and shout that she was the victim, while another part of her wanted to huddle in a corner and cry. Neither of those actions would help, however, so she wiped away the tears before they could fall and focused on her surroundings, holding up her candle to better see.

The window of the room was large enough to fit through, and it faced toward the dark forest. But further inspection showed that even though it did open, she was too high off the ground to escape that way. The room was luxurious, meant for well-paying guests. The bed was an actual feather-stuffed mattress covered in heavy blankets. She considered knotting the blankets together and lowering herself out the window, but they might not hold a knot securely, and she wasn't sure what she could fix them to in the room and still have enough length to reach the ground safely. She stored the idea in case things got desperate.

A light thwap on the outside wall of her room pulled Karyna from her thoughts. Frowning, she ventured to the open window and peered out. She heard several more thumps, these much louder, and then a man's face appeared in her window. She leaped back in alarm, a scream forming in her throat.

"Please, please don't be frightened," the man said, "I'm not here to harm you, Karyna. I'm here to get you out of there."

The scream died in her throat, and all that escaped her lips was a stuttering croak. By the gleam of her candle she saw that the man was handsome, with dark brown hair and dark eyes that were very familiar. Closer inspection revealed that he was clinging to a rope that must be attached to a chimney. He had another rope tied around his body like a harness, and she could see that he was using this to keep from falling.

Karyna let out a gasp. "Prince Ritter? What are you doing here?"

"So you do remember me." Ritter grinned. And remember him she did: Prince Barend's younger brother, always the handsome rogue even when they were children. How long was it since she'd even thought of him? Of course she had assumed he would be in Norvue, preparing to step into his older brother's role as Crown Prince; for as time passed and the curse remained unbroken, the world would have to continue turning without Barend.

Yet here was Ritter hanging outside her window, quite impossible, and grinning as though this was the finest of jokes.

"As for what I'm doing here," he continued, "I should think that would be obvious. I'm looking for my brother." His grin faded. "I don't mean to rush you, but if you'd like to escape, *now* would be good. This harness is not the most comfortable thing I've ever worn."

Karyna eyed him skeptically. "You want me to . . ."

Ritter twisted until he was facing away from her. "Climb on my back. I'll lower us down."

"I don't think so." Karyna gazed at the rope with distrust.

"I remember you being more adventurous when we were younger." Ritter glanced back over his shoulder, raising a mischievous eyebrow. "Don't worry, I won't let you fall."

Still she hesitated.

"Look, Karyna, I don't know what they're planning to do with you, but do you really want to wait around to find out?" All trace of mischief left his face, and his eyes became serious.

Footsteps and voices in the hall outside her room galvanized Karyna into action. Setting her candle aside, she clambered up to the window and perched herself precariously on the sill. "Are you sure?" she asked.

"For the few seconds it will take us to reach the ground? Yes, I'm sure," he huffed.

Karyna eased her way through the window and wrapped her arms around his neck. She pressed her face against his shoulder and squeezed her eyes shut. "I'm ready," she said, her stomach lurching.

She pictured the rope giving way or Ritter losing his grip as they plummeted to the ground. The idea was almost enough to send her lunging back to the window. But they began to descend, and it was too late to change her mind. Ritter lowered them easily, his makeshift harness holding strong. They landed so gently, Karyna was not aware they had reached the ground.

"You can let go now." There was a hint of amusement in Ritter's voice. Karyna loosed her hold on his neck and dropped a few inches. Her feet touched the solid ground, and she opened her eyes and looked up to see Ritter's white teeth flash in a grin.

"That was terrifying," she admitted.

"But good sport." He chuckled. "Come, our horses are just down the road a bit. I already liberated your mare."

They raced away from the inn, the darkness of the evening enveloping them in its cool embrace and hiding them from anyone who might have been watching. The sky was overcast, so neither the moon nor the stars betrayed their passing. They reached the spot where Ritter had tied their horses and clambered up into their saddles.

Ritter reined his horse toward the road, but Karyna stopped him. "Not that way," she said.

Ritter pulled his horse to a halt and looked back at her. Karyna could barely make out his face, but she could tell he was startled. "Where to, then?" he asked.

"I'm going to Rivenloch Palace. I think the answer to breaking the curse is there, and I remember the way."

Ritter paused. "A servant at Thorndale Castle mentioned Rivenloch. Do you have reason to think the answer is there?"

Karyna nodded wordlessly. She did not know whether he would believe and accompany her or simply think she was crazy, but she found she did not care. No matter what Ritter did next, she was going to see this journey through.

"You think the curse can be broken? My brother could come home?"

Karyna squared her shoulders and nodded. "I do."

"Right. Lead on, then."

CHAPTER SEVEN

KARYNA FOUND the overgrown road leading off the highway, and she and Ritter walked their horses into the darkness. "How far from the highway is this palace?" Ritter inquired after a time.

"A long way. I don't remember exactly," Karyna admitted. "We always traveled in a carriage." How different those journeys with Princess Bellenya had been, filled with girlish laughter and anticipation!

Finally, after they had put a good distance between themselves and Mirhaven, Ritter halted his horse.

"We cannot ride farther tonight, we might lose our way in the dark," he said. "Besides, it's getting late and I could use some rest."

Karyna did not want to stop, but she had already twice caught herself dozing off in her saddle, so she agreed. They found a sheltered spot where Ritter built a small campfire.

"I'll make us something warm to drink," he offered. He pulled a wineskin from his saddlebags and set to warming the red liquid in a pot over the fire.

Before long they sat together on a log, with steaming pewter cups warming their hands. Karyna felt the weight of Ritter's curious gaze on her. "What do you want to know?" she asked.

"Everything. Is it true Barend was transformed into a beast? That he cannot leave Thorndale Castle without losing his mind?"

Karyna nodded.

"Does anyone know how it happened? Or why?"

Karyna took a small sip from her cup and shook her head.

"Were you there that night?" Ritter's expression was strangely hopeful.

While the fire crackled and sent sparks skyward, Karyna stared off into the night. She did not often dwell on the events of that fateful night. She preferred to push such memories to the periphery and focus her attention on more present and pressing matters. But now she let it all come back. The memory no longer threatened to crush her like it once had, but it still pressed down on her shoulders, a load much too heavy for one person to bear alone.

"The palace staff spent weeks getting everything ready for the ball," she began. "As you know, the royal family of Suvall has always had a strain of magic running through their veins, the gift of a fairy godmother from generations ago. At eighteen they begin to see their powers manifest."

"I remember Bellenya talking about that when we were children."

Karyna sighed as memories of happier times swirled through her thoughts and vanished. "On the day of her birthday, Bellenya had worked herself into a frenzy. It was more than just her birthday and the ball. She talked all week about a 'special guest' and hinted that something even more exciting than magic might be in store for her. She never came right out and said it, but I assumed she expected Barend to propose. I know how much she admired him."

Ritter gazed steadily into the snapping fire. "Everyone admired Barend," he agreed. "Do you know if he did propose?"

Karyna hesitated. "I don't know. I never asked him," she admitted. "He doesn't remember much about that night."

"I see." Ritter frowned at the fire, a strange expression for the habitually cheerful prince. "Please, go on."

"The night of the ball, everything was perfect. Bellenya was radiant in the gown I had helped her choose." Karyna smiled at the memory. "It was lovely. Plum satin with a short train that flowed to the ground and swirled around her feet when she walked. The neckline was worked with pearls and silver embroidery. It had sheer hanging sleeves and a silver belt . . ." Karyna trailed off with a chuckle. "Forgive me, I'm sure you don't care about her gown. You must understand, it was all we talked about for weeks."

Ritter grinned. "Bellenya always loved dressing well. If you were at the ball, how did you escape the curse?"

"Bellenya," she replied. "She was going to walk in the gardens, so she sent me to fetch her a shawl. She claimed it was because the night was cool, but I knew she just wanted a few minutes alone with Barend." Karyna wrapped her arms around herself. "I was on my way back to the Throne Room when . . ." She felt her throat close of its own accord. Cold washed over her along with the memory. She wanted to run to her father and have him wrap his strong arms around her and make the world safe again. Her voice trembled as she continued, "I'm sorry, I cannot describe what happened next. I felt the floor shudder beneath my feet, and the air grew icy. The candles flickered. And then the screaming started."

"The people in the ballroom were screaming?" Ritter asked, now staring at her, his eyes wide.

"No. Just one person," Karyna shivered and took a sip of warmed wine, remembering. The sound had been terrifying and otherworldly, yet also filled with grief. Even now she felt a twinge of sympathy for the screamer. "I don't know who it was, but it was horrible. I dropped the shawl and raced to the open doors. The curse rolled in from the garden like a great cloud of smoke. The queen started to rise, but before she could take a step the curse lashed through the room. I did the only thing I could think to do: I shut the doors and ran." Karyna grimaced. "I didn't get far. I tripped over the shawl I had dropped. I don't know how long I lay there, but when I got up . . ." Karyna paused, unable to speak past the lump in her throat.

The light from the fire flickered in Ritter's eyes, revealing there a deep sorrow. "I know the rest," he said. "Barend sent a message home, explaining what had happened and how he could not return. Our parents hired every wizard and enchantress in the land. They offered a reward to anyone who could break the curse."

"At least they had a sensible plan," Karyna replied. "The minor nobles of Suvall decided that true love was the cure. They began sending their daughters to the castle, hoping one of them would fall in love with the prince and break the curse."

Ritter's lips twitched. "Interesting theory. I'll bet Barend loved that."

"Don't laugh!" Karyna wrinkled her nose at him. "It was awful. There was no order to it at all. Sometimes we'd get half a dozen girls on our doorstep all on the same day."

Ritter laughed anyway. His laughter worked a soothing effect upon Karyna, a magic of its own. She felt her heavy heart lifting and discovered a smile upon her face, as unexpected as a rose in winter. She put a hand to her cheek, oddly embarrassed that she should be laughing when the curse was still so dreadful, still so strong. But she remembered now how Ritter always managed to bring out the best and brightest even in the worst situations.

"Why are you here, though?" she asked him.

He took another sip from his cup then stretched his legs out before him, groaning a little and rubbing one knee. "Same as you: I want to break the curse. I turn twenty-one in a week, and my parents want to name me Crown Prince in Barend's absence."

"So they agreed to let you take a dangerous journey by yourself right before they hand you the kingdom?" Karyna eyed him. "What aren't you telling me?"

Ritter had the grace to look abashed. "I'm not exactly here with my parents' blessing." Karyna said nothing, and Ritter squirmed. "Or their knowledge," he added.

"I see."

Uncomfortable, Ritter set aside his cup and leaned forward, resting his elbows on his knees. "Why are you undertaking this journey? Surely there are others who could be sent."

"No. After the curse fell, the servants began leaving. Nobody wanted to stay in an enchanted castle or have a beast for a master—especially since he's from another kingdom."

Ritter sobered. "You stayed."

"My father is inside the Throne Room," Karyna replied.

Ritter winced at this unexpected bit of news. It was bad enough knowing that his brother had been turned into a monster, but at least Barend could still move and talk. What would it be like to have a loved one trapped forever in unyielding stone? "I'm so sorry." Ritter's tone held equal parts of sympathy and horror. He did not know what else to say. "My brother . . . It feels selfish to ask, but is he . . ."

"He is well," Karyna replied, understanding the unspoken question.

"But he's so . . ."

"So what?"

"Frustrated. He tries not to show it, but he can't hide it from me. He's homesick and angry . . . and he tends to take it out on the furniture."

Ritter's keen eyes lingered on Karyna speculatively. "You've been close to him, haven't you?"

Karyna felt her face grow warm and hid her discomfiture by pretending to take a long sip from her empty cup. Ritter watched her, his expression amused, as if he knew exactly what she was doing.

Karyna avoided his gaze. It was true. Bellenya had not been alone in her admiration of Barend. But Karyna had always known he was meant to marry a princess. Even as Bellenya's lady-in-waiting, she had no reason to think Barend would ever look at her. Could it be that part of her was grateful for the curse, for keeping Barend close to her? She would never be able to live with herself if that were true.

She stood up suddenly, dusting off her skirts, and prepared to pack up her cup and Ritter's. "I must sleep. I can't keep my eyes open any longer."

Ritter grinned but did not press the matter. "I'll keep watch for a bit. Tomorrow I'd like to hear more about this plan you have for breaking the curse."

CHAPTER EIGHT

THE NEXT morning, Ritter and Karyna resumed their journey. The weight lifted from Karyna's shoulders as they traveled. Having someone to talk to besides her horse felt like seeing the sun burst from behind the clouds after a long winter storm. Ritter had always been a charming companion, and his presence and easy friendship made the journey far more enjoyable. He turned everything into an adventure, and his smile was infectious.

The forest was deep and dark, but sunlight filtered down through the emerald canopy and dotted the ground. As they rode, Karyna explained to Ritter about her dreams, the roses turning to stone, and how she believed the curse had been cast by an enchantress who had kidnapped Bellenya and was hiding in Rivenloch Palace.

"You mean you were planning on facing this enchantress alone?"

Ritter asked, incredulous. "You don't have any idea how to break the curse, do you?"

Karyna picked invisible burs from Pippa's mane. "I thought I'd figure something out along the way." She gestured expansively. "I sort of believed the dreams would tell me what to do, but they stopped the night I left. I've only had one since, and it wasn't particularly helpful."

"I guess I shouldn't be surprised," Ritter said at length. "After all, you're the one who convinced Barend, Bellenya, and me that it would be a good idea to climb that pine tree so we could slide down the branches and land in the snowdrifts."

"It was a good idea," Karyna retorted, but her eyes sparkled at the memory. "In fact, it was an excellent idea! Especially when you consider that I was only eight years old at the time and the youngest in the group. I'd never seen a tree like that before, or that much snow. It looked perfect for sliding, and it was. Admit it—it was great fun!"

"It was . . . until Bellenya got the sash of her dress caught on a branch and none of us could get her down." Ritter chuckled heartily, his dark eyes alive with laughter. "I'll never forget the sight of her hanging there, arms sticking out of her cloak sleeves, legs kicking. I thought she would be stuck there forever!"

Karyna laughed. "Barend was the only one of us with any sense. He ran straight to your father."

"Who came running through the snow with a groundskeeper and a ladder."

"I couldn't believe it when the king went racing up the ladder to rescue Bellenya." Karyna shook her head. "I always was a little in awe of your father after that."

Ritter grinned. "We're not quite as formal in Norvue. I remember the day Barend and I learned that the hard way."

"Oh?" Karyna's eyes widened. "You're talking about the time you visited during the Feast of Christouge? I've always wondered: Wherever did you and Barend find all those frogs?"

Ritter's laughter rang through the forest. "I'm not telling. We were sent home in disgrace. No desserts, no free time, just lessons and chores for weeks on end. It was worth it, though, to see all those stuffy courtiers jumping up and down and trying to scream politely!"

Karyna smiled at the memory. "It was certainly one of the more interesting balls I've attended." She and Bellenya had always looked forward to Barend and Ritter's visits, and they had enjoyed traveling north to visit Norvue, as well. The brothers had always been full of fun ideas, and both girls were more than willing to dive into whatever adventure the young princes planned. They had spent many afternoons wading in the creek, panning for gold, climbing trees, and digging holes. They had sparred with sticks and played at being knights. Even though Barend was five years older than Ritter and Bellenya, he had never hesitated to join them in their various exploits. "Tell me this, then: Were the frogs your idea or Barend's?"

"Barend's," Ritter admitted. "But it was Bellenya who told us where to get them."

Karyna snapped her fingers. "I knew it!" she said. "Bellenya would never confess, but I knew she was involved. She was always showing off for Barend, always going that extra step to impress him."

"We all were," Ritter replied. "Admit it: Even you were constantly looking for his approval."

"I was simply glad to be included at all," Karyna admitted, her cheeks turning pink. "But Bellenya . . . she went further out of her way to get his attention than anyone else."

"Do you think Bellenya is being held prisoner at Rivenloch?" Ritter asked, an inscrutable expression on his face. "Do you believe the curse can be broken?"

"Yes," Karyna said, her tone firm. "I have to. Anything else would mean . . ." She trailed off, feeling less confident than she sounded. If Bellenya was not at Rivenloch, then the dreams had meant nothing and all her efforts had been in vain. The curse would continue; Barend would remain trapped in a land that was not his home, and her father would be lost to her forever.

Karyna pressed her lips together, defiance rising in her spirit. That could not be true. She refused to let it be true.

Ritter winced apologetically. "I'm sorry. I forgot about your father."

"No need to apologize," Karyna said, waving a hand. "I know most people have given up on a happy ending. But I can't. I have to hope."

"Me too," Ritter replied.

The beast prowled through the forest just out of sight, following her and the scent of roses that clung to her. His massive paws made no sound as he stalked through the underbrush, silent as a fawn. He knew not where she was going, and he cared not. He followed. That was his duty.

Laughter rang through the forest and the beast crouched close to the ground, his senses wary. The other who now traveled with her was not wholly welcome, but he was not a threat like the first. This one seemed to make her happy, and so the beast allowed him to stay. He wished he could make her happy, wished he could be the reason for her laughter. But he seemed to be only a source of sadness for her, so he remained in the shadows, allowing her to catch small glimpses of him through the trees when the other was not looking.

He did not know why he made her sad, but he wished her to know he was there, still protecting her.

Finally, after taking a few unintentional detours, Ritter and Karyna came within sight of their destination on the third morning after leaving Mirhaven. It was not a sight either of them expected. A thick hedge of thorn bushes ringed the palace. Hanging on the living vines were roses in full bloom, each one turned to stone. Above this thorny barrier they could see that the palace itself had fallen into a sorry state of disrepair. Snaking vines climbed its walls, cracking the stones in various places.

Ritter glanced at Karyna, his eyes wide. "I thought you said Rivenloch has only been empty for a few years. What happened here?" he asked.

Karyna felt numb. The palace held many happy childhood memories for her; it was painful to see it so dilapidated. She and Bellenya had spent pleasant summers here when they were younger, visiting Bellenya's grandmother. Her Majesty Queen Noureen, the dowager queen of Suvall, had always been very kind, and had treated Karyna like a second granddaughter.

"I have no idea," she breathed, her heart aching.

"I'm guessing we need to go inside?" It was not really a question, but Ritter disliked the look of the thorny hedge and was uncertain he trusted the palace not to collapse on top of them once they were inside. "Why would the enchantress bring Bellenya here?"

"I wish I knew," Karyna replied. She stared at the thorns before them, feeling overwhelmed. The weight she had struggled to bear since the curse first fell now crashed with renewed power on her shoulders, sending her spiraling down into despair. She had no idea how to proceed.

Ritter noticed Karyna's plight. He drew his sword and, in spite of the somber atmosphere that clung to the once-beautiful palace, he threw a grin

Karyna's way. "It's a good thing I came along when I did," he teased. "You never would have finished your quest without me."

"Apparently your brother got all the humility in the family," Karyna shot back, just barely refraining from sticking out her tongue.

Ritter raised an eyebrow and then shrugged. "He can keep it," he said. "I got all the good looks."

Moved by Ritter's twinkling eyes and casual humor, Karyna's firm control over her emotions finally snapped. She began to laugh. Many conflicted feelings raged in her breast, a tempest that threatened to overwhelm her though she struggled to regain control. Everything about her journey suddenly seemed absurd. She had traveled all this way because of dreams. If, indeed, the dreams were true, they promised that the enchantress within was wrathful and cruel, and possibly quite mad. The thought of facing such a being, even with Ritter and Barend at her side, frightened her. Even more terrifying was the thought that they would find nothing at all inside. She took a deep breath and managed to stop the fit of hysterical laughter.

Ritter looked at her askance. "Nothing for it, then." He grimaced and raised his sword—hoping what he was about to do wouldn't irreparably damage its blade—and began hacking at the thick, thorny vines.

Branches fell. Wood chips flew. Ritter chopped and swung his sword, its blade biting into the vines that barred the way.

"Ritter! Stop!" Karyna said.

"What is it?" he asked, turning toward her and wiping his face on his sleeve.

"It's not working."

Ritter looked at the vines. She was right. Branches lay on the ground all around him, but the hedge was just as thick as it had been when he started. He blinked.

Karyna touched one of the vines gently. "There is magic here," she said.

Ritter stuck the tip of his sword in the dirt and leaned on it wearily. "Wonderful. How do you propose we get through it, then?"

"One moment, please." Karyna hurried to her horse and rummaged through her saddlebags. She made a triumphant noise and returned wearing her gloves and holding her pruning shears.

"You thought you might have time for a little gardening on your journey, did you?" Ritter asked, arching an eyebrow.

"Of course not." Karyna did not so much as look Ritter's way, focused on the task at hand. "These were in my satchel already; I forgot to take them out before I left." She knelt at the base of the nearest rosebush, excitement and nervousness clashing together inside her. She was sure this was the way in, as sure as she had been that Rivenloch was where she needed to go. And yet, the enormity of the task before her was like an insurmountable wall. But she had to try.

She set to work, removing the dead wood. Ritter helped her pull the dead vines and branches away, tossing them into the forest as Karyna directed. Next she removed the stone roses from the vines with tender care. They might be in full bloom, but she could not believe they were good for the plants. When she finished, she looked with a critical eye at the bush she was tending and began snipping off the tallest branches, giving the bush a more pleasing shape. The thorns rustled and parted, allowing Karyna to enter the barrier and work on the next part of the hedge.

Ritter made a startled sound behind her. "Did you see that?" he asked.

Karyna nodded but did not stop. She was wholly focused on her task. It was tedious, exhausting work, but with each bush she tended, the hedge opened a bit more until they emerged on the other side and were standing before the thick wooden doors of the palace. Karyna laid down her shears and pulled off her gloves with a weary sigh. She glanced back, half-expecting to see their passage blocked.

Behind them, the path remained open, and Karyna was startled to notice that the plants she had so gently tended were already bearing new buds near blossoming. These buds were living, with the barest hint of red petals peeking through. Hope sprang afresh in her heart and she started forward, but Ritter held her back with a steadying hand on her shoulder.

"Wait," he said, and patted the hilt of his sword. "Though it didn't help against the thorns, perhaps I should go first, just in case." He pushed the doors open.

Time had been far kinder to the interior of the palace, though the air was cold and smelled musty. Four lit torches hung in sconces on each side of the large entryway. A suit of armor stood below each torch, all eight polished to a bright shine.

"Someone has been caring for . . ." Karyna broke off, blinking in disbelief. "Did that suit of armor just move?"

Ritter eyed the offending knight and then shook his head. "Might have been a draft," he muttered. "The armor's empty."

Even as he spoke, every helmet in the hall swiveled toward them in sharp, military precision.

Karyna yelped, her eyes wide. "Are you sure?" A prickling sensation crawled down her spine. The barrier of thorns outside was one thing, but facing suits of armor that moved on their own was quite another.

"Um." Ritter drew his sword then motioned with his other hand. "Get back. I'm not sure these empty suits are a threat, but there's no sense in taking chances."

Karyna darted behind him as the "knight" nearest them drew its own sword and stepped away from the wall. Others followed suit, and a wave of terror washed over her. The first knight reached them and swung its sword at Ritter's head. Ritter ducked and whirled then stabbed his own sword into a vulnerable space under the arm. The knight did not notice but attacked again, swinging its sword with vicious and terrible force.

"There's nobody inside!" Karyna shrieked. "You can't fight as though they can be wounded!"

"Right," Ritter shouted back, sounding embarrassed. He brought his sword down again, this time severing the clasps holding the right arm to the breastplate. The arm and sword fell to the ground with a deafening clatter.

The knight did not acknowledge the loss but continued its determined stride. It punched with its left fist, but Ritter dodged the clumsy blow and swung his sword at the knight's legs. The entire suit of armor collapsed and rolled across the hall with loud clangs and crashes.

There was no time to rest, for there were seven more suits of armor converging upon them. Karyna scrambled forward and picked up the fallen knight's sword. Together, she and Ritter faced their lifeless attackers. The sword was heavy in her hands, and Karyna had no idea what to do with it, but she felt that having a weapon was better than nothing.

The other suits of armor were quicker than the first, descending upon the two travelers with deadly intent. But Ritter moved like a whirlwind. His sword spun and slashed and sliced through the air with precision and power. Another knight fell to the floor as Ritter parried and dodged and stabbed, all while keeping his body between the enemy and Karyna, shielding her from harm with his every move. Though the knights appeared to have little in the way of initiative, they were many, and Ritter was only one.

Karyna saw the strike that made it through Ritter's defense. Crimson blood fell on the white marble of the floor, and Ritter growled in pain, stumbling. The misstep threw him into danger from another knight, and Karyna acted without thinking. She swung her sword like a club at the knight's legs. Her technique was raw, but her aim was true, and the knight collapsed to the floor, falling to pieces. One of its comrades tripped over the leg of the suit of armor Karyna had felled, and it also clattered to the floor.

Recovering himself, Ritter faced the remaining four knights. He stood, breathing heavily, and surveyed his opponents. His arm pained him, and he knew he could not face so many opponents alone. A breeze tickled the back of his neck, and an idea lifted his spirits. He let out a shrill, piercing whistle. The knights hesitated at the sound, but when nothing happened, they began to move toward Ritter as one.

A moment later, Tarak burst into the palace through the still-open door, his hooves clattering on the marble tiles. At a word from his master, the sorrel stallion reared and crashed down on one of the knights, sending it rolling in pieces, while Ritter swiftly took out another. The two remaining knights put up a determined fight, but they were no match for a well-trained warhorse. Ritter and Tarak made short work of them.

When the last piece of armor lay inert on the ground, Ritter patted Tarak's cheek, and the horse nickered affectionately. "Thanks, old friend," the prince said, leaning his forehead against the stallion's neck. "I owe you one." Stepping back, he ordered, "Now head on out and tell Pippa what a great hero you are." He gave the horse's red rump a parting slap.

Tarak shook himself with a tremendous rattle of leather and metal then clopped down the front steps with massive dignity.

Only then did Ritter glance at Karyna. "That was quick thinking back there. Thank you."

Karyna dropped her sword, her limbs all atremble. "I, um . . . You're welcome. You're hurt?"

Ritter looked down at the wound on his arm and winced. "It's not deep."

"I'd still like to look at it, if you don't mind."

The prince sank to the floor and submitted to Karyna's gentle ministrations. He was correct: The wound was not deep, but it was a sizable gash. She bound it tightly with cloth from her satchel.

"Thank you." Ritter moved his arm around. It still hurt a bit, but he was satisfied that it wouldn't be a hindrance. "Well, now we're inside. Do you have any thoughts on where we should look for the enchantress?"

Karyna closed her eyes and concentrated, straining to remember every detail of her dreams. A sense of peace flooded through her, and she opened her eyes. "The Queen's Parlor. It's at the top of the southeast tower," she replied. "We should start there."

"Lead the way," Ritter said gamely.

Karyna led them down lavishly decorated hallways. Everything was just as she remembered it. Tall white columns soared from floor to ceiling. Elaborate chandeliers covered in diamond pendants caught the light streaming in through the large windows and cast sparkles on cream-colored walls. Paintings of roses and forest scenes hung in the rooms they passed. It was all so very familiar. The enchantress did not seem to have disturbed anything. Karyna marveled at how clean the passages were, especially when she considered how hard she and Setella struggled to keep Thorndale Castle in good repair. She had not expected an evil enchantress to be so concerned with tidiness.

At the end of a hallway, between two large open rooms, they arrived at the base of a spiral staircase. Karyna pointed, indicating their destination, but she paused before beginning the climb.

"What is it?" Ritter asked quietly.

"It's probably nothing," Karyna replied. "I was just remembering that the Queen's Parlor was Bellenya's favorite room. We'd play Nine Men's Morris and Fox and Geese up there on rainy days, while Her Majesty did needlework and told us stories." She felt wistful and a little sad, but she straightened her shoulders. "Up we go."

"Let me go first," Ritter murmured.

Karyna stepped aside, and the prince mounted the stairs, his soft-soled boots making little sound on the steps. Just before she followed him, Karyna caught a glimpse of a dark shape passing outside the window of the room to her right. She knew instinctively that it was Barend, and she was comforted, knowing he was still with them.

Upon reaching the door at the top of the stairs, Ritter tried the latch. It lifted with ease, and the door swung open on silent hinges. They entered the large room and peered around. The parlor was darker than the rest of the palace, and it took their eyes a moment to adjust to the gloom.

The interior was far simpler than Karyna remembered. Nearly all the furniture and decor had been removed. A thin pallet lay against the far wall, covered with rumpled blankets. To their right was a wooden table, upon which rested a glass vase.

And suspended above the vase, as if shunning any attempt at containment, floated a brilliant red rose. The flower cast a soft pink glow around itself.

Entranced, Karyna crossed the room, her quest momentarily forgotten at the overwhelming, enchanting beauty of the rose. Without thinking, she reached out her hand to caress its petals.

"Don't touch that!" a voice hissed, and what they had taken for a pile of blankets exploded to life and crossed the room with surprising speed. Karyna found herself yanked backwards by a powerful arm around her neck. She tried to pull away, but the hold on her throat tightened.

"That's *mine*," the voice snarled in her ear.

CHAPTER NINE

R ITTER RAISED his sword, preparing to spring to Karyna's defense.

"Take one step and she dies." The words flew at him like daggers.

Ritter froze, assessing the scene before him. Karyna's eyes were strangely calm, cloaked in the steady composure he had grown to admire over the past few days. Holding her by the throat was a pale woman, taller than Karyna by several inches and terribly thin. Long dark hair cascaded over hunched shoulders in unkempt, tangled waves. The remains of an exquisite plum-satin gown hung from her frame in rags and tatters. Her gaunt face was heart-shaped and could have been lovely but for the expression of rage and hatred etched there in harsh lines.

It was a face Ritter recognized, despite its twisted features.

"Bellenya?" Ritter's throat and mouth suddenly went dry. Confusion made his head swim, and the ground beneath his feet seemed to spin. He licked his lips, fighting the sudden throbbing in his temples. "What . . ." He locked gazes with Karyna and saw his own bewilderment mirrored on her face.

"Drop your sword!" the woman cried, her eyes flashing.

Ritter complied then raised his hands in a gesture of peace. "We mean you no harm, Bellenya," he said hoarsely. "We are here to help. Just . . . please, let her go."

A rasping, mocking laugh escaped Bellenya's throat.

"Bellenya?" Karyna's voice wavered. "Princess? It's me. Karyna."

There was a startled intake of breath, and then Bellenya shoved Karyna away and retreated. Karyna stumbled forward and would have fallen, but Ritter moved swiftly to catch her. He helped her regain her balance, and she rested a hand on the corner of the table, catching her breath. Her eyes flicked to the vase in the center of the table then toward Ritter, her gaze confused and troubled.

"Are you all right?" Ritter asked.

Karyna nodded and turned toward the princess. "Bellenya!"

"What do you want with me?" Bellenya's voice rasped as she recoiled into the shadows beyond the glow of the rose. The ruined train of her gown snaked in her wake.

"We've come to bring you home," Karyna said, holding her hands out as if to embrace the princess. "You're safe now. Come with us before the enchantress returns."

"Karyna," Ritter spoke softly; his voice held a note of warning. "I don't think there is an enchantress."

Her brow furrowing, she cast him a sideways glance. "What do you mean?"

His head had stopped throbbing, but the ache was still there. He saw the denial in Karyna's eyes, denial he wished he could embrace, because the truth was too painful to bear. He spoke the words though he feared they would sear his tongue. "Bellenya cast the curse."

"That's not possible," Karyna argued, but her protest was weak. "It can't be."

"Bellenya," Ritter said, feeling as though his throat might close around the words. "Why?"

The shadow beyond the rose leaped forward, and the pink glow illuminated a haggard face, a weird mask of the beauty Bellenya had once been. "Why?" she snarled. "You ask me why? In all this time, has he admitted how he wronged me? He never came to find me! No one came, no one cared. Has he come to beg forgiveness? Well, he will never have it!"

"What are you talking about?" Ritter demanded. "What happened to you, Bellenya?"

"He rejected me!"

The words exploded from the broken princess's throat like thunder roaring across the sky. Her face crumpled in pain, and her wrath spread out from her like a terrible tempest. The air in the chamber grew chill, and a wind howled around the room, catching Karyna and pushing her off balance. When she caught herself on the table, the impact knocked over the vase, which fell to the floor and shattered into a thousand tiny fragments.

The rose that had hovered above the vase also fell to the floor and lay amid shards of glass.

Bellenya let out an anguished wail and threw herself upon the rose, her hands scrabbling for it, lifting it tenderly and cradling it to her bosom. Karyna and Ritter backed away, uncomprehending.

Then the shadow of the princess stood, and darkness shimmered around her. Ritter watched, helpless, as her aspect wavered and changed.

She seemed to grow taller, looming over them. Her skin became even paler, and her fingers warped into long, wicked claws. Shadows like wings sprouted from her shoulders, and her eyes grew wild and fierce. She was still Bellenya, but she was no longer the princess. Now she was every inch an enchantress.

Holding the rose in one clawed hand, she cast a murderous look at Karyna. "You!" she hissed. "You will pay."

Bellenya raised a hand and motioned ferociously. The shards of glass whirled in a sudden tornado and spun toward Karyna. Ritter was helpless to stop it. He heard himself shouting at Bellenya as he tried to reach Karyna in time, but before he could take a second breath, a huge shape crashed through the window and landed in front of Karyna, shielding her from the glass.

"Barend, no!" Karyna shouted, and Ritter stared in wonder at the beast who was his brother.

The glass shards did not appear to penetrate the beast's thick fur, and Bellenya hissed in fury. Barend reared up as Bellenya leaped forward and struck him with a raking sweep of her clawed hand, knocking him out of the way with surprising strength. She lunged toward Karyna, who scrambled back, tripped on her long skirt, and fell to the floor. Ritter moved to defend her, but Barend was quicker, leaping to interpose his body between the enchantress and Karyna yet again.

The large room seemed quite small as the two foes clashed together, their growls and screams resounding off the walls as they battered against one another again and again. Bellenya hissed, and orange fire blossomed in her hands. With a snarl she hurled the fire at Barend. It washed over him, and he gave a howl of agony. The air filled with the acrid stink of sulphur.

Ritter coughed and choked as smoke filled the room. Once more he tried in vain to reach Karyna. Part of him desperately wanted to stand and fight alongside his brother, but he knew in his heart that he could do little good against such a foe in open combat.

Bellenya attacked again, hurling Barend across the room. He landed on the table, and it collapsed into kindling beneath him. Seeing an opening, Ritter darted to Karyna and pulled her toward the window as Barend picked himself up off the floor and charged at Bellenya with an inhuman roar.

"When our path is clear, make for the stair and run!" Ritter whispered in Karyna's ear.

She nodded, her face pale, her eyes wide and terrified. Together they awaited their chance.

Though Barend was strong and fierce, much larger than the enchantress, Bellenya was clearly more powerful than he. Their whirling, furious dance of death filled the room. Another burst of magic knocked Barend to the ground; and then Bellenya turned on Karyna, blood dripping from the hand clenched around the stem of her rose. She raised her hand to strike, but Barend was there once more. His jaws clamped down around Bellenya's arm, yanking her to one side.

"Now!" Ritter shouted, and he and Karyna darted across the room, through the door, and down the steps.

The sounds of battle continued behind them as they emerged into the wide hall below. Karyna continued running until she reached one of the doorways to an open sitting room, but there she paused and looked back, trying not to gasp for breath. Ritter had stopped, drawn his sword, and stepped to one side of the stair, where he now stood listening. There was a crashing above, and then the sounds of pursuit came pounding down the steps. Barend burst out into the hall, his claws slipping and skittering on the marble floor. He came to a stop before Karyna and stood staring at her, his sides heaving, then dropped to his belly and laid his heavy head at her feet.

Karyna had time only to murmur, "Oh Barend!" and fall to her knees beside him before Bellenya came hurtling down the final steps, her eyes wild and her entire focus on Barend. But Ritter swung the flat of his sword at Bellenya's legs, tripping her. She sprawled to the ground with a shriek of rage; and before she could rise, Ritter pressed one knee into the middle of her back and pinned her wrists to the floor with his hands.

"Bellenya, stop!" he shouted. His arm ached where it had been wounded, but he ignored the pain. "This isn't you! It's the curse!"

Bellenya snarled and writhed, trying to free herself. "Let me go!" she screamed.

"Stop this!" he shouted again. "Look what the curse is doing to you! Look what it's turned you into! That's Barend and Karyna you're trying to kill, do you hear me? That's *Barend!*"

Bellenya froze, and the fury and hatred drained out of her face. The shadows around her flowed away, shimmered across the floor, and vanished; the enchantress was gone. She quieted, and Ritter slowly backed off, allowing her to rise. She rolled over and sat up, obviously confused, and her gaze met Ritter's.

"What? Ritter?" she whispered. Her gaze fell on Barend, and her face paled. "Oh!" She gave a tiny sob. "W—what have I done?" She cradled the rose to her breast, staring down at its petals, her eyes glassy.

Ritter wearily stood up. He looked at Karyna, who nodded to let him know that both she and Barend were all right. Then he reached down, took Bellenya by one elbow, and lifted her to her feet.

"Bellenya." His stern voice cut through her daze, and she looked up at him. "Can you break the curse?"

She shook her head and raised an arm as if to ward off a blow. "I don't know! I don't know," she moaned. "What have I done? I didn't mean to . . ."

"Can you tell me what happened that night? The night of the ball?" Ritter asked, his tone relentless.

Bellenya turned her face away, shame spreading across her features. "I thought Barend was going to propose. I had dropped hints all evening. We went for a walk, and he picked me a rose, said it was a birthday gift." She paused and took a shuddering breath. "Then . . . he told me I was like a sister to him, that he loved me but could not care for me in that way. He rejected me." Her eyes brimmed over with pain. "I couldn't bear it. I was angry, embarrassed, and hurt. I felt the magic take shape. It spilled out of me. I couldn't control it. I was terrified, so I fled. Darkness closed over me, and when I could see again, I was here."

"Why didn't you come home?" Ritter asked.

"How could I go back to that humiliation? How could I face the gossip, the jeering? I knew they would all be laughing at me behind my back. I couldn't face it. When no one came looking for me, I knew the truth: Nobody cared at all." She stared at Barend, her eyes wide. "I never imagined . . ."

"It's worse than that," Ritter added. "Nobody came looking for you because everyone who was in the Throne Room that night, including your parents, was turned to stone. They've been trapped there as stone statues for the past two years."

Bellenya stared, shocked into silence.

"Can you free them?" Ritter demanded.

Bellenya hid her face in her hands, clasping the rose to her cheek, oblivious to the sharp thorns embedding themselves ever deeper into her skin. "I didn't do it on purpose. I don't know how to undo it!" she wailed.

"Is that the rose Barend gave you?" Ritter asked, his voice thoughtful.

Bellenya gave a tiny sob. "Yes."

"How has it stayed alive all this time?"

"Magic," Bellenya whispered. "I couldn't let it go. It was all I had left of him."

"I think it's time to give it up now, sweet lady," Ritter said quietly, placing his hand over hers. "It's time to forgive my brother and move on."

A shudder passed through the princess's body. "How?" she cried, her voice despairing.

"You've been holding so tightly to your humiliation, your bitterness. That is what has been feeding the curse and keeping the rose alive. Let go of it! It's destroying you. Come home to the people who love you. This," he gestured at her, "this is not you."

Bellenya's whole body convulsed again. Then, closing her eyes, she opened her hands and let the rose fall to the floor.

The air around them turned golden, blinding and brilliant, almost too brilliant to bear. Ritter closed his eyes and flung up his hands in a vain attempt to block the light. But when the light cleared and he dared to look again, he found himself standing beside the rosebush in the Queen's Garden outside Thorndale Castle, along with Bellenya, Karyna, and the beast.

The bush was in full bloom, every rose a brilliant, living scarlet.

Ritter looked down and saw the rose that Bellenya had dropped. He bent down and picked it up, staring in wonder. It had turned to stone.

CHAPTER TEN

BEFORE THEIR eyes the form of the beast blurred and dissipated like fog when the sun kisses it. There stood Barend, dressed in his best raiment as he had been on the night of Bellenya's ball, with no sign of the wounds he had sustained while in beast form. He blinked at them, his expression confused. He took a step toward Karyna and then stopped, staring down at his hands and plucking at his own waistcoat, an expression of wonder on his face. Barend looked up at Karyna, his eyes wide.

"Dear one." He took her hand and held it to his heart, full of emotions he could not express. He had so much to say to her, though just in that moment he could find no words.

"Barend," Karyna breathed, her face alight with joy.

He turned to his brother next. "Ritter!" The two men embraced, their voices inarticulate with exclamations and laughter.

Barend stepped back, holding Ritter at arm's length. "You've grown up," he accused.

"Tried not to." Ritter grinned, a twinkle in his eye.

Barend's eyes found Bellenya at last, and the laughter died on his lips. She had turned away, fingering a leaf on the rosebush. Her shoulders were hunched as if she were trying to turn herself invisible. Barend approached her cautiously.

"I am sorry," he said in a low tone. "I'm so sorry that I could not be what you wanted me to be."

Bellenya kept her eyes fixed on the ground. "I'm the one who's sorry," she whispered. "You offered me friendship, and I paid you back for it with misery. I'm . . . I cannot begin to . . ."

"I forgive you," Barend said simply.

A tear trickled down Bellenya's face. "I don't blame you for not loving me. No one could ever love such a beast as I am." Her eyes filled with anguish as she turned to Karyna. "Karyna, dear friend, can you ever forgive me? I wish I could say I didn't know what I was doing, but . . . I would be lying. A part of me did know."

"Of course I forgive you." Karyna stepped forward and put her arms around Bellenya. Bellenya stiffened for a moment at the embrace, and then she put her face into Karyna's shoulder and sobbed. Karyna patted her back gently.

"There was another reason I could not love you as you wished," Barend said quietly.

Bellenya lifted her head, her face twisted with pain. "Why is that?"

"Because I knew of one who already loved you better than I ever could."

Bellenya startled, pulling back from Karyna, and wiped away tears with one hand. "What? Who?"

Barend hesitated.

"Me. I do." Ritter stepped forward, looking awkward. "I've loved you since we were children. I never said anything because it was obvious your heart was set on Barend, and I didn't know how he felt. I know our parents all hoped for a match between the two of you, and I didn't want to get in the way. But I loved you anyway."

Bellenya swayed wearily. "I . . . I see. Oh, I've been such a fool!" A whimper escaped her lips and she wilted, sinking to the ground, her body shaking with sobs of remorse.

Ritter knelt next to her, his arms wrapping around her. He smoothed her hair with a gentle hand and whispered, "I will always love you."

Bellenya quieted; she continued to weep, but her sobs of heartache were transformed into silent tears of unmerited joy. Barend took Karyna's hand and led her away, leaving Ritter and Bellenya in peace.

On the far side of the garden, the doors leading into the Throne Room opened and people began to emerge, stumbling as they blinked in the sudden light and wearing extremely confused expressions. Happiness filled Karyna's heart, a sweet ache she could hardly bear.

"Papa!" she whispered. "Oh Papa!"

She pulled her hand from Barend's and raced across the garden into the throng of people. She ducked between lords and ladies, past dukes and duchesses, ignoring their exclamations and wrestling her way past those who reached out to stop her and demand answers. Her eyes searched the faces, frantically seeking.

And then she stopped, her heart pounding, her breath catching in her throat. The next instant she threw herself into her father's strong arms, and the floodgates she had tried to hold firmly in place for two years burst open, and she wept and laughed all at once as he held her tightly and whispered her name into her hair. There would be time later for questions and answers and the work that would need to be done to set all to rights. For now, her father was alive, and that was enough.

Pandemonium reigned for several weeks. Emissaries were sent to Norvue to inform the king and queen that the curse had been broken and their son was free, and that both their sons were safe in Thorndale Castle. Word returned swiftly, conveying the royal parents' relief at the news. There was a stern reprimand for Ritter, though the sting of it was lost in their joy at having their elder son returned to them and in their following congratulations on Ritter's engagement to Princess Bellenya.

Those who had been trapped in stone for two years wished to return home, and there was general uproar across the country as news of the curse's end spread. Many rejoiced, though a few were resentful. Lord Fredrig numbered among the latter; he grumbled and tried to stir up trouble, but it never amounted to anything. Ritter and Barend were sequestered away with the king and queen, bringing them up to date on events of the past two years.

The day the curse broke, old Willem the gardener discovered Tarak and Pippa grazing on the royal lawn. The horses gave him and Henry a merry chase before surrendering to a bucket of oats in wise Setella's hands. Both Ritter and Karyna were relieved to learn that their faithful steeds had not been left behind at Rivenloch.

Through all the bustle and activity, Barend longed to speak with Karyna, but he found it difficult to get a moment alone with her and began to fear she might be avoiding him. Finally, after three weeks, life had settled down enough that the princes felt they could return to Norvue. They would be traveling home together, although Ritter would soon return to Suvall for the royal wedding.

On the last night before the princes were to leave Suvall, Karyna took refuge on a bench in a remote part of the garden and stared up at the stars.

A shape loomed out of the shadows—a tall form with a white shirtfront, not the familiar bulk of the furry beast. "Ah, here you are. May I?" Barend asked, gesturing at the spot on the bench beside her.

She nodded. "Of course, Your Highness." She felt strangely shy and uncertain how to act around him now that he was back in human form. The easy friendship they had shared seemed to have vanished forever along with his beast-like form.

He sat, then reached over and took her hand in his. "No, please, you must always call me Barend. We are friends, you and I."

Karyna felt an almost painful stirring in her heart, but she pulled her hand away gently. "I cannot do that, my prince."

Folding her hands in her lap, she resisted the urge to brush imaginary dust from her skirts. She had been reinstated as Bellenya's lady-in-waiting, and the queen had given her an accolade for helping break the curse. It was strange returning to her old position after having once been treated as mistress of the entire palace, albeit by a very small household. Karyna felt a pang of longing. It had been hard work, but a part of her missed those days.

How odd it was, sitting so close to Barend this way. Although the man he was inside had not changed, she could not deny the difference now that he was human again. They had been so close throughout his imprisonment, and though she rejoiced at his transformation, her heart ached at the thought of his leaving.

She could never tell him that, though. She was, after all, simply a baron's daughter, and he was a prince.

"I half expected to find you tending the roses," Barend said quietly.

Karyna sighed. "No, the new gardeners tend them now. There isn't anything for me to do out here anymore. There's even a servant making sure roses are picked and dried to place in the princess's room." She stared at the ground, wondering if she would ever matter again. She would not wish the curse back, yet life now stretched before her in an endless stream of dull, monotonous days. She could easily envision herself buried in obscurity.

"How is Bellenya?" Barend asked.

"She seems well. Things haven't been the same between us though." Karyna hesitated, then added, "She's healing, and I think she's embarrassed. She won't ask me to do anything for her, and she won't talk to me, either. Not that she needs me. She has Ritter."

"A friendship like the one you two shared . . . it isn't easily discarded," Barend replied slowly. "I'm sure you'll be friends again one day."

"I hope so." Karyna sighed.

Barend shifted on the bench. The silence stretched out between them. He looked down at Karyna, studying her as though seeing her for the first time. She wondered what he saw but dared not ask.

"I wanted to thank you," he said hesitantly. Puzzled by his tone, she looked up. "For your friendship when so many others left," he continued. "You kept me sane."

"Oh." Karyna made a small gesture with her hand. "I—"

"That's not all," Barend rushed on. "I know you have a life here—your father, your loyalty to Bellenya . . . It would be wrong to ask you to leave all that."

Karyna frowned, still confused. "What do you mean?"

Barend continued as if he had not heard, his voice impassioned: "I can imagine leaving you tomorrow no more than I could allow you to travel to

Rivenloch alone. Even though I knew the beast would take control of me, I had to go with you. I could not live without you."

Karyna's heart began to race as the glimmer of hope she had allowed herself to entertain only in her most precious of dreams shone through her thoughts. "Barend, I don't—"

"I'm making a mess of this," he interrupted, running a hand through his dark hair and scratching the back of his head. "I can't seem to find the right words. I'm no Ritter." He made an exasperated sound deep in his throat then took her hand in both of his, cradling it tenderly. Even by starlight she recognized the longing, fear, and love in his expression, and her heart responded with leaping bounds.

"Karyna, you are like my own heart. I thought, hoped, dreamed, that perhaps you felt the same, that I had seen in your eyes some gentle feeling toward me even when I was a beast. In the past few weeks I have come to fear that I imagined it. I am a man without hope, yet . . . Do you think you could . . . My dearest girl, could you love one who was once a beast? I know you believe your station is too low for marriage to a prince, but please believe me when I say it does not matter to me, or to my people. They will love you because I love you."

Karyna thought she understood what the fledgling dawn had felt when the sun burst over the horizon for the very first time and bathed the world in its warm light. All shadows vanished from her heart as her most longed-for secret wish was suddenly placed in her hands. She raised her face, and her answering smile was glorious in its brilliance.

The fear in Barend's eyes dissolved into purest joy. Gently taking her face in his hands, he leaned forward to kiss her. The sweet smell of roses hovered about them, filling their senses. When they finally broke apart, Karyna leaned her head against his shoulder. Her heart overflowed with more emotion than she had words to express, but there was one thing she felt she had to say:

"Dearest Barend," she whispered, her voice bursting with love. "You are many things. But you were never a beast."

ABOUT THE AUTHOR

JENELLE SCHMIDT grew up in the northern-midwest. She now resides with her husband and their three adorable children in North Carolina where the summers are too hot and there is never enough snow. Jenelle fell in love with reading at a young age during family storytimes. To this day she enjoys creating exciting adventure tales filled with poignant themes and compelling characters in the fantasy and sci-fi genres.

To find out more about Jenelle, visit www.JenelleSchmidt.com.

DORIAN TSUKIOKA

ROSARA
AND THE
JUNGLE KING

For Bonnie and Dwain:
Grandmother and hero,
Brother and best friend,
Always in my heart, until we meet again.

THE KNIFE in my hand flies in an arc, felling the unfortunate vines and foliage blocking my escape. Quick and quiet, my strokes cut through the thick underbrush of the jungle, but I worry that using the stone knife will lead a path straight to me. That's the last thing I want to do.

I stop for a moment, crouch down low to the ground, and attempt to keep my breathing silent. I need to hear how closely I'm being followed. The sound of another knife hacking through the jungle tells me that my pursuer, though less careful than I, is not far off.

I have to make a choice. If I continue to cut a path, I can move much more quickly through the dense undergrowth, but I will no doubt be followed. The jungle is too thick for me to crawl through quickly, though I'm small enough that I can probably make it through the tangled vines and saplings without giving away my location. It would be a very slow escape. Or . . . I can climb.

I look around for a suitable tree and sigh in frustration when I spot one close by. A young wimba tree is making its way toward the top of the canopy, and according to the legends of our tribe, it is cursed and filled with evil spirits. The sound of my pursuer closing in behind gives me the impetus to ignore my fear and scurry my way through the ferns and liana vines.

In a few moments I reach the base of the tree. Its smooth bark and straight trunk would normally be difficult to climb, but I am in luck—this tree is being slowly suffocated by a strangler fig. Thick vines have wound their way down to the earth, enveloping the tree in a deathly embrace.

I waste no time. The bark tears at my skin as I climb the tree as silently as possible. I watch out for howler monkeys, fearing my climb may set them off and their alarm would enable whoever is following to catch me all the sooner. Luckily, I seem to be alone. I secure a spot in the tree that will hide most of me and pray that my pursuer does not look up.

A few minutes later the steady *whack-whack* of the knife comes to a stop not far from where I stopped cutting vines myself. Whoever it is was closer than I thought or faster than I had anticipated. The jungle is as silent as I've ever heard it. The animals of the forest must be as frightened as I am, for they seem to be holding their breath too.

I know I should not look, should keep my face hidden in the shadows of the tree, but curiosity maddens me for a moment, and I feel my body shift forward to get a look at the person following me. I see him and stiffen.

Maor.

The strongest man of the village is standing just under the wimba tree. He is also the cruelest. And he is looking right at me. Or so I think until his gaze shifts and he peers into the tree next to mine and frowns. Now that I know who is following me, I want to shrink back into the shadows of my hiding place, but I'm afraid that movement will draw attention to myself. So I wait.

Before long he alters his course and is gone. I take a moment to thank the spirits for hiding me. I had intended to offer prayers at the river this evening. Alone. The men of the village should be still accompanying my father, the chieftain, on a hunt while the moon is bright and nearly full. The extra light gives them an advantage in the hunt for peccaries, deer, and other wild game, allowing them to see into the dense foliage. They must have returned early.

When I was a child, my father allowed me to accompany him on the week-long trek through the forest, but once I reached womanhood it was no longer appropriate. In fact, if a man is found alone with me now he can claim me as his wife, and I will be bound to him. Whether I like it or not.

Not even my father can break the traditions of our tribe.

This reason alone is exactly why my father forbade me to leave the village and enter the jungle by myself even when the men were supposed to be far away. I want to obey my father, but life in the village is so dull and monotonous. Each day I must help the other women tend to the gardens, weeding away saplings and vines from a jungle attempting to claim back the small plot of land that makes up our home. I try to help with the women's work, but the jungle calls to me, beckoning me to leave the village behind.

Today I needed time to listen to the sound of the river under the great canopy of life and to offer my prayers up to the karawara, the spirits of the jungle. Maybe they would give me peace and help to soothe my restless spirit. Such had been my intention as I forayed into the jungle, but my plans quickly changed when I noticed I was being followed.

I shift my body into a more comfortable position and wait. I do not wish to leave the tree too early and chance running into Maor. Neither do I want to wait too long and run into him as I return to the village. I'm not sure what action to take.

Maor's face passes through my mind, and I shudder. Only my father, as chief, has more standing in the village. Maor already has two wives. I see them in the village sometimes, tending to their children, helping with the garden, and cleaning the kills that the men bring back from their hunts. I also see where their skin is bruised, their limbs battered due to Maor's short temper and quick use of his club to beat them into obedient submission.

I have no desire to become Maor's third wife.

As chief, only my father has permission to have so many wives. If Maor claims me it would be a direct challenge to my father for control of the village. I know Maor is cruel, but I didn't know he was also so devious. Claiming me would not only be a challenge to my father, but would be a personal insult. I vow to never allow myself to be claimed by him.

Time passes and my stomach rumbles. I have been hiding long enough, I think. I poke my head out slowly from behind the trunk. A green-haired sloth hangs upside down from a branch of a neighboring tree and winks a sleepy eye at me as a pair of brightly colored macaws take flight, startled by my movement. The sound of a twig snapping on the ground below freezes me to my spot, but it is only a lone anteater that waddles out from the underbrush and over the thick maze of roots littering the jungle floor. I exhale in relief and begin a search for fruit-bearing trees.

Pushing back a cluster of hanging flowers as brightly colored as a parrot, I am rewarded with a jaboticaba tree nearby. It is just within arm's reach of the branch above me, its plump, purple fruit ripened to perfection, growing directly on the trunk of the tree. I climb higher up into the wimba tree and wonder if I will tell my father of the lack of evil spirits when I return to the village. This tree has so far provided me with shelter and access to food; it seems lucky instead of cursed.

I reach out and pluck the jaboticaba fruit, taking enough to fill my hands, then I crawl carefully back to the sturdy trunk of the wimba tree. My teeth break through the crisp skin, and a rush of sweetness fills my mouth. I take a second bite, and that's when I see it.

A jaguar. Sitting in the branch just above me and looking right at me

My eyes travel the length of its immense body. Easily as large as any man in my village, it is the most enormous animal I have ever seen. My stomach knots as I realize that I have been hiding right under this creature and never knew it. His paw dangles off the branch where he perches lazily, looking as if he is ready to put his head down for a nap. I am unconvinced. The tightness of his hindquarters and a twitch of his ear indicate that he is just as alert as I am. Perhaps more so.

I have no weapon other than the short stone knife. I hope it will be enough if he decides to pounce. I try to calm my quickened heartbeat, telling myself that jaguars rarely attack humans, and if I seem to pose no threat to it I will probably be safe. My heart doesn't agree and continues to drum at a maddening pace.

The tip of his tail flicks back and forth, and his nostrils flare as he sniffs at the air. Does he scent my fear? Undoubtedly, he does. I try to relax my muscles, to appear unthreatening, but I cannot quite will my eyes to tear away from the beast. If I am to die in the next few moments, I want to know that it's coming.

His ears fold back, and his thick, powerful legs lift his body up into a crouch. My body stiffens, and I sit farther back into the cursed tree, pushing as far from the beast as I possibly can.

He yawns, shakes his head, and breaks our eye contact for a brief moment. I hope that he has grown bored of me and will leave. Instead, he fixes his gaze on me once again. Whiskers flick. He opens his mouth, baring his teeth. And then he speaks.

ICOULD finish you in three small bites, little bird," he says. "Hardly worth the trouble."

I sit slack-jawed, unable to comprehend what I am hearing. The largest jungle cat I've ever seen is speaking to me. And I think he has just insulted me.

"Calm yourself," he says. "I can practically hear your hummingbird heart beating its way out of your chest. I have no plans to harm you. I'm not even the slightest bit hungry."

A rush of air escapes my lips. I hadn't even realized that I'd been holding my breath. Somehow I find my voice. "Forgive me, jungle king, if I find it hard to relax. I'm not used to meeting a jaguar who can . . ."

"Speak?" he asks.

"Eat me in three small bites," I answer.

His lips curl back and his mouth forms what I can only guess to be a smile. With his long yellow fangs exposed, it is the most horrifying smile I have ever seen. Fear makes me giddy and I begin to laugh.

"Do you find me amusing?" he asks, pushing himself up with his massive front paws and stretching his lithe body out to its full extent. My hysterical giggles die away as he sits across from me. Likely he can bound from his branch onto mine with a single leap. The thought is sobering.

"Forgive me, jungle king. I am just nervous. I am not laughing at you."

"Are you hiding from the man I smelled earlier?" he asks as he begins to groom himself, licking one of his massive paws. Despite his assurance that he has no reason to harm me, I find that I cannot take my eyes off of his powerful jaws.

"Yes," I answer truthfully. "His name is Maor."

"And what is your name, little bird?"

"Why do you call me that?" I ask and then shrink back into myself, hoping I do not sound insolent. Obviously he is more than a mere jaguar, and I wonder if he might be one of the evil spirits of the wimba tree, or perhaps a karawara. I hope for the latter. Though I have never met a forest spirit myself, I have been warned that they are sometimes mischievous and often capricious. But I would rather deal with a mischievous spirit than a malicious one.

He pauses his cleansing ritual and looks directly at me. "Because you flew up the tree like one when the man came close. And you're quite small."

"I see." I'm not sure what to make of the big cat. His voice is terribly deep, and though it seems that he is teasing me, he does not seem to be unkind. "My name is Rosara, daughter of Rapau, chieftain of the jungle dwellers."

"Indeed?" His golden eyes seem to widen. "Well, Rosara, I am honored to meet you," he says and dips his head in a small bow. Tension fills me again, and another small giggle escapes my lips. The jaguar smiles his fang-filled grin.

"Are you a forest spirit?" I ask. "Have you heard my prayers?"

A deep rumble explodes through the jaguar's mouth, and his jaws open wide. I'm terrified until I realize he is laughing. At me.

"No, little bird . . . Rosara. I am not a spirit of the forest. Right now, I am merely a big cat. Please do not pray to me. But be careful of praying to the spirits of the jungle. Sometimes an answered prayer can be a dangerous thing."

I'm not sure what he's talking about, but I nod as if I agree. It seems unwise to disagree with the huge beast and take the chance of angering him.

"What does the man, this Maor, want with you? Why was he hunting you?" he asks.

"Hunting me?"

"I know a predator pursuing its prey when I see it," he answers. "You were most definitely the prey. Why?"

I duck my head and begin a thorough study of the calluses on my hands. I don't know why I feel ashamed, but I do. The thought of Maor taking me as his wife makes me feel humiliated and dirty. I choke on the words as they leave my mouth: "He wants to claim me. To take me as his third wife."

"Ahhh . . . I see. I thought that might be the reason. Males in pursuit of females have a distinct odor. His was quite distasteful."

I look up and see the jaguar smiling at me. I shudder a little. "I cannot be the wife of such a man," I say. "I'd rather die."

"If that man has his way, then death might be your lot. You should be careful."

I nod, not knowing what to say next until I realize there is something I want to ask the jaguar. "Do you have a name, jungle king?"

"Of course," he replies. "My name is Tupa."

Tupa. I'm surprised to hear such a name. It sounds too soft, too innocent to be the name of a gigantic beast who could kill me with one swipe of his paw. I see he is smiling at me again, and I briefly wonder if he can read my thoughts as well. Perhaps he lied about not being a jungle spirit.

Though I cannot see the sun through the great canopy of trees, I know that dusk is near. It is too late to make my way to the river and offer prayers to the karawara now. If the hunting party truly has returned, then father will be worried about me. I must return to my village. I hope the jaguar will let me.

As if he can read my thoughts he says, "You should be getting back now, little bird. Time to fly home to your nest."

I am not eager to get back to the village. I cannot decide whether my reluctance has more to do with having to deal with Maor or with being stuck in the village and unable to leave. Once my father finds out about Maor, I know he will expressly forbid me to leave the village, and I will be stuck working in the gardens and doing the women's work indefinitely. I'm certain that father will ask his second and third wives, Tatuie and Hana, to keep their eagle eyes on me. If my mother were still alive, she would no doubt help me to escape into the jungle for at least a little while, but since she's been gone . . .

"Are you sad?" Tupa asks me.

"A little," I answer truthfully.

"Don't you wish to go home?"

"I'm not sure."

"It's probably better that you return to your people rather than spend the night alone in the forest. Don't you agree?"

"But I'm not alone," I say, wondering where this boldness inside me has come from. "I'm with you."

The jaguar's whiskers twitch. I have the distinct impression that he is trying not to laugh. He begins to groom his other paw. "I'm sorry, but it's nearly time for me to go home to my family as well. I will walk with you awhile, but I must leave soon. I, too, need to get back home before night falls."

I feel the frown form on my face and wonder why I should feel sad to lose the company of the most frightening of beasts.

"Do not worry," he says. "I will see you tomorrow if you are once again brave enough to enter the jungle alone."

I smile. Morning cannot come soon enough.

Tupa begins to climb down the tree, his claws holding him vertically in the air until he takes a great leap to the jungle floor below. I am far less graceful and take much longer to navigate my way down the twisted vines ensnaring the wimba tree. My stomach growls, and I find that I am glad to be going home, at least for something to eat.

We walk side by side through the jungle. Tupa's head bobs near my waist when the path is wide enough. When it is narrow he slinks ahead, all silence and deadly grace. Goosebumps grow on my arms as I watch him. He is soundless as we proceed through the jungle, and I feel that I'm as loud as a pack of monkeys traveling next to him. I do not have his grace or stealth, and every step seems like an announcement to the world of where I am.

The dying light filters through the trees and dapples the path in shades of gray. It is about to rain, as it often does this time of day. I usually try to be under the roof of my village's shabono, our communal house, when the rains come so I do not get drenched in the sudden onslaught. Today I will not be so lucky.

Tupa stops and sits facing me. "I must go before it is too late for me. Will you be all right to make it back to your village from here?"

I nod just as the rain begins to pour in sheets on top of us. The jaguar rises and begins to walk away, back into the depths of the jungle. "I'll see you tomorrow then," I say.

The great cat pauses, turns his head, and smiles at me with a grin that makes me both frightened and elated. Within seconds he has vanished. For the second time, I wonder if he really is a jungle spirit and is testing my faith. Perhaps he is part of my imagination.

I shake my head, unable to understand it. I know only one thing for sure: I'll be returning to the jungle tomorrow.

I pick up my feet and try to jog back to the village, though it is slow going with the damp ground sucking at my feet with every step I take. As I walk, I try to decide whether or not I should tell my father about Tupa. I think he should know, but I am concerned that he will worry too much and not believe that Tupa is safe.

Safe? That's not the right word. Undoubtedly, Tupa is not safe. He is anything but safe. He seems good, though, and kind. I weigh the pros and cons of telling my father about him as I continue to pull my feet out of the mud. I am concentrating so hard on treading through the muck and on what I shall say to my father about Tupa that I don't see danger until I'm nearly standing on top of his feet.

Maor.

III

THE CLUB comes flying out of nowhere. In the rain, I don't see it. I only hear the swoosh of raindrops and wind flying toward me, a precursor to the pain just before the club strikes me alongside the head. I spin and crumple to the ground, the mud softening my fall. My mind has gone blank, paralyzed by fear, and I must force myself to move. I cannot simply lie there in the mud and let Maor assault me.

My head pounds with pain, and my vision is not quite right. Everything is darker than it should be. Nevertheless, I push myself up to my hands and feet and prepare to stand and run.

A second blow hits me on the back, crashing between my shoulder blades and throwing me back down to the soggy ground. I know what he is doing. He is demonstrating the extent of his power and of my weakness. He will claim me and then rule me, keeping me in his thrall with his club and fists if I dare object.

I scream when the next blow strikes the back of my legs. Something cracks. I scream even louder. I hope I am close enough to the village for someone to hear me, but the deluge of rain is so strong that I can barely hear my own voice.

"You are mine now, Rosara," Maor says, standing over me, his feet planted in the mud next to my head. "It's useless to fight back. I claim you as my own."

He grabs my hair and flips me over. The pain is so great, I cry out again and try to pry away his hands as he drags me farther into the jungle, away from the village. He leaves the trail to the village and pulls me into the deep undergrowth. My screams never stop, but I know that no one can hear me. I am alone.

He releases the clump of my hair, and I fall against a tree root. My head cracks against it and I see nothing. No rain. No man. No jungle. Only darkness.

When my vision returns, I know I have been unconscious for only a few moments. Maor has lowered his club, and I see him kneeling next to me through my barely open eyes. I hear a groan and hardly recognize my own voice.

"This will be easier if you don't fight, Rosara," he says.

At first I think perhaps he is right. Perhaps I shouldn't resist, should give in to the inevitable.

But when he puts his hands on my shoulders, panic wells up through my chest, hot and quick. Of course I will fight. I will fight and I will die. I will not *let* him claim me.

I struggle, trying to push Maor away from me. He pins my arms down and I thrash my legs. I open my mouth for another scream and bite at him. His shoulder is just out of my reach. He is getting angry, frustrated that I will not cooperate.

He lets go of me and sits back on his heels. I try to push my body away from him, try to get my feet under me, but the moment I put weight on my foot a searing pain runs up my leg. I collapse, defeated. I will not be able to escape from him. He bends down, keeping his eyes on me, and grabs his knife. I can see it in his eyes—if he cannot have me as wife, then he will kill me.

A blur crosses my vision, and in an instant Maor is no longer in front of me. He is lying on the jungle floor, not moving, and the rock-hard root of a tree next to his head is covered in his blood.

I do not see where the jaguar has come from, but instantly he is there, as if he has magically appeared out of the rain. Tupa, the jungle king—my new friend—pads across the ground toward me and lowers his face to mine.

"Are you hurt, little bird?" he asks me in his frighteningly deep voice.

I stare at him. How is he here? How can he be here? I am shaking hard, no longer from fear but from immense relief.

"Rosara, are you hurt?"

I snap out of my daze, and nod. "A little," I say. "My ankle . . . it may be broken."

"You will not be able to walk, and I can't leave you here with that man in case he awakens. I think you must ride upon my back, and I will take you back to your village." The great beast sits down completely and stretches his legs out in front of his body. "Can you pull yourself onto my back?" he asks.

I nod my head, yes. The great cat maneuvers his body close to mine and I roll toward him until I am able to throw my arm around his neck. I marvel at how soft his fur is beneath my fingers. I have never touched a jaguar before. I expected his hair to be rough like his voice. It is anything but. I stroke his hair for a moment, lost in the feel of it.

Tupa purrs. "That feels wonderful, but I think it's time we got you home."

Heat flares in my cheeks. I'm not sure why I feel so embarrassed. I gingerly lift my hurt leg and push it over the beast's back. A moment later, I am lying on top of him. I don't know how I will keep from falling off.

"Put your arms around my neck and hold on," he says.

I obey. The moment my hands clasp together around his thick neck, he rises up. My legs slide down either side of his middle, and my body rocks in sync with his sleek gait as he walks slowly and silently through the jungle to my father's village.

For the first time in my life, I am thankful for the daily downpour of afternoon rain. It means that no one will be loitering about the village. Everyone will be under the semi-circular roof of the shabono, waiting until the clouds pass and the rain lets up. There will be no one to interfere as Tupa carries me into the village.

With the rain pouring, I cannot hear the villagers' gasps of astonishment as Tupa walks into the village, but I see surprise in their faces. Everyone rises to watch as Tupa carries me through the center of the village and around the curve of the shabono to where my father is standing with his spear in one hand and his club in the other. A quick glance shows me that all the men are standing ready with their weapons. Many of the women, too, hold weapons and push their little ones behind them. Tupa doesn't seem to notice, or if he does, he does not care.

We reach my father's plot, and Tupa lies down on the ground. He speaks just loud enough for me to hear: "I will leave you here and let your family care for you. I must go now before it is too late, but I am eager to see you again."

The jaguar's body shifts, and I slide off his back onto the sopping, muddy ground. He stands and stares at me a moment before his head bows down to mine and he licks my cheek. His sandy tongue is rough and soft all at once, and I am filled with warmth.

I look up and he is gone. I catch only the briefest glimpse of his tail as he bounds back into the forest. I place my hand on my cheek where he touched me. So tender, just like a kiss.

The moment passes, and my father is kneeling next to me, the rain snaking down his bald head and onto his face. "Rosara," he says, "what happened? Why were you . . . Never mind, you're hurt. There will be time for questions later."

Father lifts me into his arms and carries me under the protective shelter of the shabono, where his second and third wives begin to fuss over my wounds. I am hurt worse than I realized. Bruises spot my skin black, not unlike my jaguar friend's. Though I see the marks where Maor wounded me, I do not yet feel their pain. I am still in shock. I lie back and rest on a straw mat while my father's wives apply healing herbs and salves to help seal my wounds.

Father shoos away curious villagers, promising to explain all after I have been cared for. He sits cross-legged next to me on the ground. He doesn't speak, just watches. But I know questions are whirling through his mind.

I think back over how Tupa walked through the village and brought me directly to my father's plot without having to ask me where to go. I have questions of my own as well. Chiefly, how did Tupa know which man was my father? How did he know where to take me?

THE RAIN finally stops. My father speaks only five words. "Tell me what happened, Rosara."

I tell him then. Everything. How Maor hunted me through the forest. How I hid right next to a jaguar without even knowing. How Maor attacked and tried to claim me as his third wife. How he is lying in the jungle right now, unconscious, perhaps dead.

I feel only a bit guilty for hoping he is truly dead. I've never wished that about anyone before, but I do now. Part of me hopes that Tupa goes back to finish him off. Part of me fears that he will.

Father's frown grows deeper as I tell my story, but he doesn't speak or ask any questions. He only listens. This is what makes my father such a good chief of our village. He waits until I am finished with my tale before he speaks, and even then he thinks long and hard before he says anything.

"Something will need to be done," he says, and then stands and walks across the village grounds to tell the villagers what has happened. I am not sure what Father means. Is he speaking of Maor? Or Tupa? And what does he think should be done?

Several men gather around as he relates what happened to me in the forest. The men take their weapons and follow my father into the jungle. I wonder who exactly they are hunting—Maor or Tupa.

It isn't long before gossips share my story with everyone in the village. But, other than my father's wives, no one comes to talk to me. No one offers sympathy for the treatment I experienced at Maor's hands. I am sad but not surprised. This is the way of our tribe. Men have claimed their wives thus for many generations, perhaps from the beginning of time.

Most claimings are not so violent anymore. Many are even consensual, between two adults who love each other, choosing to be together. This was the way of my father and his three wives. But some are not. Some are about power and position. If a man is powerful enough to take a woman against her will, then she is lucky to have such a strong husband.

The thought of it makes my stomach clench. I close my eyes and will myself not to vomit. Images of Maor attacking me fill my head, but I force them away. Instead, I concentrate on the memory of Tupa's soft fur, his rumbling voice, and his golden eyes. I do not even notice how tired I am, but soon I fall asleep.

When I awaken it is to the whoops and hollers of men emerging from the jungle, carrying Maor on their shoulders. The night is dark, so I cannot see if he is dead. Whispers from the women fill the air, and soon I learn that Maor is not dead, merely unconscious. They think he will be fine and even wonder what great strength he must have to survive the attack of a jaguar.

This news fills me with dread. In attempting to take me as his third wife, Maor was obviously asserting his desire to become head of the village.

Now, with villagers proclaiming that he possesses superhuman strength, it will not take much for him to convince them that he should be chief. I shudder at the thought of Maor as leader of our tribe.

When Maor awakens, he is surly and quiet. He makes no great boasts of his strength and ability and says nothing of trying to claim me. He returns to his plot under the shabono, where his two wives minister to his needs. Father returns to our plot and, though he says nothing, I see the concern in his eyes.

It is only a matter of time before Maor makes his move against both of us.

The birth of the new moon has come and gone again before I can walk unassisted, and even then I am painfully slow. After so many days of lying under the eaves of the shabono and watching the rest of the villagers move freely, I am bored to tears of frustration. Father doesn't want me to step out from under the shabono, but Tatuie and Hana vow not to let me out of their sight in the garden. I am even glad to be able to help work in the garden and pull weeds away from the young plantain trees and cassava roots.

Though I am grateful for their kind watchfulness, I would much rather be strolling through the jungle. I try to continue to be thankful when my back and ankle are throbbing from the work of pulling weeds. The jungle is so near that I have difficulty concentrating on my work as I sense its pull. A glasswing butterfly flits through the air and catches my eye, dragging my gaze along its path to the flowering jungle blooms in the trees surrounding the village. I see a blur of golden fur coated in spots, and then it is gone.

Tatuie hollers at me to stop my daydreaming, and I tear my eyes away from the jungle that I love so much. I look up to see Tatuie staring at me. I was not the only one to see the jaguar.

Forcing myself to concentrate on pulling weeds, I can't help but smile to myself. Tupa is waiting for me.

I grow stronger each day as my ankle sets and continues its healing process, but inside me the pain of not visiting my beloved jungle is festering like a disease.

I catch a few more glimpses of Tupa hiding in the trees or crouching in the undergrowth, watching me. I long to speak with him, but I am afraid to draw attention to my friend. I am not the only one who has noticed him lingering around the village, and even though every one of the villagers watched him bring me to safety, there is talk that he is dangerous.

Whether Tupa knows about the villagers' talk, I do not know. But if he does, he does not seem to care much, as he continues to come and watch over me every day.

The moon continues through its cycle once again. Birth, life, death, and then rebirth. The rising tension is so thick that I can almost see it hovering in the air. Though Maor has not mentioned his failed attempt at claiming me and is still just one of the village warriors, other villagers are seeking his counsel much as if he is chief. I see the worry in my father's eyes.

I have also caught Maor's gaze on me several times. Though he always looks away, I know my ordeal with him is not over. I fear he will try to claim me again the moment he has a chance. Even with Tupa watching over me, there is no guarantee that I will be so lucky a second time.

Father reveals that he shares my worries as well. "It is no longer safe for you here, Rosara," he whispers to me one evening as the village is settling down for the night. "It is time for you to go."

"Go? Where? Where will I be safer than here with you?" I ask, fear welling up inside me. All my former wishes of being somewhere other than in this village crumble like dust as I think that I may be sent away.

"You are not safe from Maor," Father says. "He is growing in favor with many of the villagers. If he tries to claim you again I may not be able to stop him. I'm not sure your jaguar friend will be able to either." My father's words echo my own fears. "You will never be safe as long as you are without a husband."

My breath catches in my throat. I cannot breathe. A husband? So few of the men here are eligible to take me as a wife even if I wanted one of them. Most are too young, too old, or already have claimed their two wives. I search my father's eyes. Would he force me into a marriage with another man of our village, even though I love none of them?

"Rosara," he says and then pauses. I can see that he is carefully choosing his words. Again, one of the qualities that make him such a good leader. Would Maor be quick to listen and slow to speak? I doubt it. "I know that none of the men of our village are meant for you. Many of them support Maor, and I have no doubt that they would simply give you to him. The others are weak and would probably do the same thing in their fear."

My heart beats rapidly in my chest. I'm not sure what my father is going to say, but at least he agrees that no man here is right for me.

"You need a husband who is strong," he tells me. "A husband who will treat you as the priceless treasure you are."

My eyes brim with tears. My father has never before spoken to me with words like these. He has always been kind but never so tender and affectionate. I realize suddenly that he is saying goodbye.

"There is a place far away where you can be safe," he continues, "with a man who is worthy enough to protect you. He is the son of a chieftain, young and strong. When you were still children, his father and I agreed on your betrothal to help strengthen both of our tribes. It is time to invoke that betrothal. I am sending you to the tribe of the river people. Their ways are different from ours. There is no claiming there. They only marry if both consent, and they almost always marry for love."

"What if *I* do not consent?" I ask, wondering who is this man I've been betrothed to. "What if the man you have betrothed me to does not love me? What if I cannot love him? What happens to us then?"

"Please understand," my father persists. "This is the only way you will be safe. We have no other choice. I cannot bear to have you matched with Maor. I know you cannot bear it, either. You will leave just before dawn with Hana and Tatuie. They will accompany you through the jungle to the village of the river people. I will stay here to make sure Maor does not try to follow."

He is silent then. I know he is waiting for me to say something, but what is there to say? I am being banished from my own village to marry a man I have never met and will probably never love. There are no words to express how heavy my heart is at this moment.

"You are my treasure, Rosara," he says and leans down to kiss my face just as Tupa did not so long ago. "Be safe."

I try not to cry, but I cannot stop the hot tears from betraying me. Father leaves, and I lie alone in my hammock, wondering if what he said is true. Is it the only way?

No, I decide, it is not. There is another. I need only to wait for the right moment.

TATUIE SHAKES me awake. The jungle is still dark in the predawn hours, and I wonder if my father's wives slept at all in the night. Father lies in his hammock pretending to sleep, but I see his eyes shining in the darkness.

Hana hands me a cloth filled with provisions for our trip, and we slink away from the shabono and into the embrace of the jungle.

The tension of the last few weeks peels off me with every step I take under the great trees. The effect is immediate. I breathe more deeply and walk more assuredly under the green canopy of life. My heart is still heavy from saying goodbye to my father, but it also rejoices in being free.

Free, that is, until we reach the village of the river people. The thought threatens to weigh me down again, but I push it away. I have a plan.

The moment I see Tupa I will make my move. Somehow I will elude

Tatuie and Hana, and, with Tupa's help, I know I can find a home for myself in the jungle. My family will grieve over my decision, but I know in my heart that I can never be married to any man who I do not love, even if he is a chieftain's son.

It will be very dangerous to try to live on my own in the jungle. My tribe is not the only one that forcefully claims women as wives. I have heard rumors of other tribes that do unspeakable things to their women. But I am willing to risk the danger of living in the jungle, so long as Tupa will help me. He has been watching over me since the day we met, and I cannot help but think of him as my protector.

I keep alert for any sign that Tupa is following along with us, but I see none. Perhaps he is not here. The first day I saw him, he spoke of returning to his family. Likely he is there now with his jaguar wife and cubs.

For some reason the thought makes me uncomfortable, and I try to ignore the tension in my body. I will see him when I see him—that is all I can do.

We walk for nearly an hour through the jungle before we need to pull out our stone knives to force our way through the tangle of vines. I recognize that we are heading parallel to the river, not far from where I hid in the wimba tree on the day I first met Tupa. The sky, what little of it I can see through the thick canopy of leaves, has begun to lighten. Dawn is here. It won't be long before the village is fully awake.

I wonder how soon the villagers will notice that I am gone. Will Maor accept his defeat silently, or will he take this as his moment to challenge my father? I hope with all my heart that it is the former and not the latter.

I slash away at the vines and branches hiding our trail to the river and nearly slice into Tatuie as I jump back and cry out in alarm.

An arm is lying in the bush, fingers curled as if it is holding a secret in its hand. It is not moving.

Tatuie steps forward and pulls back some vines. Enough of the body is revealed. We know who it is: Pucu, Maor's first wife, lies dead on the ground.

Hana, Tatuie, and I sit next to her still body, too stunned to do anything. I try to think of when I saw Pucu last. Wasn't it just yesterday I noticed Maor slapping her? How could she be here, this far into the jungle? How could she be dead?

"We should untangle her," Tatuie finally says, taking charge. "She needs to be cleansed and then buried. We will have to go back."

I understand. Pucu's spirit is in danger of not being led to the iwa, where the spirits of our ancestors rest, unless we cleanse her body and say the proper ritual prayers. We have only until sunset before her spirit will be lost in the forest, forever haunting us. It is for the good of all that we go back and bury her.

"How did she die?" I ask.

"I don't know," Tatuie responds. "Let's pull her out onto the path."

Hana chops away at more of the vines hiding Pucu's body while Tatuie and I pull. A collective gasp escapes our lips as Pucu's body rolls onto the ground, revealing the cause of her death.

Deep gashes cover her body. The skin of her arms, legs, and torso is shredded. Tatuie and I drop Pucu's legs, and her body rolls farther, her head lolling to the side. Claw marks cover her face. One of her eyes is missing.

I turn away and cannot stop myself. I vomit up everything I have eaten recently, heaving until nothing is left.

"What kind of animal could do this?" Hana asks, though we all know the answer. The marks are those of a jungle cat. A jaguar. A very big jaguar.

Tatuie's eyes meet mine, and I know she is thinking the same thing. She says nothing other than "We need to wrap the body with what we have and try to keep animals from getting to her as much as we can. Help me," she adds, kneeling down to the ground, opening her cloth satchel, and pulling out the supplies inside. Setting aside provisions meant for our journey, she unrolls the cloth to its full length. Hana and I follow her lead, discarding our supplies and unrolling our own cloths. Expertly, Tatuie folds all three pieces of fabric around Pucu's body.

I know that our efforts are likely in vain. Wild dogs or other beasts will probably get to the body before we are able to bring her family to carry it back to the village for the burial ceremony. Certainly, the three of us can carry Pucu's ravaged body ourselves, but our custom is that only family members carry the dead. Already we have broken too many taboos by moving her. We can only hope that Pucu's spirit knows our intent and will honor us for it.

We lift the wrapped body off of the path and back into the undergrowth as gently as we can, then stand to leave. Hana's scream jolts me as an enormous jaguar walks out of the jungle and onto the path beside us.

"Run!" she yells, and escapes down the path, pulling Tatuie along with her. Tatuie turns back for an instant and tries to latch on to me, but Hana's grip is too tight, and Tatuie is forced to follow along behind her. I watch them disappear around a bend and back the way we came.

My feet are stuck, though my body is shaking violently.

"Hello, little bird," Tupa says in his deeply frightening voice.

"Hello, jungle king," I say.

VI

I SMELL death," Tupa says. "What has happened? Are you all right?"

My brain tries to comprehend his questions. Why is he asking me? Is this a test? Does this mean he had nothing to do with Pucu's death after all? I want to believe that. I want to believe my jaguar friend innocent, but the image of Pucu's mangled body fills my mind, and I do not know what to believe.

"Rosara, are you all right?" he asks again when I say nothing.

"Yes, Tupa," I finally answer, "I am."

I tell him what happened to Pucu. He stands as still as a stone while I relate what I saw. "Claw marks," he asks, "from a jungle beast?"

"Yes. A large jungle beast." I think about showing him the tears in her skin, but I cannot bring myself to unwrap her body. It seems wrong to expose her again. I also don't think I can stomach seeing her mangled form one more time.

"Did you think I did it?" he asks.

I can't answer at first, but then I whisper, "I hoped not."

"Do you still think I killed her?" he asks, his whiskers flicking in the still morning air, his body tense.

"No," I answer truthfully, realizing in that moment that I mean it.

His body relaxes. "Your friends seemed to think that I am responsible, though," he says as he sits on his haunches next to me. "They left in quite a hurry."

"Those are my father's wives," I say. "You frightened them."

"Your father has two wives?" he asks.

"He had three, when my mother was still alive," I answer.

"Interesting. In my tribe, males are allowed only one mate. For life. I think it would be very confusing to have more than one wife," he says as he begins to scratch his ear with a hind leg.

The image I had of him earlier with his jaguar mate and cubs comes back to my mind. I want to ask him if he has a mate, but I hesitate. This is not the time for that conversation. Besides, I feel awkward and cannot form the right words to ask.

Instead, I say, "What kind of animal could have done this to Pucu?"

He sniffs around the body for a few moments. I'm not ready for the word he says.

"Man."

Man? A human being did this? I cannot fathom the viciousness of such a person. How could anyone do such a thing? And why? How did Pucu end up being the victim, and why out here, so far from the village? None of this makes sense to me, and I shake my head to clear it.

"Are you certain it was a man?" I ask Tupa.

"Yes, little bird. There is no animal scent on the woman. Only the scent of a human. One that we both know well."

"A man who wanted to make it look as if a jungle beast killed her," I say. My head is spinning. Only one man I can think of is devious enough to make Pucu's death look like an accident. "Maor."

"Yes," Tupa says.

"Pucu was his wife."

A deep, guttural growl vibrates in my ears as Tupa responds to what I have said. I tell him everything then, of how the villagers are looking to Maor to become the next chief. How I've caught Maor watching me.

And then I tell Tupa of my father's plan to send me to the village of the river people to marry the son of the chieftain, a man I have never met and have no desire to marry. Tupa's whiskers flicker as I finish my story, his ears flitting back and forth.

"Would it be so bad to be married to the chieftain's son?" he asks me, his head cocked to the side. "You've never met him. Perhaps you would fall in love with him after all."

I feel my face flush with my anger, and the words come spilling out before I can stop them. "Would it be so easy for you? Could you accept a wife you had not chosen?"

At first Tupa is silent, and shame colors my face an even deeper red. I did not mean to lash out at him.

"No, little bird, it would not be easy for me either," he concedes.

Silence grows thick and tangled like liana vines between us. I am about to apologize for causing the tension when Tupa asks, "If you do not wish to marry the chieftain's son, what do you intend to do?"

I am grateful for a break in the silence.

"First I planned on escaping from Tatuie and Hana, but your arrival made that happen more quickly than I had anticipated. After that I thought . . ." I stop. My plan sounds so childish to my ear now that I am standing before the great jungle cat. How could I possibly ask him to take care of me in the jungle? He is a jaguar. A mammoth of a jaguar, but still just a beast. But perhaps . . .

"Tupa, do you remember that day in the wimba tree?" I ask.

"Certainly. I will never forget it," he says, and with his lips pulled back to show his fangs I can tell he is smiling.

"I asked if you were a karawara, a spirit of the jungle, and you said you were not."

"That is still true. I am not a karawara. Right now I am nothing but a beast."

"Have you ever met a karawara though?"

Tupa's smile vanishes. "Why do you ask me this?"

"I want to ask the spirits of the jungle if they will help me so that I can remain in the jungle forever and not have to worry about living in the villages of men," I say with conviction. My heartbeat is rapid but firm. I know that this is what I want.

"You don't know what you are asking for," Tupa says as if I am a child. "The karawara do not make simple bargains. I fear you will not be happy with what they give you."

I think over his words for a few moments. He speaks the truth, and I know it deep inside. Though the jungle spirits can be generous, they can also be mischievous, even cruel at times. If I strike a bargain with one I may live to regret it. Or I may not live at all. There is no way of knowing.

"I would rather take my chances with the karawara than with Maor," I declare boldly. "Please take me to them."

"But, Rosara . . ." he begins to speak, but his words change into jaguar growls and I no longer understand him. Tupa jerks his head from side to side as if he's trying to shake out the words he wants to speak. He stops, rubs at his mouth with a massive paw, and opens it. All that escapes are the sharp grunts and growls of a jungle cat.

"Tupa, are you all right?" I ask, holding my hand out to touch him. He backs away from my fingers with a loud hiss, and I retract my hand quickly. Something has changed.

Tupa paces back and forth in front of me. The early morning sounds of the jungle are muted, and silence presses down around us as I wait for his voice to return.

"Please, Tupa," I beg. "Help me."

His eyes meet mine. I don't want to cry in front of him, but I can feel tears begin to pool in the corners of my eyes. If Tupa refuses to take me to the karawara, I am out of options.

His shoulders slump and his head drops as he puffs a rumbling sigh. I finally hear his human voice return, its timbre tight and strained as if he is fighting to push out the words. "All right."

The great jungle king walks a few steps into the jungle and pauses. "Follow me," he says. And I do.

We walk through the jungle without speaking. I'm glad for the silence and a chance to explore my feelings more deeply. I'm afraid and elated all at once. Will the jungle spirit grant my wish? Will it simply laugh at me, or worse, punish me for soliciting its favor? Will Tupa even be able to find a karawara?

The jungle grows thicker around us, and I use my knife to chop at the vines and bush to make my way forward. Tupa waits as I do so. I know he could easily maneuver his lithe body through the brambles, so I am thankful for his patience as I hack my way through slowly.

My thoughts flicker back to Pucu's mangled corpse. I feel guilty about leaving her alone in the jungle, but I know that Tatuie and Hana will get help from the village to fetch her remains before sunset. The guilt settles deeper in my breast as I think of how they will interpret my disappearance.

"Tupa!" I gasp. "They will think that you did it!"

"Did what?" he asks. Of course he is not thinking of Pucu as I am. His mind must be on other things—his family, perhaps.

"The people of my village will think that you killed Pucu. We thought it was a beast, and then you showed up and scared Tatuie and Hana away. And now that I'm gone they will think . . ."

He finishes my thought: " . . . that I have devoured you."

VII

AS THE day wears on I begin to tire. Tupa helps me find food in the jungle, even climbing a tree to gather fruit for me. I wish I had thought to bring some of the provisions we removed from our satchels when we found Pucu's body, but I did not have the foresight to do that, nor did I have anything to carry them in. Tupa helps provide for me though, and rests beside me as I eat.

"Aren't you hungry?" I ask him. "Shouldn't you eat as well?"

"I don't think you would really like to see me eat, little bird. I am not nearly as . . . dainty as you are."

I blush and feel embarrassed for asking. I'm surprised at how considerate he is. And I am glad he is not tearing into his prey right in front of me.

"Besides," he continues, "I usually wait until after sunset to eat." I want to ask him why, but he has laid down his head as if ready to fall asleep. I lay my head on his side and stroke his soft fur. I can hear his fierce heart beating steadily. It is fast and sure. My eyes close, and drowsiness overcomes me. As I fall into sleep, all I hear is Tupa's heartbeat and the sound of his purr.

"Rosara." I hear Tupa's deep voice pull me out of sleep. "Rosara, it's time," he says, and my eyes open wide.

I'm curled against his body, and one of his great paws is resting on my shoulder in a warm embrace. Tupa stands. "Follow me," he says quietly. I wonder if that is sadness I hear in his voice.

The light is fading. We continue on through the jungle until it is nearly twilight. In the distance I begin to hear the rush of water. A river is nearby. We approach it and follow the current along its banks, walking downstream until we come to a place where the river widens. The current is slow and lazy here, forming a gentle pool. A group of capybaras wade at the edge of the water, grazing on river reeds. They scatter into the jungle, squeaking, when they see us.

I look all around for a jungle spirit but see nothing out of the ordinary. Tupa notices my staring and says, "Don't worry. The karawara are particularly fond of the brief moments when it is neither daytime nor night. They are most easily found at twilight or just before dawn when the world is not yet quite awake or quite asleep. I'm sure we'll find one here."

I look around but still see nothing other than jungle and the river. My hand lifts, and I feel Tupa's head duck under my arm. I scratch the skin between his ears, and he purrs once again, the breath rushing from his mouth as he exhales. Even if the karawara does not come, I wonder if Tupa would help me to live in the jungle. I know it would be difficult, but perhaps with his guidance I could somehow manage.

I consider asking him when I hear his growl, a deep rumble in his chest that makes the air vibrate in my ears. He is looking up into the sky. My eyes follow his gaze upward, though I hear the sound of what is coming long before I actually see it.

Wings. Hundreds of wings beat and stir the air. And then I see them as they rush out of the forest and sail overhead. Every color of the rainbow fills my vision as scarlet and blue-winged macaws fly alongside green-feathered parrots, their long tails floating behind them in the wind. Black-and-white toucans join the throng along with smaller crimson topaz birds, their iridescent plumage gleaming in the dying light. Miniscule yellow- and orange-breasted hummingbirds zip and dart in circles, stopping to hover before us as if they are appraising me. Although the air is filled with the sound of their beating wings, I hear only one bird's voice. It is a deep, throaty, warbling sound.

Out of the jungle appear the massive wings of a great white egret. They lift and fall in slow, powerful beats until the bird lands on the firm branch of a young wimba tree. Though the arms of the tree stretch out wide, the tree is not so tall as its brothers and sisters, not yet towering over the canopy of the forest. The hundreds of other birds follow and find places to perch in the tree. Its branches are thick with their crowded bodies, except for the branch with the great white egret. It sits alone, a single white star flanked by every imaginable color.

The rumble in Tupa's chest lessens but does not diminish entirely.

The egret walks along the thick branch and reveals beautiful plumes draping from its back, as wispy and delicate as a spider web. The slender plumage sways in the wind with each step of its black, spindly legs. I'm enchanted by the beauty of this bird. Surely this is a holy animal, a true spirit of the jungle. Its snake-shaped neck stretches and bobs with each step until it stands just above us.

It opens its knife-sharp beak, and I expect to hear the deep, throaty warble once again. Instead I hear the egret say, "It's a little late for you to be wandering the jungle, isn't it, Tupa?"

The egret says this in a soft, silky voice. I am not certain how I would expect an egret's voice to sound, but it would not be so gentle and smooth, like a breeze through the rainforest carrying the coolness of the mountain mist.

Tupa growls in response and does not answer.

"I'd expect you to be crossing the river by now. It is nearly dark, after all."

I have the distinct impression that the great bird is teasing my friend. Or taunting him. Tupa says nothing, though the rumble in his chest continues.

The egret tilts his head, bobs, and tilts again the other direction as if waiting for a reply. Tupa does not grant him one. The bird takes a few preening steps then jumps from the tree, his wide wings catching the air as he floats to the ground.

Tupa shifts his body in between mine and the bird's. The egret is indeed the largest bird I have ever seen. However, my friend is the largest animal I've ever laid eyes on, and I'm fairly certain he could easily eat the egret in a few mouthfuls if he wished to. Nevertheless, Tupa keeps himself solidly between us.

"Is this the karawara?" I whisper in Tupa's ear. He nods, and I am suddenly afraid. Perhaps seeking the help of a jungle spirit is not the best idea. I put my arm around Tupa's neck and squeeze. He pushes back against me, and my fear abates a little.

"I will not let him harm you," Tupa says, never taking his eyes off of the giant preening bird.

"Harm you? Harm you?" the bird asks, his tone incredulous though his voice remains silky smooth. "I have no desire to harm you, child. Tell me what you seek, and I will try to grant your wish."

Tupa turns his head to me, and I look at him before I speak. "You do not have to do this," he says. "You can—"

"Enough!" the great bird says, and a chorus of squawks and calls from the host of birds in the tree echo his cry. Tupa's mouth continues to move, but only the growls of a jaguar escape his lips. His human words are gone, just as before. I understand now: It is the karawara's magic keeping Tupa wordless.

I wonder what the karawara doesn't want him to say. Or doesn't want me to hear.

"Why have you sought me, girl? What do you desire?"

I swallow my fear. "I wish to be able to live in the jungle freely. My father is forcing me to marry a man I have never met in order to escape marriage to a man who is a monster. I have no desire to be married to anyone if it will keep me away from the jungle I love so much. Please, great jungle spirit, I beg you to help me."

The magnificent bird tilts its head again and regards me silently for a moment then looks at Tupa. "She is not so different from you, is she, Tupa?" Tupa growls again. "As I recall, you came to me to escape from a life you had not chosen as well. How interesting that you two have found each other."

The words make little sense to me. Did Tupa make a bargain with the karawara as well? If so, what did he bargain for? How is it that we are alike? I want to ask Tupa my questions, but now is not the time. Questions can wait.

"Please, mighty one," I beg, "grant me your favor." I step away from Tupa and toward the great white egret, careful to keep my eyes lowered in reverence and respect. When I am standing before the mighty bird, I prostrate myself on the ground and wait for him to speak.

I do not wait long.

"Arise, human," the spirit says. "I will grant your request."

I stand, both elated that he will help me and terrified about what he will do.

"You humans call us forest spirits fickle, as if we enjoy bringing both harm and joy to those who seek our help," the karawara says, staring at Tupa. "It is not true that we delight in the pain our magic creates. But, in truth, all magic requires sacrifice. And sacrifice leads to pain."

Sacrifice? Pain? My heart begins to race.

"Are you willing to make a sacrifice to gain what you most desire? Are you willing to bear the pain of your action?" the karawara asks me.

I turn back to look at Tupa. He shakes his head. "You do not need to do this," he whispers.

But he is wrong. I do.

"Yes," I answer. "I am willing."

The egret struts up to me, its plumy feathers quivering in the gentle breeze. "Take one," it says.

After a moment of hesitation I select a feather whiter than all the stars in the sky and pull. My hand meets slight resistance, but the feather finally releases from the body, and I hold it before me. A drop of the karawara's blood hangs off the tip of the quill.

"I have given my sacrifice," the bird says. "Now you must give yours. Let the blood drip onto your hand."

I hold the feather over my open hand. The blood dangles briefly then drops into my palm. It shines there, a bulbous dot of crimson before the color drains from it, turning it white. It then sinks into my skin, disappearing from sight.

He continues to instruct me. "Follow Tupa to the river. He will show you what to do."

I turn to my friend. His head is low and it seems that a great weight presses down upon his strong back. The sun is setting beyond the jungle, and the twilight world descends for the few moments remaining before darkness falls completely. Tupa says nothing more to me, only turns his head toward the river and begins to walk.

He leads me to the pool where the water is calm, pauses for a brief moment, and then plunges into the middle of the river. The water surrounds him, and in seconds it is nearly level with his head.

"Come, little bird," he says, his voice strangely hollow.

I obey and walk into the river as well. The water is cold but not so much that it shocks me. Instead it causes me to be even more alert. I wade in next to him until the water covers my shoulders.

"Go under," Tupa says, then dips his own head below the surface of the water and disappears from my view. I take several deep breaths. When I have gained my courage, I dip my head under the water as well.

I feel the power of the river rush into me, stretching my skin, my bones, my muscles. I think it should hurt, but the experience is pleasurable and calming. I feel the soul of the river flow around me, through me, mingling its essence with my own.

I long to stay in this embrace forever, but too soon my lungs ache for air, and I break the surface of the water. The spell of the river breaks as well, and I no longer feel its power flowing all around me. I am simply standing in the river.

Directly in front of me, where my jaguar friend should be, stands a man I have never seen before. I step back in surprise, but my feet do not move correctly. They bend strangely beneath me, thick and powerful. I jump away from the stranger and swim back to the river's shore.

When I step out of the water, I understand why my legs do not feel quite right. They are shorter than before, thicker, and covered with fur. My feet are no longer my own; they were replaced with padded paws and claws.

The fur covering my skin is short and completely white save for black splotches and rosettes dotting it randomly.

I know now what my sacrifice is. I am no longer a human girl. I am a jaguar.

The man walks out of the river and sits down beside me on the bank. *Who are you?* I try to ask, but a deep, rumbling growl escapes my lips. I cannot speak. The man seems to understand me just the same.

"Rosara, it's me," he says. "Tupa."

UPA? I try to say, but I growl again instead.

"It will be a while before you're able to speak," says the man. "It was seven days before I was able to speak with anything other than the roar of a jaguar. It will come to you, though. This may even be easier for now, if you're not able to talk. Just listen."

I shake my head and the rest of my body follows, spattering water into the air. I can feel my ears, no longer on the sides of my head but on top, twitch back and forth in sync with the sounds of the forest. The man's voice sounds strange to me, more musical. I can hear all the different tones layered on each other that make up the harmonious whole of his voice. I'm lost in the melody of it until he stops speaking completely and stares at me with a smile on his face.

"Are you listening to me, little bird?" he asks, and I know without a doubt that somehow this is my friend Tupa, the jungle king.

I growl in response, frustrated that I cannot communicate what I am thinking.

"Everything will be strange at first," he explains, "as you adjust to your jaguar senses. You will see, hear, and smell differently."

As soon as the words are out of his mouth, I notice that my eyesight is much keener than before, and that I can clearly smell the sharp tinge of human skin and sweat.

I want to ask how he knows this. What happened to him? I tilt my head to the side as I regard him with a look that I hope expresses all the questions tumbling through my brain.

"It grows late," Tupa says, standing. "I must return to my home. Will you walk through the jungle with me, Rosara?"

He wades back into the river, swims across, and stands on the opposite bank, looking at me until I follow. We progress through the jungle along paths I have never walked before, as the evening rain begins to pour. Tupa remains silent through most of our journey, which I don't mind. Everything feels so new and different, and the whole of my attention is focused on absorbing it all.

The rain ends quickly, and before long night has fallen. I have no trouble seeing in the dark, and I use the cloak of darkness to surreptitiously steal glances at Tupa as we walk through the jungle. He is tall, thin, and muscular. His hair is dark as night, but he wears it cut short, unlike the men of my village, who keep their hair long. I sense the jaguar in him as he walks along, silent and agile. It is strange how utterly foreign he is and yet so familiar at the same time.

He catches me studying him, and I quickly look away, but not before I notice his smile. It is small and sad. And yet, sad though it is, his smile makes his face all the more beautiful, and I think of it long after I look away.

I hope to see him smile at me again . . . but then I remember that we are nearing his village and the family he has waiting there.

I have no business feeling giddy for his smile. I tell myself not to mistake his friendship and kindness for something more than it is.

I smell the village long before I see or hear it. The scent of man is pungent and easily recognizable.

Tupa slows as we reach the outskirts. Torches have been lit, though even without their light I could easily see everything. The structure of this village is nothing like the shabono of my own tribe. Rather than situating a central, semi-circular hut on razed jungle ground, this tribe has embraced the jungle, building structures that seem to sprout up out of the trees themselves. Wooden braces hold palm-thatched huts and wooden walkways high above the ground and against the trunks of the thickest trees. Swinging rope bridges made of jungle vine and wooden planks connect dwellings together and even span to the far side of the river, where more huts populate the trees. A bevy of canoes sit tethered on the river's banks.

Turning in circles I gaze up in awe at how the people of this village have joined with the jungle instead of struggling against it. Children run across swaying bridges. A young girl swings from one hut to another by a series of vines. The people here seem to share more in common with monkeys than with men. I love it.

"Welcome to my home, Rosara," Tupa says, his voice breaking the silence that has grown thick between us on our journey. His arms spread wide as if to encompass the entire village, and the smile on his face reveals his love for his home.

There are many questions I wish to ask. A growling, mewling sound rolls off my tongue instead of the words I long to say.

Tupa seems to understand my need to communicate. "I know how frustrating it is to be without your voice. I'll tell you what I know, and you may ask me more questions in the morning if you'd like." His statement raises even more questions.

"Every day before dawn, you must enter the river in the exact place where you transformed into a jaguar. Swim to the middle of the river and duck under the water, just as we did this evening. Your body will return to its natural form. It is most important that you do this before the first rays of sunlight break over the forest. If you miss that moment between dark and dawn, you'll remain a jaguar forever.

"At dusk you must repeat the process and enter the river again just before nightfall. This is part of your sacrifice. From now on you will live half of your life as a jaguar and half as human."

My heart thuds rapidly in my chest. I had thought that I'd been made a jaguar for all time, but now I am glad to know that at least for half of each day I will become human again.

"I also must return to the pool before dawn or else I, too, will forever be cursed to remain a beast."

I think how odd it is that Tupa lives as a jaguar during the day and I will live as one during the night. We will never be human at the same time. Perhaps that is also part of the sacrifice, to live our lives unable to share this strange experience with the one other person who understands it.

"I have much more to tell you," Tupa says, "but now come and meet my people. They are used to my being a jaguar by now. I'm sure they will get used to you as well. That is, if you choose to stay with us."

Tupa leads me to a vast wimba tree, larger than any I have ever seen. I look up and up until its trunk disappears into the canopy of leaves and branches above. Around the trunk hang several rope ladders that lead up to a wooden platform fanning out around the tree.

"Do you think you can beat me?" Tupa asks with a wide grin on his face. He grabs onto a rung of a ladder hanging from the tree and pulls himself up. He ascends the tree faster than I thought possible, and before I know it, he is looking down at me from the platform. I haven't yet tested my jaguar legs and claws, though I feel the power in them as I pace back and forth underneath the tree.

"What are you waiting for, little bird? Come on. Fly!" he calls.

His teasing gives me the courage I need. I pounce onto the trunk of the tree and bound up its side, my mighty back legs launching me upwards. In moments I am standing next to him on the platform high above the ground.

"This way," he says, and I follow him through the tree village. A few people stare momentarily as I walk past, but most of them hardly pay attention to me. Instead, the people of the village greet Tupa with warm smiles and waves. I wonder who he is to them. The people of my village do not greet each other so enthusiastically. Life is too difficult, and too much tension exists between us to allow for easy smiles and happy faces. The feeling of calm and acceptance in this village warms my heart.

Tupa leads me to the largest dwelling of the village, lifted high above the ground and resting in the midst of several grandfather trees. A torch provides light at the entrance, and an older man, nearly the same age as my father, sits in the entrance of the dwelling. He stands as we walk across the rope bridge leading to the structure and greets Tupa with open arms and a warm embrace.

"Welcome home, Tupa!" the man cries jovially. Tupa returns the embrace and stands back for the man to see me clearly.

"Allow me to introduce my friend Rosara, daughter of Rapau, chief of the jungle people," Tupa says. He turns to face me. "This is Trumak, chieftain of the river people."

The briefest of moments pass as understanding fills my brain. My father betrothed me to the son of the chieftain of the river people, whom I have never met, but who he believes will protect me from Maor. This man's son is the man I refused to marry; to escape him I ran to the karawara for help. My heart skips a beat. Where is he? Inside the hut, perhaps? My curiosity rises. I wish to catch a glimpse of the man my father hopes I will wed, but I see no one.

Tupa speaks instead. "Trumak is my father, Rosara."

I look at Tupa and finally see the man I am betrothed to marry.

IX

THE SMILE on Tupa's mouth does not reach his eyes. Does he realize that my father meant for me to be betrothed to him? Surely he must. Does he care? Of this I'm not so sure. I do not know my sometimes-jaguar friend well enough as a human to guess what he is thinking.

"So this is your maiden friend," Trumak, Tupa's father, says as if he knows me already.

"Yes, this is my friend, Father. Rosara. She met a karawara this evening, and he helped her to escape a terrible fate." Again, the smile that does not reach his eyes. Does he refer to my being claimed by Maor or being betrothed to him? Or both? I wish he would elaborate, but he says nothing more.

"A karawara? It must have been a very terrible fate for you to seek a jungle spirit, my child," Trumak says kindly to me, stroking the fur on my chin. I'm momentarily distracted by how pleasing that feels. "You are welcome to stay here in our village for as long as you need. Our home in the jungle is yours as well."

Trumak stops rubbing my chin, and I regain my focus. I'm warmed by his invitation though uncertain what to make of it. I imagine what would happen if our situations were reversed and I brought Tupa to my village. Without a doubt he would meet with hostility and suspicion. Likely he would be challenged by another man in the village and possibly killed. This is the way of our village, and so it has been for generations. I don't know how to respond to Trumak's warm hospitality.

Tupa embraces his father again before Trumak leaves us alone, crossing the bridge and entering another dwelling. "Come, little bird. Let's get something to eat," Tupa says, and I follow him into the hut. A small fire sits atop the center of a large, concave stone, its smoke curling up and out of the hut through a small hole in the palm-thatched roof.

Hanging from the curved branches forming the structure of the roof are thin liana vines holding several fat fish over the fire. Tupa releases several of the fish, cupping them in large, waxy leaves. He places them on the floor for me.

"Please eat," he says.

I try to eat slowly, appreciatively, but the fish are gone instantly. I swallow them whole, bones and all. Tupa has barely begun to eat his. My jaguar stomach growls. Evidently it finds a few fish to be a meager meal. Tupa smiles and hands me his as well.

"Don't worry. I can find something else to eat."

I finish the rest of his meal and decide to try out my voice again. I make several attempts, but I only manage a rather weak roar. Tupa chuckles at me. "Give it time," he says, "I know it will come."

I still have so many unanswered questions. He looks back at me, frowns, and looks away. I wonder briefly if I have done something to offend him, and then he speaks.

"There is something I must admit to you," he says in a voice barely above a whisper. My jaguar ears pick up every word clearly. "I, too, sought out a karawara to escape a fate that I thought I could not live with. My father revealed to me many moons ago that I was betrothed to a girl of another village, and if her father invoked the right of betrothal, then I would be bound to her in marriage. It was a bargain my father made long ago, when I was just a child. I had no say in the betrothal, no choice, which is so important to my people. I thought I could never love a woman I had not chosen for myself. I did not know it would be you."

For the moment I am glad that I cannot speak, for I'm not sure what I would say if I could. I want to know more. Does he wish he had not become a beast? Does he wish I had not?

"The day I met you in the tree and realized who you were was the first time I regretted my choice. Until then I thought you were just the spoiled, chieftain's daughter of a backward tribe. I'd met your father on occasion and had come to respect him, but the stories of the jungle dwellers . . ." He pauses and I look away.

It isn't until this moment that I even consider the situation from his point of view. What must have it been like for him to find out that he was betrothed to a girl of a faraway tribe, used to a life of savagery? What must he have thought of me before we actually met? The karawara's words from earlier ring in my ears: "She is not so different from you, is she, Tupa?" No wonder he, too, sought out the magic of the karawara. He was just as scared as I.

"I tried to tell you who I was this morning, when I found you in the jungle. I wanted to. But the magic of the karawara keeps me from revealing my true self while I am in my jaguar form."

I bring the memory of this morning to my mind. It feels like a lifetime ago that I found Pucu's slain body hidden in the jungle.

"And then you said the words that made it impossible for me tell you more," he continued. "You asked me to take you to the karawara. Their magic has bound me to them as a servant. If anyone requests an audience with a karawara, I must obey. I tried to fight against it, but ultimately I had no choice.

"You are bound to them now too, Rosara. I am so sorry. I wanted to tell you, to protect you from this, but . . ." His voice trails off into silence. We sit together, neither of us saying anything, while the fire burns down.

Trumak enters the hut. "It is late, son. We should sleep."

Tupa nods at his father, and before long Trumak is snoring in a hammock. Another empty hammock hangs loose in the hut, but Tupa does not climb into it. Instead he slides his body down to the floor. I lie down next to him, but he does not touch me. Though there are only a few inches between us, the distance feels much greater. Was it only this afternoon that I woke up next to his jaguar body with his arm embracing me? It feels so long ago.

"Goodnight, little bird," Tupa says, closing his eyes.

I stay until I know he is asleep. The change in his breathing indicates when it is safe to go. My jaguar paws are silent as I exit the hut and leave the village to enter the darkness of the jungle.

It is as if I have entered a new world. Everywhere, I see and hear the heartbeat of a jungle that I never knew existed. Even though I've lived in the midst of the jungle my entire life, I had no idea how much life exists here. The flora and fauna overwhelm me with beauty, and I feel deprived that as a jaguar I cannot cry for joy. I expect I will shed many tears in the morning when I return to my natural form.

What will I do in the morning when I return to normal? I cannot go to my father's village. That was the whole reason I sought the karawara for help. But in my human form I will not be safe in the jungle, at least, not without help. Perhaps I should return to Tupa's village during the day. His father is so warm and inviting; indeed, his entire village is quite unlike my own home.

A great need fills me as I think of my father and the village I have known my whole life. I do not wish to return there to live, but I long to see it with my jaguar eyes. Just for a moment.

I move through the jungle with purpose, following the scent trail left behind when Tupa and I traveled to his village. I'm amazed by how obvious the trail is to my nose, even more than to my eyes, though I can also see every blade of grass that bent beneath our feet as we walked. No wonder Tupa knew where I lived in the village that first day we met.

I follow the trail all the way to the river, and then wade across the pool where I transformed into a beast. How quickly my life has changed—how my world has changed. It is difficult for me to consider all the implications of my decision to seek the karawara for help.

The trail continues through the forest, though this time the human scent is my own. How strange I smell to my own nose. Stranger still is Tupa's jaguar scent. Its muskiness wafts through the air like perfume, impossible to ignore. It is everywhere. This land has been clearly marked as his territory. I approach the village and find that his scent is strongest in the trees nearest my father's plot under the shabono. Tupa was here many times, watching me from the safety of the jungle.

Movement from the shabono catches my eye, and I push aside thoughts of Tupa and concentrate my other senses on what is happening in the village below. Men are gathering in a corner of the village. Weapons are being stacked. Someone is sharpening the stone blade of a spear. I leave the safety of the tree and silently tread around the shabono to crouch where I can more clearly see what is happening.

"We'll start the hunt at first light," I hear my father say.

"We should go now!" a man yells, challenging my father. I know his voice as well. Maor.

"It will be safer to wait until dawn," my father explains.

"My first wife is dead! None of us are safe. Even your daughter was not safe from the beast. No doubt it killed her as it killed Pucu. Would you leave her body to rot in the jungle and have her spirit walk in agony for eternity? We must avenge our women and kill the beast!"

Men's voices ring in the air in support of Maor. My heart sinks.

"Rosara's body was not in the jungle. My own wives showed us where the great jaguar walked out of the jungle near Pucu's body, but we do not know for certain what happened to my daughter. It is possible she is still alive. We do not even have proof that the great jaguar killed your first wife, Maor. You have quickly forgotten that it was the beast who saved my daughter from—"

Maor interrupts before my father can finish. "What more proof do you need than the torn body of my first wife? What other monster could do that besides the one we have seen stalking our village? We should kill the beast!"

More men join in the cry, echoing Maor's words: "*Kill the beast!*"

I do not realize that I have been walking closer to the village until the voices stop and I see the terrified eyes of my father staring into mine.

"I am not dead!" I cry out, but my voice is not my own. The men step back, fear etched across their faces.

"Rosara?" my father says. I turn my head to look at him. He is the only man who has not stepped away from me in fear. How he recognizes me I cannot guess. He holds his hand out as if to touch me.

"A white jaguar can mean only one thing. It is her ghost!" Maor yells. "Rosara's spirit is here to punish us for leaving her body to decay in the jungle."

"No!" I yell, but instead my roar sounds like an affirmation of Maor's proclamation. The men nod their heads and then lift their voices in agreement. "We must avenge her death. Kill the beast!"

Frustration seizes me. If only I could talk, tell them what happened. Tell them I am still alive and that Tupa had nothing to do with my death or Pucu's. But of course Maor knows that Tupa did not kill Pucu. He is only using this opportunity to his advantage, and I've practically handed him another reason to hunt Tupa.

Anger wells up within me. My muscles grow taut. Maor raises his spear toward the sky above with a war cry, and I can hold back my rage no longer. Anger pours out through my roar as I spring, knocking him to the ground. His hands and feet are quick to push me off, but I am quicker, and I graze him with my claws, leaving a red gash oozing across his chest.

Maor scrambles backward out of my reach, but my anger is not yet satiated. I lunge again, and he barely escapes my jaws as another tribesman jumps between us. This man is not so lucky though—my jaws clamp down on his forearm. The unfortunate man's scream rips through the air along with the crunching of bone as his arm snaps between my teeth.

I open my mouth, horrified at what I've just done. Then pain explodes in my side. I turn my head and see a spear jabbed into the haunch of my leg. The hand holding it is my father's. He pulls it out and I roar in agony.

The men of the village begin to surround me, their spears held high to strike as well. In a moment I will be dead. And after me, they will likely hunt down Tupa. Though I would happily give my life if it meant stopping Maor, I cannot allow them to harm Tupa. I must warn him.

I stumble backward toward the jungle as waves of pain flow from the wound down through my leg. Maor stands with difficulty but then grabs his spear and trains it on me. Father grasps his shoulder, giving me the chance I need. I turn and leap back into the jungle and allow the darkness of the night to cloak me. Several thrown spears follow me into the jungle, but the men are frightened and do not take careful aim. They miss.

I flee to the outskirts of the village and listen to the men plot their revenge. Maor speaks, and I hear his voice rising in the night, mingled with pain and rage:

"This is a sign, brothers! Rosara's spirit is angry and must be avenged. As soon as my wounds are bound, we will hunt. Then we will kill the beast that caused all this misery."

Voices of men agree and cry out for Tupa's death. I listen closely for the voice of my father to disagree and contradict Maor's attempt to lead the men of the village. This is his village. He is the chief.

But I do not hear his voice. I realize that my father is the chieftain no more.

X

MY HAUNCH aches and my leg stiffens more and more as I make my way back through the jungle. I know I am bleeding out, but I cannot stop moving. I need to get to Tupa. Warn him. Stop Maor.

I hear the river calling me, and I follow its gentle voice until I can walk no further. I'm near the pool where I saw the jungle king become a man. Where I made my choice to leave my village forever. I don't regret that decision even now, when I can no longer walk. No longer move. No longer open my eyes.

I don't know how much time has passed when I hear the sound of splashing in the river and catch Tupa's human scent. I smell it long before I hear his voice call out my name.

But my eyes will not open. It hurts. I hurt.

Tupa's arms encircle me, lift my head and shoulders off the ground and into his lap. "Rosara, what happened?" he asks.

I want to laugh at how ludicrous his question is. Even if I could muster the energy to answer him, he would not be able to understand my jaguar voice. Fighting against the inertia of the dull pain that wants to pull me back into sleep, I open my eyes.

Tupa's face is only inches from my own, his eyes glassy with tears threatening to spill out at any moment. His hand strokes my cheek, and he murmurs soft, comforting words into my ears as his other hand tentatively searches the skin surrounding my wound. The jungle is lighter. It is nearly dawn. Tupa and I must get to the river before it is too late.

I try to stand, but my hind legs will not work. Tupa attempts to help me to my feet, but I collapse with the first step.

"The magic of the river will help to heal you," he whispers to me. I hold onto his promise, hoping it is true and not just his wishful thinking.

He encircles my torso with his strong arms and begins to drag me to the river. He struggles to heave my body across the ground until we enter the river and the buoyancy of the water lifts my body, making it easier for him to carry me to the slowly moving pool. My head rests against his shoulder, and we wait for the moment when the world is neither day nor night, but that magical moment in between. The colors of the forest sharpen. A hush falls as newly woken animals stop their chattering in reverence for this magical moment.

Tupa smiles down at me. "It will be all right," he says, and then he pushes me under the water.

I thought I knew pain.

I was wrong.

My jaguar body convulses and spasms as my limbs elongate and change. I can feel my bones break, reattach, and break again. I can't breathe.

I can't see. I feel nothing but pain.

I don't understand. My transformation to a jaguar was completely painless. Why does it hurt so much now?

I know it has been only moments since Tupa pushed me under the water's surface, but the agony makes it seem like an eternity while I'm awash in wave after wave of pain. Finally it begins to subside. My body stops jerking in Tupa's arms. I am able to relax in the buoyant embrace of the river.

Tupa pulls me up out of the water, and I stand.

It takes me a moment to realize that he no longer needs to hold me. My legs are working perfectly fine. The pain of the transformation is gone. The pain of my injury is also gone. I put my hand to my hip, expecting to feel a hole from where my father's spear pierced me, but there is nothing but smooth skin. I am healed. Tupa's arms are still around me though.

"It's a little different when you've been injured, isn't it?" he asks with a smile, and I see that the tears are still in his eyes. I nod in answer, still too shaken from the experience of becoming human again to speak. "Rosara, what happened?" Tupa asks. "Why were you hurt? Who did that to you?"

Memories of the previous evening slam into me. I must warn him. "It doesn't matter what happened to me. Tupa, I have to warn you—"

I stop. The light is growing more intense. Dawn is nearly here. "You must change!" I yell at him. "Now!"

Realization ripples across his face. A few more seconds and it will be too late. He will change into his jaguar form forever and never again become a man. He slips wordlessly into the water, and I wait impatiently for him to surface. I have to warn him. Maor is coming with men from the village to kill him. We must run deep into the heart of the jungle and hide.

I am anxious to speak to him. Time passes, and I begin to wonder if something has happened. Finally the jungle king's jaguar head lifts out of the water, and he begins to swim back to shore. I follow him, eager to tell him what we must do. Just as he climbs ashore, a cry rings from the trees. A spear flies through the air and lodges in Tupa's shoulder.

He drops to the ground. One paw bats at the spear while he unsuccessfully attempts to pull it out with his mouth. I run to him, trying not to care about the sound of someone rushing toward us through the jungle. I grab the end of the spear but cannot see its head; it is embedded too deeply.

Tupa's eyes roll back in his head. Fear overwhelms me. I don't know if I should dislodge the spear or if that will cause more damage. I know I must decide quickly. I grip the pole and pull it out with a quick jerk. Tupa's body spasms briefly, and blood pours from the wound.

This cannot be happening. The words have only an instant to pass through my mind before I am struck in the back of the head and fall to the ground. I do not lose consciousness, though black dots dance before my eyes. A hand yanks me onto my back, and for a moment all I can see is the canopy of jungle trees until a face hovers above my own.

Maor bends down and lifts me off the ground by my hair. "Good morning, Rosara. I'm glad you are not dead. Yet."

He drops my head, and it slams back into the ground. The black dots spin again.

"I've been watching you for some time, you know," I hear him say above me. "It wasn't difficult to track you through the jungle. I knew that the beast would come for you. For a while I thought you might die, but then that man arrived and pulled you into the river. I didn't know who he was at first, but when you walked out of the river as a girl, with the beast beside you, I knew what you both were." He leans down and presses his cheek against mine, and whispers into my ear. "You are demons. And you must be destroyed."

My vision clears just in time to see Maor pick up the spear from the ground and hold it above me, preparing to plunge it into my chest. I don't even have time to shout out before he pulls his arm back.

From the corner of my eye I see Tupa lift his head, and then his whole body flings through the air and crashes into Maor. The whoosh of the air parting around the tip of the spear sounds in my ear as it embeds itself in the dirt just a hair's breadth away from my head.

A loud hiss comes from Tupa, and tension ripples through his body. He has knocked Maor to the ground, and now he stands between us. Tupa's head is tucked low to the ground, and his shoulders roll, indicating that he is waiting for the perfect opportunity to pounce. I scramble to my feet and brace my legs, ready to run in any direction.

Maor pulls himself off the ground, his eyes huge with fear and fire. A lonely beam of sunlight has made its way through the canopy above us and shines on the knife in Maor's hand. I know that someone here will die.

Tupa growls but then begins to back up, pushing against me, forcing me back toward the river. Maor follows. Taking slow, deliberate steps, he holds the knife in front of him, swinging it back and forth.

I step back into the water of the river. A shriek escapes Maor's mouth. His lips curl back, exposing his teeth, as he rushes toward us with his knife flying through the air. Tupa rears onto his back legs and catches Maor between his great paws. I see the knife for an instant and watch as it impacts skin, muscle, and bone.

Tupa roars and falls backwards onto me. I see the blade protruding from his chest before I plunge backwards into the river.

Water covers me. It isn't deep, probably just over my knees if I were standing, but on my back I'm completely covered. I see nothing, though I feel Tupa on top of me, pinning me down. In my surprise, I gasped in a mouthful of water, and my lungs ache to expel it. My throat burns. I push against Tupa's body, but he is too heavy. Frantic, I beat my hands against him. Finally he moves.

I sit up and cough out water. Wet hair plasters my face, and I push it aside just in time to see Maor dislodge the knife from Tupa's body and strike him once again in his side. I've never heard a jaguar scream before. The sound of it sends a sickening shiver down my spine.

I don't realize what I'm doing, but suddenly I'm flying through the air, grabbing, kicking, punching, scratching, biting—anything I can do to bring Maor down. I target his chest, reopening the wounds I gave him in my jaguar form. My human body is no match for his, and after his initial surprise, he is easily able to fend me off, and he pushes me back down into the river.

I look to Tupa. His mangled form lies half in the river, half on the bank. I cannot tell if he is still breathing. Please, still be breathing!

Maor stands between us and speaks. "I would have made you my wife, but you would rather be with this demon beast. You belong together then. In death."

He walks toward me, and I try to get to my feet, but he is too quick. I feel his hands grab my arms from behind. His foot hooks my legs and I fall, face first, back into the river. Maor pins me to the floor of the riverbed, his knee jammed into the small of my back, my body sinking down into the muddy sand of the river bottom.

My throat and chest ache for air. I need to breathe. I struggle against the need to take a breath, but my body acts on reflexe, and water rushes into my lungs, burning all the while. I thrash and twist, but there is no escape. I know I am going to die.

After the longest moment of my life, a peace settles over me. Darkness comes. Just a few moments more, I tell myself. It will soon be over. Tupa and I will be together after all, in death.

The pressure on my back lifts. A moment passes. Something grabs on to me. It's sharp. Painful. It pulls on my arm. I break the surface again. My body is dragged out of the river, and my lungs heave. I vomit out water and hungrily suck oxygen deep into my burning chest.

I sit up on the riverbank and see Maor's face staring at me with vacant eyes, his body floating in the water, making its way into the current where the river will carry it downstream. I watch his carcass disappear from view and let out a breath of relief.

XI

I HEAR Tupa release a sigh, wet and gurgling. I turn away from the river to see him lying on the bank just behind me. His beautiful fur is coated with blood. I'm not sure whether all of it is his, but certainly much of it is. Gashes all over his beautiful body bleed freely. He breathes in great heaving pants. I rush to him, eager to help but afraid I might hurt him further.

There is so much I want to say to him, but the only words I can muster are "Tupa, you saved me." I bury my head in his neck and wrap my arms around his great body. A sob escapes my lips. "Don't leave me. Please," I beg him.

His voice is quiet and raspy, his body shaking with effort. "I'm sorry, little bird. It seems I am bound for the great iwa. I promise to look after you from there. Always."

"No," I argue. "It's not your time yet. You belong here with me."

"I don't think it's up to you," he says with an agonized rumble in his throat. His eyes close. I shut my own tight and pray more fiercely than I've ever prayed before.

Oh great karawara, spirits of the jungle, hear my cry! My heart lifts my prayer to the canopy, and I hear it echoed in the call of the birds, the breezy shaking of the leaves, and the ripple of the river waters. Tears stream down my face as Tupa's breaths become more and more shallow. It will not be long now.

Please, please deliver him. I will sacrifice myself. I will sacrifice!

The throaty warble of a bird rings in my ears, and I look up to see a ghostly white egret standing on the lowest branch of a tree just beside me. He stretches his head toward me and speaks. "Would you truly give your life for this beast?" he asks.

I can barely see the bird for the tears in my eyes but nod in its direction. "Yes," I say, "I'll give anything I have to offer if you'll save him."

"I told you that magic always requires sacrifice," the bird says. "In order to save his life, you must give up yours."

I speak without reservation. "I give it. Gladly."

The bird's feathers rustle. He unfolds his wings partially and refolds them again. He is agitated or excited, I'm not sure which. "Do you love him?" the bird asks.

Love? The word itself had never entered my mind before. Admire, respect, treasure? Yes. All of these words come easily. I gaze down at Tupa's face. I can see through his jaguar form to the man within—a man who has saved me more than once. A man who has fought for me. Who may die for me.

Love him? How can I not?

I nod. Tupa's breath rattles in his chest. There isn't much time. "Tell me what to do."

The bird's head bobs a few more times as his long neck snakes back and forth. He finally answers, "Pull him into the river. The magic will heal him there."

I waste no time and haul Tupa's heavy jaguar body into the river a few inches at a time until the water helps lift his body fully into the river. I pull him close to my chest.

The karawara signals me. "Now. Push him beneath the surface and allow the magic to heal him."

I bend my head over his, kiss his forehead, and say, "I love you, Tupa. Please live."

I push him under.

Nothing happens at first, and I fear I am too late. Then Tupa's body jerks and tenses beneath my hands. I feel his back arch, and I remember the pain I felt when the river healed my own broken body. I thought I was dying. My heart aches for Tupa as he undergoes the same pain, but I continue to hold him down until the healing is complete.

He changes in my hands. The fur on his body recedes, leaving behind the smooth flesh of skin. His muscles roll and twist beneath my fingers, snapping into place in their human form. Finally Tupa stops jerking. His hands lift above the surface and clasp my arms. I release him, and he rises up out of the water. I think I have never seen anyone as beautiful in my life.

"Rosara," he says, "you saved me."

I can only nod. There is too much in my heart to speak. I know I do not have long. I made a bargain with the karawara, and I will be held accountable for it soon. I may have only seconds left with Tupa before I die.

He pulls me into his arms and holds me tightly. I relish his embrace and can no longer hold back the sorrow of nearly losing him. He steps back and looks into my eyes. His seem like great pools of darkness that I could swim in forever.

"Is it true?" he asks. "Do you truly love me?"

My voice has lost its strength, but I am able to whisper, "I do."

He pulls my face to his, and his lips are on mine. I press against him and hold him tightly, fighting against the fear that threatens to overwhelm me. His embrace is as forceful and wild as my own, and I wonder if he knows what I've chosen to give up for him.

Although I am afraid, I do not regret it. I love him. I will always love him. I will love him from beyond, and vow to watch over and protect him when I reach the great iwa where our ancestors rest.

Our lips part too soon. I yearn for more. But I have made a promise, and it is time to keep it. I turn my head to the shore and see the karawara's feathers splayed out in all their majesty. He is beautiful indeed.

Tupa takes my hand in his, and together we walk to the water's edge.

"Rosara has made a great sacrifice for you, Tupa," the karawara says. "She has given her life for yours. It is time for her debt to be paid. The magic of the river demands its payment."

Tupa's hand clutches mine tightly. I see anger flash across his face, quickly replaced by fear. He is about to speak when the great white egret says, "Come, child."

Nothing in my life has prepared me for this. I don't want to die, but more powerful than my fear of death is my need for Tupa to live. I tear my hand from his and walk to the bird.

"Take a feather," he says, and I remember living this moment just yesterday. It seems a lifetime ago now, when I became a jaguar. The lacy feathers quiver as my hand catches one. I look at Tupa. I know from his expression that he can see my love for him. I hope it will be enough. I know it can never be enough. I pull.

There is a slight resistance, and then the feather comes free from the bird's body. I hold it in front of me. A droplet of blood sits on the tip of the quill.

The karawara tilts his head toward Tupa. "Now you," he instructs, "take your turn."

Tupa's surprised expression matches my own. Why should Tupa have to partake in this? I don't understand. I made the bargain with the karawara, not Tupa.

He doesn't hesitate, however, but pulls out a feather as well. We stand staring at each other. I am wondering how much time we still have together. I wonder if Tupa is thinking the same thing. These moments are precious. I do not want to waste a single one.

"The sacrifice has been made," the bird says. "Throw the feathers into the middle of the river."

Tupa and I walk out into the river and release the silky egret feathers. As soon as they hit the surface they melt into a burst of inky color that travels through the water toward our bodies. Light surrounds then envelops us. It's warm and not unpleasant. I hope it won't be painful to die. I look to Tupa. He is smiling and holds out his hand to me. I grab it and hope to continue holding onto him as we step into our afterlife together.

The light fades and recedes back through the water to two brown feathers floating on the surface. I don't understand. Shouldn't I be dead by now? Shouldn't I be walking through the misty land of the iwa?

I turn around in time to see the karawara fly up and into a tree. He turns and looks at us as if he is studying us. Perhaps that is what he is doing. Perhaps for him it was just a game. Or a test. "I don't understand," I say to him. "I thought I was going to die."

"Yes, well . . . life is completely predictable only in its unpredictability. Besides, you did die in a way," he says in his silky-smooth voice. "Your life as a jaguar is over forever. It has been sacrificed."

It takes a moment for the karawara's words to sink in. By the time I realize what he has said, he is gone and Tupa is pulling me against his chest in a tight embrace. His lips press down hard against mine, and joy fills my heart as I understand the gift we have been given. No longer must we live half-lives, part beast, part human. We will no longer be subject to sharing only a few, brief moments together in the twilight of day and night. We've been given a chance to start again. Together.

I pull back from Tupa and gaze into his eyes. I will never be tired of staring into them. I have to force myself to look away from him, just for a moment. I need to give thanks. I look to the tree where the karawara stood just a moment ago and offer up a prayer of thanksgiving.

I turn back to Tupa and delight in his embrace. Together we cross the river to the other side and begin the journey to his village. Hand-in-hand we walk into the heart of the jungle.

ABOUT THE AUTHOR

DORIAN TSUKIOKA writes fairy tale retellings, young adult fantasy, and science fiction with just a dash of romance thrown in. When she's not writing, Dorian teaches 5th graders in Kansas City, MO, or she can be found chasing after her two pixie-esque daughters. She has a love of learning and teaching, and loves to talk about books with anyone who will listen, especially if the conversation includes cinnamon-chip scones and caramel lattes.

Visit www.DorianWrites.blogspot.com to learn more about Dorian and her work.

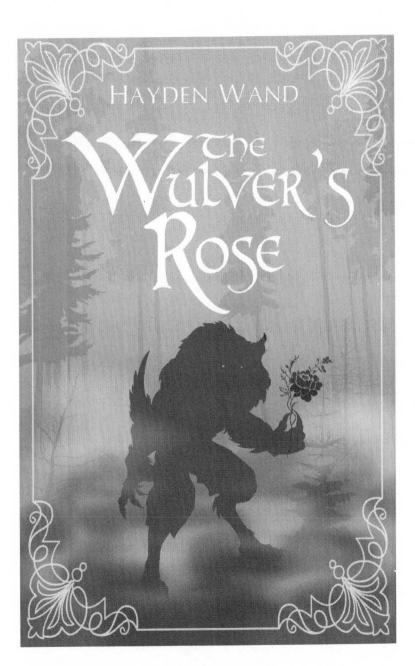

For my grandparents:

Carol & Norman Parker
Robert & Shirley Sorensen
Alvin & Patricia Wand

and my great-grandmother,
Alice D. McGee

who tell the best stories from my family's past

PROLOGUE

1 FORGET things more easily these days.

It seems that the older I get the more scattered my mind becomes. Yet as my present memories escape my grasp, my older ones only grow stronger. My eyes have gone dim with age, and my hands feeble and stiff; yet when I close my eyes I am a little girl again, and I can still remember everything about that day. The day my world was stolen from me and I was thrust into the depths of a living nightmare.

It was early spring, and the wind howled around our family's stone castle, warning of an approaching storm. I wasn't cold; the fire crackled by the hearth, and my father held me in his arms as he so often did. I was the only child of my widowed father and, looking back, I realize now that I was probably a bit spoiled.

He kissed my forehead, but I paid little attention, not knowing it would be his last kiss for a long time. I slid out of his lap to find my doll and took her to play on the rug in front of the fire, intent on my own small musings. It had begun to thunder outside, and rain pounded on the roof. I glanced up from my play for a split moment just as lightning flashed into the large room; its momentary illumination revealed the presence of a woman in the corner across from me.

I screamed in surprise and scrambled to hide in the shadows; my father sprang from his chair and spun to face the direction of my startled gaze.

"Well, well," the woman said. "Isn't this a warm and invitin' picture?" Her voice was cold and elegant, yet her appearance had a primitive aspect that clashed with her refined air. I had never seen her before, and something about her terrified me.

"Morag," my father said, his voice hard and unwavering. "Yer not welcome here."

"Oh, is that the way ye treat yer family, Lauchlan? Really, I'd 'ave thought better of ye." She swept past him and approached me. I stiffened up against the stone wall, unable to move. She leaned in close, put her index finger under my chin, and lifted my face to meet her gaze. Her face was rather ordinary, but a beautiful mass of black hair fell loosely down her back.

Her dark eyes glittered in the firelight as she surveyed me. "And is this me sister's child?"

"Stay away from Róis!" my father barked. But he, too, seemed rooted to the floor.

She slipped her finger from beneath my chin and turned to address him. "She's a beautiful bairn, Lauchlan. I'm so sorry. Mayhap if she were plain I would have more sympathy for her." She arched one brow. "After all, I understand how concerned with appearances ye are."

Though I could not tear my gaze away from the strange woman, from the corner of my eye I saw my father shifting on his feet. "Ye've always thought what ye liked about me, Morag. I have no interest in arguing with ye."

She laughed. "I thought ye'd say somethin' of the sort. After all, what was it ye said when ye rejected me for my beautiful elder sister?"

"Morag—"

"Oh yea, I remember. 'I've chosen the most beautiful girl in all of Alba.' For of course I was but a slug compared to the paragon of beauty that was me sister. Yet who is the beauty now?"

Suddenly she seemed to alter before our very eyes. She appeared to grow taller. Her eyes grew bigger and lightened into a deep blue while her nose straightened and her cheekbones became more pronounced. She had transformed into an unnatural, terrible beauty, bitter and wild. The fire sputtered, and I was too frightened even to cry.

"Morag," my father gasped in horror, seeming to grasp what I had not. "What have ye done?"

"I have embraced me destiny, Lauchlan, and the faith of me mithers before me." Then, all at once, she reverted back to her old self. Her voice was different now, almost pitying, but its lilt seemed to invoke some ancient evil I was as yet too young to understand.

"Ye've embraced the devil, ye have, woman! Ye've no idea what ye've done!"

"I know exactly what I've done, Lauchlan! I've unlocked the powers of the druids. I've felt power, a power that leaves beauty in the dust! And I've come to give ye one more chance. Ye can embrace it with me." For the only time that night, she gazed openly—almost hopefully— at him.

But my father stood as firm as stone, unmoved by her desperation. "I don't care whit ye'll offer. I loved yer sister; that's why I married her, God rest her soul! And I would have loved her no matter whit she'd looked like. Her soul was beautiful—that's whit I saw." His voice broke, and when he regained his speech it was hard and angry. "And I saw yer soul, Morag. I didn't reject ye because of yer appearance. I saw yer soul, and it was black. And it has only grown more polluted!"

The woman Morag lifted her chin, and the cruelty of her gaze returned. "So be it." A breeze blew from the corners of the room and tickled the fire. "Ye say appearances don't matter. Shall we put that to the test?"

I looked around, fascinated yet terrified as the rising wind snuffed the fire with a single gust and began to circle the room until we were in the midst of a whirlwind.

"Morag!" my father yelled. "Stop this at once!"

But Morag continued speaking, her voice growing louder. "I call on the power of Cernunnos! For the powers of terror, revenge, and war!" The wind whipped her hair. A crack of thunder shook the room. I covered my ears and cowered on the floor.

"Cailleach, hear me cry!" The woman began to scream words in old Gaelic that I didn't understand. But my father did, and the wind closed in around him until it was moving so fast I couldn't see him. Sobbing, I crawled into the corner of the hearth and curled into a ball, hiding my eyes from the terror around me. The screams and wind grew louder and louder until they reached a pounding crescendo . . . and then stopped completely. I slowly uncovered my ears but didn't dare look up.

"Love." The woman laughed. Her laugh sounded young and beautiful and genuine, and I shivered. "Can love *really* see past appearances, Lauchlan?" Her voice was playful and condescending, as though she spoke to a baby, but then it turned cynical. "If a woman can love ye—agree to wed ye—as you are now, ye shall be uncursed. Then yer misery will end. If ye cannot win yerself a bride"—she gave a mockery of a smile—"then ye and all yer household will die. Until the time of me reckoning I will be watching ye, drawing power from a hundred years of yer pain."

I opened my eyes and saw her skirts twirl past me and then stop.

"Róis. *Rose*. How appropriate." As I glanced up, she flicked her wrist. I saw a flash of light and knew no more.

CHAPTER 1

Scotland, 1752

1N THE years when Scotland was only just recovering from the uprising known as "The Forty-Five," an astute merchant took advantage of his opportunities and began to make his fortune through trade with the royal houses of Europe.

This merchant, one Gregor Alleway by name, had years ago been married to a young lady of great affluence, whose wealth only increased his own. Though this woman of merit had been struck down in the prime of life by a sudden, violent sickness, she left behind five handsome children who were all beloved of their father and a comfort to him in his bereaved state.

The youngest of these children was a beauty of a girl with wild curly hair and eyes as gray as the mist above the moors. Her given name was Seònaid, but as she was the youngest bairn of the clan, her father had never called her anything more than his "wee bonnie lass," and as the years flew by, this was shortened simply to Bonnie. A childish name, and long before her thirteenth year Bonnie felt that she had outgrown it, but she was too fond of her father to tell him so.

The family lived in a large house in the town of Burntisland, on the east coast of Scotland. Despite his wealth, the expense of raising five children often drained the merchant's plentiful coffers. Still, there was money enough for pleasure as well as necessities, and the family's existence was more than comfortable. The eldest children enjoyed education abroad, and the merchant knew that he could do no less for his youngest girls.

"I'll never leave you, Da," Bonnie told him determinedly. She was nearly fourteen years of age and had grown up observing her older siblings. Only a few years ago she'd watched her oldest sister, Sorcha, go away to school, returning as what seemed to Bonnie an entirely new person. This prospect frightened her. "I don't want to go away."

The family were gathered that night in the drawing room of their beautiful stone-front, terraced house located on one of the best streets in Burntisland. Bonnie sat at her father's feet before the fire, but she now rose to her knees and looked at him, the firelight emphasizing the pleading in her eyes.

"Oh Bonnie," Sorcha chided from her place across the hearth, where she sat playing draughts with their middle sister, Maisie, by firelight. "You're too attached to home. It's not healthy in a young lady!" Sorcha had only just returned from France and was grown so elegant and aloof. Bonnie could not imagine this new creation of a sister—who sipped her tea with a genteel air and spent her afternoons embroidering cushions—running around the stables the way she had been wont to do in the past. She spoke differently, too.

Bonnie ignored Sorcha, keeping her attention fixed on her father. She hated to admit that she was afraid to go, afraid to change. Afraid that she might no longer know herself after a few years in France. She took her father's hand. "Please don't make me go."

"If Bonnie doesn't go, I don't want to either," Maisie, the sister closest to Bonnie in age, asserted, distracted from plotting her next move—a distraction which would surely give Sorcha the edge.

"Now, my Margaret," their father said indulgently to Maisie. "You were quite excited about the thought of school yesterday."

"But that was before Bonnie said she didn't want to go! I don't want to be sent to France by myself!"

"Don't be silly, Maisie," Sorcha said, shaking her head dismissively. "Your move."

Maisie moved her draught without thinking, and Sorcha swooped in for a victorious finish to the game. Bonnie only half-heard her two sisters' respective cries of triumph and despair as she continued to squeeze her father's hand. "Please, Da," she said one last time.

"It's already been arranged, my sweet lasses," Mr. Alleway said, gently patting his daughter's hand. "And you have a full summer with us still before you must leave. You'll be glad you've had your education when the time has gone by. And you'll be back before you know it, even as we now have our Sorcha home with us again." He beckoned Maisie close and, rising from his chair, kissed both his younger daughters' foreheads. "I don't want either of you to leave for my own selfish reasons. But sometimes we must do things we do not like for the greater good. Now you'd best be getting off to bed."

Bonnie sighed, momentarily defeated. She took up a candle and lit it at the candle on her father's table, holding the light high to illuminate the way as she and Maisie made for the door. "Good night, Da. Good night, Sorcha."

"Don't forget to say your prayers!" Sorcha reminded her. "And be certain to blow out that candle when you're done."

Bonnie, who was a good girl but not entirely outgrown of childish foolishness, stuck her tongue out at her sister and then hastened from the room before she could be scolded. Cupping her hand around the flame to protect it from drafts, she led Maisie up the stairs to the room they shared on the third floor of the townhouse. Obedient to Sorcha's injunction, both girls made for the prayer closet at once—which was not truly a closet so much as a little bench near the window, set aside for pious reflection. Bonnie placed the candle in its brass holder on the bench, and the two sisters knelt on the floor to whisper prayers into the chilly spring-night air. "*Lighten our darkness, we beseech thee, O Lord; and by thy great mercy defend us from all perils and dangers of this night . . .*"

Upon whispering a hasty *amen*, they helped each other out of their dresses and into their nightgowns, leaving the candle burning so that they might have some light by which to change. In a hurry to get her bare feet off the cold floor, Maisie made a flying leap to the bed and slipped under the covers, huddling into a ball for warmth. Eager to join her sister before she froze half to death, Bonnie climbed into bed, quickly drew the curtains, and slid under the blankets.

"School might not be so bad, Bonnie," Maisie whispered between her chattering teeth. "We'll get to wear fine dresses and have all sorts of lovely things to eat. And maybe we'll meet husbands, like Sorcha did."

"I don't like John," Bonnie said, thinking of her oldest sister's intended. "And she didn't meet him at school. Finishing school is just for girls. How dull must that be?" Bonnie couldn't imagine life without her brothers. "Besides, Calum says Hetty will foal later this summer, and we'll miss that if we leave."

"Oh." Maisie sounded disappointed. "I hadn't thought of that. He promised we could name the foal." She smothered a yawn in her hand and burrowed deeper under the covers.

"Maisie?" Bonnie asked, poking her sister. But Maisie had always been able to fall asleep in an instant and already began to snore. Bonnie smiled to herself, wondering if a French finishing school could do anything to combat snoring.

For an hour—by the count of the clock chiming in the drawing room below—Bonnie tossed and turned in her bed. Through a gap in the bed curtains she saw the glow of the candle she'd left burning on the bench across the room. She really should slide out from under the blankets and snuff the light. But the night was so cold, and the candle would gutter eventually.

She kept thinking of the changes coming up in her life, wishing she might somehow cling to her childhood a little longer. At least Father had decided to keep Maisie back from school for an extra year so that the two sisters might travel together when Bonnie came of age. But the thought brought meager comfort to Bonnie's fearful heart.

She dozed at last, but awakened when the drawing-room clock downstairs struck eleven. The air felt thick in her throat, and she struggled to draw breath. Her eyes flew open and immediately began to stream and sting. She sat up in bed and shoved aside the curtain, only to see brilliant flames climbing the draperies at her window.

The very window under which she had left her candle burning.

"Maisie!" she cried out, grabbing her sister and violently pushing her from the bed. "Maisie, wake up!"

Maisie woke as she hit the floor, screaming before she even knew what was happening. She gasped and choked on her own scream as smoke filled her lungs. Bonnie slipped to the floor as well, keeping low to the ground where some air still lingered. She could not find the will to move, and the fire climbed her curtain and ate into the wall.

Suddenly her door slammed open, and her brother Calum stood in the doorway. He took in the sight in an instant and, putting his arm around his face, rushed in. He nearly fell over Bonnie, but caught his balance at the last. Grabbing her by the back of her nightgown, he hauled her out into the hall. "Make haste!" he cried. "Tell the others the house is afire and get outside!"

Bonnie obeyed even as Calum darted back into the room after Maisie. Not waiting to see him drag his other sister to safety, she pounded on the doors of the other rooms, shouting at the top of her lungs. In moments, the household was awake. Smoke began to fill the hallways, and terrified servants poured down the stairs from their rooms in the garret. Mr. Alleway put sheltering arms around Sorcha as he led the way out into the street.

Bonnie, caught in the flow of people, cried out for Maisie and for Calum. But not until she stood shivering on the stone street outside the house did she realize that neither her brother nor her sister were with them. "Where are they? Where are they?" she screamed, almost incoherent in her terror. The upper rooms of the terrace house were alight with hellish flames.

"Who? Who do you mean?" her father demanded of her, as yet unable to discern in the strange red half-light which of his family members had escaped from the house and which had not.

"Calum! Maisie!"

Hardly had the names left Bonnie's lips when she saw movement in the house doorway. The next moment Calum crawled into the street, dragging Maisie behind him.

Instantly the men of the household, including Mr. Alleway, rushed forward and hauled the two figures away from the house, onto the stones. Bonnie hastened to Maisie first, collapsing beside her sister where she lay on the cobbles, soot-covered and struggling to breathe. But she did breathe! Oh, thank God above, she *did* breathe!

"Calum!" Sorcha's scream brought Bonnie's head jerking up, and she turned to where her brother lay but a few feet away, her older sister crouched over him. Even in the weird light cast by her burning home, Bonnie could see the terrible, blistering burn that ravaged the whole left side of Calum's face.

The streets of Burntisland echoed with sounds of terror—shouts, screams, and the crackle and roar of the ravening fire. A rattling filled Bonnie's ears, and she felt her arm grabbed by someone—her father perhaps—pulling her out of the way as the fire pump, dragged by a powerful horse, appeared in the street before her home. Volunteers, and men from the houses on either side of the Alleways', ran with buckets to fill the trough then set to work pumping the handles as hard and fast as they could. A jet of water shot from the copper spout, streaming into the upper windows of the house where fire blazed.

Bonnie wept uncontrollably, not once realizing she did so. The horror of the night washed over her in wave upon wave. She distantly heard someone shouting for the doctor to be brought, someone else shouting for a horse. Two arms wrapped around her, pressing her close, and Bonnie closed her eyes and wept still more.

"We're all alive," Sorcha whispered into the top of her head. "We're all alive. We're going to be fine. We're going to be fine, dearest."

She said the words like a mantra, over and over again, perhaps trying to convince herself as much as her sister. But Bonnie, the screams of the townsfolk resounding in her ears, could think only of the terrible vision she'd glimpsed of Calum's face.

With a roll of thunder, rain began to fall.

ChApter 2

HE NEXT morning Bonnie found herself standing outside a strange bedroom door in a strange house. One of their kind neighbors up the street had offered the family shelter until they found another place to stay. Bonnie knew she should feel grateful. But for the most part, her spirit was so numb with loss and fear, she hardly felt anything.

Anything other than guilt.

Why did I not put out the candle? she asked herself again and again, her own inner voice like a scourge. *Why didn't I get out of bed when I noticed its light?*

For inside that strange bedroom, Calum now lay in agony, attended by the doctor. All because of her irresponsibility. Sorcha's comforting arm around her shoulders could do nothing to alleviate the pain in her heart.

The door opened at last, and Mr. Alleway emerged, his face grave as he met his daughters' anxious gazes. "He'll live," he told them, keeping his voice down. "He'll be scarred, and he'll know much pain for some while. But Doctor Campbell believes he will live."

"Thank the Lord!" Sorcha whispered.

But Bonnie, recalling the horrible glimpse she'd had of Calum's face the night before, began to weep again. "It's all my fault," she whispered. "I left the candle burning—"

"Hush, Bonnie," her father said. "'Twas an accident."

His words made Bonnie feel worse. She wished he would scold her. She wished he would punish her, and that his punishment might somehow atone for her wrongdoing. But ultimately she knew that no chastisement her father might inflict could compare to the lashings of guilt she already endured.

Before she could ask her father what the doctor had said about Maisie, a servant of the household approached, a letter in his hand. "For you, Mr. Alleway," he said with a bow.

Surprised, the merchant took the letter and quickly opened it. His eyes scanned its contents, and the further he read, the more disturbed his expression became. By the time he finished reading, he looked so pale that Sorcha urged him to take a seat before he collapsed upon the hall floor.

"What is it, Da?" she demanded even as she led him to the sitting room and pushed him into a chair. Wordlessly, Mr. Alleway handed her the letter. Bonnie watched her sister's brow furrow as she read, and halfway through the letter, she said a word she could not have learned from her elegant French schooling days.

"It's gone," Mr. Alleway whispered, resting his elbow on the arm of his chair and burying his face in his hand. "All gone."

Through the fire of her tormenting guilt Bonnie felt a sudden sickening of cold. What new sorrow was this that could make her father's face turn gray? "What's gone?" she asked, afraid to hear the answer.

"All of our ships have been lost," Sorcha answered. She tossed the letter to the table by her father's chair and stomped to the window. Resting both hands on the sill, she stared out into the rain-drenched street. From this vantage, one could still see the smoke rising into the air from the ruins of the Alleway home. It was only by the grace of God—and the timely thunder-shower of the night before—that this whole street had not been damaged, possibly destroyed.

But this thought could bring little comfort now.

Mr. Alleway, his voice broken, said, "We have nothing left."

"Nothing?" Bonnie repeated. She looked from her father to her sister and back again. "What about your investments, Da? You have money in other places, don't you?"

Sorcha cast her father a tortured look then returned to her contemplation of the street.

"We did," the merchant replied but could not bring himself to say more.

Bonnie opened her mouth to pursue the matter, but Sorcha turned to her and silenced her with a motion of her hand. So instead Bonnie merely whispered, "What is going to happen to us?"

"I do not know," her father said quietly. "I simply do not know."

Bonnie's eldest brother, Donald, came home from school a week later. Mr. Alleway closeted himself away with Donald and his solicitor the next morning, discussing the family's options. During all this time, Sorcha insisted that she and Bonnie keep themselves busy.

Sorcha tended to Maisie, who, while not burned, suffered from smoke inhalation and lay uneasily in her borrowed bed, breathing roughly and sometimes vomiting from nausea. Sorcha saw to her comfort as best she could and sent Bonnie to sit with Calum.

Because he could not be on hand to treat her brother every day, Doctor Campbell taught Bonnie how to apply a salve of linseed oil, lime water, cerusa, and vinegar, using a soft feather to spread the medicine across the burned area. He then showed her how to apply the dressings, warning her that they would have to be changed every day and the salve reapplied for many weeks to come. "The bad humors will leak out in pus," he told Bonnie, "and we must keep the damaged area clean."

Bonnie's stomach roiled in horror at the sight of those dreadful burns, but she listened with great care to the doctor's instructions, her hands trembling as she struggled to mimic his actions. Throughout all of this, Calum slept, heavily drugged so that he might not experience the full extent of pain. "He must be kept asleep," the doctor advised, "or the pain may well make an end of him."

With those words echoing like mourning bells in her head, Bonnie redoubled her efforts to learn the doctor's treatments. And after Doctor Campbell left, Bonnie sat beside her brother's bed, watching him breathe. Sometimes she slipped to her knees and tried to pray but found she could hardly remember the words she had learned as a child.

Mid-afternoon the day after Donald's arrival, Sorcha put her head into Calum's sickroom, her gaze first resting on her brother's sleeping form then finding Bonnie kneeling at his side. "I'm stepping out, dearest," she whispered when she caught Bonnie's eye. "Maisie is asleep. I'll be back soon."

Bonnie nodded and returned to her attempted prayers.

Later that evening, Mr. Alleway summoned Bonnie to the small drawing room of their neighbor's house. The family who owned the house had retired to their country home to allow the Alleways some privacy as they struggled to regain their lives. Nevertheless, the room and its unfamiliar furniture felt strangely unwelcoming to Bonnie as she joined her father and her brother Donald, taking a seat on a low stool near the fire.

"Where is Sorcha?" Mr. Alleway asked.

"She stepped out," Bonnie replied. "I did not see if she returned."

"We'll wait for her, then," her father said, and they all lapsed into uncomfortable silence. Bonnie wished she might slip away to Calum's room or perhaps to visit Maisie. But she remained where she sat, sometimes watching Donald, who paced the room, and sometimes watching her father, who gazed into the fire like a man lost in a dream.

Suddenly a door slammed open and closed downstairs. Footsteps sounded in the passage, and Sorcha appeared in the drawing-room doorway, her face white and her eyes terrible to behold. She took one look at her family and burst into tears.

"Sorcha!" their father gasped. "My child, what is the matter?"

"The wedding's called off." Sorcha wiped her nose with the back of her hand, something just days ago she would never have done. "I told John I would understand if he didn't wish to marry me anymore, now that our fortune's gone. I said it was only honorable for me to release him from our engagement." She sucked in a breath before sobbing out, "He wasn't supposed to say *yes!*"

"Oh Sorcha!" Bonnie exclaimed from her low seat. She wanted to rise and comfort her sister but found she hadn't the strength to move.

Donald, however, strode across the room and put an arm around Sorcha, leading her to a chair and urging her to sit. Even as she took a seat, he growled, "I'll have a word with that maggoty—"

"Donald," their father said warningly. He offered his daughter a compassionate gaze. "Sorcha, pet, I can try to speak to John. If I tell him—"

"Don't!" Sorcha yelled, leaping up from the chair in which she had only just rested. "I never want to see him again! He was supposed to love me! He was supposed to *love* me." Her voice broke, and she pushed Donald away and ran out of the room. Her wooden heels clattered on the stair, and the door to her borrowed bedroom banged shut in her wake.

Mr. Alleway rested his head in his hands and groaned. This last was a small blow compared to the others so recently fallen, but it was a bitter one. Bonnie sat wordlessly, observing all from her low seat near the fire. Sorcha had always been strong and fearless, with an ability to contain her emotions. She *never* cried. Not even the night of the fire. Not even when they waited to learn Calum's fate. And to see her weep now . . . Bonnie felt as though the world had spun out of control, leaving her no firm footing.

And it's my fault. The words echoed through her mind. Had they a house, they would have at least been able to sell their possessions to clear their debts. Now they had nothing. Even the clothes she now wore were borrowed.

"Father," she managed to whisper at last, "why did you call us in here? Did you have something you wanted to say?"

Mr. Alleway cleared his throat, his eyes shiny. "I had wanted to tell you with Sorcha present, but she will have to learn later. I have a second cousin up in the Highlands, near Inverness. A crofter of some moderate success who owns his own land. Not a man I've spoken with in years, yet he has kindly made arrangements for us to take a cottage near him. It'll be a roof over our heads at least."

"The Highlands?" Bonnie felt her heart sink even lower, though she had not believed it possible. She knew little enough of that wild country up north but had always assumed it was peopled with savages.

Mr. Alleway shook his weary head. "We have no choice, my Bonnie wee lass."

"I have a choice." Donald came and stood before his father. "Mr.

MacDougall offered me a job with him as an apprentice cartographer. And I accepted, which means . . . I'll be staying here in Burntisland."

Bonnie looked down at her hands and twisted the edges of her apron. It was stained with the salve she had applied to Calum's burns only a few hours before.

How foolish I was, she thought suddenly. *To think how I dreaded going away to school! How gladly I would go now if it meant we could regain some of what we have lost.*

Bonnie drew a deep breath to steady herself, looking up at her father, at his face so worn and drawn in the firelight. He met her gaze and smiled wearily. She wondered how he—or any of her family—could even bear to look at her after how much her carelessness had cost them. The sinking of the family's ships had come so swiftly upon the heels of their last misfortune that the two seemed irrevocably intertwined.

Though it was a foolish thought, Bonnie felt that if she were responsible for one tragedy, she must also be responsible for the other. Her reason told her how ridiculous the idea was, but her heart and emotions wouldn't stop convincing her otherwise.

I will never cause them such pain again, she vowed to herself. *Never.*

CHAPTER 3

ETTY AND the other fine horses of the Alleway stables fetched a good price, enough, in fact, for Mr. Alleway to purchase a cart, a massive carthorse (not so handsome as his former steeds but able to haul a loaded cart with little effort), and other necessities for the journey to Inverness. And so he and his family set out from Burntisland only two months following his fall from fortune.

For the first many days of travel, Maisie and Calum rode in the cart, propped on top of the family's sparse belongings. Mr. Alleway drove, but there was room for only one other on the seat beside him. So Sorcha and Bonnie took turns walking. Walking and walking, on and on, mile after mile, day after day, until Bonnie wondered if she could bear to take another step.

As the days passed, Calum often joined his sisters in their trek. He still wore the dressings on his burns, and Bonnie knew he experienced much pain though he never complained. And he seemed to gain strength as they traveled, his long limbs taking the strides with ease. Maisie, however, remained in the cart. Her lungs were not yet strong enough for such exertion.

They spoke little on the journey; what was there to say? They could not guess what life awaited them in the cold, wild north. They could not bear to contemplate the past they left behind along with Donald. Sorcha bit out the occasional grumble, but Bonnie dared not make a sound. What right had she to complain of any hardship or trial after what she had done?

Weeks of slow progress led them farther from the civilized landscapes they had always known, deeper into the wild north. Summer rains poured down upon them, drenching their clothes and thickening their boots with mud. And whenever the rain cleared, a heavy fog wrapped about them like a clammy blanket, hiding all from view except the road at their feet. Still they plodded on, stopping only to purchase supplies or to sleep. By the time they saw the first stone marker reading *Inverness*, Bonnie had not the strength or heart to feel anything. Neither relief nor sorrow. Nothing at all.

Under her feet, the wide military road was paved with local stone taken from the rocky heath surrounding. Heath, heather, stony waste . . . all spread before her in storm-gray magnificence and desolation. How, she wondered, could her family make a new home in this land?

"Not far now," her father said from his seat beside Sorcha. He indicated the stone marker with a nod, but there was no need. Little else in the landscape could draw the eye.

Calum stepped up beside Bonnie and put an arm around her. "We're almost there, Bonnie lass," he whispered.

She stiffened and moved out from his embrace quickly. Though she still tended to his injuries every evening when they stopped for the night, performing what she could remember of Doctor Campbell's treatments, she avoided Calum otherwise, choosing to walk on the other side of the cart from him when she could. The bandages on his face were a painful reminder of her terrible fault—her sin which, she still believed in her heart, had caused their sorry state.

They pushed on through the day, passing by the town of Inverness without stopping. It was hardly what Bonnie would consider a town: Inverness Castle loomed high and impressive on its hill, but other than a few stone buildings the town was made up mostly of simple thatch-roofed huts. Mr. Alleway, following the directions sent to him by his second cousin, took the west road away from the town. "Only eight more miles," he told his family, his voice as encouraging as it could be through the rain. "We'll be there by nightfall."

And so they were. Even as the rain clouds dispersed and the sun set, the Alleways stood at the gate of a rundown yard, gazing upon the crofter's cottage that would be their home: a hut, such as Bonnie had glimpsed in Inverness, built entirely of local materials, from the stone foundation to the timber framing to the walls of wattle-and-daub panels. The turf roof boasted a thatch of heather, and the low windows and gaping doorway were dark and unwelcoming. How isolated and lonely was the prospect, set in that rocky landscape!

Sorcha led the way inside, braving the dark threshold, and discovered that their father's second cousin had left a peat fire burning in the fire ring in the center of the cottage; a trail of smoke rose through a hole in the roof. Rude furniture lined the walls, and Sorcha found a small stool and placed it near the fire. "Sit here, Maisie," she told her sister.

"The walls are made of mud," Maisie said, her voice disbelieving as she studied her new home by light of the peat fire. "It's all so . . . small. And dark." She coughed as she finished speaking and huddled into her damp shawl, taking a seat on the stool.

"At least we have a roof over our heads," Sorcha said, briskly returning to the yard to assist with the unloading of the cart. Wordlessly Bonnie joined her, and together they, their father, and their brother managed to bring most of their few belongings into the house. They discovered that a cobbled section divided the interior of the cottage in two, and the second side had been used as a stable of some sort. Calum decided to house the horse there for the night, but declared that he would set to work making it into a second living space on the morrow.

Cold, exhausted, heavy-hearted, the family gathered around the central fire and ate the travelers' fare that had been their diet the last several weeks. As they ate, Mr. Alleway murmured, "I'll pay a call upon my cousin tomorrow and thank him for his kindness. Perhaps he can tell me where I might sell the carthorse and purchase a few chickens. Maybe a sheep."

"We're not to have any horse at all, Da?" Maisie queried, her voice very small in the darkness.

"We cannot afford to keep a horse," Sorcha snapped, and pressed her sister to eat more. She hid her own fear and unhappiness in managing those around her, and her family had not the strength to resist her stern dictates.

Bonnie did not draw her own seat as close to the fire, but remained a little outside its warm glow. Her meal tasted like ashes in her mouth, and she raised her eyes to the beams overhead which supported the turf roof. She could not have imagined a dwelling more primitive, more horrible. And this was their new reality? It was worse than a nightmare!

She lowered her gaze, looking instead across the fire at Calum and his bandaged face. He would need a new dressing this evening. She would need to tend him, need to . . . need to . . .

Suddenly she found herself at the door of the cottage. No one saw her slip out into the darkness of the Highland night, and she passed through the humble yard, through the gate, and out to the road beyond. There she stood a moment, spinning in place, taking in what she could see by light of the half-moon, which burst through the dissipating rainclouds. All was wild and bare, as far as the eye could see.

She began to walk. Then she began to run, leaving the cottage and the road behind as she fled up the first of the rolling hills. She ran through late-blooming heather, the rain-soaked blossoms breaking as she passed by, petals clinging to her skirts. Paying these no heed, she climbed to the top of the hill, descended into the valley beyond, and climbed again up the next hill, well out of sight of the cottage.

Here she fell, first to her knees, then to her face. She did not even realize she wept until that moment. But her grief poured out of her in torrents she could not stop. She tried to pray but could not recall any of the words she had learned from the *Book of Common Prayer* as a child. So she simply wept: for Calum and his scars, for Maisie and her breathing, for their lost home, for their new horrible abode . . . even for foolish things, like Hetty, whose foal she would never see, much less name. For Donald, who had stayed behind, making a new life for himself without them.

And all of it . . . all of it was her fault. Her doing.

At last she rose up from the damp ground, wiping her tear-streaked face and streaking it still more with mud. A large craggy rock jutted out from the landscape, and Bonnie, on an impulse, hiked up her skirts and crawled atop it, standing tall and allowing the wind to caress her flushed face with its cold fingers. The moon illuminated the world around her, and she once more turned in place to take it all in.

Her gaze came to rest on a distant forest. Much of this country was forested, but for some reason her eye lingered particularly upon that dark expanse of trees to the south.

Even as she looked upon it, a strange prickling touched the edge of her conscious mind. A sensation she could not quite define, like the creeping shadow of illness upon a household, or the scent of a bad storm blowing in from the sea. The feeling pulsed from the forest, throbbing across miles of dark landscape.

Bonnie shook her head and told herself it was nothing more than the heaviness her heart had suffered these last many weeks. With a shudder down her spine, she turned to climb back down from the rock.

But suddenly she gasped and fell to her hands and knees, her fingers scrabbling for purchase on the stone. She could not see the stone, however, nor anything else around her, for her mind exploded with a sudden image— the image of a bleak castle rising up from a fog-shrouded forest, its iron gates swinging open. She had never before seen this castle, and yet she could swear that she heard the creak of the gates themselves, that she smelled the wetness of rain upon the great stones of the wall.

The image passed, replaced at once by another. She saw a gloomy dining hall in the style of generations past, lit by a huge fire upon an equally huge hearth. Her ears roared with the crackle of that blaze. Something moved in the corner of her vision, something standing beside her. Some great shadow which breathed so heavily.

Then that image vanished and she stood in a snow-covered yard, gazing upon a yellow rose. Snow fell from the sky around this rose, mounding in a circle all about it. But where the snow touched those blooming petals, it melted away in an instant.

And in her ear a voice whispered—a child's voice, clear and soft and unmistakable. Bonnie heard the two words it spoke with utmost clarity:

Help us.

The breath rushed from her lungs as she landed hard upon the ground, having slipped and fallen from the stone. The jar was enough to banish the visions from her mind, but Bonnie, picking herself up, using the stone for support, still felt the pulsing darkness emanating from that far-off forest. She could not deny it now, not with the child's voice still lingering in her mind.

She dropped to her knees, clasping her trembling hands as she had been taught since childhood. The only prayer that came to mind was the same one she and Maisie had said together the night of the fire. She spoke it now, the words spilling from her lips: "*Lighten our darkness, we beseech thee, O Lord! By thy great mercy, defend us from all perils and dangers of this night!*"

Even as the words fell fearfully into the night air, the darkness upon her soul lifted. By the time she spoke the *amen*, she was able to rise and face the forest once more. No longer did it strike her as evil. It was only a forest several miles away. Nothing to fear.

"Bonnie!"

With a gasp Bonnie whirled about, only to see the familiar lanky form of Calum scaling the hill. The moon shone bright upon his bandaged face. "Foolish lass, what are you doing?" he demanded, catching hold of her hand as he gained the summit beside her. "You can't go wandering out alone like that, leaving us half-mad with worry! What were you thinking?"

"I—I'm sorry," Bonnie gasped. Her relief at seeing her brother and feeling his hand in hers was so great, she forgot for a moment her crippling guilt. "Oh Calum, I . . . I . . ."

The next moment she flung her arms around him, clinging as though she would never let go. "Calum, forgive me!" Her words came out muffled against his shoulder, but she knew he heard them. She felt him stiffen and then embrace her, holding her tight.

"Oh sweet Bonnie," he said gently, "I forgive you. You know that, right? I forgive you, and I want you to be as happy as you can be." Gently he pushed her away, holding her at arm's length. His good eye searched her face in the moonlight. She knew then that neither of them spoke of her foolish wanderings that night. Not anymore. "Do you believe me, dear sister?" he asked. "Will you now forgive yourself?"

With an effort of will, Bonnie nodded. "I will try," she agreed. "I promise, Calum. I will try."

"Good lass," said he. In the distance both of them could hear Mr. Alleway and Sorcha shouting Bonnie's name as they searched for her nearer to the cottage. "Come on then," Calum said, wrapping an arm around Bonnie's shoulder and leading her down the hill. "We'd best get . . . home."

He hesitated briefly over the word, but when he spoke it, he did so with conviction. For the first time since that horrible night of the fire, Bonnie felt her heart begin to lift with something like hope.

That night, however, as she lay upon her crude bed of piled blankets and sacking, she could hardly bear to close her eyes. For every time she did so, she saw again in her memory the image of the forbidding castle . . . and that strange rose blooming in the snow . . .

CHAPTER 4

Five Years Later

HELP US!

Bonnie woke with a start, gasping as she tried to scream, but her lungs could not draw enough air. Her heart thundering in her breast, she stared about her, at first unable to comprehend where she was. Her mind was so alive with the vision of that fire-lit hall . . . the shadow beside her she never could see . . . that garden shrouded in snow . . .

But there was no hall, though there was indeed a fire: a small peat fire burning in the center of the cottage room, close to where she and her sisters slept at night. The peat harvested from the surrounding landscape could burn on indefinitely with little tending, and the Alleways had grown used to using it as fuel rather than wood. The flames had scarcely lessened throughout the night, even as the family slept, and its light now illuminated the cottage, seeming to emphasize rather than lessen the pre-dawn gloom.

Bonnie breathed a long relieved sigh. Her sisters lay asleep around her on their straw pallets. In the other room, beyond the cobble divider, her father snored, sometimes accompanied by a snort or two from Calum. She heard the sheep muttering in their pen outside, and she knew that at any moment the rooster would crow, summoning the family to wake and start their day.

There was no massive dining hall. No garden. No child.

Nevertheless, Bonnie did not try to snatch even a few more moments of sleep. She rose and very quietly began preparing the morning meal. Action and activity were better than lying in the semi-darkness, thinking about those visions.

Ever since moving to the crofter's cottage—ever since that first night out on the heath—Bonnie had periodically experienced these same dreams and visions. Sometimes they came to her in sleep, as in this instance. Sometimes she might be in the middle of a daily task and suddenly find herself incapacitated, unable to move until the images passed from her mind. Bonnie never could predict when they might come and, though she had labored over the question for five years now, she could not guess why they came at all.

She stoked the fire and hung the iron kettle over it, heating water for porridge. As she worked, she whispered the prayer she had grown to depend upon throughout the years: *"Lighten our darkness, we beseech thee, O Lord."* As though in answer, the sun rose on the horizon.

A few hours later the household was awake and busy as the new morning brightened the sky. Mr. Alleway and Calum ventured out to the sheep pen and worked to separate from the small flock those lambs they would drive into market at Inverness that day. "You can come along, my dears," Mr. Alleway told his daughters. "Take a walk with us into town."

Maisie declined, a little sadly. Though her health had improved dramatically in the five years since the fire that nearly claimed her life, her lungs never would be as strong as before, and a long walk into town was more exertion than she could well manage. Sorcha, however, declared her intention of selling eggs and, if she made a good price, purchasing new needles from the town needle-maker.

"And you, my Bonnie wee lass?" Mr. Alleway asked, turning to Bonnie just as she stepped out of the cottage into the sun, wrapping her shawl about her shoulders. "Will you be joining us?"

Bonnie hesitated. She hated to leave Maisie alone. But her sister stepped into the cottage doorway and smiled at her. "Go along, Bonnie," she urged. A mischievous glint lit her eye. "Perhaps you could persuade Sorcha to buy us some golden silk thread as well."

"We have no need to be extravagant now!" Sorcha protested as if on cue, and glowered when everyone laughed at her sharpness. Rolling her eyes, she adjusted the basket of eggs on her hip and demanded, "Are you coming then, Bonnie?"

So Bonnie found herself walking the road to Inverness beside Sorcha, following her father and brother and Calum's collie dog as they herded the sheep. Calum no longer needed the heavy bandages and dressings, but he always wore a broad-brimmed hat as if its shade might somehow hide the disfiguring scars covering the left side of his face. His left eye was blind, but he moved lithely as he whistled directions to his dog and guided the sheep down the road, and one would not know to look at him that he often still experienced pain from his burns.

Bonnie eyed him now, and a pang shot through her heart. *He told you to forgive yourself,* her inner voice whispered as it often did. *You promised him you'd try.* And she did try, truly she did! But nothing could undo the damage she had wrought, however accidentally. Nothing could ever repair Calum's face.

The day was fine, however, and Bonnie's spirits lifted as they came at last into Inverness. Although nothing like so fine as Burntisland, the town did boast a thriving market square. While Mr. Alleway and Calum made for the butcher's to discuss the sale of their sheep, Sorcha took Bonnie's elbow and guided her toward the market, eager to make her own sale.

The market was even more exciting than usual this day, for the sisters soon discovered that a caravan of gypsies had rolled into town, bringing with them their foreign ways and foreign wares. A musician sang at one end of the street, and gypsy children danced, as delightfully strange as fairy-folk to Bonnie's eyes.

"Scarves for sale! Beautiful patterns from all over the world!"

At the sound of the gravelly voice, both sisters turned to see a booth overflowing with fabric in myriad colors and shades. The woman hawking her wares was small and frail, almost hidden by the pile around her.

The girls glanced at one another. "I need to sell these eggs . . ." Sorcha began, but Bonnie smiled encouragingly. "All right, I suppose we could *look* at them," her sister said, and they hastened to the stall.

"They're very beautiful," Bonnie said kindly to the old lady. Her voice was a tiny bit sad as she spoke. After all, she had once worn scarves much finer and never thought twice about them. Now her garments were all rough-woven and faded, handed down many times over before they became hers. She did what she could to stifle such thoughts and simply enjoy the beauty before her.

As the two girls admired the scarves, taking care not to dirty them as they fingered the soft fabrics, they heard a sudden commotion. Both Bonnie and Sorcha turned to see a street magician pull a bouquet of flowers out of thin air as excited village children surrounded him. The children applauded.

Bonnie, however, felt her pulse suddenly quicken. For upon first glimpsing those glorious flowers, she had momentarily thought the man held a bouquet of yellow roses. But no, his hand clutched a bunch of daffodils. Nothing like the glorious blossom she witnessed in her strange visions, ever surrounded in its veils of snow.

"Witchcraft!" Sorcha muttered, startling Bonnie from her reverie. "Don't look at it, Bonnie."

Bonnie, surprised at her sister's unexpected vehemence, studied Sorcha's frowning face. "Do you believe in magic?" she asked, curiously. "Not that sort, of course. It's only tricks. But *real* magic?"

Sorcha sniffed, cast a brief glance back over her shoulder at the street magician, then turned away, lifting her nose, as dignified and disapproving as the day she first returned to Scotland from her elegant French school. "If magic wasn't real, why would the Bible instruct us not to practice it? It must be real, and those who dabble in sorcery are wicked and dangerous!"

Even as Sorcha spoke, Bonnie felt an uneasy darkening in her soul. Her eyes momentarily clouded, and for a moment she feared her strange vision would return, right here in the streets of Inverness.

"Will ye buy anything?" the scarf merchant asked. At the sound of her voice, Bonnie turned to her, really looking at the old woman for the first time. And old she was indeed! Eighty years at least, with iron-gray hair straggling about her hollow cheeks, and endless wrinkles spreading out from her deep-set eyes. But she smiled at Bonnie, a toothless sort of smile.

As she smiled, however, the same darkening passed over Bonnie's vision. For a moment she thought she saw in that old woman's face . . . something else.

Bonnie backed away, blood draining from her face. "Not today, thank you," she murmured, hoping her voice did not sound as frightened as she felt. Sorcha had moved on already, seeking the right place to sell her eggs. Bonnie hurried after her and grabbed her arm, whispering urgently, "Did you see that?"

Sorcha frowned at her, perplexed. "See what?"

"That woman. For a moment she looked . . . young."

Sorcha looked over Bonnie's head toward the scarf-seller's stall. "What do you mean? She *is* young."

"No, I'm talking about the woman with the scarves. The old one."

"I didn't see an old woman," Sorcha persisted. "Just the one who called us over. She is about my age, I think. And very pretty, really."

Bonnie sighed, frustrated. "No, I mean"—she turned to point—"that one at . . ." Her voice trailed off.

Sorcha waited expectantly for her to finish, but Bonnie stood quite still, staring. The woman stood beside her wares, wearing the same clothing and surrounded by the same colorful scarves. But this woman was young and beautiful, with glorious black hair and clear blue eyes. Her face had nary a wrinkle. Indeed, it was unnaturally smooth. There weren't even any crinkles about her eyes when she caught Bonnie's questioning gaze and smiled.

Bonnie sucked in a breath, too taken aback to speak. Slowly the woman's smile faded into an expression of narrow-eyed suspicion.

Bonnie turned away hastily. "Never mind," she whispered once she regained power over her own tongue. She tightened her grip on Sorcha's arm. "Let's go find Da."

"I don't want to find Da. I want to sell my eggs. Bonnie!" Sorcha struggled against her sister's grip as Bonnie, demonstrating surprising strength, dragged her from the market center. "Bonnie, you're hurting me!" She pulled her younger sister to a stop. "What is the matter with you?"

"Nothing," Bonnie said, but she could not convince even herself. All she knew was that she felt an almost frantic need to escape the marketplace. "I'm tired all of a sudden. That is all." She glanced over her shoulder toward the booth one more time.

The woman was gone.

Bonnie all but ran from the market square down the side street toward the butcher shop where her father and brother had taken the sheep. Sorcha, unwilling to leave her sister alone in town, followed after, scolding all the while.

They had not yet reached the smelly yard belonging to the butcher when they saw Calum running toward them along the narrow stone-paved street, his broad-brimmed hat nearly flying from his head in his haste. The look in his good eye was indecipherable, and Bonnie stopped in her tracks at the sight of him, uncertain if she should be afraid. "Calum, what is it?" she demanded as he drew near.

"A letter!" he replied, holding up an already-opened missive as though in proof. "A messenger just rode in from Burntisland with a letter from Donald. And you won't believe what he says, Bonnie lass, you won't believe it!"

The seller of scarves hung about the shadows along the edges of the marketplace, her eyes keen and narrowed. There had been something different about the red-headed girl, something that set her on edge. Not the prim young miss with her nose so high in the air she might drown if it rained! No, the other one . . . the one with sorrow in her eyes . . .

She looked at me as though I were old.

No one had looked at her that way in years. She had kept a wary eye on the lands about these parts, changing her appearance every so often, and traveling a bit to remain undetected. Nothing had ever given her reason to worry. Nothing had ever given her cause to fear that the isolation of her victims might come to an end. Her plan must surely come to fruition.

His time is running out, she reminded herself. *One girl who can—and only for a moment, mind—see through my sorcery will not stop me. Am I not Morag, the last true priestess of Alba? What can a mere peasant girl to do me?*

The corner of her mouth turned upward in a facsimile of a smile. She would not be thwarted.

But she saw something in me . . .

No matter how powerful her magic, true evil could not be entirely disguised, and well she knew it. But few—very few people—could see through her charms. Unless something else was at work. Something more powerful than she.

The girl might not be a threat. But she was certainly a concern.

CHAPTER 5

ATER THAT same evening the Alleway family gathered around the peat fire, scarcely able to stomach the meal of pottage and oat bannock Maisie served to them. Their excitement was simply too great, and they stirred their wooden spoons around their servings of pottage without often remembering to lift food to their mouths.

"What do you think, Da?" Calum asked at last. None of them had spoken much on the long walk back from Inverness, the money from the sale of the lambs jingling unnoticed in Mr. Alleway's pouch. A day ago that small income would have seemed a fortune. Now they scarcely remembered it.

Mr. Alleway, upon reading the letter from Donald, had fallen into a deep contemplation which his children hardly dared to break. From the look on his face, Bonnie thought perhaps he was afraid . . .

Afraid to believe that Donald's words were true.

"He doesn't have much information," Calum persisted. He took up the letter from where it lay on a nearby table, scanning its contents again by the dim light of the fire. "Did you even know this uncle who died and left us this fortune?"

"I knew his name." Mr. Alleway broke an oat cake in half and watched it crumble into his pottage bowl but never once took a bite. "He's a great-uncle, my grandmother's brother. I never would have thought I'd be his last living relative."

"It sounds as though he named you quite specifically in his will," Sorcha said, her voice tight and tense with unexpressed longing. Though earlier that day she had been as frugal and sharp as any crofter lass in the Highlands, now her eyes danced with the memory of fine gowns, fine cutlery, fine balls. Bonnie, sitting quietly beside her older sister, glanced at her uneasily. Such a longing could only turn to bitterness if disappointed!

"It should pay off the rest of our debts if it proves true," Calum said, frowning over Donald's letter.

"I should think it would do a great deal more than that," their father answered, his voice scarcely more than a whisper.

"Oh!" Maisie leaned back in her stool to rest against the cottage wall and sighed suddenly. "It *would* be nice to have a real house again!"

Bonnie remained silent. For the past five years their lives had been simple and constant. Aside from the occasional letter from Donald, the outside world had gone on without them. Her family had adjusted to the world as it now was and rarely spoke of their previous wealth, never with such longing.

It cut Bonnie to the quick. Over the years she had grown accustomed to life here in the crofter's cottage and had even, for the most part, blocked out the guilt she'd harbored over her own role in their financial undoing.

Had she been a fool to believe her family could be happy here? Were they all secretly longing for their old lives as they went about their daily tasks?

Had they truly forgiven her? And more importantly, had she truly forgiven herself?

"I must travel to Burntisland at once," Mr. Alleway said. "I must speak to Donald and my solicitor and find out the truth of the matter. If enough is left over to clear my debts entirely and possibly to reinvest . . ." He shook his head quickly as though afraid to walk that road. "Meanwhile," he continued, smiling around the fire at his children, though the smile was drawn with anxiety and hope mingled, "there should be enough money set aside to bring you all a little something back from the city. What would you like, Maisie?"

Maisie considered a moment then shrugged. "A new bonnet, Da. A wide-brimmed straw bonnet with silk flowers and a ribbon. I know it's impractical for our life here, but I'd wear it to service every Sunday, and otherwise I'll hang it up on the wall and just *look* at it each day!"

The family laughed at her choice, but no one mocked her. Mr. Alleway addressed his son. "You'll want a book, I know that," he said with a smile. "And you, Sorcha?"

"Shoes," Sorcha answered at once. "And I do not mean anything with lace or silk or little wooden heels! No, no. I want a stout pair of boots that will bring me through the winter. There will be time enough for . . . if . . ."

She could not bring herself to finish, and Bonnie once again felt her heart sinking as she realized how desperately her family wanted this promise of a new fortune to be true. Of course she had been a fool to think they were content with these reduced circumstances, living under a roof of turf, surrounded by mud and wattle walls! Oh yes, she was a fool . . .

"And you, Bonnie lass? You're awfully quiet," Calum said suddenly, turning his smile to her. The left corner of his mouth did not lift when he smiled, the dead flesh simply twisting grotesquely. He did not seem to notice or remember his ugliness, however, and his good eye twinkled. "What do you want Da to bring you?"

Bonnie tried to think of something she might request, but her spirits were too heavy. At last she said the first thing that came to mind. "I miss the roses we used to have." She surprised herself when she spoke. Why, she had scarcely thought of the roses in their garden in Burntisland in years! Or perhaps it wasn't those roses springing to her memory at all. Perhaps it was one yellow rose shining bright though surrounded by falling snow.

Her family watched her expectantly, so she hurried on. "I wouldn't mind a cutting or two to plant outside the door. I don't know if it would survive the winter, but . . ."

"Is that truly all, me bairn?" her father asked, slipping into his thick brogue, which, even after their move to the Highlands, Bonnie rarely heard him use.

She nodded, trying to smile. "That is all, Da."

Calum set aside his half-eaten pottage and stretched his legs out to one side, avoiding the fire. "Will you be setting out tomorrow, Da? Shall I run over to our cousin's and ask about borrowing a horse?"

"Aye. I think that'd be best. Take the money from the sheep sale today and offer to pay him for loan of a horse and gear."

Calum hopped up at once, fetched his father's pouch, and set out into the deepening evening. Maisie began to clear away their meal, and Sorcha reached out to grab their father's hand. "We'll wake with you in the morning," she said, giving his fingers a squeeze. "Give you a proper send-off."

Bonnie said nothing but stared into the fire. Why had she asked for such a foolish gift? She knew roses would not bloom in this soil, would not thrive in this harsh weather. And why did she see yellow blossoms blooming in the twisting flames before her eyes?

She dreaded her father's going more than she could explain, even to herself.

The weeks after her father left passed in excruciating slowness. Bonnie felt restless and apprehensive. The summer lengthened into autumn, and soon it was too cold for her even to walk out into the heathery hills for privacy, as was her practice. She performed her duties in the cottage yard, her fingers blistered and lips chapped with frost, then quickly hastened back into the stifling warmth of the cottage.

She and her siblings rarely spoke of Da, as though somehow to speculate on the success of his trip would be to call down ill-fortune. They tended the sheep, harvested the meager offerings of their garden, and smoked the meat of small game Calum snared, storing up for the long winter. And they waited.

"We cannot expect him for another month, I think," Sorcha said suddenly one evening as they sat huddled close to the peat fire. Their father had been gone for over a month already. Bonnie knew that she turned her eyes to the road more often than she should, searching for some sign of Mr. Alleway's tall figure on his borrowed horse. "Once he arrived in Burntisland, he'd have much work to do, so many meetings and processes and suchlike," Sorcha continued. "And then it's a long road home again."

"The ground frosted last night," Maisie said softly, leaning her shoulder against Bonnie's for warmth. "If Da doesn't return soon, will he winter in Burntisland?"

"Don't believe it," Calum replied. "He'll come home to us as soon as he can."

But Bonnie, thinking of the heavy snowfalls of the last few winters, hoped Calum was wrong. She did not like to think of their father traveling through snowstorms to reach them, whether or not his journey to Burntisland was a success. She hoped he would be safe and warm, perhaps staying with Donald. "If he's not coming himself, he'd have sent a message, don't you think?" she said, avoiding the eyes of her siblings.

"Of course," Sorcha agreed. "But even if he did, we can't expect to receive it for another few weeks. So don't fret yourself, my dears!"

Sorcha could boss and command all she liked. But Bonnie, wrapped in her shawl, leaning against Maisie, could do nothing but worry.

Two weeks later, as a light snow fell, Bonnie followed in Calum's footprints out to the shed with his shaggy dog frisking beside them. Evening fell, and they must feed the sheep and make certain the shed was secure before the night grew dark. Ordinarily, Mr. Alleway would have assisted Calum in this work, but in his absence Bonnie had taken over the task.

Once the sheep were fed and comfortable, she ducked through the shed's low doorway and stood in the yard, blowing on her rag-wrapped hands to keep them warm, waiting for her brother. The snow now swirled around her, and she knew it would turn into a real storm before the night ended. The first real snowstorm of the winter. They may need to dig a path from the cottage to the shed in the morning.

Her thoughts trailed away, and she stared through the falling snow, her brow knitting in a frown. Was that a horse she saw coming up the road? And was that figure clinging to the horse's back, shoulders slumped against the cold . . . was that . . . ?

"Da!" she cried and ran from the yard, through the gate, out into the road. She caught the horse's bridle first, then reached up to grasp her father's hand. "Da, it's you!"

And indeed those were his eyes gazing down at her between the brim of his low-pulled hat and the wrappings of his scarf. But were those tears she saw forming in his eyes, spilling out upon his frozen cheeks?

Before she had time to wonder at this, Calum joined her. He had scarcely reached the horse's side when Mr. Alleway fell from his saddle, collapsing into his son's strong arms. Bonnie's joy turned to alarm. "Da!"

"Get the horse, put it in the shed," Calum commanded and began to half-carry, half-lead their father through the snow up to the cottage door, shouting for Sorcha and Maisie all the way.

Bonnie obeyed, her fingers trembling with fear as well as cold as she removed the horse's tack, rubbed it down hastily, and made certain it was made properly comfortable among the sheep. Only then did she race back to the cottage, her feet kicking up snow.

Her father lay upon a pallet by the fire. She had never before seen him so ill, so gray in the face, not even when their misfortunes had befallen them. His eyes were bloodshot and his cheeks pasty. He seemed unable to speak, and any time Calum or Sorcha tried to ask him anything, he shook his head despairingly.

"His coat is wet. Help me, Maisie," Sorcha said, taking charge and motioning to her sister. The two girls assisted their father out of his coat, and something fell from inside it.

Bonnie, still standing just inside the door, stared at that which lay upon the floor: a single yellow rose.

Mr. Alleway sat up on the pallet and reached out to pluck the rose from the ground. Though it must have been crushed inside his coat throughout the journey, as he held it up it seemed to blossom anew in the light of the peat fire, unfurling glorious sunny petals.

Bonnie could not move. She could scarcely breathe.

"For you, my Bonnie wee lass," Mr. Alleway said, holding out the rose to her. Even as he spoke, his eyes rolled up into his head and he fell into a faint.

The rose landed once more upon the ground and was nearly trampled as Sorcha and Maisie hurried to tend to their father. But Bonnie, moving as one in a dream, knelt on the dirt floor and picked it up, holding it with fear and trembling as she might have held a snake. For she knew it at once, more clearly than she would know her own face in a glass.

It was the rose from her dream.

Chapter 6

THEIR FATHER slept straight through the night and most of the morning. Bonnie remained at his side, watching his haggard face and the rise and fall of his chest as he breathed. She did not look at the rose, which Sorcha had plucked from her hands at some point the evening before and placed in a chipped cup on the table.

By mid-morning Mr. Alleway opened his eyes. His first words, before he had even sat up, were "Where is Bonnie?"

Bonnie immediately leaned over him, taking hold of his hand. "I'm here, Da. What is it?"

"The rose," he whispered. "Let me see the rose."

Though she hated to go near it, Bonnie fetched the broken cup and held it so that Mr. Alleway could see the blossom. "Da," she whispered, kneeling in the dirt beside him, "it is beautiful, but . . . I don't understand. How did you come by it?"

"It is the rose of a wulver, my lass," her father replied. "Such a small, lovely thing. But how much it has cost me!"

Darkness like unto that she had experienced on her first night in this wild country, when she gazed upon that distant forest, washed over Bonnie. She drew away from her father.

Sorcha, however, overhearing, came to kneel on his other side. "Nonsense!" she scolded, feeling his forehead with the back of her hand. "You're delirious, I think. A wulver, indeed!"

But Bonnie, seeing the look in her father's eye, could not take her sister's view. She got up and backed away from the bed, still holding the cup and the rose in her hands.

Calum and Maisie, realizing their father was awake, drew near, and Maisie offered him oat bannock, which he refused. "What happened, Da?" Calum pressed him, his voice gentle but urgent at the same time. "What happened in Burntisland? What brings you back to us now?"

Slowly, haltingly, the merchant began his tale. "When I went to the city," he said, "my uncle's clerk had arrived. Donald and I went to see him, but when we got there . . ." He coughed, the sound painful to hear, and it was some moments before he could continue. "My uncle had made a shambles of his business. There was nothing left."

Sorcha and Maisie exchanged glances. Maisie quickly bowed her head and a few moments later wiped away a single tear. But Calum shook his head and spoke firmly. "It's all right, Da. We knew it was only a hope. You need not worry yourself so cruelly! We will get by as we always have—"

But Mr. Alleway cut him off. "That's not all!" He coughed again, and Sorcha rushed to pour him a cup of water. He drank, and it seemed to give him strength.

"On the way back home," he continued, "I got caught in a storm. I couldn't see through the wind and snow. I lost the road to Inverness and found myself in the midst of a deep wood. I discovered a path, however, and my wanderings led me near an old castle."

Bonnie drew still further back into the shadows. She felt as though she could almost, though not quite, predict what her father would say next. And she knew she could envision the very castle he described.

Mr. Alleway told his tale, his audience listening in a rapt silence.

"It was old and run down, but not ruinous, and I saw a light in one of the upper windows, beyond the wall. The gate was open, so I passed inside and knocked at the entrance door. No one answered, but the door was unlocked, so I stepped inside out of the snow.

"It was unlike anything I'd seen before! Beautiful, and kept as though for royalty. Nothing like the outside, not at all. Candles lit the passage before me, illuminating a richness of furnishing and moldings and beautifully woven carpets that might have been new! And yet it all gave me a strange sense of oldness.

"I called out, but no one answered. So I stumbled on until I came to a room, a great dining hall with a table spread as though for a feast, and an enormous fireplace with a fire built up like blacksmith's furnace. The warmth was welcome and the food as well! I ate and I stretched out before the fire, resting my head on my own coat. How long I slept I do not know, but when I woke, I found that the table had been cleared and replaced with new food. Someone had come and gone while I slept.

"I searched for my host again and found no one. By this time I felt uneasy. I wanted to leave, to hasten my way home to my dear children. So I took up my coat, ate hastily of the new food—which had been so kindly presented, so surely it must be all right for me to eat it?—and sought my way out.

"But as I stepped out into the courtyard, something most unexpected caught my eye: a garden, tucked almost out of sight. And a rosebush bright with summer blooms and green leaves despite the snow all around! I stared at it, wonderstruck. You may laugh and say it is an old man's raving, but it seemed to me as though the snowflakes melted as they touched the bush.

"I—I don't know why I did it. It seems so foolish to me now. Oh, forgive me, my dear ones! Forgive me! But as I looked upon that rose, I thought of my Bonnie and her request. I thought of all of you, and the gifts I had promised and been unable to bring. But this gift . . . this rose for my youngest child . . . and the bush bore such plentiful blossoms, would anyone miss a single bloom? I took hold of a stem, on the end of which bloomed the most beautiful of all the roses, and I twisted it until it broke.

"And that is when I met the owner of the castle. The *wulver*.

"I see by your faces that you do not believe me. I scarcely believed it myself. But there was no mistaking that which stood before me. Before I saw him I heard his voice howling with a noise that rattled the windowpanes. And then he appeared on the other side of the rosebush, clothed and upright like a man, but with the head and body of a wolf! I thought I might die of fright, but I did not know true fear until he spoke.

"'I have offered ye nothing but kindness and hospitality,' said he in a terrible snarling voice. 'And ye repay me by stealing that which is of most value to me?'

"I tried to apologize. I tried to say that I only wanted a present for my daughter, that I meant no harm. He asked me to explain, and I found myself telling all . . . telling of our misfortunes and our lives here in the wild north. I told of all my brave children, who have made the most of their loss, who have grown strong and hearty enough to make any father proud. I told of my wee Bonnie, my lovely youngest though now a woman grown, and her desire for a rosebush to brighten our lives."

"Oh, I can hardly bear it! For that beast told me that if it was my daughter who wished for the rose, it was my daughter who would pay."

Mr. Alleway's words hung in the stifling air of the cottage as though suspended on darkness. Bonnie, her heart racing, felt suddenly lightheaded, though she could not yet fully comprehend what her father had said.

"He told me," Mr. Alleway continued, his voice breaking though he struggled on to finish his tale, "that I was to bring my daughter to him within the fortnight, or he would come to collect her himself."

"Da," Maisie spoke gently, touching her father's shoulder, "You're not thinking clearly. Wulvers aren't real—"

"Do you dare doubt me, child?" Mr. Alleway's voice was so sharp, Maisie startled back, her face paling. Sorcha felt her father's forehead again for a fever. He pushed her hand away. "I am not ill, Sorcha! I did not imagine it, nor am I delusional. I saw what I saw, I heard what I heard."

"We just find this a little hard to believe," Calum said, crouching across from his father and trying to meet his gaze.

But Bonnie, staring at the rose in the cup, did not disbelieve. Not for a moment. Even as her siblings continued to protest and Mr. Alleway continued to defend his mad story, she remembered every one of the visions she had seen over the last few years, starting that night when she first gazed out upon that distant forest. She did not doubt that this was the same forest in which her father had been lost. Nor did she doubt a word of his tale, for the rooms he described and the rose he had brought her were too perfectly matched to everything she had dreamed time and again.

And the shadow breathing in the corner . . . the one she always turned to in her dream but never quite glimpsed . . . must be the wulver himself.

"True or not," Calum declared suddenly, "it makes no difference. Bonnie is going nowhere. And if perchance some monster comes knocking at our door, I'll kill it myself!"

Sorcha agreed, speaking as violently as her brother and even taking up a carving knife as though ready to do battle then and there. But Maisie whispered in tremulous terror, "What if it curses us?"

"I'd like to see it try!" Calum answered, his fists clenching and his good eye bright.

Mr. Alleway protested, throwing up his hands. "It's no use, don't you see? This monster is much older, much more powerful than you know! I will return to it myself before the fortnight is up and pay for my theft. It is the only answer."

At this his three older children put up still greater objections. Through it all, Bonnie listened silently, hardly able to lift her gaze from the yellow rose.

I vowed I'd never cause them pain again, she thought. *It's my fault. I asked for this gift.* She should have bitten off her own tongue before requesting a rose! And now, once more, she brought doom upon the heads of those she loved.

She knew then exactly what she would do, and it did not matter how her family might argue. So she kept her peace and watched them quietly, all the while making her own plans.

CHAPTER 7

O NCE HER mind was made up, Bonnie knew there could be no use in waiting. The pain of leaving her family behind—not to mention the unknown horrors that awaited her at the end of her journey—would become too much, and she might, despite her guilt and her conviction, talk herself out of going.

No, she must leave that very night, as soon as her family slept. Calum had not yet returned their cousin's horse to its rightful owner, so she would ride it into the forest. She did not doubt in which forest her father had discovered the beast and the rose. It had to be the same dark wood she had observed from a distance years before.

Her father, weak from exhaustion and sorrow, remained quiet all the rest of that day. Sorcha and Calum whispered much, and Maisie wept now and again, though she put on a brave face. They all wondered if perhaps Mr.

Alleway had lost his reason due to this last crushing disappointment in Burntisland. Only Bonnie did not doubt the truth of his strange tale.

The dreams were sent so that I would know I have to go, she told herself as evening fell upon the snow-covered world. It made sense to her now—after all, she had been the one to cause her family grief. So she must be the one to suffer for their sakes now.

After a bleak meal together and a quick tending to the animals, the Alleways took to their pallet beds, all sleeping in the one main room near the fire for warmth. Bonnie lay for some time, listening to the sounds of their breathing. At last, when she was certain that even her father slept, she rose up, wrapped a thick shawl around her head and face, and slipped out into the night. There could be no goodbyes, and well she knew it. She must go in silence and secrecy, and hope that her family would remember her with kindness. And that they would understand why she chose this course of action.

Shaking with fear more than with cold, she saddled their cousin's horse, led it from the shed, and mounted in the yard. There she hesitated, gazing upon the humble cottage that had become dear to her over the last five years. She never would have believed that such a poor abode could feel so full of love and good cheer!

Perhaps he . . . the creature . . . will let me send the horse back, she thought even as she turned her mount's head and, taking the south road, began her journey. If this beast of the castle agreed, she might even be able to send a letter back to them, explaining herself. She could only hope.

The moon shone brilliantly that night on the new-fallen snow. As this was the first major snowfall of the year, the drifts were not yet terribly deep. Nevertheless, Bonnie was obliged to ride with caution for fear of driving the poor horse to a misstep and sending both of them tumbling to earth. But the wood was not many miles off. She thought she could make it well before dawn.

Sure enough, after a few frozen hours of steady riding, Bonnie rounded a hill and found herself facing the very forest she sought. She knew it was the right one immediately, for the moment she set eyes upon it she felt again the same pulsing darkness she had experienced that first night in this region, so long ago. She half expected the visions to return as well, but they did not. The dark pulse was potent, however, and she felt sick with dread as she urged her horse up to the edge of the trees, where the snow was not so thick on the ground, caught as it was in the branches overhead.

She turned to look back, where the moors spread out for miles. A quick breeze tickled her hair, which had escaped her long braid and now fell freely down her back. Bracing herself, she faced forward in the saddle once more.

For several terrified heartbeats she did not think she would be able to go on. Not for lack of willingness! But the pulse of darkness was so great, she feared she would not have the strength to push through.

Almost without realizing she did so, Bonnie whispered into the night air: *"Lighten our darkness, we beseech thee, O Lord! By thy great mercy, defend us from all perils and dangers of this night."*

As she spoke, she urged the horse on, and it progressed into the shadows of the forest. A terrible moment during which Bonnie thought she might be pushed from her own saddle by the darkness itself left her sweating despite the cold. But the moment passed, and she was through, riding into the wood of the wulver.

As she made her way through the trees, her eye lit upon something unexpected—something made of stone resting almost hidden beneath a broken branch, half-covered in snow. On an impulse of curiosity, Bonnie slipped from her horse and bent down to brush away the snow. To her surprise she discovered a paving stone. Brushing away more snow, her brow furrowed in concentration, she discovered a paved path gleaming with unearthly light, as though somehow the stones drank in the moonlight through the trees and reflected it back.

The moment she recognized the path, it seemed to glow all the more, bright enough that she could follow it with ease.

"Lighten our darkness," she whispered again, and climbed back onto her horse, nudging it into a plodding but steady pace. She had ridden but a few minutes when the forest abruptly opened, and she found herself not more than a quarter mile from the edge of a cliff over the sea. This surprised her greatly, for she would not have guessed this forest lay anywhere near to the sea! *But then, it must certainly be enchanted,* she reminded herself. Far below, waves lapped on rocks and the sea murmured in its many deep voices.

The path turned sharply to the left, and Bonnie followed it until she approached an imposing gate, worn and beaten down with age. Beyond stood an old stone castle, large and beginning to crumble. She noticed that one side of the castle was so close to the edge of the cliff that one couldn't walk around it without falling. Bonnie thought that it might have been beautiful once, but it was now a shell of what had once been.

She slid off her horse. Now that she no longer had the protection of the forest, the wind from the cliffs whipped at her and blew her hair into her eyes. She pulled the horse up to the gate and examined the lock, which, she wasn't surprised to discover, had rusted away.

Her hands shook as she pushed the gate open and led the horse through into the silent courtyard beyond. She let out an unsteady breath, and once more feared her courage would fail her. For before her loomed in reality the exact vision of the castle she had glimpsed many times in her dreams. And she did not merely see it; she smelled it, the ancient corrosion of its stones. She tasted the dust of time upon the air. She heard the wind sighing round the tall turrets, blowing in from the sea.

Her dream was become reality, even as she had known it must from the moment she saw the yellow rose her father had brought home to her.

Leading the horse deeper into the courtyard, she approached the tall front entrance. Uncertain what to do with the horse, she tied it to a spindly tree near the castle. Then, drawing a deep breath to steady herself, she approached the door and knocked.

It swung open easily at her touch, as though she had been expected. Warm candlelight, just as her father had described, met her eye, but she found herself reluctant to leave the moonlight behind. Still, what good would it do to linger here on the doorstep?

She passed inside and heard the door shut behind her but refused to look around. Iron sconces lined the stone walls on either side of the passage, their tall candles lit as though whoever lived here—the wulver, presumably—did not concern himself with the expense of burning so many candles at once. A luxury Bonnie herself had once enjoyed, but not for many years.

The light from those candles illuminated fine furnishings, somewhat old-fashioned but not ancient by any means. This surprised her, though in retrospect, she could not say what exactly she had expected. Her visions had never shown her the castle's entry hall.

She moved on, walking quickly as though trying to outpace her own fear. Somehow she felt she must find the dining hall with the long table and the huge fireplace, the one her father had described. That chamber she had certainly seen in her dreams, and perhaps there she would—

"Ye have come."

Bonnie almost choked on her own heart as it leapt in her throat. She whirled to face in the direction from which the voice had come and saw a figure dressed in a dark cape descending a huge staircase. It was difficult to discern much about him, for he stood beyond the candlelight and carried no light of his own. But his eyes gleamed bright amber in the shadow of his face.

Bonnie said nothing. Her pulse quickened to a maddening rush as the beast reached the bottom of the stair and stepped at last into the full light of the nearest candle sconce. She saw then that his body was not unlike that of a man, though he towered over her by more than two heads. His clothing was loose and ill-fitting though finely made, and he wore no shoes on his large, fur-covered paws. His hands were also covered with thick, coarse fur, and long, razor-sharp claws tipped each finger. Worst of all was his face—for though his head was that of a wolf, his eyes were terribly *human*.

So at last Bonnie beheld the shadow she had only ever sensed in her dreams. And he was beyond anything she could have imagined.

Realizing that he had spoken and she had not yet given an answer, she valiantly fought to find her voice. "Aye. I have come," she said, and how young she sounded, even in her own ears! Like a foolish, frightened child. She tried to steady her voice, to show some strength, though she felt none in that moment. "I have come to repay my father's debt."

"Whit is yer name, maiden?" the wulver asked.

His voice was so deep, so growling, and simultaneously so thickly accented that Bonnie almost did not understand him. She guessed as much as anything and quickly dropped a curtsy, saying, "They call me Bonnie, milord." Though she tried to meet his eyes, she could not bear to, and dropped her gaze to the floor at his feet.

"Are ye afraid to look at me, Miss Bonnie?" said the wulver. He stood so perfectly still, it was almost uncanny. One could have believed he was a statue had he not spoken.

"Aye, milord." Bonnie tried again to look into his eyes and failed. "But I am sure I shall grow used to you."

At this the wulver nodded as though satisfied. "Come with me," he said, turning away so abruptly that Bonnie again scarcely understood him.

She gathered herself quickly, and took two faltering steps after him. "Milord, my horse is outside . . ." She stopped as the wulver turned to look at her over his shoulder. Her throat tightened with fear, but she forced herself to speak on. "I need some way to send him back to my family. He's not our horse, you understand, and my father cannot afford to pay—"

"I will make certain he is returned," said the wulver.

How trustworthy was the word of a beast? What choice had she but to trust him? "Might I . . . might I send a letter back, telling them that I have arrived?" she asked.

The wulver stood silent for so long, Bonnie feared she had overstepped her bounds. After an agonizing interval, he nodded toward an elegant side table near the door, which she had not noticed before.

"Ye'll find a pen and ink in the drawer," he said.

Bonnie hastened to the table and, her hands fumbling with the drawer, found the tools even as he had said. She could feel his powerful presence at her back, and her spine crawled with terror that those great jaws of his might close upon her neck from behind at any moment. The terror was so great that she could barely remember how to write. It had been many years since her hand held a pen.

She managed to scrawl out a short note. *I am safe; I have found the castle.* A tear escaped her eye, and she wiped it away quickly, not wanting it to fall on the paper and betray her emotions to her family. *Forgive me. I love you.*

What more could she say? She had wanted to explain her actions but now could not manage another word. Not with the wulver behind her. She signed her name and gently folded the paper in half.

"Leave it on the desk," the wulver said before she could ask what to do with it. "I will ensure that it is delivered."

She placed the letter on the desk and forced herself to turn and face the wulver again. Though she had thought it terrible to stand with her back to him, seeing him was hardly better. She stared dumbly at the pattern of an ornamental rug on the floor.

"Come with me."

His voice was not angry, but neither was it kind. If she sensed anything at all in that voice it was fatigue. He turned from her, leading the way down the hall, the candlelight shining on his dark fur. Bonnie followed him silently for some time, her mind racing with questions she could not begin to comprehend. Finally, the most pressing question billowed up from inside her and burst from her mouth before she could quite think to stop it.

"Please, milord, could you tell me . . ." He turned at the sound of her voice and looked at her. The words fell from her tongue beyond her control. ". . . could you tell me if you are going to eat me. Please, I'd rather know to begin with."

"Eat ye? *Eat* ye?" The wulver's human eyes widened with honest surprise and horror. Then his lip curled, and he looked animal again. "Do ye think I would do such a thing as *eat* ye?"

The strange combination of man and beast so unnerved her, Bonnie feared her knees might give way. She braced herself and tried to speak with courage. "I—I am sorry if I have . . . offended you. I shouldn't have—" She flushed at her own stammering and stared at his enormous feet, ending so quietly that she didn't know if he heard her: "I shouldn't have said it."

The wulver didn't speak, and after a short but uncomfortable silence, she looked up to find him studying her with those human eyes of his.

"In truth, 'twas not an unfair supposition," he said at last. He heaved a heavy sigh, and his awful visage seemed to soften. "But know this: I say no harm will come to ye here, and I mean it. Ye have no need to fear me. Now come."

Oddly, Bonnie felt calmed by his words. She did not know why, but she found that she trusted this beast. Her courage rising, she followed as commanded, and he led her down a labyrinth of passages. Candle sconces lighted their way as they walked, and Bonnie could not help wondering whether they were always lit at night or if some unseen servant ran in advance of the wulver, lighting them before his approach.

Finally the wulver stopped and opened a large wooden door. When he entered, Bonnie saw a winding staircase. Lifting her skirts, she hastened after him, around and around to the top, where they reached another door. This he opened and stood to one side, indicating for her to pass through.

Bonnie hesitated but reminded herself that he had promised no harm would come to her. Drawing another long breath, she stepped through, passing so close to the wulver that she could feel the warmth of his breath on her hair.

At sight of the chamber beyond the door, a small gasp of wonder escaped Bonnie's lips. She had been expecting something dark, damp, and gloomy, a prison of some sort. By contrast, the room before her was bright and cheerful. A warm fire lit the hearth, and through an arched window she saw the sky over the sea begin to lighten with coming dawn. The furnishings, like all she had glimpsed in this place, were fine, though old.

"Rest yerself," the wulver said gruffly and moved to leave. "Ye'll be expected downstairs for the midday meal."

"Wait!" Bonnie spun to face him, meeting his gaze and holding it for the first time. She clutched her arms tightly around her shivering body but kept her head upraised. "I—I only wish to know . . . What shall I call you, milord?"

"Call me whit I am." The light from the fireplace played on the darkness in his eyes. "A beast. Anything else is a lie."

He backed from the room and shut the door. She listened for a latch or a bolt but heard only the sound of his footsteps fading down the stair.

The finality of her position hit her, and she sank to her knees and wept.

Chapter 8

ELP US! Help . . . us . . .

Bonnie she sat bolt upright in bed as she so often had in the last few years, her heart racing, her lungs struggling with a scream she could not utter. But this time, as she stared about, trying to recover her consciousness, she did not find herself in the safety of her family's humble cottage. She did not see the sleeping forms of her sisters on their pallets, she did not hear her father's snore through the cobble divide.

Instead she sat upon a large bed, much grander, much richer than any she had ever before known, even in Burntisland. How dirty and poor did her garments look, spread out upon that rich counterpane! This she thought dully, for her head felt groggy and her ears still burned with the dream-voice of the child.

This time the child had not whispered. Indeed, as Bonnie shook her head and tried to rub exhaustion from her eyes, she recalled that she had heard the voice speak loudly for the first time. As though the child had stood beside her bed and leaned over to speak right into her ear.

But the only sound she heard now was the *tick-tock* of a tall Dutch clock standing in the corner of the chamber. Its rhythmic voice served to emphasize the silence all around her. She could not even hear the voice of the sea outside her window.

Climbing out of the rich bed, she ran a hand through her mass of curls. The . . . *beast* had told her to come down for the midday meal, but he hadn't told her when that would be. The clock's face indicated eleven in the morning, but how could she know if it was accurate?

Discovering a mirror on the wall near her bed, she inspected her face. Her bloodshot eyes stood out starkly in her pale face. She sighed, thinking how little she resembled her moniker, and, yawning, walked over to open the door.

The handle wouldn't move.

Bonnie frowned and tried again. Then she frantically jiggled it and, her anger suddenly rising, pounded on the door. She had not heard a bolt drop when the wulver left her a few hours before, but apparently he had locked her in after all.

"Let me out!" She felt as though her voice struck the door and bounced back into the room, unheard by any who might lurk without. She called again and again to no avail and wearied her hands with pounding.

At last she groaned and slid to the floor. A prisoner! How foolish she had been to hope she might be treated as a guest. Despite the lovely room and comfortable bed, she was still nothing more than a prisoner.

Head aching with both physical and emotional exhaustion, she leaned against the door. She wanted to weep, but more tears would not come, only a sharp stab of overwhelming homesickness. All she wanted was the embrace of her family's comforting arms.

What have I done? she asked herself again and again. But her heart reminded her: *The only thing you could do. You vowed not to cause them more pain.* A shudder ran through her body, and she feared that she would be sick.

It seemed like hours but may have been mere minutes before Bonnie heard a heavy tread upon the stair. At last! Relieved and terrified at the same time, she scrambled to her feet and stared at the door.

The footsteps stopped and nothing happened. No pounding, no sound.

And then the wulver's voice growled, "Yer late, Miss Bonnie."

"My door is locked," Bonnie replied, her voice so soft that she wondered if he could hear it. So she spoke again more loudly. "My door is *locked*. I could not come down." This time she sounded almost as angry and frightened as she felt.

Another silence. Then she heard a rattle of keys, a *click*, and the door slowly opened. The beams of late-morning sunlight pouring through Bonnie's window revealed her captor standing without, but to her surprise he did not look angry or even particularly ferocious. Instead he looked rather embarrassed.

"I apologize," he said in the strange, emotionless tone he had used a few hours before. "Ye must be hungry." His eyes on the floor, he backed from the doorway, offering for her to pass through before him, as polite as any fine gentleman could ever be. At his quiet demeanor, Bonnie's terror dissipated, replaced by a vague uneasiness which she found easier to stomach.

She picked up her skirts and made her way across the landing to the staircase. It was strange descending the stairs before the wulver, but when she arrived at the passage below he took the lead once more. For a moment she thought he would offer her his arm like a proper escort and was relieved when he seemed to change his mind, merely indicating with his claw-tipped hand the direction they would take.

He led her to a room that she recognized as clearly as she had recognized the castle at first sight—a huge dining room with an enormous fireplace, which was blazing despite the midday light pouring through the windows along the opposite wall, the fire necessary to drive away the cold of winter. Bonnie knew the room as well as she would know the confines of her family's cottage. And now she also knew who the shadow beside her was.

The wulver pulled out a chair for her. Bonnie took her seat, noting that the only other place setting was at the far end of the table; and as she watched the wulver take this place she felt grateful for the distance between herself and her captor. Dishes piled with food filled the table. Most of it was the simple, hearty fare she had grown used to in the Highlands—oat bannock, porridge, and the like. But she spied several more elaborate dishes that she remembered eating in richer days.

She had not realized until that moment how hungry she was.

"Eat yer fill, lass. Please," said the wulver with a gracious nod.

Bonnie hesitated only a moment before serving herself, attempting to balance decorum with the extreme hunger she felt. She chose the simpler food, knowing it would be more sustaining. Besides, she suspected her palate would no longer appreciate the more sophisticated fare offered.

As she began to eat, she glanced down the table at the wulver. His plate was empty. Her stomach clenched, and the first several bites she had swallowed seemed to turn to stone in her gut. Was the food poisoned?

"Why don't you eat?" she asked.

"A beast's meal is not a pretty thing," he replied.

Something in his voice convinced her to believe him. She could not say what, exactly. Neither could she starve herself. So she forced down more of the oat bannock, though her anxiety made it taste like dust on her tongue.

They sat there in silence for some while before the wulver spoke again. She looked up sharply at the sound of his voice and at first could not even comprehend the words he spoke.

"Miss Bonnie, will ye marry me?"

She went cold all over. Once more she wished she had not eaten, and her head went light with sudden terror. When she did not respond, the beast cleared his throat and repeated his question more loudly. "Miss Bonnie . . . will ye marry me?"

She tried to speak but could not find words. Her mouth moved, and her hands clutched the edge of the table for support.

"Answer truthfully without fear," the wulver said in a tone Bonnie might have recognized as kindness had she been more coherent.

"Oh *no*, Beast!"

She flushed at the haste with which the words spilled. The flush turned to deathly pale as she wondered what the consequences might be. With an effort of will, she forced herself to look the wulver's way, to ascertain his reaction.

He rose from the table and bowed with strange elegance. "I will leave ye to finish yer meal. Guid night."

After her meal, Bonnie found her way back to her own room almost too easily. Her memory told her that she had followed the wulver for much longer on the way to the dining hall, but when she had finished dining she stepped out into the passage and found the door to the winding stair only a few paces away. Too tired to reflect on this for more than a moment, she hurried up the stairwell and back to her room, shutting the door with some relief. As though she could somehow shut out her fears.

If he were truly a monster, he would not have asked, she told herself as she stood in the center of the room, trembling. *He would have taken me by force.*

She could not consider that thought any longer, but shook her head fiercely and looked around the room. A wardrobe stood in one corner—large and elegant and carved with an intricate pattern of roses and thorns. Feeling how drab and dirty her own garments were, Bonnie opened the wardrobe, curious to see what it might hold, and discovered that it was filled with richly embroidered gowns cut in an old-fashioned style with voluminous sleeves and wide portrait necklines, very little like the styles of her own day. But they were beautiful, stunning even.

Bonnie looked down at her own rumpled frock, which seemed even dirtier and more provincial next to the garments in the wardrobe. She touched a certain blue gown and wondered to whom it had belonged, possibly a hundred years ago . . . .

Shaking her head, she shoved the gown back into the wardrobe. The idea pressed upon her mind that other girls may have been held captive here before her. But this she could not bear to consider, so she shut the wardrobe doors and turned away, rubbing her arms to ward off a chill although a bright fire blazed upon her hearth.

Her gaze turned to the fire. Who had lit it? Surely not the wulver himself. And he certainly could not have prepared the food she had so recently eaten! But she had glimpsed no sign of anyone else in the castle.

Trying to silence her questions, she moved to her window and gazed out upon a fine prospect of the sea. Who would have thought this castle stood so near the coast? It gave her an uneasy feeling, as though the forest she entered the night before had somehow shifted around her, leading her to places far away from all she knew. Though she had only ridden through the night, she suspected she was many days away from her family now.

The day passed slowly, and evening fell. Though the wulver had not said as much, Bonnie guessed he would expect her to join him for an evening meal. A part of her did not wish to leave the room, for it seemed a sanctuary compared to the rest of the house. *But if I don't come down and he comes to get me* . . . Little though she liked the idea of seeking him out, the thought of waiting for the beast to come to her was even worse.

So, after running her fingers through her tangled curls and doing what she could to make herself presentable, Bonnie opened the door of the bedroom. The stairs were clear, and she took a deep breath before venturing out, knowing full well that once she left the confines of her room she was bound to run into the wulver.

She found the table in the dining hall set less formally than at noon but still with more food than she could ever eat in a week. The wulver, however, was nowhere to be seen. Uncertain whether his absence relieved her or worried her all the more, she picked at her food. Upon finishing, she decided she would rather wander the castle and get her bearings than return to her silent room.

And the castle was truly a marvelous place! Old and frail, yet somehow enchanting all the same. Again, someone seemed to walk before her, lighting the candles in each passage down which she turned, but vanishing before she caught any glimpse of who it might be. She opened one door and looked into a room filled with every musical instrument imaginable. Although she had never learned to play an instrument, she examined each one closely, admiring its beauty, before moving on to the next room. This was a library, but the light was too dim to read by even if she could settle her nerves enough to open a book. She passed through the room to the far end, where stood a tall curtained window. When she pulled back the curtain, she saw the castle gates and, beyond, the forest she had ventured through the night before. The sky was darkening and the moon beginning to rise, casting the trees' shadows long and dark.

"Guid evening, Miss Bonnie."

Bonnie startled and whirled about, dropping the curtain back into place. The wulver himself stood in the doorway, his great clawed hands clasped behind his back, his shaggy head bent. He bowed to her.

"Good evening, Beast," she replied, dropping a nervous curtsy.

"Did ye find yer evening meal to yer satisfaction?" he asked, remaining in the doorway.

"Aye. Thank you." She gripped her skirts tightly in both hands, wishing she could escape the room somehow. But he blocked her exit. "I . . . I did not see you at supper."

"I thought to let ye eat in peace," he replied. After a moment's silence he added, "Ye may explore the castle as much as ye wish. Every door is open to ye. But ye may not leave the grounds or pass through the gate. Do ye understand?"

Bonnie nodded wordlessly. If only he would step away and let her pass! She wished now that she had returned to her room at once following her meal.

"Will ye marry me, Miss Bonnie?"

Breathless, she answered at once, "No, Beast."

The wulver nodded. "Very well. Guid night."

"Good night," she whispered, the words spoken to his retreating back. Then he was gone, and she stood alone in the library, her hands seeking the back of a tall chair for support. *Why isn't he angry?* she wondered desperately, unable to comprehend. Though the wulver was imposing and, indeed, even terrifying to behold, he behaved with such control and courtesy, even when she turned down his proposal a second time.

So why had the theft of a single rose driven this calm, quiet beast to such rage that he'd imposed his terrible will upon her father?

More confused than ever, Bonnie hastened from the library and, following the candlelight, retreated up the stairs to her room.

Chapter 9

T HAT NIGHT, Bonnie entered her room to find the fire blazing and a nightgown draped across the chair before it, warming. After changing, she slipped into the bed, trying to enjoy the luxury of fine blankets but instead finding herself longing for the rough straw pallet she had slept on for the last five years.

Nevertheless, she closed her eyes and slipped into dreams . . .

Someone was crying.

Bonnie bolted upright in bed. The crying only grew louder, so she ventured down the hall, still in her nightdress, trying to follow the sound with the assistance of a lit candle. The halls lengthened and twisted every which way. Every time she thought she had found the right way through the maze of corridors, she found herself back in the castle's entry hall.

For what seemed like hours she struggled to follow the sound of that sad weeping. At last she asked in desperation, "Where you?"

The cries softened. "I am here," the voice responded quietly.

It was a voice Bonnie knew at once.

She turned and watched as the wall behind her opened up, revealing the snowy garden beyond, the same garden Bonnie had seen in her dreams a thousand times. But now, where she had only ever seen the rosebush before, she saw instead a small girl, rolled up into a tight ball, weeping.

"What is the matter?" Bonnie hastened to the child, knelt down, and laid her hand on her shoulder.

The girl looked up, tears gleaming in her blue eyes. "Help us!" she said.

Bonnie woke with a start, clutching the blankets tightly to her breast. She stared up at the canopy of her bed, struggling to draw breath. Never before had the dreams been so vivid! Never before had she seen more than brief glimpses of scenes!

And never before had she seen the face of the child who made that desperate plea.

"How can I help?" she whispered into the cold night. But there was no one to answer.

The next day Bonnie descended the stair to the dining hall and found the beast waiting for her, standing beside the table. She said nothing but nodded politely and sat as he held her chair for her. As he moved to the far end of the table to take his own seat, she studied the pattern of the cutlery beside her bowl. Would it be better to say nothing and endure an interminable silence? Or should she try to alleviate the loneliness and speak?

"Are you . . . are you really a wulver?" she asked at length even as she served herself from the crock of humble porridge near at hand.

The wulver, who had been gazing into the fire, looked her way, surprised perhaps that she addressed him. "Not of legend, no," he said, shaking his heavy head. Light reflected off the golden brocade of his doublet, an antique piece of clothing that fit with the appearance of everything else in the castle . "I am entirely . . ." He paused for a moment as if searching for the right word. "I am entirely unique," he finally finished.

Bonnie nodded, half-sorry she had asked. His answer was far from satisfactory. She began to eat.

"Why did ye come?" her host asked abruptly.

Bonnie looked up in surprise. "My father said . . . That is, you wanted—"

"Ye could have refused." He gazed across the table at her meaningfully, and Bonnie realized that he knew she had come against her father's will. Perhaps he had read her letter.

"I could not leave my father to your mercy. And . . ." Bonnie stopped.

"And?"

"I don't know. I've caused my family so much pain and maybe . . . maybe I wished to redeem myself." She shook her head, feeling the intensity of the wulver's studying gaze, and knew she would have to offer more of an explanation. "My thoughtlessness once hurt them greatly, and I've been unable to truly forgive myself for it." Calum's injuries—his scarred face and ruined eye—haunted her. Even in that moment she felt her heart sicken at the memory, and she feared she might disgrace herself with tears. Steeling her spirit, she closed her eyes, trying to drive back the memory. But she could not forget Calum's dear smile, ugly though it may now be.

"Ye are honest."

"I suppose so," Bonnie whispered in response. She picked at the rest of her meal, and another long silence fell between them. As she laid down her spoon, the wulver, observing, rose to leave.

"Milord," she said quickly before he could bow and exit the room, "if I saw you at times during . . . during the day, I mean . . . it would not bother me."

His strange face seemed perplexed, and she wished she could better explain. Explain that she dreaded another day alone with her thoughts and fears far more than she dreaded his company. For in his presence she found the wulver far less intimidating than he was in her mind.

Perhaps he read some of her meaning in her face. "I'll be in the garden then," he said. Was that *hope* she heard in his growl? "If ye wish to join me later, I'd be glad of yer company."

In that moment Bonnie realized that the wulver was lonely. Maybe this was why he had demanded her presence at his castle? A strange way to find a companion, and it did not incline her to forgive him. But she might begin to understand him a little.

CHAPTER 10

FOLLOWING HER meal, Bonnie returned to her room and, after some consideration, opened the wardrobe once more. Her frock was dirty and rumpled, and she could not well live in it the rest of . . . of her stay here, however long that may be. If the wulver protested her wearing gowns stored in her own room, well, she'd apologize and make do. Otherwise, she decided she must wear them.

The blue dress fit her well, though it felt odd and uncomfortable. The undergarments were strange to her, and the skirt was intended to be worn with panniers. When she discarded these as too uncomfortable for daily living, the mounds of skirt fabric and petticoats hung oddly from her waist. Still, it was a fresh gown.

She moved to the little table beneath the mirror she had seen the day before and discovered there a hairbrush. As she brushed her hair before the glass, she frowned suddenly, tilting her head. The mirror's frame was engraved with an inscription she had not noticed before:

TRUST YE NOT THINE EYES
APPEARANCES ARE NOT WHAT THEY SEEM

"An odd sentiment for a mirror," she whispered. With a curious shake of her head, she replaced the hairbrush and, holding the heavy skirts of the new gown up so as not to trip upon them, made her way out of the room and down the stairs.

The castle was large and rambling, and it seemed that no matter how far she wandered, there was always some new passage or chamber she had not yet discovered. Sometimes it seemed to her as though the winding halls were rather too like the dream she had experienced the night before, and once she caught herself listening for the sound of a child's weeping. But no. This was no dream. And there was no child.

She took a turn and found herself in a large, elegant hallway filled with portraits. Some were very old, all were dusty, and Bonnie had a feeling that this was a part of the castle even her captor avoided. She had seen no pictures in any of the other rooms, and this was the first hint she had found that anyone else had ever lived there.

One painting in particular caught her eye. It was of a fair-haired gentleman, handsome and dressed in the fashion of a century past, with huge sleeves and a tall, stiff collar trimmed in lace. He had a face Bonnie deemed extremely likable, and she wondered what had happened to him— what had happened to all the faces gracing either side of the hall.

Next to the gentleman's portrait was another painting. At the sight of it Bonnie gasped, for this was a face she knew, though it took her a moment to realize why. It was the portrait of a little girl who shared the man's blond curls and blue eyes, clearly related to him somehow.

She was the child from Bonnie's dream last night.

Bonnie took a step back, her eyes still on the painting. Once more she caught herself straining for some sound of a child's voice, the familiar pleading she had heard these last five years. Only silence lingered in the halls of the castle, however.

She moved on, eager to escape the soulful gaze of the girl in the portrait. There were more paintings—one she especially noticed was of a beautiful, kind-looking woman with dark hair and a sweet smile. But Bonnie did not like to linger here any longer and hurried out of the hall as swiftly as she could.

She progressed to the end of a dim hall, pushed aside the heavy curtains draping a tall window, and looked out into the gardens. Oh yes! The wulver had told her that she might find him there. Very well. Join him she would.

She found a door with little difficulty, as though the castle itself offered her a way out once it knew her intention. Her gown was of thick fabric, and she was only slightly cold as she walked through the garden, which was bare and brown from winter frost. Its stark appearance contrasted with the only blooming plant—the large rosebush covered in yellow blooms, which Bonnie recognized at once and without surprise. After all, she had known it must be here.

And beyond the rosebush stood the wulver, just lifting his head to see her approach. His expression was difficult to read, but she thought she glimpsed delighted surprise flash through his eyes.

"Good day, Beast," Bonnie said, drawing near.

"Guid day, Miss Bonnie," he replied. His claw-tipped fingers gently tested the leaves and stems of the rose, as though he searched it for some sign of blight or rot. But though he feigned busyness, she saw how his wolf's ears twitched toward her more often than not.

Uncertain what to say now that she had found him, Bonnie maintained her silence. She admired the rose. Indeed, it was very beautiful. In her dreams she had never taken the time to notice or appreciate its beauty. She remembered the sight of the little child curled up in this very spot in her nightmare of the night before, but shook this away and tried to focus on the moment at hand.

"Ye said ye were called Bonnie," the beast said suddenly without looking at her. "Whit be yer Christian name?"

"Seònaid," she answered. "After an aunt of my mother."

"Seònaid. A true Gaelic name," said he.

Bonnie nodded. After a moment, she asked, "Do you have a name? A real name, I mean?"

The beast's movements stopped, and Bonnie regretted her question. "I did once," was all he said, and then he returned to his work.

Feeling as though she had intruded upon his privacy, Bonnie searched for something else to say. "The blooms are lovely," she said.

"Aye, they are."

"You tend them very well. I've never heard of a rose that would bloom in winter."

The beast glanced her way, uncertainty in his strangely human eyes. "Are ye well tended, Miss Seònaid? Do ye have everything ye need?"

Bonnie offered something close to a smile, the first she had managed since setting out from her family's cottage. "Everything but company," she said. A small stone bench stood nearby, and she brushed a layer of snow from it and sat, her ample skirts spread about her.

The beast grunted at her words, obviously ill at ease. "I dinnae ken if ye'd want *my* company," he said, and shook his head.

This surprised Bonnie as much as anything else she'd experienced since coming to this strange place. After all, she was *his* captive, was she not? Why would it matter to him what *she* wanted? Why would he send for her in the first place if, once she came, she might decide for herself whether or not to be in his presence? Was she or was she not a prisoner?

And why did she find herself, when given the choice, preferring to seek out the companionship of her monstrous host? Was she truly that lonely or did she actually enjoy his quiet, gracious, oddly elegant demeanor? No, that certainly could not be! He was a beast, and she his captive.

Determined not to think more closely on these questions, she turned to another possible conversation. "How old is this castle?"

The beast's eyes narrowed as he looked up at the high towers and walls around them. "Several hundred years, I expect," he said, and his voice held deep sorrow and longing, neither of which Bonnie could begin to comprehend. She followed his gaze and saw how the stone of the castle had begun to crumble, how the glass in many of the gothic windows looked cracked or was missing altogether. Perhaps, Bonnie thought, the wulver remembered when the castle was as beautiful on the outside as it was within.

He continued, "'Twas taken over by a family from Norway in the early thirteenth century. They lived here for hundreds of years."

The unspoken question of what happened to the family hung in the air, though Bonnie didn't dare ask it.

"I don't suppose you fish?" she asked impulsively to break the tension. The beast looked at her curiously. "*Catch* fish," she continued. "In the old stories, wulvers would go fishing and leave their catch for the poor."

"I told ye I'm not a wulver."

Bonnie raised an eyebrow.

"Well, I am, aye, but not a *real* one."

"Are you a ghost then?" Bonnie couldn't say why she pushed; he obviously wasn't given to easy conversation.

But he seemed bemused, as though he didn't quite believe her efforts at friendliness. "I'm no ghost. Have ye nothing better to talk about?"

Hearing his growling tone, Bonnie felt the corners of her mouth turn up in another smile. "You sound like my sister Sorcha. She can be rather . . . difficult, when she chooses."

"Aye, I remind ye of the difficult one, then?"

She laughed. This surprised her as much as anything. How long had it been since she laughed, truly laughed? Indeed, when she stopped to think about it, she could not remember. Not since before her father set out for Burntisland. Possibly not for some time before that.

"Ye have other siblings?" the wulver asked, drawing her out of her reverie.

Bonnie opened her mouth and suddenly found herself telling him about her siblings at home: Sorcha, Maisie, Calum. She told of Sorcha's bossiness which scarcely disguised her giving heart. She told of Maisie, who concealed her frailty behind determined good cheer and smiles. She told of Calum, even of his scars, though she did not dwell on those. Mostly she told of his kind smile and the way he always did what he could to keep the family strong, even when their father sometimes lost himself in despair, reminiscing about the past.

To all this the wulver listened quietly, no longer even moving to tend his rose. He simply stood, his head tilted to one side, drinking in every word. When Bonnie found her voice trailing away at last, a heavy silence followed.

But this silence the wulver broke, saying, "Sometimes it is difficult for a man not to despair when he thinks upon the past."

Bonnie looked up at him sharply, meeting his eyes over his blooming roses. Were those . . . Heavens above! Were those tears she saw glistening there?

The wulver blinked and passed an ugly hand over his face. Then, without another word he turned and strode away swiftly, as though he could not bear her presence another moment. Bonnie remained seated upon the cold bench, feeling the coldness of the winter air, which felt colder now that she was alone again.

The wulver waited uneasily for his guest—he hated to use the word *prisoner*—to come down to the dining room. He did not doubt that she would come, but he worried that her face might display displeasure upon seeing him waiting for her. Perhaps he should leave before she arrived? Give the poor young lady peace . . .

Finally he rose, prepared to hasten away. But before he could move, Bonnie appeared suddenly in the doorway and, with no greeting or acknowledgement or even a glance his way, hastened to her seat at the opposite end of the table. After a moment she took up her cutlery and began to serve herself a portion from the bounty spread before her.

The wulver stood awkwardly, uncertain whether he should reclaim his seat or disappear as he had intended. Before he could quite make up his mind, however, he found himself fixed with Bonnie's intense gaze.

"Milord," she said, clutching a spoon as though it were her one weapon of defense, "did I . . . did I anger you earlier today? By something I said?"

Nonplussed, the beast shifted upon his feet. "Why would ye think so?"

"In the garden, you left so quickly, and I . . . Are you upset with me?"

Was that honest concern he saw in her face? Concern for him? No, certainly not! She must fear only the beast's displeasure, must fear that his vicious wrath would fall upon her head. She certainly could have no other worry in her heart for one such as he.

"I am sorry," he said and, after an uncertain moment, took his seat. His social skills were sorely lacking; he hardly knew how to behave around young women anymore. "I dinnae think . . ."

She sighed. Then in a small, timid voice, she said the last thing he would have expected or even hoped to hear from her: "I simply thought . . . I thought maybe we could . . . be friends."

The beast sat back in his chair. "Ye want to be friends? With me?" His voice rang with disbelief. "The one who stole ye from yer family and bullied yer da? Who locked ye in a tower room? Ye wish to be friends with a monster like me?"

He hadn't meant to raise his voice, but by the time he'd finished, his questions were echoing off the walls. *Now ye've gone and frightened the lass*, he scolded himself. But he couldn't help butchering the conversation; he was too out of practice in understanding other human beings or their reactions. And now he'd sabotaged his only chance to right Morag's wrongs, for Bonnie stared at him in startled terror.

Before he could say more, he saw something flicker in the girl's face. He could tell she had made some sort of decision. But just what the decision was, he did not know.

She set her jaw, any trace of her earlier timidity gone. "I am trying to make the best of a wretched situation," she said. "Yes, maybe you are horrid. You'll get no argument from me on that score!" Her voice was calm, though a small tremble betrayed her following words. "Do you know what I feel for you? *Pity*. Pity because you're a lonely old creature with no friends and nothing to love but an old rosebush. But I refuse to be frightened. I refuse! Do you hear me? I refuse!" Her eyes glimmered and, to the wulver's consternation, tears began to trail down her face. This seemed to frustrate her all the more, and she dashed them away with angry swipes of both hands.

The wulver rose and stumbled over to her. He carried no handkerchief, so he took one of the table napkins and handed it to her.

She smacked away the napkin. "I don't want that!" she said crossly.

"Take it," he said softly. The words came out in a growl.

She stared up at him, her eyes glassy with unshed tears. Then she obeyed, snatching the napkin from his hand, and blew into it loudly. Embarrassed, the wulver backed away several paces, not yet returning to his seat but standing with his hands behind his back, his shoulders bowed. "I apologize for raisin' me voice at ye," he said as gently as he could. "Ye offered me the precious gift of yer friendship, and I threw it at ye with a vengeance, like an idiot of the worst kind."

Her silence was the only answer he received.

"Might we start this conversation anew?" he asked.

She swallowed, mangling the damp napkin in her hands. "I—I suppose." She dashed at her face once more with her hand. "I shouldn't have lost my temper. I apologize as well."

"Apology accepted," said the beast. He bowed then, very elegantly, and extended a hand to her like a gentleman at a ball. "Will ye do me the honor of bein' my friend, Miss Seònaid?"

She nodded quickly and attempted a smile. Then, as though coming to a decision, she reached out her trembling hand and lightly rested her fingers in his palm for several moments before drawing back and folding both hands in her lap.

The wulver straightened and returned to his place at the other end of the table. Taking his seat, he said, "Tell me more about yer life in the country with yer family. How did the lot of ye take to shepherding?"

She began to talk again, speaking of lambings and shearings, of the struggles of learning a new and difficult trade. She spoke of her and Maisie's joy when the first lamb was born, and of how Sorcha pretended hard-hearted indifference only to be caught holding the lamb and crooning lullabies to it when she thought no one was near. Bonnie spoke long and easily, her eyes alight with love for the family she had left behind, and the wulver listened and asked occasional questions.

All the while he clenched his hand tightly around the warm place in his palm where her fingers had so gently rested.

CHAPTER 11

SEVEN DAYS later, Bonnie relaxed after her evening meal before a crackling fire in a large sitting room. Much to her surprise, the wulver joined her, seating himself in a large chair. When he leaned back, his face was hidden. Though she wouldn't have admitted it for fear of hurting his feelings, a part of Bonnie preferred that he remain in that attitude. Then she could simply listen to his voice and pretend that he looked like something—*someone*—else.

And she did like the sound of the wulver's voice—like a roll of thunder, dangerous and yet comforting all at once.

"I haven't been out in the world fer, well, a verra long time," the wulver said as they sat together admiring the blaze. "I suppose 'tis too much to hope that our land is at peace?"

Bonnie sniffed derisively. "I think you already know the answer to that question." She grew somber. "There were talks of Jacobite uprisings when I left." She played with the fabric of the bountiful blue skirt she wore, tracing the elegant lines of embroidery. Oh, how Sorcha and Maisie would have appreciated its beauty!

"I hope my family is well," she said softly. Seated in a chair so large that it swallowed her, she felt strangely safe here in this castle where she was a captive. She found she did not like to think of her loved ones out in the cold world beyond these sturdy walls.

The wulver was silent for some while before changing the subject. "Yer speech is very English." Bonnie heard him shift in his chair. "I take it ye are not native to the Highlands?"

"No, but my mother was. Her family was Catholic, and they were furious when she turned Protestant to marry my father and move to the Lowlands." Bonnie shrugged. "We attend a Protestant service at a small church just outside Inverness. We're not the only ones, but it is a precarious position all the same."

"And do ye still pray, Miss Seònaid?"

"Still?" Bonnie asked in surprise.

"I would think ye'd believe it useless, after . . ."

Bonnie bowed her head, a soft smile on her lips. She thought of the desperate prayers she had uttered on her journey to this castle, to a fate she could not guess. It seemed to her that the Lord God had indeed lit her way through darkness, protecting her from the perils of the night. "You cannot shake my faith, milord," she said with a smile. "Even you are not quite *so* terrible." She made sure she said it laughingly, so he was not offended. Truly, she did not find him terrible at all. Not anymore. "*You* speak English well, though many here speak Gaelic."

"My mither was English."

"Truly?" Bonnie could not keep the surprise from her voice as she gazed across at the shadow of the wulver.

"Does it shock ye that I had a mither, lass?" he asked, his voice rumbling in his throat. "Did ye think I sprung from beneath a rock?"

Though he could scarcely speak without a growl, she thought he sounded amused. "No—I suppose not." Bonnie felt her face flush. "Perhaps I was just surprised your mother was . . . English."

He gave a bark of laughter. "Aye, 'tis nearly as unbelievable, methinks."

Bonnie smiled in spite of herself. "Aye. I suppose it is."

The creature that was once the man called Lauchlan stood in the archway of the balcony doors. From this vantage point he could see the young woman there on the grounds below, her ginger hair blowing in the wind as she stared out to sea. She was a pretty lass, and kind.

She was not difficult to love.

But his emotions would not help him. They never had. The lines of Morag's curse were deeper and more complex than even his invisible servants knew. She had twined her life with his, and he felt her mocking presence. Haunting him. Scorning him.

In taking away his life she had ensured her own. He knew she was still alive somewhere, spiraling deeper into sorcery and witchcraft.

How the Hand of Righteousness had not yet struck her down he did not know! And over the years his belief in a Higher Power had waned. Could a loving and good God allow that witch's wickedness to continue? How could such a thing happen to him, a good, God-fearing man?

The beast sighed and leaned his head against the window frame. He was not so sure the word *good* described him anymore. He truly did not know what he was anymore. No one had come to the castle in decades.

Then, when someone *had* come, his fury had overtaken him. Then when the merchant, in his fear, began rambling about gifts and roses and his beautiful youngest daughter, the answer had seemed clear. With only months left to break the curse, it was his last chance. A desperate effort, but a *chance*.

But her arrival had panicked him. He hadn't seen a woman for almost a century. For one to suddenly stir up the sort of feelings he'd thought he would never experience again . . .

It was terrifying.

Yet he couldn't quite pull himself away from her. Nor could he entirely give up hope. Their conversations at dinner were growing longer. The beast found himself talking—and talking much—as he unburdened his ninety-odd years of solitude onto the girl Bonnie. After being alone for so long, it had taken him days to grow accustomed to the sound of his own voice (such a horrible, changed voice as it was!). But slowly, as they spoke of her life, of the castle, even of history and gardening, he began to remember what it was like to have companionship. He had been a sociable man, once upon a time. A man who loved an evening's conversation over a cup of hot grog. He had almost forgotten that man's existence.

He felt young again. He felt a little less like an animal. Perhaps Bonnie was bringing out the man he still was inside.

Help us!

Bonnie jerked upright in her bed. It was still black outside, and she pulled the covers close around her shoulders. The days had been steadily growing warmer as the winter turned to spring, but nights were still chilly and unforgiving.

And the dreams . . . they grew stronger.

This last dream had been short enough but no less worrisome. The same nightmare of searching the empty halls of this castle, searching for the rose . . . searching for the child . . .

But this time, no matter how she sought, Bonnie could find neither the little girl nor the rose. And the voice calling out to her was more distant than ever before.

Bonnie breathed heavily, drawing cold air into her lungs and expelling it in gasps. She whispered into the silence of her chamber, "Where *is* she?" The more important question pressed upon her mind, and this time she whispered, "*Who* is she?"

Bonnie was pensive at dinner the following evening, and the wulver noticed. "Whit be troubling ye, Miss Seònaid?"

Bonnie hesitated, unsure whether or not she should ask. But the time had come, and she needed to learn answers. "The portraits on the wall in the hallway . . . Who were they?"

The wulver looked away. His face looked so sorrowful, so wounded, that Bonnie instantly regretted asking. "Never mind," she said quickly.

But the wulver shook his heavy head. "No, I'll . . . I'll tell ye." His claws dug into the wood of the table. "They were the family that lived here before me. The man was called Lauchlan."

"And his family?" Bonnie asked quietly.

"His wife died young, and his daughter was taken from him. But that was long ago."

The uneasiness Bonnie had felt when she first came to the castle returned. Sometimes she almost forgot the beast was, well, a beast. She was used to his savage appearance by now, and she enjoyed his gracious company. But once in a while something would prick her, and she'd remember that she knew little about him. At other times, she'd catch a glimpse of him from the corner of her eye and see his wolfish form anew.

The portraits disturbed her. She hated to think that the creature who had somehow become her friend was in any way responsible for the unknown fate of Lauchlan and his family. But what *else* could have happened to them? She often wondered if she was a foolish coward for trying to pretend that the beast had no connection to them when he clearly did.

"Miss Seònaid, will ye marry me?"

The first time he had asked, Bonnie was terrified; the second, apprehensive. As the days and even weeks wore on, his subsequent offers had made her feel uncomfortable. But now she felt regretful, almost guilty.

"No, Beast," she said quietly, wishing he would stop asking. Couldn't he see that her answer would always be the same? Why must he torture the both of them with his relentless request?

That evening as she walked past the hall of portraits, the beautiful, dark-haired lady seemed to regard her with disappointment. Bonnie looked at her in annoyance. "Well, what would you have done?" she asked the unresponsive image sourly.

She leaned with her back against the opposite wall and slowly slid to the floor, her skirts ballooning about her. She put her head in her hands and sighed. Why had it suddenly become so hard to answer his question? She felt the painted gazes of the man, girl, and woman staring down at her. Suddenly she couldn't stand the accusation in their eyes, so she leapt up and all but ran back to the safety of her room.

"Did he hurt them?" she wondered even as she shut her door and turned to the solitary silence of her rooms. "Is he responsible for their deaths? It's the only thing that makes sense! Even if he wasn't . . . what he is, I could never marry a murderer."

The word *murderer* slipped from her tongue, and she frowned as though she'd tasted something vile. Oh, how could she even think such a thing? The wulver couldn't be a murderer. He simply *couldn't!*

"But then what *is* he?" Bonnie's anguished voice seemed small and childish in her own ears as she stared at the high ceiling of her bedchamber. No answer came to her.

Morag stood in the shelter of the forest. From her vantage point she could see the light in the tower room. Sometimes she saw the shadow of the lass's form flicker across the light.

Stupid, stupid girl! How had she, of all people, been found by Lauchlan? Oh, by Cailleach the dreadful, she should have done away with the child the moment she laid eyes upon her in the market of Inverness! Set a hex upon her, made certain she never stepped anywhere near this castle.

Morag ran her tongue under her teeth. Though her former brother-in-law might believe her curse to be nothing more than pure revenge, it was actually the only thing keeping her alive. The curse she had enacted was necessary to her very survival, for it fed her as she, draining her victims' hopes and humanity, filled herself with their strength. Its breaking would cause her instant, painful death.

And even worse torment to her soul afterwards.

Slowly, she retreated farther into the forest. She would watch silently for now. *But soon*, she thought, *I may have to interfere.*

CHAPTER 12

"MISS SEÒNAID, will ye marry me?"

Bonnie closed her eyes in pain at the question. "Beast, I—"

"Dinnae answer," he said abruptly.

Startled, Bonnie opened her eyes as he rose from his place at the table and stood there, as if fighting some inward battle. When he spoke again, his gruff words surprised her even more: "Think about it. I shall—I shall not ask again."

Bonnie stared at him, feeling as though she wavered on the edge of some great precipice, where her next move might mean either salvation or destruction. "I shall think about it," she promised. He bowed and left the room.

Bonnie returned to her own rooms, her heart pounding in her throat with as much anxiety as it had on her very first night in the castle. The air began to smell musty and old, as though the interior of the castle were suddenly decaying to match its exterior. Something was *wrong*. She had noticed a crack in her window the other day, and the tapestries grew discolored and frayed, their age finally catching up to them. Fissures appeared in the stone walls, and even her borrowed gowns had faded, their elegant embroidery becoming tattered.

The next morning when Bonnie went out into the garden, the sight that greeted her deepened her distress. Over the past few weeks the yellow rosebush, which had bloomed throughout her stay, had begun to wilt. Now, almost overnight, it had deteriorated so dramatically that Bonnie could only stare in shock. After regaining her ability to move, she fingered its brittle branches. Only two flowers remained on the entire plant, and these were wilted and brown. As she watched, another leaf fell to the ground.

"It's dying."

Bonnie turned to see the wulver staring at the rosebush despondently.

"But how can this be?" she asked. "It bloomed all winter, even in the snow. I don't understand." Her voice trembled as she spoke, for she thought back suddenly on the last several nights . . . nights strangely empty of dreams, even of the child's whisper.

With one claw the wulver gently touched a withered petal. "The rosebush was meant to last for only a hundred years. Its time now approaches."

Bonnie took two paces back. She felt a single tear slide down her cheek but didn't know why. Quickly she wiped it away.

"Do ye like it here, Miss Seònaid?"

The abruptness of the wulver's question surprised her. Sudden resentment, perhaps strengthened by her concern over the rose, welled up inside her, and she struggled to keep her voice civil as she replied. "You are . .

. very kind to me, Beast. I have everything I need, everything I could want except . . ."

"Except?"

Bonnie's hesitation did not come from fear. She knew he would never hurt her. Instead, she found herself reluctant to say anything that would cause him pain. Nevertheless, the resentment pushed her, and she answered softly, "I have everything except my freedom."

The wulver's facial expressions were difficult to read, being something other than human. Yet Bonnie knew that he was unhappy and wished she could somehow express her feelings without hurting him. But the truth of the situation remained glaring and painful. "I miss my family," she said as though to explain.

"Of course, Miss Seònaid," he said in his deep voice. He gave the resigned growl that Bonnie had come to recognize as his sigh. "Of course ye do."

Before Bonnie could say another word, he was gone.

The wulver stood in his room and leaned upon a sturdy wooden desk. His self-loathing threatened to overcome him entirely as he considered the creature he had become. The *beast*. For a beast he was, due not to his appearance but to his deplorable actions.

He prayed to the God that Seònaid loved so well, struggling to recall the prayers he had known long ago, begging for some guidance. How could he keep her against her will? But then, how could he let her go? For to do so would be to give up on all those who depended on him. To do so would be to let his servants suffer their final doom . . . to let his daughter fade away . . .

"Guid evening, Lauchlan."

The wulver stiffened. Though he hadn't heard her voice in years, he knew it immediately. "Morag." He spoke the word as though it were poison in his mouth.

Turning, he saw the sorceress leaning against the wall and wearing an air of nonchalance as she examined her nails.

"How did ye get in here?" he snapped.

She laughed, bestowing a frighteningly beautiful smile upon him. "I turned ye into a hideous beast, and ye ask how I kin get into yer room unnoticed? Fer shame, Lauchlan. I almost feel insulted."

"Why are ye here? The hundred years are not yet completed."

Her smile disappeared, and she straightened then wandered leisurely about the room. His hackles rose as she examined the draperies and furniture. "This castle used to be so beautiful. 'Tis a shame to see it die along with ye."

He watched her with a glint of confusion in his eyes, and she gasped in mock surprise. "Oh dear. I thought I told ye. Dinnae ye remember? When the curse is fulfilled, the castle and all who are in it shall collapse into nothingness. Haven't ye wondered why everything seems to be fallin' apart at once?"

His heart grew leaden in his breast. "Even . . . even Miss Seònaid?"

"The girl?" Morag smiled. "'Tis a pity to have *finally* met someone so close to the end of the curse, isn't it? Yet her presence here only endangers her life as the day draws nigh. Ye have . . . oh . . . three more weeks. Perhaps." She pretended to think. "I seem to have forgotten the exact date." She turned to the door and opened it, pausing before she stepped through into shadows. "Guidbye, Lauchlan. I doubt we shall see each other again."

With one last triumphant look thrown over her shoulder, she vanished.

"Morag!" he growled and ran to the door. But when he looked out into the hall, she was gone.

The following two weeks felt strained, almost unbearably so. Bonnie, who had become attuned to the wulver's moods, didn't believe he was upset with her, yet something troubled him. Not that he neglected her; on the contrary, he sought her out. But his movements were agitated, and once in a while she caught him watching her with an inscrutable look in his eye.

Finally, one evening near the end of one of their meals, she heard the beast exhale a shaky breath—evidence of anxiety she had never before seen in him—and she knew that whatever the matter was, she was about to learn of it.

"Miss Seònaid," he said, "would ye like to go home?"

Bonnie choked on her food. When he began to speak, her stomach had twisted in knots. But *this* had never crossed her mind. "Go home?" she repeated, too stunned to form a complete sentence.

He smiled gently at her bewilderment. The expression should have been dreadful on his animal face, but Bonnie had learned to read the difference between his smiles and his snarls. "Aye," he said.

Bonnie couldn't keep from smiling. Indeed, the smile rising inside her would have burst had she tried to contain it. "I would. I would! Oh *Beast!*" She laughed and then choked as the laugh turned to a sudden sob. Why did she feel this sudden sorrow, this terrible foreboding? No, no, she must simply be overwhelmed with her own happiness, that was all! "How long might I stay?" she asked quietly, hardly trusting her own voice.

"Fer as long as ye like," he said softly. He bowed his great head, staring at the empty plate on the table before him. "I canna keep ye here anymore."

Her foreboding redoubled; she could no longer deny its presence. "I don't understand," she said.

"I canna keep ye here, Miss Seònaid." The wulver lifted his gaze, staring across the table at her. Candlelight shone in his eyes, which seemed to beg her to understand, to discern some secret meaning in his words.

Bonnie felt hopelessly stupid. "What if I don't wish to go?" she asked, closely watching his reaction.

The wulver closed his eyes. "I'm sorry," he said hoarsely. "But if ye don't—" He paused.

"Beast!" Bonnie cried, suddenly frightened. She rose and came around the side of the table, approaching him with some trepidation despite the friendship they had developed over time. "Beast, are you—"

He looked up and, seeing her approach, sprang from his chair as though afraid that her extended hand might touch his own. "I'm fine," he said weakly. "I shouldn't have spoken." He backed away from her, making for the door and an escape. Bonnie watched these actions, her heart twisting with so many conflicting emotions, she scarcely knew how to feel.

The wulver paused in the doorway. "I have gifts for yer family," he said, "to serve by way of an apology."

"Beast," Bonnie persisted, "what are you not telling me?"

But he refused to answer. "There'll be a horse waitin' for ye in the mornin'."

Before he could vanish, Bonnie leapt forward, closing the distance between them, and caught his ugly hand to hold it in both of hers. "Please," she pleaded, trying not to let the tears come to her eyes, "tell me what you mean—"

The wulver froze at her touch as though struck to the heart. Then, with no further word, he slipped his hand from her grasp and fled the room. Bonnie stood where he left her, wondering if she would ever see him again.

In the morning the horse—her father's cousin's horse, the very same she had ridden to the castle so long ago—awaited her, its saddlebags full of gifts, just as the wulver had promised.

Bonnie, clad in her old gown and shawl once more, approached the horse in some surprise. "What will our cousin say when he finds you are missing?" she whispered, taking hold of the bridle and stroking the animal's broad cheek.

She looked back toward the castle one last time. Something moved in one of the upper windows, and she knew the wulver had pulled back the curtain to watch her departure. As soon as he realized she had seen him, he released the curtain and disappeared from her view.

But she was free to go. Free! And here was the horse, ready to carry her back to her family. How could she refuse such a chance?

Help us . . .

The memory of the child's voice lingered in her mind. Bonnie mounted the horse and, from that high vantage, looked around at the castle yard, even at the small garden where the rosebush stood brown, its final rose fading fast.

"I'll come back," she whispered, promising herself, promising the wulver. Promising that poor withering rose. The promise still on her lips, she urged her horse through the gate and away into the forest.

CHAPTER 13

ONCE BONNIE had traveled far enough from the castle to step from the forest into the open heath not many miles from home, she found herself strangely apprehensive. That morning she had been too focused on the wulver's melancholy to fully grasp the fact that she was returning to her family. Now the reality dawned, and she considered the many questions they were sure to ask. How was she to explain the complicated relationship she shared with the wulver? She couldn't help but think of his pensive look the night before.

You're going to see your family again! she scolded herself. *He's released you! There's no reason to feel . . .* Her thoughts trailed off. No reason to feel what? Bereft? Lonely? Rejected?

For one breathless moment she considered turning back. *But what sort of person longs to return to her captor instead of her family?* she asked herself uncomfortably and continued homeward.

As she rode on, finding the road and covering the miles that separated her from home, she remembered suddenly her long-ago fear of leaving home, of going away to school and returning as a different person. How desperately her child self had longed to keep her family together, to allow for no change.

But now her worst fear had come to pass—she was no longer the Bonnie who had ridden away in the dead of night. She was a new person. Would her family be able to understand?

Suddenly she glimpsed the crofter's cottage ahead. As the sun shone down from high above, she saw the familiar dooryard showing the first signs of spring. She saw Maisie out with the chickens, her back to the road, as yet unaware of her sister's approach.

"Maisie!" Bonnie called.

Her sister spun about, spilling chicken feed from her basket as she did so. She recognized the figure on horseback at once, dropped her basket— much to the delight of the chickens—and ran down the road, crying out, "Bonnie! Bonnie!"

Bonnie leapt from her horse and fell into her sister's embrace, and the two of them laughed and wept. "Our cousin came by yesterday," Maisie said, wiping tears from her eyes suddenly and shaking her head. "He said his horse had run off and wondered if it had come here. I remembered how it returned to us with the message from you all those months ago, and I . . . I started to hope . . ."

She laughed then, and Bonnie did as well. By that time, others had heard the commotion in the road, and Mr. Alleway's joyful shout carried through the air. Bonnie found herself wrapped in her father's arms and felt him plant a kiss on the top of her head. "Oh, my Bonnie lass!" he exclaimed.

Soon she was surrounded by all of them—Sorcha, Calum, her father,

Maisie—and smothered in their affection. As though from a distance, she heard Sorcha's firm voice declaring, "Settle down! Settle down, all! We must get Bonnie inside, and she's not to answer a *single* question until she's had a chance to catch her breath and down a cup of warm milk!"

"There are gifts in the saddle bags," Bonnie managed to interrupt. Calum attended to the horse while Bonnie was practically carried inside. "How are you all?" she asked as she settled onto the stool Sorcha pulled forward for her, close to the peat fire.

"We all want to know about *you*," her father insisted, drawing another seat close to hers and taking her hand as though he would never let go.

"Do tell us!" Maisie pleaded, closing in on Bonnie's other side. "How did you escape?"

"I didn't," Bonnie said. "He . . . let me leave."

"The wulver?" Maisie persisted. "Was he indeed a wulver?" She winced at her father's sharp glance and said, "I'm sorry, Da! I just want to know."

"Yes," Bonnie answered, patting her sister's hand. "Yes, he was indeed a wulver. But—"

"What did he want of you?"

"Now, now!" said Sorcha sharply, pressing the promised cup of milk into her sister's hands. "I thought I said no questions?"

"It's all right," Bonnie said, though she hated the question. She knew she had been brought to the castle for a particular purpose. She knew it even as she had always known, from the moment she first glimpsed the rose her father brought to her and first determined to pay his debt. The visions she had seen all those years were a promise of some kind . . . a promise she had failed to fulfill.

Realizing her family still waited for her to answer Maisie's question—even Sorcha, whose curiosity overrode her insistence that they allow Bonnie to rest—Bonnie whispered, "I think he's lonely."

"Isn't that just typical Bonnie," Sorcha said. "Held captive by a wolfish monster, and all she can say is *I think he's lonely*." She shook her head, trying to be scornful but not quite succeeding. Not even Sorcha could completely hide her relief and gladness over her sister's safe return.

"Tell us *everything*," Maisie pleaded.

This was what Bonnie had most dreaded about her return. "I don't know where to begin," she said honestly. "It wasn't at all like I expected." She furrowed her brows.

"Did he mistreat you?" This from her father, spoken with great dread. Bonnie realized suddenly the guilt he must have suffered all these long months. She knew too well how painful guilt could be, how torturous.

She quickly shook her head, smiling at her father, wishing to soothe his pain. "Not at all! Indeed, he was kind to me. He became a friend. I don't know . . ." She paused, taking in the heartbreak in Mr. Alleway's face, heartbreak scarcely alleviated by the sight of his daughter returned to him. "I am sorry I ran off without telling you," she said. "I couldn't think what else to do. I couldn't bear to let you suffer for another of my mistakes."

"We were worried sick!" Sorcha scolded, taking a seat on a stool across the fire. "Goodness knows how long we looked for you. The horse finally wandered its way back here with your note in the saddle." Her jaw twitched. "'Twas a foolish act, Bonnie."

"But brave," Calum said, entering the cottage in time to hear the last of Sorcha's tirade. He laid a hand on Bonnie's shoulder and squeezed.

The family stayed long about the fire that night, simply relishing being together with their reclaimed sister and daughter. Bonnie felt a strange combination of gladness and guilt, and her vagueness caused several awkward lapses in the conversation. She was glad to be home, but . . .

. . . just as she had feared, home was no longer the same. And neither was she.

It would be unfair, she knew, to expect her family's lives to stop simply because she was gone. But she was unprepared for everything to be so different. She felt as though she'd been left behind while everyone went on with their lives without her. They spoke of people she didn't know, of events she hadn't attended. Even jokes passed over her head as they laughed about things she hadn't witnessed. *Can so much change in a matter of months?*

She disliked talking about the beast—not because she found it painful, as her family's attitude seemed to suggest, but because she felt she was breaking the beast's trust by doing so. She owed him nothing. At least, most people would think so. Yet she had given him her friendship, and to discuss him behind his back seemed wrong in her mind.

She looked at one of the low windows, where the wulver's rose still rested, propped up in the broken cup. Miraculously, it remained in bloom, even after all this time! But even this rose, like those at the castle, had begun to brown about the edges. Soon it too would crumble into dust.

Sometimes during the next few days, for brief moments as she did her chores or laughed at something Calum said, Bonnie forgot she had ever been away from home. She could pretend that her life was the same as it had been before. But a brief glimpse of the rose on the windowsill was enough to bring her back.

She couldn't look at it without thinking of *him.*

Bonnie wondered again why the loss of a single, insignificant rose had enraged the wulver so much that he would tear her away from her family. She knew him well enough to be certain that such behavior was unusual for him. So what about this rose would drive him to make such a blindly wrathful decision?

She touched the flower gently, but the slight pressure was enough to cause another petal to fall.

Help us!

As the petal drifted to the floor, the child's voice assaulted Bonnie's mind with sudden desperation. She recoiled with the swiftness of one who has accidentally touched a hot fire iron. Knowledge tickled the back of her mind, as if her heart knew something her head did not yet comprehend.

"Calum?" An unfamiliar feminine voice drifted in through the front door, and Bonnie turned in surprise.

Calum, who had just been stoking up the peat fire in the middle of the cottage, spun about suddenly. He had just removed his wide-brimmed hat upon stepping through the door, and Bonnie watched as he hastily grabbed for it now. "That'll be Abigail, come for her wool," he said, tugging the brim of his hat low, as though to hide his ugly face.

Bonnie followed her brother to the door and found a pretty, dark-haired young woman standing in the yard and carrying an empty basket.

"Good morn, Abigail," Calum said, touching the brim of his hat respectfully. "Allow me to introduce my sister Bonnie."

"Guid mornin', Bonnie," the girl said pleasantly to Bonnie, but her attention quickly returned to Calum. She blushed just the slightest bit. "Mum said I'd need to get a bit extra today. I hope it's all right? We have much spinning to do before market day."

"Of course." Calum's words were all politeness but almost stiff. Bonnie watched as he led Abigail out to the barn and then saw her on her way with a basketful of sheep's wool sheared but a few days before.

Calum seemed pensive when he came back inside. He stood by the front window and watched Abigail walk away until she disappeared around a curve in the path.

"Why don't you talk to her, Calum?" Bonnie asked, watching her brother carefully. "She's lovely. And I think she would welcome more conversation than you were offering!"

Calum grimaced and turned away, removing his hat and hanging it on a peg.

"What is it?" Bonnie asked, though she already suspected the answer.

"I guess I don't think a woman could like me, not when I look . . . like this." Calum turned to Bonnie, and she saw his scarred face clearly by the light coming through the window.

Once more she felt the sorrow in her heart that so often assaulted her when she looked closely at her brother. Yet she saw no resentment in his eyes. He had forgiven her long ago; she doubted he even remembered the part she had played in his disfiguring.

"Calum," she said softly, "you are a wonderful man. And I say it not because you're my brother but because it's the truth!"

He answered her smile with a tentative one of his own, the right side of his mouth curling at the corner, the left side merely twisting. "So you're saying you think a fine woman such as Abigail could look past . . . *this*?" He indicated his face with a wave of one hand.

"Of course," Bonnie replied confidently. "When someone is good and kind and honorable, it doesn't matter what he looks like. Love can see past all that. It can . . ."

"It can what?"

Bonnie looked away. "I . . . Never mind. But try for Abigail, will you? I need . . . I need some air."

With this, she slipped from the cottage and began to run. Out from the yard she sped, out through the gate. She followed the same path she had trod on her first night in this country so many years ago, up to the top of the not-too-distant hill where the jagged rock jutted to the sky. She placed her hand on this rock, resting against it to catch her breath.

"What have I done?" she whispered. Then, setting her jaw, she climbed up onto the rock even as she had on that first night, standing there in the wind and the sun, gazing out to the far forest.

She felt again the pulse of darkness, even though the sun was bright. And she thought of the wulver, whom she had left behind. Alone in the midst of that darkness. In the midst of that evil.

"Oh, what have I *done*?" Bonnie asked herself.

She focused on that distant forest, her mind searching for something. Perhaps for the visions, perhaps for the voice. Perhaps for some sense of the wulver himself, calling out to her from across the miles.

She heard nothing. But she felt the power of that darkness, and it frightened her, even here, even in the safety of her family's home and land.

Help us, the child had pleaded. And what had she done instead? She had abandoned them. The wulver. The child. All of them. Given the first opportunity, she had fled, though she knew—she *knew*, Heaven help her!— that she had always been meant to go to the castle, to rescue them from that darkness somehow.

Suddenly she turned and leapt from the stone, flying back down the hill and on to her family's cottage. She saw Maisie in the yard, tending to the chickens even as she'd been when Bonnie first returned.

"Maisie!" Bonnie cried. "I have to leave. I must go back to the castle!"

"What?" Maisie turned to her, horror written clearly across her face. "Bonnie, what are you saying?"

But Bonnie hadn't time to explain. She darted into the cottage and, on an impulse, snatched up the wilting rose from its cup. Tucking it into the bodice of her gown, she darted back into the yard and gave her sister a quick embrace. "Tell the others I've gone," she said. "Tell them there is something I must do, something I should have done long ago. I know now, you see . . . *I know*, Maisie! And I'm going to make it all right!"

"Bonnie, you've gone off your head," Maisie said, trying to catch her sister's hand as Bonnie pulled away. "Wait until Da comes back from the fields, at least! Wait until Sorcha—"

"I can't wait!" Bonnie said. "I love you, Maisie. I love all of you! But I must go."

Maisie's eyes brimmed with tears. Then suddenly she sprang forward, caught Bonnie in a last tight hug, and whispered fiercely in her ear: "*Hurry, Seònaid!*"

Bonnie's heart stopped for an instant. "What did you say?"

"I told you to hurry." Maisie frowned. "Why did I say that?"

"And you called me . . . you called me Seònaid." Bonnie breathed faster. "You never call me that. Only one person calls me that." *I have to get back!* "I must go. Say a prayer for me, Maisie," Bonnie told her. "Say a great many prayers!"

Then she turned and ran on foot down the road. She had no horse, but this could not stop her. She would run the whole way there if necessary, the yellow rose tucked close to her heart.

CHAPTER 14

S HE SHOULD not have been able to run that whole long distance, all those endless miles. But it seemed to Bonnie as though angels took hold of her arms and carried her along, giving her miraculous strength and endurance beyond her own ability. With every step she took, she felt her heart beating a wordless prayer, and she could only trust that God in His heaven heard and understood and made the path clear before her.

Night had fallen long before she drew near to the forest, a starless night pulsing with evil far stronger than she had ever before experienced. Indeed, even as she left the road behind and scrambled up an incline to the forest's edge, she suddenly stopped as though she'd struck a wall.

"No!" she cried out, pressing into what appeared to be empty air . . . empty air that resisted her, striking her again and again with nausea and despair. "No, let me in!"

What was that fleeting shadow she glimpsed in the trees? A lithe woman's form? A bent and hobbling hag? No, just a deeper shadow . . .

But the darkness fought her, and she could not push through. And her beast lay beyond, in peril. Perhaps dead!

Bonnie looked down at the rose she had taken from the cup on the windowsill. Several of its petals had fallen since she began her mad run, and what remained could scarcely be called a rose anymore. But those last remaining petals were still bright gold like sunshine, and the sight of them gave her hope.

Her heart trembled with terror, however, when a woman's laugh, cruel and cold, rolled out from the depths of the forest to strike her with a redoubled force of wickedness, driving her to her knees. This, however, was a dreadful mistake on the part of whoever sought to keep her out. For Bonnie pressed her hands together, cupping the shredded rose between them, and boldly cried out the same prayer which had comforted her so many times over the years:

"*Lighten our darkness, we beseech thee, O Lord; and by thy great mercy defend us from all perils and dangers of this night!*"

Something warmed between her palms. Bonnie opened her eyes and stared down at the last rose petals. Glowing with their own inner light, they drove back the darkness.

The wicked laughter turned to a furious scream even as Bonnie leapt to her feet and pushed into the forest, which no longer resisted her. Holding the gleaming petals high, she found the winding path and ran on, her heart beating with hope and fear and, most of all, with love.

She passed the cliffside falling down to the sea, and came upon the open gate. Beyond loomed the wulver's castle, darker and more desolate than ever, without a single candle shining in its windows. Bonnie's wilting rose cast the only light around, for the stars still feared to shine. The castle, what she could see of it, appeared to have aged a decade for every day she had been away.

Bonnie ran into the courtyard and across to the great front doors. Pushing them open, she shouted, "Beast? Beast, I am home!"

No candles flickered to life. No voice answered her. She sensed no sign of life, and her fears almost overwhelmed her in that moment. Holding high the rose, she ran through the great hall and into the winding passages of the castle, searching the rooms, to no avail. "Beast? Beast!" she cried.

The castle was in complete decay. What was left of the furniture was rotten, and the roof of the dining hall had collapsed into rubble. She couldn't even get to her bedroom, for the stairs had begun to crumble.

Truth be told, she knew where to look. She couldn't deny it, not for long. Even as she wandered the corridors, calling for the beast, desperately hoping he would answer her, she did not doubt where she must go to find him.

So she made her way out into the garden. And there he lay, prostrate on the ground before the dry and desolate rosebush.

Bonnie gave a cry and flew across the garden path, falling to her knees beside the wulver. She dropped the rose stem and clutched him by the shoulders with both hands. He was terribly heavy, but she hauled at him until she managed to roll him over. How still he was, and how cold! But when she pressed her ear to his chest, she could just discern a faint heartbeat.

"Beast!" She shook him then, her voice ringing through the night. "Beast, wake up! *Please!*"

His eyes fluttered opened. "Seònaid?" he asked faintly.

She almost sobbed in relief. "I'm here, Beast. I'm here."

"Ye weren't supposed to come back," he said in confusion. There was a hint of something else in his voice, something Bonnie couldn't quite name. It was almost annoyance. "Ye weren't supposed to see this," he continued, his voice cracking. "I sent ye away. It isn't safe for ye—"

"I don't care," Bonnie said, wiping away her tears with one hand while she clutched his great clawed fingers with her other. "I don't care if it's safe or not. What is happening to you?"

"I am dying," he said simply. Bonnie now realized how old he looked, as though he had aged a hundred years in those few days she had been gone. His muzzle was gray, his eyes faded and cloudy.

"Then why did you send me away?" Bonnie's voice was pleading, the tears back in full force. "How could you do that? How could you send me away, knowing I'd never see you again? Knowing that when I returned I'd find you dead?"

His voice became agitated. "Because ye'll *die*, Seònaid. Ye must leave! The castle is falling in. Any moment she'll be here—"

"I won't leave you!" Bonnie said stubbornly. And she knew then that she spoke the absolute truth. Nothing could frighten her away now. She had always been meant to come to this place, to kneel here beside him. Perhaps she was meant to die with him, and not even that could cause her fear. Not now.

"Oh Seònaid." His voice was sad and loving and resigned. "Please let me fade out of your life as though I were never in it to begin with. I never should ha' been in it at all."

"How can you say that?" Bonnie's tears dissipated, and she found suddenly that she was smiling and warm, as warm as the glowing light of the dying rose she had carried into the forest. "I cannot imagine not knowing you. Oh *Beast*," she said, and the last of her fear vanished as she spoke, "I *love* you. Don't you know that? In fact"—she tenderly stroked his forehead—"I wish to marry you."

The words had barely left her mouth when the ground rumbled amidst the sound of a furious scream. Bonnie's head jerked up and she turned swiftly to see the woman from the market running toward them, aging before their eyes with every step she took. Her legs began to blur into a ghostly mirage that rapidly moved upward until she had completely vanished. The echoes of her scream lingered a moment longer than her body did, and the beast shuddered beneath Bonnie's touch.

Bonnie, still on the ground, felt the earth below her shift, and winds from every direction swept past her and around the wulver. Too startled and amazed even to scream, she moved backward, her hair whipped in every direction, as the twirling tower of wind enveloped the beast.

Then, all at once, the gust dissipated into a soft breeze. Even as Bonnie brushed the hair from her eyes, the darkness lifted like a curtain, revealing a sky pale with the touch of dawn. Bonnie found she could hear again, though the only noise was that of waves lapping at the base of the cliffs below.

Her wondering gaze fell upon a small object near her feet. It was the rose she had carried into the forest . . . only now it bloomed in golden perfection there upon the ground.

She bent and picked it up gently. As she stood upright again, she realized that the castle too had transformed into a splendor she had never before seen.

But where was her beast? Where was her dear wulver? And who . . . who was this man standing with his back to her?

Slowly, ever so slowly, the man turned. "Seònaid?"

Bonnie gasped. *His voice . . .*

As he faced her, Bonnie recognized the man from the portrait. Just as handsome, though perhaps older and wiser. Bonnie stepped closer. "I'm sorry—I don't—that is . . ." She rubbed the heel of her hand against her temple. "*Beast?*" Her stomach felt as though it had jumped to her throat.

"'Tis I, Seònaid." The beautiful stranger with the familiar voice took a step toward her. "Ye broke the curse!" He seemed to scarcely believe it himself, and he looked down at his hands in wonder.

"Da!"

Both the man and Bonnie turned. The rosebush behind them was gone. In its place stood a small girl with curls as yellow as sunshine, a heart-shaped face, and bright blue eyes. Bonnie recognized her immediately.

"You!" Bonnie gasped. She had seen the girl many times, in both the portrait and her dreams. Breaking the tension of the adults, the girl flung herself at the man, who swept her up into his arms and buried his face in her hair.

"Róis," he whispered, and when he looked up, Bonnie saw tears in his eyes.

The girl scrambled out of her father's embrace and looked to Bonnie. "Ye saved us," she said in wonder. "I kept calling, and ye heard me. Ye saved us!"

"Aye," her father said. "She did save us."

"You're Lauchlan," Bonnie said, stepping closer to the man. "It was *your* story the whole time. Why didn't you tell me?"

"I couldn't." His jaw tightened. "'Twas one aspect of the curse. I could never tell ye; ye'd have to decipher it all yerself."

So many things began to make sense. Bonnie looked into Lauchlan's eyes and recognized them—the human eyes that had haunted and disturbed her so deeply in the face of a beast but felt so *right* in the face of the man before her. She desperately wanted to stare at him, but oh! What did he think of her, such an immature, gawky young woman? She looked away, feeling shy and uncomfortable.

Lauchlan seemed to understand. Tentatively he touched her arm, and she looked up. Something in his eyes set her fears at rest, and her nervousness abated. They stared at each other, unblinking, before Róis spoke up softly.

"Will ye be my new mither?" she asked, startling the two out of their reverie.

Lauchlan laughed. "If she will still have me." He looked to Bonnie, a question in his eyes.

Bonnie felt the edges of her mouth begin to turn up, but she steadied herself. Or tried to, anyway. Her voice couldn't quite keep from shaking with happiness and excitement and nerves. "There was one question you said you'd not ask again. But could you, one more time?"

Slowly Lauchlan sank to one knee. "Seònaid—my sweet, bonnie Seònaid—will ye marry me?"

Bonnie's joyful laughter rang out as she answered. "*Yes!*"

EPILOGUE

A SINGLE rose in a glass vase sits by my window. It's the same rose, the one that started it all. The one the merchant stole and gave to his beautiful youngest daughter.

Years ago, my children used to ask me about it and, carefully, when they were old enough, I told them the story behind it. The story I've told to my grandchildren, and one I know I will tell yet again.

They were always curious about it, this rose, and why it never wilted. It has been a constant presence in my life, taken with me on all my wanderings across the cities of Europe and the sands of the Mediterranean.

I carried it down the aisle on my wedding day.

I've traveled often over the years, to countries as varied as the stories they tell. Stories of poisoned apples, trails of breadcrumbs, and slippers made of glass. And yet the element that binds many of them together is the exact opposite of my own story, for my stepmother is not the villain of my tale but the heroine.

I gaze again at the rose, unchanged for so many years, but now wilting. Drooping.

As I am.

"It won't be long," I whisper to myself. I, like the rose, have little time left on this earth. But what a glorious time it has been!

"Gramma Róis?"

A small voice calls to me, and I see my oldest great-grandchild, a tiny wisp of a thing with curls as blonde as my own once were.

"You said you'd tell about the rose. I want to hear about the rose." She tilts her head and stares at me intently.

I smile. "And you will hear it, Little One."

ABOUT THE AUTHOR

HAYDEN WAND is a Christian and a homeschool graduate who has loved the classic story of *Beauty and the Beast* since the age of three, when she saw the Disney movie for the first time. When she's not writing, reading, or bribing her siblings to read the classics, you can find her baking, crafting, practicing her archery skills, or watching her favorite shows on the BBC. She lives in South Carolina with her parents and four energetic younger siblings.

Visit www.EveryStory-StoryGirl.blogspot.com to learn more about Hayden and her work.

More stories by the authors of:
Five Enchanted Roses

Les must accept her place in the world as Ember Flame, one of the six Leverage. If she cannot find her destiny and the other Leverage, the souls of the people will perish. Will she sacrifice her desires for a world that has been nothing but cruel to her? Or will she succumb to the will of a tyrant and live a life of numbness?

EMBER FLAME by Kaycee Browning
www.KayceeBrowning.com

Before *Wither*, a Spook risks everything to protect his streets from the undead and a mysterious assassin . . . even as he himself is becoming one of the creatures he hunts.

BOOK I *in*
THE NEVERWAY CHRONICLES
COMING DECEMBER 2015

AFTER by Savannah Jezowski
www.SavannahJaysWorkshop.blogspot.com

When Dark Warriors invade her country, it is up to Princess Kamarie to seek out the legendary king's warrior and request his aid. Whether or not Kamarie trusts him, the hope of their world rests on this mysterious man and the steel he wears at his side . . .

KING'S WARRIOR by Jenelle Schmidt
www.JenelleSchmidt.com

When a fairy godmother offers her a pair of glass slippers that not only transform her ragged dress to an elegant gown, but also remove the mark that covers her face, Adelaide believes her life is about to change for the better. However, she soon learns that the beautiful slippers can steal away more than just her birthmark, leaving her cursed in a far worse way . . .

CURSED BEAUTY by Dorian Tsukioka
www.DorianWrites.blogspot.com

When an unexpected letter sends her on a voyage across the Atlantic, Constance Steele's experiences affect more people than she ever could have realized. From the lives of her sister Margaret and cousin Jack, to a band of notorious pirates, no one could have guessed how Constance's adventure would change them all . . .

HIDDEN PEARLS by Hayden Wand
www.everystory-storygirl.blogspot.com

Looking for more fantastic fairy tale retellings?

TAKE PART IN THE NEXT CONTEST

An all-new collection releases *Summer 2016*

www.RooglewoodPress.com

Great titles from
ROOGLEWOOD PRESS

Like us on Facebook
www.RooglewoodPress.com

A timid stepsister.
A mistaken identity.
A disinherited princess.
A seething planet.
An enchanted circus.

Here are five
beautiful retellings
to bring new life to the
classic Cinderella tale!

Stories by: Elisabeth Brown, Emma Clifton, Rachel Heffington,
Stephanie Ricker, and Clara Diane Thompson

In the early days of the
French Revolution, Colette
dreamed of equality for all.
But those days are gone,
and the bloodshed creeps
ever closer to home. Can
Colette find the strength to
protect her loved ones . . .
even from each other?

UNTIL THAT DISTANT DAY by Jill Stengl

59832165R00299

Made in the USA
Lexington, KY
21 January 2017